THE HUMAN SCRIPT
a novel in 23 chromosomes

Johnny Rich

Praise for
THE HUMAN SCRIPT

'Hands down my book of the year. Brave, intelligent and gloriously unsettling. Tackling the big, beautiful, murky questions of science and genetics, "nature/nurture", love, life, death ... there are few books I finish and have to start at the beginning again but this was one of them'
BookSmoke

'Incredibly clever and smart ... really made me think, while keeping me entertained to the end ...
truly different and unique'
Stephanie Cox

'Intelligent, thought-provoking and profoundly moving'
Byte the Book

The Human Script
a novel in 23 chromosomes

JOHNNY RICH

Red Button Publishing

This paperback edition published in 2015 by Red Button Publishing

First published in Great Britain in 2013 by Red Button Publishing

ISBN: 978-0-9576116-6-5

Cover design by Red Button Publishing

www.redbuttonpublishing.net

Contents

Part One

'Is not our future already determined by our past – by the goals we have pursued, the habits we have formed, the relationships we have established, the countless choices, large and small, which we have made over the years? Is not each man's life a book, written by his own hand, and from the chapters concluded, cannot the next chapter be predicted?

And yet our destiny is not unalterable. For God has made us free. However strong may be the shackles of the past, we can break its hold. We can change course and so escape from the sequence of events which we ourselves have set in motion. We can write a new and better chapter.'

Rabbi John D. Rayner

Chromosome 1
Genesis, Genetics and Gemini

'And God saw everything that He had made. And, behold, it was very good.'
Genesis I, 31

'There is no human nature, because there is no God to have a conception of it. Man simply is.'
Jean-Paul Sartre

In the beginning, Chris Putnam believed. Believed in God. God on a cloud with his father's frown. Then Chris Putnam believed God was without form and, eventually, void. Then Chris Putnam believed in science. And he believed in freedom.

None of this is important, however, because no one believes in belief anymore, not in these days of knowledge. Besides, belief in freedom is only another way of saying belief in uncertainty. So Chris Putnam thought perhaps he believed in uncertainty.

Uncertainty is the scientist's domain. Belief is not. Scientists build knowledge on what they cannot show to be doubtful, not on what they can show to be certain.

One thing, however, is certain in life. No one survives it. Nevertheless, in the meantime, for Chris, the future was uncertain.

Although, by the end of that day, the never-ending chain of events would have begun to challenge his uncertainty.

*

Because there's freedom in the air, 'Good morning,' I beam to Peter the old security guard who sits in his hut at the Gower Street gate and who told me once he still likes to fish at weekends and who looks up to see which person is bothering to talk to him. I smile again and I've already turned right in through the double doors of the redbrick lab building and up the stairs three at a time. One – two – three – four times three is twelve in all to the landing with the lockers and I can still feel the warm of the sun, even indoors, even in the shade, with the vitamin E or D or whichever it is, I forget, and all its little reactions cascading through me, so, ultimately, this is the joy of a sunny Bloomsbury good morning.

And it's good because I'm turning over a new leaf and today I'm starting a new chapter in my life and I'm free to do it because now, finally, I'm in the clear again. I'm not sure what I'm free to do yet, but that is what I've decided to decide today and I'm thinking about how I haven't thought about Gill at all since last night, well, since now, but now I really feel the whole thing's not an issue anymore. Gill's just a control freak and, see, it's even possible to be bitter about it all now which is progress. As Elsi said last night in bed, get bitter, get better.

And things are getting better, getting better all the time. And all you need is love and I'm humming that to myself. That's all I need now in my life, someone to love who'll love me back and I can start to do something about it now because the whole Gill thing's not an issue anymore. I can start to think about doing something about it. I can decide what to do with all this freedom.

A girl comes down the flight of stairs above with long hair and legs and turns to carry on down and doesn't really notice me and I don't know her but 'Hi' I say anyway and she looks back over her shoulder and says, 'Oh, hi' without stopping and carries on down. I think she's a research assistant too, but she may be a postdoc, and anyway she's with plants not humans.'Human Genome Laboratory' it says above the door by the lockers where I take out my lab coat and where I put my bag and now take it out again to get out the mugs and now again to pluck out the apple. And now in white and with some chemical stain now permanent on the pocket, I push through and swing to the left immediately and into the galley kitchen where there's a sign above the fridge says, 'You don't have to be mad to work here, but it helps' and someone's crossed out 'be mad' and written 'watch Star Trek' and I decide to cross that out and I write 'eat beef'.

I put down the apple and the mugs and pick up the kettle which is still warm from the last round of first coffees of the day and fill it up. 'Anyone for coffee?' I say loudly over my shoulder without knowing who's there to answer and there's no answer, so I step back a couple of paces and say it again and get no answer again. So I switch on the kettle anyway and walk through to the main lab room with the bench tops and the stools and the windows along the far-side wall with sunlight streaming in and the three centrifuges in front of me with tippex names on them which say 'Crick' and 'Watson' and the new one, 'Spinning Jenny'. The room's empty apart from Colin E. – as opposed to Colin Ng – and he's sitting in the corner with his back to me and I'm making my way over to him and his sadly unattractive ponytail although he could look okay if only he knew it and with goggles on top of his head but with his specs on, typing or rather not typing at his monitor.

'Where is everybody?' I ask and he doesn't look up but shrugs and now pauses and says, 'Don't know. Sir Hugo's in Zurich or Amsterdam or somewhere.'

'Again? So I suppose while the cat's away ...'

'... Everyone turns up late. Except me because I've got this sodding fragile X data to get through before Friday.'

'Come on, Colin,' I say, 'it's only Monday morning.'

'Yeah. So I don't know what you've got to be so happy about.'

'Joys of spring,' and it's more than that, I'm released, back to normal, and so I add, 'and because basically I'm a happy person.' But he seems down. 'You okay?'

'You're like a bunny in heat.' He's fine. Busy.

'Coffee?'

'Thanks. Black. Two sugars. Three parts hot to one part cold. Here,' he says and looks away from the screen. 'It's half empty.' He hands me his mug which is half full of cold black coffee and which says 'Wellcome' and 'Trust'.

'Coming up,' I say and twist my way between the benches and stools back to the kitchen where I tip Colin's mug into the sink and give it a rinse and rub the stains which record the many levels of undrunk coffee and tea this mug has contained. It might be possible to calculate the average depth of coffee or tea Colin drinks from his mug by these geological striations, by their levels and their intensity. Of course you'd be assuming the length of time the mug's been left unwashed on each occasion would even out, but then, assumptions are inevitable.

I shake the water off Colin's cup and now decide to dry the outside properly. He doesn't know what I've got to be so happy about and you don't often realise you're happy when you're happy, but I am. It's as simple as that. I wonder why? Basically I'm a happy person, but I haven't been happy lately. Does that still make me a happy person? If I'm not happy? And why today, why today am I happy again? The vitamin D or whichever, maybe. Sunshine. One way or another, the sun provides all the Earth's energy and so ultimately, the sun is the reason I'm happy. Although there's also energy from the Earth's core, the magma in the mantle and so on. But that's because of pressures which are only there in the first place because of the gravity of the solar system which forged the planets and so that's because of the sun too. Indirectly, it's all to do with the sun in the end. But then, it's not all because of the sun – there are also the planets themselves to include in the equation and the rest of the Milky Way, the entire universe for that matter. How far back do you have to go? The Big Bang.

The kettle clicks. Cosmology: not my speciality. Who cares? The universe or whatever has conspired to make me happy this day.

The cloud of steam expands and gradually condenses into droplets and maybe it doesn't matter why I'm happy. It just matters that I am and that it makes me feel free and full of opportunity and full of everything I'm going to do next with my life, even though I don't know what that is, but that's half the fun, deciding. I have decided to decide. And what should it be that I decide to do I wonder as I turn one of the new mugs right-side up. So that's it. I'll decide today what to do and it should be something that makes me happy every day. I feel closer to a decision already.

But what makes me happy? If I knew why I'm happy today, I could decide. So it matters why after all.

One thing I have decided – that all I need is love. And I hum the opening bars of 'The Marseillaise'.

I *am* happy, but I'm out of practice. That's why I need to analyse it. Then I can make decisions. My life becomes an open book.

Maybe, I think as I pick up the teaspoon and the coffee tin, I'm happy because the good dose of Elsi just hasn't worn off. That depends whether it's just this morning or last night.

Last night, I think as I prise the top off the tin with a spoon, I may have gone to sleep like this, after I talked to Elsi, who always makes me feel good, snuggling in my bed and talking it through over how much wine between the two of us – too many to measure in glasses, bottles rather – why haven't I got a hangover? No after-effects. Slept it off, slept it all off. I scoop up granules and put them in the mugs. Anyway, Elsi said last night that four months' mourning was long enough for Gill, who may be sexy as hell and all that but kept me on a short leash anyway, too parental. It's just, as Elsi said, I was finally ready to reach some kind of closure, strike out on my own. I cried a lot. Last night. That can't be happiness, can it? But maybe I'm happy because I was able to sleep well for the first time since Gill dumped me, flushed me and watched me spin round the bowl. And that was the thing I cared about – how it ended, not the fact that it did. I didn't love Gill, not really. I just liked the protection of being with someone. At any rate, it wasn't the love I need. And now I'm in the clear. Bunny in heat. Possibilities.

In the end I had to kick Elsi out to go to sleep, back to her red room with all its wall-hangings. Probably would have stayed all night if I'd given her the chance.

I put just a few more granules in Colin's. He takes it strong. I had to rush this morning so I can't say whether I started out happy or whether it was the sunshine? Had to rush but I remembered to bring in the mugs anyway. I must look a mess. Didn't even shave.

I remember to fill Colin's only as far as one of the higher layers of the striations which I haven't been able to rub off. I suppose it was bound to come one day, a day when I'd realise I was over Gill. Or near enough. I run the tap cold and fill up Colin's mug. Maybe it's not over yet, but today it feels like it. Is it all that bad to never let go?

I never let go of Mummy. And I won't. I think of her brushing my hair after a bath, the way the brush would catch in a tangle sometimes but I wouldn't flinch to show her what pains I could bear, would bear, but instead I breathed in medicated shampoo, warm skin and the end-of-the-day rumour of her scent, which I'd never normally smell except when playing at the dressing table in my parents' room or at intimate moments, moments such as this. Dan watching and waiting his turn. I put my head against her breast, the breast that killed her. There are some things you don't want to let go of, even though they hurt.

Still, death, that's life. Today I'm happy.

So, today, I decide as I add sugars – one – two – to Colin's coffee and milk to mine, I am over Gill. Today, I decide as I take up the mugs and carry them through to the lab, the strands of my life are recombining. Today, I decide, the story is over. I am free.

But to do what?

*

I'm sitting at a screen and checking my email and typing in my password which is 'Sartre', not that I really know anything about him, only what Elsi told me the day before I had to choose a password and it sounded good and I'm thinking that, today, I can define my own essence, for the first time for four years, because, like Elsi said, I'm no longer letting Gill make my decisions for me. Elsi is wise. A bit loopy, perhaps, but that's what you get from studying too much philosophy. All those questions, never any answers.

But how, I wonder as I wait for the message software to load, does all this essence relate to reality, to what I'm going to do, to be? I'll decide in a minute.

Was I happy earlier, when I woke up? I take a sip and try to remember and can't, because all I remember is rushing because I wanted to be in before Sir Hugo, which, it turns out, wasn't necessary. I wasn't properly awake yet. It can take time when you've had a good night's sleep, but I remembered the mugs anyway and I didn't think I would. The computer beeps to tell me I have no new messages but reminds me Dan's message from last week is still unopened. It's called 'dad'. I couldn't face it then. I'm not going to read it now. I'm happy now. Whatever it is, it won't be good. Later.

It's a good mug – I take another sip – the right weight in

the hand and the rim isn't too thick and it feels right on the lower lip and it says 'Chris' on it so that whole situation where I don't have a mug won't happen again.

All this protectiveness about the mugs is a bit unnecessary. Maybe it's because we share workspaces that we feel a need to mark our territory so we do it with the mugs, not that I need to, or I didn't at first, but I guess I do now or else I wouldn't have got a new mug with my name on it. But at first I didn't even realise and kept using any mug and then I realised and felt terrible because people were probably just being too polite to say. But that meant I had no mug, so I got a couple of extras, but thinking about it, I never said that they were mine, never claimed my territory. That was where I went wrong, I suppose, on reflection. Because I didn't feel the animal need. I wouldn't make a good baboon, never an alpha male, maybe a good dog, a puppy.

I must do some proper work.

Should I read the email first? I think of my father and decide not to, not yet.

I finish my coffee and I make a decision.

I decide I don't need another one. I suppose I should have explained the etiquette with regard to mugs to Eve when she started and adopted one of the ones I'd got. But I had got two deliberately so that there would always be a spare. Although then there wasn't any more and she was new at the time and I didn't like to bring it up, but it would have meant that when that guy from Hinxton broke the other one I'd got, she would have felt, might have felt, she should get me one, but I didn't like to mention it. Especially not after so long. Especially after it was now *her* mug. It would have seemed so petty. And it's all better now. And we have a spare again.

Maybe, I think, I'm just a happy person and that's it, that's why I don't care about having my own mug, why I'm happy today. Today, I am returned to my natural state. From today things start to go right. That's what the horoscope said.

Gemini, I remember as I take a pair of twin gloves from the box, something about important events, pivotal changes, the strands of life recombining.

It's all junk, of course. I know that perfectly well. A magazine left in a tube compartment, unread it was and not a freebie. *Cosmo*, *Marie Claire* or *Elle*, maybe, I didn't even notice. Somebody, I think as I pull on the sterilised gloves from the inside out, had spent money on it and left it behind. She'll be upset now. She'll be in some office now thinking she wishes she hadn't spent that money and what a waste and maybe she can't afford it really, it's just one of those little luxuries she indulges in to make her job as PA to some pompous lecher seem less dead and then she forgot it on the tube. She's probably standing at the photocopier right now, cloning paper and blaming her boss for her mistake. She lacks freedom, that's her problem. If I were her, I'd put toner in his tea.

Maybe she doesn't care all that much. There are one – two – three – four lids on the PCR block and two have got samples in which someone's left on a three-hour programme to run overnight and I switch it off and the fan shudders and stops. I click open the front-right lid and I lift out the plate and I take it to a bench and peel off the rubber mat on top, a grid of little pink samples, each with their own neat well in the flimsy plastic tray. Twelve rows – eight columns – ninety-six wells – ninety-six samples – 20 µls each.

Maybe it was her horoscope made me happy. I think of her unknowingly across London somewhere doing such good. Maybe she left it there deliberately, an act of charity, multiplying happiness throughout the capital like so much DNA, dividing but never lessened, always multiplying, amplified, cloned.

I'm not so different. The lab's just another office. Polymerase Chain Reaction is just xerox by another name. I start sucking up the cloned samples with the Eppendorf syringe. Eight at a time – ninety-six samples – twelve rows. Trained monkeys could do this shit. I'm a qualified biologist. I'll be twenty-four in June. I've learnt how to investigate and consider rationally. No wonder my mind wanders. I'm a trained chimp, 98.9 per cent chimp anyway, DNA-wise. What's 1.1 per cent?

*

I wonder, as I pour a little chloroform in each of the samples, whose project they're for. No one ever tells me. They could be anything – haemophilia, Favism, colour blindness. I don't even know if they're all from the same person. Rows of eight, samples to be cleaned before I make more copies in the PCR block and then I'll have to sequence them, reading off the string of letters. I wonder about the people, the ones the samples belong to. Or maybe it's the people who belong to the samples? I wonder about them now as I realise that I do sometimes. I never see more than a few drops of their blood and, whatever else we carry in our blood, it isn't our essence. I know, I've looked, I would have seen. Usually I don't even see their blood, just frozen DNA.

Who am I trying to convince? I leave the first set of samples to stand and go to fetch the next ones. Just do the job, don't bother what any of it's about. But I know the answer and I believe I know why I'm happy – I'm not actually nodding because I'm checking on the panel on the front of the PCR block that the programme is over. I think I know – it's because of the horoscope which I want to be true because it's good and maybe that's why I'm happy, but I don't want it to be true because I'd have to be mad to believe it. I mean, how can astrology work? Show me cause and effect. Offer a scientific explanation of how this influence might operate.

It's all balls and gas. Balls of gas in certain juxtapositions at the time of birth, albeit unimaginably big, but also unimaginably distant. It's just because people don't want to feel so free. They're scared of the responsibility.

The universe, though – and I know I'm trying to see both sides of the argument, typical Gemini – is all interconnected. The slightest movement of particles, butterflies flapping or Pisces up Uranus – they're all causes and they amount to Bloomsbury is sunny this morning and I am happy and free today. So, maybe, then.

But, come on, and I remove the next set of samples and take them to the bench and the rubber and the syringe and the chloroform. It's all negligible compared to direct effects closer at hand.

But, then again. Maybe this isn't physics, it's psychology or sociology or whatever. I leave them to stand and go to the freezer to fetch primers and more samples which need to be cloned, need to be subjected to cycle after cycle of repetitive reactions building up copies.

Maybe, enough people believe in horoscopes for them to be a self-fulfilling prophecy. Autopoiesis. I tug at the heavy metallic door and with a suck the door opens and clouds spill out like I'm standing on them. Parents expect children to be such-and-such and bring them up such-and-such and they read into it such-and-such and ultimately, along with everything else, of course, there's some truth in it. Chilly.

Or there's the time of the year. I take the samples and the primers from the freezer. Maybe that has an effect on personality, like an autumn baby grows up to be more – what would they be? Gill's birthday's in September. Virgo. What are they like? Uptight?

I set them down, cold they are, -70°. Maybe there's a kind of evolution of understanding over the centuries. People have classified the personality types from different times of the year and the better the classification, the more it was accepted until it's a true hypothesis and maybe there's some truth in it after all although it's got nothing to do with the stars and on the Northern line I read Gemini: *This month will be a period of pivotal change in your life. Important events are about to happen, but don't let the past decide the future. You must choose to leave relationships behind and feel free to seek a new path. Don't let your tendency to see both sides of the argument get the better of you. Listen to those closest to you and beware of people who don't have your best interests at heart. Romance: With Venus entering your sign, your love life is about to take off. Prepare to meet someone special and for affairs to hot up.*

The samples need to defrost. Love life to hot up. Bunny back in heat. Those closest to you: that's Elsi. I know she's right – she always is and she knows that too – and I know it was largely because *I* didn't end it with Gill. Even when I knew it was over. Not that I would have anyway because I'd never want to cause anyone pain, least of all ... well, I don't know, Gill deserves it, swanning around, lording it and telling me what I can't do all the time. I'm a pushover, I know, too easily controlled. Elsi said I should just stop feeling sorry for myself and realise I can be happy now I'm free and I should be embracing it. Which, apparently, I am. I should decide for myself, she said, and she's right and that's what I have decided to do. I am setting out a sterile well plate for the next ninety-six reactions and trying to work out what someone's done with the syringe tips.

I can't believe I'm wasting time thinking about a horoscope.

I've got to wait for the samples to defrost anyway, so I'm going to make a list of hypotheses. Always the best way to start an analysis, I think, as I go into the common room to do it and sit by the fugu fish in its tank and turn over a photocopied article from *Bioinformatics News* to write my list on the back.

HYPOTHETICAL CAUSES OF MY GOOD MOOD
(In chronological order)

1. Talk with Elsi last night re: Gill leading to possible closure of mourning period through emotional release aided by the consumption of much alcohol. Went to bed happy.

2. A fully restful night's sleep for the first time post-Gill (aided by emotional release and the consumption of much alcohol, see 1 above). Woke up happy.

3. Sunshine: physiological effects thereof (increase in levels of vitamin D leading to increase in uptake of seratonin and levels of neuropeptides).

4. Horoscope: good horoscope (with promise of love), despite lack of belief, provides positive outlook owing to desire to believe anyway (because it would be nice if horoscopes came true even if it is silly). Became happy on the Northern line (*c.* 9.15 a.m.).

5. Got a seat on the Northern line (see 4 above).

6. Four days away from lab (including Thursday and Friday at the Sanger Centre). Gradual effect. (Should have been at the top of the list chronologically.)

7. Got to lab ~~before Sir Hugo~~ and discovered Sir Hugo is away. Became happy *c.* 9.45 a.m.

8. Any combination of, or all of, the above.

And I'm looking at the list and I add:

9. General freedom: from Gill; from what other people expect from/of me.

And I am smiling at the list because it's a good list. My thoughts are always jumbled until I write them down, but it doesn't constitute the basis for an experiment because the conditions could not be repeated. A bit of amusement, but nothing in there to advance understanding. I hear someone come in through the lab doors and I make a ball with the list and they poke their head round the corner and it's Eve's head and she says, 'Hiya, gorgeous. You're lookin' good – the sexy, stubbly look, very hot. How you doing?' and I say, 'Great,' but I don't want to go into depth or show her my list because she wouldn't really want to know. 'You all right?' I say.

'Hmm, so-so,' she says. 'Rotten weekend. Hold on, I'll get a coffee and tell you about it.' And her head's gone and I am hoping that it's nothing really bad, but she doesn't seem upset, so I guess it's not too important. I hear her in the kitchen with the kettle and flatten out my list again. The critical piece of missing data is the timing of the onset. Now I have to laugh because this is so ridiculous making a list like this. I'm analysing it all way too much and that's exactly what Elsi was saying had been stopping me from being happy as we analysed it all together and she did add that it was a bit rich coming from a philosopher and everything. She is right, though, I think to myself and I tear up *Bioinformatics News* into two – four – eight – sixteen because I wouldn't want anyone to find it and I sprinkle the pieces in the bin and they spin around like sycamore seeds or more like angels' feathers falling.

Eve's head pops round the corner again and so does her arm this time and she's holding up the apple and she says to me, 'This anyone's?' and I say, 'Well, I brought it in because I missed breakfast, but it's okay, you can have it, if you like. I'm going to get some lunch soon anyway.'

'You sure?' she says and I'm smiling back at her and nodding and she's already taking a bite and 'mmm' she says as it's still in her mouth and now kind of half laughs, but she has to take the apple out to say anything properly and she says, 'It's good. Want a bite? Go on.' And she steps out fully from round the corner and she holds it out to me and I think that I guess I am hungry and it will take away the stale aftertaste of coffee I've got so I take it from her and bite.

The phone rings and Eve says, 'I'll get it' and I am trying to give her back the apple but she's gone to the phone, but I don't want to eat any more because, although it is good, I feel it's her apple now and so I hold on to it for her and wait to see if she comes back immediately and now I think, now I can make another list because the choice is mine. A list of what to do. So I won't be listless ever again. I know the happiness won't last forever, not unless I catch it and decide quickly what to do with all this freedom. Now, I think as I watch the fugu turn around in his tank and mouth something to me, pivotal change, feeling free, hotting up.

Eve's head again is saying, 'It's your brother.'

'Who?' I say, because I didn't think it would be for me.

'Your brother.'

'What does he want?' I ask, feeling embarrassed or guilty or nervous, and there is something like a tug in my gut and my left arm hurts. I put down the apple. 'Why's he calling?'

'Dunno mate, maybe you should ask him?'

*

'Hello? Dan?' There is no voice, but a kind of sigh, a rearrangement of sound, at the other end of the line. 'Dan? Is that you? You okay? What's up?'

'The old man's croaked, bro. Gene's dead.'

Chromosome 2
The Calvinist Tulip

'No, no, he is dead;
Go to thy death-bed,
He never will come again.'
Hamlet, IV, v

'Moreover, whom He did predestinate, them He also
called; and whom He called, them He also justified;
and whom He justified, them He also glorified.'
Romans XIII, 30

Jesus, I say, although maybe not out loud as the taxi pulls up outside Dunmarrick Free Presbyterian Kirk. It is not a prayer.

I've just had to catch a cab all the way from Kirkcaldy station and it's costing me twenty quid and I'm paying in English notes and I'm still late for my own father's funeral anyway. It's raining – it should always rain at funerals – but it's only an April shower. I grab my black nylon overnight bag, tighten my borrowed tie and sneak in at the back, trying not to make a sound although the great wooden doors whine loudly on their hinges and everyone will turn and look I'm sure.

I do not want to be here.

But it's not a matter of choice. Being late is bad enough.

*

Chris Putnam had neither seen his late father nor spoken to him for some time, nor would he ever again. Even so, the terminal condition of Eugene Joseph Putnam had skulked in the shadows for some time. Since his birth, in fact, but it had been particularly notable during the previous four months. His imminent death was first heralded by headaches in the shower and a craving for honey, followed by a stroke just after Christmas. His decline had been fast once the prognosis was decreed, his body ceding to the edict that he should die. Since his beginning, his end was only a matter of time and the duration of the inevitable mechanism was sixty-five years.

His stroke had coincided, approximately, with Chris's break-up with Gill. No one, however, imagined that they might be causally linked.

Eugene was tall and thin with granite-grey hair across the chin, above the ears and sparsely across the head under his Homburg hat. He had been known as Gene to his friends. Among these, he would have numbered the members of the independent Calvinist congregation of the kirk, a cautious selection of other inhabitants of Dunmarrick and its neighbouring villages (mainly the managers of small local businesses) and, of course, Ian Poulson, to whom he habitually referred as 'my partner in crime'. Such an expression passed as humour among the employees and clients of Putnam, Poulson & Co. (Solicitors), although, as it happened, in rural Fife, criminal casework was less common than wills, conveyancing and the occasional commercial contract.

Many of these friends attended the funeral, presided over by the Reverend Andrew Manders BA, as well as a number of relatives.

He was also called 'Gene' by his son Dan. On growing out of 'Daddy', Dan had insisted on 'Gene' despite – indeed, because of – the thin-lipped sneer it would provoke amid the stony beard. Chris, on the other hand, tried to call him 'Dad' and then 'Father'. And then he stopped calling him.

Neither son grew out of calling their mother 'Mummy', in an attempt to cling on to her when the first tumorous rumours started to redouble, back when they were all too young.

It was more than five years before Gene died that he last spoke to his elder son. Chris was unable to remember what those last words had been, but he knew (though never would have acknowledged) that they were said more in sorrow than in anger.

*

I am not so late, it seems. I sit in a pew near the back. Bare white plastered walls and high leaden windows. Dan glances at me from the aisle where he moves among the people and he throws me a smile. He'll be all right through this. He's the star of the show, number one mourner, and, if there's anything he's good at, it's playing to the crowd. I look back at him and hope he'll know that the only thing I want right now is not to be like him, not to be the centre. Keep that look between us, just us. Don't get me down the front, Dan. Don't get me to sit with the family. Don't even let on that I'm here. Let me be a ghost. Let me be.

Dan is guiding Great Aunt Verity to a seat. He keeps saying loudly that she can sit at the front with the rest of the family so she can hear, but it's no good because she can't even hear Dan. So she's trying to sit down on every row as they move slowly down the aisle and the people already sitting in the rows move up to make space for her, but they're uncertain because everyone else in the kirk has heard Dan, except Auntie Verity. So each time she makes as if to sit down, Dan takes her arm again and leads her further to the front, saying, 'You'll hear better at the front ... I said, you'll hear better at the front.'

When we buried Mummy, it was terrible. My father sat in the kitchen and ate breakfast, coldly dipping dry toast in his egg with his wife about to go in the ground, looking up every now and then to smile at me. Stinging eyes I had and the silence was so wide I thought I'd hear nothing again until I heard the sound of my father at the grave, my father crying. Little weeps, the only time. And, by that time, I didn't believe him.

But this, this is just comic. I think I feel nothing. Except I want to giggle, to break the awful quiet if nothing else. To give these cold stiffs in their dark coats a jolt, to let them know that, yes, actually, the *other* son has turned up. But I wouldn't. Dan might, if he were me, but me, no.

Dan's voice does break the quiet to say, 'Here. Just here. And here's the order of service.' Great Aunt Verity takes the folded, stapled sheets from him. There is sound, I realise. There has been all along, I just didn't hear it before. The sound of the organ playing dully and low, echoing in the cold grey nave. It doesn't sound like music, just random sighs of sound. Also, there are people talking. I didn't notice before, or maybe they weren't talking then. I watch lips chatter incessantly and steamy wisps of breath, but all I hear is murmur, and I watch them solemnly nod. None of these sounds is distinct from silence.

Probably not even thirty-five people. What's that? Barely one for every two years of my father's life. And look at them, like the walking dead themselves. Reverend Manders is in the pulpit now, from somewhere. The congregation rises and bows. I rise too.

My father is there. Or, at least, his coffin is. I had not noticed it before. It had seemed an extension of the altar, some kind of furniture, but he is in there. Or, at least, his body is there. That box surely cannot be large enough to fit the corpse that was my father. I could just run up there and shove it and then he'd spill out and I picture him staring at me in horror from his box.

There can't be a body in there. No one would know if they filled it with weights.

But his body is in there, within that thin wall of wood. What else survives now? Dust to dust. Systems shut down, till only the hair and fingernails carry farcically on. It's all reflex, just like twitching frog's legs in dissections I did at A Level. Is there a draft in there that might make the hair twitch? His grey hairs will still be growing or lengthening as the skin recedes, but slow, no twitching.

How bizarre, how pagan it all is, bringing a cadaver into a place of worship. Did I ever believe in any of this?

'I am the resurrection and the life: he that believeth in me, though he were dead, yet shall he live. And whosoever liveth and believeth in me shall never die. Let us sing together Psalm 16.' The organ starts off-key, I think, and a few bold-hearted stalwarts know when to join in:

> *Lord, keep me; for I trust in thee.*
> *To God thus was my speech,*
> *Thou art my Lord; and unto thee*
> *My goodness doth not reach.*

'Where are we?' says Great Aunt Verity loudly enough to be heard over the dirge to my uncle Gordon who is sitting next to her.

'We're in the kirk, Auntie,' he whispers as loudly as possible so she might hear him and the rest of the congregation might be able to pretend they haven't.

'No. In the thing.' She waves her order of service and he takes it from her, turns it the right way up and hands it back to her, pointing.

It is her nephew in that box. And Gordon's big brother. Or his body at least. My daddy is not any more. If I lifted the lid, if they do not nail it down, my father's hands would be cold and grey, but my daddy is a warm, dry hand holding mine on a walk on a cold, fresh day when the air tastes like peppermint and I kick through leaves in red wellingtons. People don't own wellingtons in London and piles of leaves always contain dog shit.

An old man is singing too loudly. As if it helps.

> *Because my soul in grave to dwell*
> *Shall not be left by thee;*
> *Nor wilt thou give thine*
> *Corruption to see.*

So my father wins, in the end, and he knew he would. He always knew that one way or another he would get me back into this kirk. He never said so much, but I can picture it. 'Chris, you'll come back. You'll come back in the end. Back to a knowledge of Christ. Such things are foreknown, Chris, predestined. *I* will bring you back, if it's the last thing I do.' And I can imagine his stern ironical smile, the laughter lines. I can remember the humiliation of being teased.

We said family prayers and I used to like it, giggling with Dan at the big table in the dark kitchen every morning, and as we spoke often it was cold enough for the words to form brief clouds and I would pretend I was breathing fire. But family prayers are for families. I don't remember what we did when Mummy died and then, well, then I came away. Six years, more than six years, my father lived in that house all alone. If he'd collapsed there, on his own, there wouldn't even have been anyone to hear him call for help. I realise I feel nothing at the thought of it and now in a rush I feel the pain, but I am afraid it is the pain of guilt more than pity.

Dan didn't believe the prayers any more than I did, but he

could forget them the moment we said 'amen'. Even now, look at him, with his earnest look, listening to the minister who stands swaddled in his black Geneva gown and reading in sacramental monotone like an older man.

He's the other son, not me. Why am *I* sitting at the back at my father's funeral? Why do all these people think it is *me* who is so unspeakable? I did nothing wrong but I feel like an outcast. In London, it is Dan. Dan is the outrageous one. Dan is the one who sleeps around, who takes drugs and doesn't have a proper job. He is the one despised by the art establishment and even by those who despise the art establishment. They call him the *enfant terrible*. And I, I am inoffensive and nice, polite, probably there's not enough to me for anyone to dislike – I am not a black sheep anywhere, anywhere but here.

'But by the grace of God I am what I am,' reads Reverend Manders, 'and his grace which was bestowed upon me was not in vain; but I laboured more abundantly than they all: yet not I, but the grace of God which was with me.'

I am what I am. I think of Gloria Gaynor, is it? But she sings it as if it's a statement of choice, of freedom. Excuses are not needed. These people, nodding their grey heads, accept it as their destinies, saved or not, by God's irresistible grace. And they all think they're saved.

'The last enemy that shall be destroyed is death.'

Junk. It's all meaningless. My father dies. Mummy died. I will die. And that's how people, animals, plants go on living. Regeneration through recombination and selection. There is no resurrection. There is no god. Daddy isn't in that box. I know what death is, it's the price we pay for sex, every biologist knows that.

'If after the manner of men I have fought with beasts at Ephesus, what advantageth it me, if the dead rise not? Let us eat and drink; for tomorrow we die.' Reverend Manders looks up from the lectern. He speaks again in a softer tone, 'Please rise and let us read together.' And everyone stands up and everyone except me and Great Aunt Verity seems to shuffle their order of service and they start chanting together. There are tulips on the altar. It is late April, Easter Monday.

A small boy, five years old, maybe, is standing on a pew a

few rows in front of me next to a woman who is probably his mother – but I don't know these people. He gets down from the seat and his head disappears.

'Please sit,' says Reverend Manders. Up, down. Is this all necessary to commune with God? He pauses, looks around as people sit. He does not see a small boy's head bob up in the pew in front of me. The boy stares at me and smiles and I can't help but smile back and now it ducks down. 'We are gathered here to mourn the passing of Eugene Putnam, to give thanks for his life and to celebrate that he is now received into our Father's house. He was a dear friend and neighbour to us all, and this congregation, this parish, will especially feel his loss.'

He goes on – chairman of the parish council, treasurer of the parish council, chairman again. Solicitor. Freemason. Regular contributor of letters to the editor in the *Scotsman* and other newspapers. Free thinker and unquestioning follower of John Calvin in all his teachings.

'But most of all,' says Reverend Manders as if he knew anything about my father, 'he was a loving family man. By the grace of God, he joins his wife Mary who went before him into the kingdom of heaven six years ago, his father Eugene David and his mother Wendy.

'He leaves his three brothers and his two sons, Daniel' – he glances at the front row – 'and Christopher.' Who, I would point out, is also here, is also in a church, also doing his mourning, also ... I don't know. But I don't say anything. I cannot. I am what I am, but I am not one who speaks out in crowds. Hasn't he noticed me? I am invisible. I hope I am invisible. I want to be here, witness it, but perhaps to run around yanking black ties, knocking off the women's hats, strewing tulips in the air. My own commemoration of his life. My own acknowledgement of his death. My own fury that he left without a word. My own celebration, even ... I don't know.

The old man who was singing too loudly is blowing his nose. This place smells of mildew, creeping black cultures redoubling on prayer books.

'We are all born in sin. It lives in every part of us, but God, in His goodness, has chosen some of us to be saved although none of us is worthy of His love.' God's conditional love again. I want to be loved unconditionally, unspiritually. The little boy pops his head up again in front of me and smiles. I smile back briefly and look again towards the pulpit, trying to be appropriate, but the boy continues to stare at me smiling.

'He has given us His only son in atonement for the sins of the elect, as Jesus said in his suffering, "I pray not for the world, but for them which thou hast given me; for they are thine." And we are saved not by our own will, but by God's and we shall know those whom He has chosen by their acts and by their sincere knowledge of Christ. Gene Putnam was such a man.' The boy laughs, still staring at me. No one turns around. He bobs down again.

'Rarely was there a man so clearly destined by God to join him in glory. God has saved him. Gene was free to act according to the good nature with which God blessed him and the goodness of his nature meant he was never free to stray from the path of righteousness.'

He honestly believes it all. What sort of freedom is that? Freedom to do what God has made you choose to do? Why does he go on believing it? There is no God and I have no father. Take the body away. Do what you want with it. And try resurrecting the bones.

The boy runs down the aisle from the back of the kirk. 'Wooo, wooe, wooee,' he screams and it makes a fine echo between the grey walls. Everyone looks. No one speaks. A hand darts out from an aisle and grabs him and his elasticated waistband slips slightly and he falls over and starts to cry.

'We who loved him may share our grief together, express our thanks for his life and rejoice that he now resides with Christ.'

The little boy cries. People glare at his mother. My father is saved. I am not. I have no knowledge of Christ. The rest might as well be silence.

*

I follow my uncles and my brother as they carry my father's coffin to the graveside, not because I want to be there as they cover the box with dirt, but because I do not want to stand and wait by the kirk with the people who do not know what to say, especially to me.

We, the close family, stand in black above this rectangular ditch to watch this rite performed, the body in the box, the box in the hole, the dirt on the box. I know what happens. I stand with my back to my mother's grave.

'I would not have you to be ignorant, brethren, concerning them which are asleep, that ye sorrow not, even as others which have no hope. For if we believe that Jesus died and rose again, even so them also which sleep in Jesus will God bring with him.'

It has stopped raining, but I wish it hadn't. I don't want people to see that I am not crying. They will think terrible things of me. They already do. The sun has come out.

When I watched them throw mud on my mother's box and knew it was just a box, I think that was the nail in the coffin as far as God was concerned. Having no reason to believe takes you only so far, even having something else to replace it. God had his nails in me so deep, I needed a damn good reason to resent the very notion of him.

But no, my faith started to decay long before my mother did.

'Wherefore comfort one another with these words.'

No. There was never any god for me. I will comfort myself with thoughts of piggyback rides and my father whom I kissed I don't know how often. And that I won't kiss again.

I hate my father. I hate him even in his coffin. I hate him because he didn't love me anymore. I hated him. I don't know if I love him too.

*

The family home of Eugene and Mary Putnam, which had belonged to the elder Eugene and Wendy Putnam before them and which predated the Putnam family by more than three centuries, was called 'Le Noires'. It was always pronounced by its inhabitants in broad Scots as *lee-norries*. It stood about 300 yards apart from most of the village of Dunmarrick, high and alone, directly overlooking the rocks craggily tumbling down over centuries into the thick black water of the Firth of Forth below and the sea stretching blackly, bleakly all the way to Denmark, to Elsinore.

With its single tower, Le Noires cut a portentous silhouette, like a grave castle, above the high coastal brae. All around, the nipping and eager winds from the Firth kept most growth along the lofty coast to waist height: scrubby shrubs and crook-backed hedges, cowering from the gusts, except that an imposing yew stood in the front of the lonely stone house. To the back, a flagstone platform or patio looked out over the water to the south. The light at different times of the day variously made the walls look black, blue, white or even red, but the truth was that they were grey.

The living room was the largest room at Le Noires, but even this room was poorly lit. Two walls (north and east) were lined with many books with weighty and unwelcoming spines and the east wall ended in two-thirds of a circle formed by the inside of the thin round tower. French windows led out on to the patio. Only the west wall had space for ornaments or pictures, but even here there was no more than a single oil portrait of Chris's late great-grandfather, whose name, like that of his son and grandson, was, according to a gilded plaque on the frame, Eugene Putnam.

The door on the right led to the kitchen, which received almost no light in the mornings as the family prayers were said around the large wooden table every day as Chris and Dan grew up.

Upstairs, there were a bathroom and three bedrooms, two of which were identical in size and shape except that the room to the back of the house, which was Dan's, had a window to the left as one entered the room (facing south), and the other, Chris's, had a window to the right (facing north). Chris's room was therefore darker, a feature exacerbated by the yew which stood outside in the shelter of the house. The same, but different.

Chris lived in this house until October 1994, four months after his eighteenth birthday, when he went to University College London to study for a degree in biology. Believing, as he did, that God made the world and everything in it in six days, Gene's father disapproved of modern biology.

*

There are around thirty people in the living room, in the kitchen and on the patio, mostly eating small sandwiches and drinking large whiskies. It's warm outside, but there are grumbling grey clouds all across the sky out over the Firth. Rain could come down at any minute. It's dark indoors.

The sombreness of the kirk has been left in the churchyard and people are now chatting less soberly. As if my father hadn't died. Or, in my case, perhaps more as if he had.

I am not happy he is dead, but I am relieved the funeral is over. It is just as well no one knows the thoughts I have. My own father and yet I feel so little, just absence, relief and, and ... I don't know. I should be feeble with mourning. I should well up with an unselfconscious flood of tears, like when Mummy died and I did not even pause to name my feelings *grief*. I should be ashamed. I'm not, but my throat is blocked, like I'm going to choke or cry with self-pity or disgust. But I can't find any feeling inside me, nothing I should feel. Maybe it's there, I just don't feel it, but what's a feeling you don't feel?

I am still not at home at Le Noires, less than ever in fact. I do not know most of these people. I do not want to know the others. I am staying here tonight and so I have to stay for the wake, but I would like to be free to go somewhere else. I walk around the patio, the living room, the kitchen and the living room again, keeping moving so as not to talk to anyone, although they occasionally smile sympathetically, mid-mouthful, baring teeth with flakes of pastry and sausage meat mashed between them. Eventually I stand in the tower where I can haunt the room without inhabiting it and look out through the window and sip whisky. Each sip burns as it goes down, sending a potent poisonous shiver through me, but after that it is warm and honeyed and so each time I sip at it again. I have never known whether I like it.

There is comfortable talk in the room. Dan is in his element, holding court, charming a crowd of guests I doubt he knows much better than I do, putting them at ease. Even at a wake. Even at his own father's wake. He is the only one smoking indoors, a tiny roll-up which may not be alight. Our father would not have let him, but he rules here now. The other smokers stand on the patio. He has removed his tie and is now in his dark suit and white shirt. I have caught his eye several times, but we haven't spoken yet, not since I arrived. His hair is longer than mine, but only slightly and it is slicked back. It's shorter than when I last saw him. He is very lonely, right now, even as he tells a joke, just a small one, not inappropriate. I don't hear, but I know how he will smother sadness. I know how much he feels and how much more he always hides.

He darts a glance in my direction again. This time it is an apology. He is what he is though. I need to piss.

I work my way across the room, not crossing the middle where I will be drawn into the orbit of Dan's conversational huddle, but past the bookcases, where I feel camouflaged, fading into the gloom of the room's edges like just another book. I make it out into the hallway where there is a man with crumbs on his jacket between me and the lavatory door. 'Oh, sorry.'

'Och, don't worry,' he says as if it's sympathy. 'It's a sad thing, is it not?' he adds, 'But the young reverend did Gene proud. He would have been pleased.'

I doubt it, I want to say, but say something grateful instead.

'We're all right proud of you here, you know,' he says.

They are not and he is confused, but it is easier not to disabuse him and so I just say 'thank you' and give as gentle a smile as I can muster and now say, 'Excuse me, may I?' and look expectantly at the lavatory door with a gesture a bit like pointing.

'Och, of course,' and he steps aside, 'but I think there's someone in it.'

I try the door anyway, but it is locked, and I say 'thank you' to him again and decide to use the one upstairs.

In the bathroom I lock the door and let out a breath.

My urine is dark. I have not had much to drink today, I think, and now start to count the vodkas I felt I needed on the train and the couple of whiskies I felt I needed since we got back to the house. Apart from a coffee, I have drunk nothing non-alcoholic today and I haven't eaten. I may be getting drunk. But there is no one to stop me and I feel like a kid sneaking drinks while his parents are out, so why not?

I do up the flies on my dark suit and wash my hands,

staring at my face in the mirror. I look at my own face and know what I am thinking. I am alone here. It is obvious. I rest my forehead against the mirror and my reflection does the same. The cold mirror makes me feel a bit dizzy.

The hand towel is wet so I dry my hands by rubbing them damply across my face which might also make me steady again and wake me up a bit. I run them through my hair. I take off my tie.

I open the door and there is a girl outside on the landing about to try the door. We are both surprised at first, but she smiles broadly and asks how I'm doing. 'Well, you know, coping, thanks,' I say nodding, but her voice wasn't sympathetic. I think it may have been normal conversation. She leans towards me a bit. Drunk, maybe. She puts her hand on my shoulder. We are still standing in the bathroom doorway. She's some kind of cousin, I think, or the daughter of friends of the family.

'You look almost respectable in that get-up,' she says.

'Thanks,' I say again. 'Do you want to ...?' and I nod my head towards the bathroom.

'I can wait. I'd rather chat for a bit. We've hardly spoken.'

'Thanks.' Why *thanks*? Neither of us say anything.

'What would make this the best funeral of your life?' she asks and I don't know how to respond to a question like that so I say nothing but try to look as if I might be about to. We are standing very close and I can smell whisky on her breath, but it isn't strong. 'Would you like to go in there?' She is looking straight into my eyes except for a quick dart to the right as she finishes the question. I look to the right through the open door of my parents' bedroom. I can see the bed. Her hand moves from my shoulder behind my neck.

'It's not ...' I begin, but I don't know where to take it after that and don't get a chance to, because she pulls my face forward on to hers. She opens her mouth wide. I don't want to seem rude, so I part my lips as little as I can get away with and continue to kiss her until it seems okay to draw away.

'How about it, eh?' she says through her damp-mouthed smile. 'Would that do it for you? On his bed? Worship me on his altar. Honour thy father and thy mother. Come on, let's honour them on their bed. Sex and sacrilege – is that sincere enough for you? That's what you want, isn't it?' She's panting though her giggles and her left hand, the one that wasn't round my neck is undoing my jacket buttons and she is pressing herself against my left leg.

'Later, maybe, when everyone's gone.'

'I'll be gone when everyone's gone.' I am pressed against the bathroom door jamb. 'Let's do it now. I thought you liked it inappropriate. You can't get much more inappropriate than this.'

Her hand smooths down over my belt buckle to my crotch but I stop her there and grab her hand and squeeze out from under her into the middle of the landing. 'You wait for me,' I say. 'I'll be back in a few minutes.' I step back from her and, realising it would be fitting, I give her a peck on the lips but I don't look at her as I do so and now I break away down the stairs. When I know I'm out of sight, I wipe my lips with the back of my hand.

Jesus. Where the fuck is Dan?

I find him in the kitchen, sitting in my father's chair, nodding sagely as old Poulson talks to him about the house.

'Would you mind if I stole my brother for a minute or two, Mr Poulson?' I say and Dan gets up. We leave Mr Poulson sitting on his own and Dan and I, both dressed like gangsters, move through the guests into the lounge. We are a spectacle that creates confusion. We always have been and we have always known it. We head for the tower. Great Aunt Verity is in the armchair by the French windows, but she won't hear. She smiles randomly as we and other guests ignore her.

'How's it hanging, bro?' says Dan when we reach the safety of the tower. There is something about the tower which allows clandestine chats, a corner that feels like a separate room. 'Doing okay?'

'I was. I just had a close call with one of your conquests upstairs.'

'Who?'

'I don't know. There can't be *that* many here.'

'What she look like?'

I try to remember. 'Um, dressed in black?'

'Right, cheers, bro. You're hopeless. Hair colour?'

Red hair, I think I remember dark red. 'Red,' I say.

'Ah, yes. The opulent Ophelia with the pre-Raphaelite

locks. 'Red', honestly. It's *titian*. Anyway, thanks bro. What d'you do with her?'

'Nothing. But she kissed me.'

'You poor bastard.'

'She's probably still up there waiting for you.'

'Now? Really?'

'Yep, Dad's bedroom.'

'You're joshing me?' He doesn't need me to tell him I'm not. 'Christ, she's more fucking hot and ready than a Pop Tart. What did she say?'

'Um, something about sex and worship. She seemed to think doing it on Dad's bed would be some kind of act of remembrance.'

'That makes sense. Okay, sounds cool. Thanks, bro. I'll go up in a minute.' He looks around, nonchalantly. 'This is all a bit of a 'mare for you, eh?'

'Well, I thought I'd better come, you know, face the music. After all, I doubt I'll ever have to come back here again. None of them wants to know me. I definitely don't want to know them. The only ones who even talk to me are only doing it because they think they're talking to you.' I stop talking and look at all the ageing faces. I'm in a rotten state here. Dunmarrick is a prison. But this is my last humiliation. I am free of all obligation now. I'm going back to England as soon as I can.

'Actually, you may have to come back. We don't know the score on the house and all that.'

'You don't need me for that, do you?'

'I've fixed for us to go see Poulson on Wednesday about the will.'

'Jesus, Dan, I was going to go back to London in the morning.'

'If you stay another day, you may never have to come back. He says there's stuff in it you'll want to hear. He's being all red-tape about it. Christ, as if it matters.' I know he means Mr Poulson, not me. He knows even a day at Le Noires matters to me. 'Stay one more day. Then we'll go down to London together. You flying?'

'Guess again, big spender. I'm stony. Really. Forking out for the train was bad enough.'

'One more day and then you can do what you like.

Besides, we can get up to speed, bro. I haven't seen you since ...'

'Eight weeks,' I say, having already worked it out. The quick coffee in Covent Garden, the update on my life and on my father's imminent death, Dan failing to take life, or death, seriously.

'Yeah, you haven't got back with Gill, have you?'

'No. It's over.'

'Yeah, but are *you* over it?'

'Yes,' I say cautiously. 'I am.'

'In that case,' says Dan, 'there's someone I want you to meet.'

'I'm not sure. I'm not sure I'm ready yet. Who?'

'Details only if you stay for one more day. Suffice to say: tall, gorgeous, talented, clever, successful and very famous. Too good to be true. The full Mills and Boon.'

'You're kidding.' Gemini, I think. Affairs to hot up.

'*Very* famous,' he says again. 'Stay one more day. Then you're free to do whatever you want. We're orphans now, bro.'

'Jesus,' I say, probably out loud.

*

A *clone* is one of a group of organisms that are genetically identical either because they are derived from a single cell or because the genetic material of some original organism has been artificially duplicated in the clone zygotes (embryos).

Chris Putnam was a clone.

Chromosome 3
The Human Script (I)

'The human genome project became the Holy Grail of Biology and a quest for the all-revealing Book of Man.'

Robert Cook-Deegan

' "Forty-two!" yelled Loonquawl. 'Is that all you've got to show for seven and a half million years' work?'

"I checked it very thoroughly," said the computer, "and that quite definitely is the answer. I think the problem, to be quite honest with you, is that you've never actually known what the question is."

"But it was the Great Question! The Ultimate Question of Life, the Universe and Everything," howled Loonquawl.

"Yes ... but what actually is it?"'

Douglas Adams

In every living thing, there are cells. Sometimes one, sometimes so many they are beyond reckoning. And in every cell, there is a nucleus. And in every nucleus, there is DNA.[1]

In every cell[2] in every body of every member of that arbitrarily determined group called 'humans', there are two metres of DNA. Stretched out, it would be taller than most specimens of the species, but it is not. It is wound beyond the gaze of microscopes in plaited spirals, which disentangle, duplicate and recombine as each cell divides. Copies upon copies, clone upon clone of identical DNA, copied in their

---

[1] With the exception of certain simple life forms which have only ribose nucleic acid (RNA) rather than deoxyribose nucleic acid (DNA) and simpler forms yet which might not even be termed 'life'. Prions, for example, or inteins.

[2] With the exception of the 'gametes' or sex cells: the spermatozoa in the male; and the ova in the female.

trillions throughout the human frame from brain to bone and from muscle to the very marrow.

In every cell in every body in every living thing, DNA is written in a language of only four letters. A, C, G, T. Each letter represents a chemical. Adenine, Cytosine, Guanine, Thymine. In the language of DNA, there are just three letters in every word and each word means one amino acid. There are only sixty-four words, but even so, many are synonyms: there are only twenty meanings, only twenty amino acids.

Every word is an anagram and words are never meaningless. This is how to read the human script.

In every cell in every body in every living thing, strings of words make sentences, meanings locked together to make a protein. A sentence is a single gene. In every human cell, there are perhaps one hundred thousand genes. The sentences make up paragraphs and chapters: in every human cell, there are forty-six chromosomes, twenty-three pairs. These twenty-three chapters make a book: the human genome contains more than three billion letters. Three thousand million. Three thousand thousand thousand. Thirty hundred hundred hundred hundred. Twice.

If humankind has an essence, here it is writ.

*

The Human Genome Project inscribed the human manuscript. The three billion letters were written down for all time. Even some of the known variations were noted, those typographical changes that make every folio unique, that perpetually corrupt the pure text of humanity as some author might have once intended it to be. For Adam and Eve have been degraded, reduplicated forever, photocopies of photocopies, the mistakes copied, magnified, augmented. If a god wrote the human script in his own image, then it is by now a travesty. If the Script wrote itself, there was never any first folio nor ever shall there be a last. Now Man writes it out and all that can be said is that it is long.

The Human Genome Project was the most expensive scientific project ever. To travel two metres of DNA cost more than a journey of one quarter of a million miles through space to set a human foot upon the moon.

The Human Genome Project offered a new Rosetta Stone. It was the hope of deciphering those sicknesses carved on the ovum's membrane by the etching of a sperm. It was the chance to crack the icon of cancer and vanquish for evermore that ball of death inside. Someday, it was hoped, it would even smash the tablets on which mortality itself is inscribed. In the laboratories of the world the millennial explorers laboured. For they were the distillers of The Essence of Man. They were The Seekers of The Holy Grail. They Were The Ones Who Hold The Secret Of Life Itself.

They were merely copyists.

The Human Genome is three billion letters long: A, C, G, T.

*

The human genome is a life written in a book where every word has been written before. A story endlessly rehearsed. Quotations cited and recited because once they were apt, the fittest to survive.

What gives the story originality are the context and the changes, those slight misprints, inversions of words or letters, those flaps of butterfly wings that change the whole irrevocably. Those combinations of words on the page and the context in which they are read.

All books would be the same, more or less, if the authors did not switch the letters around. And all lives would be the same, more or less, if the gods of what is past had not set in stone the letters of their genes.

Read the book of life or a life in a book: it's all epigraphs and anagrams. To read a human script is to venture to know the mind of the Author.

*

No book has meaning without a reader to understand. The human genome is a script, waiting for the amino actors, the protein players to strut and fret their hour upon the stage in an intricate, interacting interplay. Who can say they saw a whole play or read a whole book? Each has their own experience, their own play, their own book.

Humankind cannot read the book of life. Who knows what levels of meaning are embedded in the gematria and temurah of the genome? Some genes are read forwards, some backwards. Some mean something different when repeated. Some only yield understanding when read in context. Some only yield understanding when words are ignored. Some appear to have no meaning at all. Ninety-five per cent, humans used to say, is junk, meaningless. But they know now that they simply do not know how to read it.

Beyond the writing of the human script is a greater task: understanding the letters on the page.

What a piece of work is a man? The human genome!

*

The Human Genome Laboratory at Queen's College, London, where Chris worked, was, in the mid-1980s, as Chris passed through puberty, one of the first frontiers of the Human Genome Project. The first scribes of the genome cloned and recorded the DNA bases: sequencing. This process, however, became increasingly the preserve of factory labs, vast white warehouses spinning threads of letters all night and day, never ceasing their duplication even while human bodies slept.

In order to maintain his laboratory's snout in the trough, Sir Hugo Huttenton, the director, specialised its activities, focusing on the sequencing of genes related to specific pathologies and identifying where they appeared on which chromosome. The glorious tradition of the Queen's Eugenics Laboratory (as it had previously been known), the rôle it had played in establishing the Human Genome Project and the almost unique scientific reputation of Sir Hugo himself afforded him the opportunity to pursue funding for research that would inevitably attract public attention. Being familiar with self-replicating systems, Sir Hugo reasoned that such attention would beget fame, fame would beget reputation, reputation would beget funding for research which would inevitably attract public attention. And so it was.

As a consequence, Sir Hugo and his staff concentrated increasingly on conditions related to single gene mutations – maybe only a single word misspelt, a single letter out of place – and, in particular, they explored the X chromosome. The X chromosome is the most easily probed, not least because, unlike chromosomes 1 to 22 which every human has in matching pairs, males have just a single X and a single Y. Females inherit an X from each parent, but the X of men is always bequeathed by their mother. Their Y is handed down from their father and from his father before that unto the thousandth generation and beyond.

Until, that is, the clerks of cell division make enough mistakes to render the script unrecognisable. That, then, is a new species. Some mistakes assist meaning: if meaning means survival, the mistakes survive. Some mistakes attach themselves to those which survive. Some mistakes are part of the wastage of life. No individual survives life, but their ancestors inherit their successes and mistakes.

*

The human genome is what every member of that arbitrarily determined species shares and yet no two humans' sets of genes are identical. The difference between people is reflected by the minute degrees of variation in their genes. Beyond a certain point of variation, the genome is no longer deemed human. No two humans have an identical genome. With the exception of monozygotic, that is 'identical', twins, as in the instance of Chris and Dan Putnam.

Chromosome 4
Inheritance

'For I the Lord thy God am a jealous God, visiting the iniquity of the fathers upon the children unto the third and fourth generation of them that hate me'
Exodus XX, 5

'I'm haunted by ghosts ... But I'm inclined to believe we're all ghosts, Pastor Manders; it's not only the things we've inherited from our fathers and mothers that live on in us, but all sorts of old dead ideas and old dead beliefs, and things of that sort. They're not actually alive in us, but they're rooted there all the same, and we can't rid ourselves of them.'
Henrik Ibsen

Chris and Dan possessed two suits each, bought for them by their father. The first were for their confirmations on the same summer day in 1992, shortly after their sixteenth birthdays, double-breasted and broad-shouldered. The next were black, worn nearly two years later, the stiff stubbornness of unfamiliar cloth no longer a matter of pride but of discomfort as in mourning they flanked their still-living father in the kirk.

By the time of their father's death, Dan was in a financial position to have bought others, but he chose not to. It was not in his nature to wear suits, he had determined. Nevertheless, out of duty, he had worn his black suit to his father's funeral, although by the next day, he had already taken on again the designer casuals to which he was more accustomed. In Dunmarrick, such sartorial exotica would normally have betokened one who did not belong, but familiar greetings, sympathetic yet cheery, at once acknowledged both his difference and his sameness. Dan belonged. Indeed, a small part of Dunmarrick was shortly to belong to him.

That Wednesday, Dan wore orange combat trousers and a pink shirt and a parka lined with a fake ermine ruff. Chris still wore his black suit. He chose to do so, not as a sign of mourning, but because of the reverence he afforded the legal profession and because he had a lack of choice.

The address of Putnam, Poulson & Co. (Solicitors) was Arras House, a legend duplicated in gold lettering in the fanlight above the entrance, which was in fact no more than a doorway between a funeral parlour and a children's clothing shop in which reluctant offspring would be dressed in school uniforms and their mothers' ideas of presentability. Beyond the door, steps ascended to the offices of the late Gene Putnam and his colleagues. The walls of all the rooms were panelled with oak to shoulder height, whereafter plain white-painted plaster stretched to the high cold ceilings. The two partners' offices were identical in size and shape and branched off a central room in which the ageing legal secretary, a Mrs H. Alving, sat and coldly welcomed visitors with grim propriety. A window looked out to the east, to the Firth, to the brae and, just visible over the yew, the tower of Le Noires.

*

I am standing at the window which is barred although I've never known why and I am looking out and down the street and I can just see the house and this is, I hope, the last time. I don't remember this view although I must have glared at it before, waiting here for my father, after school, waiting for him to finish work to drive us to Kirkcaldy to sit by her bed and feel my flesh creep at her skin like yellow latex and her thin hair that had come away in handfuls like moss.

He'd drive us back, sometimes wordless, as if we were still naughty little boys, despicable, beneath contempt. More often, he'd be full of cheery chat about tonight's tea, the foolish way people drive on country roads or something silly he heard the woman in the next bed say. But he'd never mention her. I wanted him wrought and wracked with pain and the injustice.

I remember this window sill. I used to pick at this

cracking paint. I scratch at it a little and get a crusted flake caught under my nail. It hurts and I feel I deserve it.

And one day we went in like any other and she was tanked up on morphine, her body bloated but her wrists bony and waxy and we came home. And then I woke up in the morning and he'd left the house. He'd gone back there in the night and hadn't even woken us.

I wonder again what it would have been like. A serene tableau, a look of peace descending on her, a sigh and the ECG slowing to a single, low, plaintive tone. I know that's wrong, but to be denied it, that moment – if ever I felt the need to despise him after that, I felt I had cause.

I turn back to the room which is smaller than I remember. Of course, there are computers here now and a bigger photocopier, but a smaller fax. My father is a smaller man.

It's as if he still sits, perhaps, behind that desk behind that door that bears the plaque that reads 'E PUTNAM'. My father's ghost. Neat copper plate. His name seems far away from anything I recognise, but I remember that office with the smell of the old books and the stale tobacco of the slate cigarette case on the desk. He never smoked and yet he always kept cigarettes in it. His mouldy provincial politeness. But, no, I remember noticing it wasn't there the last time I was here and realising he must have taken it away some time after ... Her ghost must have lain in his bed at night. She makes me breakfast sometimes with haunting smells of bacon and she used to phone me up until I answered and it was someone else. My father's ghost sits behind a closed door and writes out law.

He isn't there, though, and if I opened the door, I wouldn't see him. But if I did? He still wouldn't be. I imagine him only, ghosts are imaginations. He is there behind the door, I know, even though I know he isn't and I can see his frowning face as he slowly looks up at me. I would not dare open the door. People who see ghosts are just mistaken, thinking the cause of what they see is outside themselves, that's all. I know it isn't true, he's not there, in the chair, he's in my head – but it gives me no relief. Perhaps I want to know he still sits behind that door. This is grief, I suppose, but it feels more like quiet intimidation. With the door closed, I don't have to think I see him.

How do I prove my father is not at his desk behind the door and if I open it I ... Experiments and observations demonstrate what is, not what is not. How do I prove my father's dead or that there are no such things as ghosts or souls or God? Just because something isn't real, does that mean it doesn't exist? Even a projection of the mind is a kind of existence. Thoughts have physics – the electro-chemical floods and pulses that wash around the brain. Ghosts are real in their own way, but not independent of those who see them. Like fictions.

The father in my head is real. Only he has no power over me now. Nor can he forgive me. Does my father's ghost know he doesn't exist any more than I know I do?

I tug at the cuff of my suit jacket and twist my neck to get the shoulders of it straight and Mrs Alving carries on typing. I watch the blur of her fingers on the keyboard and cannot synchronise them with the speed of the click-click-click they make. Dan comes back from the toilet and throws Mrs Alving a charming grin. She stops typing and returns a ragged toothy smile. I breathe out.

Dan slumps into the low leather armchair and automatically picks up a magazine, the *Lady*.

'Are you sure you won't have a cup of tea, Daniel?' says Mrs Alving. 'Mr Poulson may be a few moments yet.'

'Go on then, Mrs A. You run a mean campaign,' says Dan and she bares the teeth again and bustles off merrily and I begin to wish maybe I'd said I would have one now, but I feel guilty about getting her to rush round making tea. I drop into the settee next to Dan.

'So where were you yesterday, then?' I ask. 'I thought we were going to do some catching up.'

'Ophelia,' says Dan, leaning forward confidentially.

'Who?'

'Don't you remember *anything* from one mo to the next? Ophelia, old man Poulson's daughter? She with the titian hair and the opulent curves? The opportunity you didn't take on Monday.'

'Oh, yeah. She's Ian Poulson's daughter?'

'And a fucking steamer. You know she's a nurse, right?' He looks at my eyes for acknowledgement he doesn't expect to see. 'Anyway, she works in Kirkcaldy on the ward

46

where Gene was—'

'Please, Dan, I don't want to know the sordid details. You ought to be careful – that's your own doorstep you're shitting on. This isn't London, remember. One peck on the cheek round here and they'll have you walking down the aisle.'

'No problem, bro. She's cool. She knows I'm just an easy lay. I'm not her type.' And he leans back again with the *Lady* on his lap. And Dan doesn't have a type. He just sits there smiling, content with the service he has provided.

'Is there anyone you wouldn't sleep with?'

'Oh sure: anyone who doesn't want to sleep with me, but beyond that, well, it all adds to the realm of experience, doesn't it? As a rule, though, I'll leave the guys for you. Talking of which ...' But Mrs Alving comes back in and Dan stands up to take a tray from her. The cup is bone china with a pattern of pansies and rosemary with a matching cream jug, sugar bowl and plate with two shortbread fingers. 'You're priceless, Mrs A.,' he says.

She looks pleased with herself and goes to knock on one of the twin closed office doors. 'I POULSON' it says. I cannot know that he's behind it any more than my father. It's an interesting thought experiment. Oh yes, it's Schrödinger and the cat and that is why ... I think again about the cigarette case. When did he stop – and I am about to ask Dan when she comes out again and looks at him and says, 'You can go on in now, boys.'

*

Chris's ex, Gill Francis, had a pretty face, no sense of humour and, being an individual of particular habits, liked to listen to jazz during thunderstorms. He was also a man. Gill, with a hard 'G'.

He and Chris went out with each other for five years and one month from the ages of eighteen (on Chris's part) and nineteen (on Gill's) to twenty-three and twenty-four (respectively). They never cohabited although after the first three weeks until the last eleven months, they rarely slept apart. They did not hold hands in public as Gill detested

47

advertising their sexuality almost to the point of denial, but sometimes they would dance together when they were on their own, but only to rock 'n' roll, never to what Gill would denounce as 'camp slush'. They would talk on their own too; mostly Gill would talk and Chris would listen. Gill drank Guinness and had a green jumper which smelled of Égoïste pour Homme and Chris spent nearly six years trying to controvert, or at least compromise, Gill's defences. Yet Chris also spent nearly six years thinking he still didn't really know Gill, who it was that brought the relationship to a conclusion on millennium night at a party in Maida Vale.

One Sunday evening the following April, Elsi, Chris's flatmate, had advised him, 'There's plenty more Gills in the sea.' She did not suppose, whenever she turned such phrases, that Chris, or indeed anyone, would appreciate them. She would have felt almost cheated if they had. They were merely a personal and private amusement when practising the art of rhetorical conversation. She had then drawn long on the joint in her right hand before bringing her thoughts to bear again on the question of Chris's emotional life and how she might be able to improve it.

*

I've never been in Ian Poulson's office before and to my surprise there is a heavy velvet curtain immediately behind the door. I pull it to one side and expose him standing there, behind his desk, an uncertain rat-like grin on his face which brightens as Dan follows me in.

He steps towards us, motioning to the chairs around a round meeting table. 'Lads, lads, come in. Sit down, you must. Dan, I can tell, for the apparel oft proclaims the man, as I always say. Take a seat. Are you both well? I'm sorry to be having to meet under such sad circumstances for us all. Sit down, sit down. Can I get Mrs Alving to get you a cup of tea, perhaps? Has she offered you one?'

It is too late to ask for one now. I don't want her to think that refusing earlier was anything personal. I sit down. Ian Poulson takes Dan warmly by the hand and Dan says, 'You're all right, Ian, Mrs A.'s been looking after us,' and I stand up to shake his hand too, but he's in the process of sitting down now, so he has to stand up again to take my hand limply. His hand is clammy. Or maybe it is mine.

We all sit down. 'Well, Dan, I hear you were stepping out with my daughter last night? I trust you two got up to nothing of which I wouldn't approve.' His great stupid grin tries to be conspiratorial. 'I should perhaps be asking your intentions as regards my daughter and her honour. What is between you? Give me up the truth.' He laughs matily and Dan laughs along. Down the aisle, Dan. Watch it.

'She deserves a better man than me, Ian,' he says and looks at me. No, Dan, don't drag me into your mess.

Ian Poulson looks at me quickly and looks back at Dan. 'Ah, there's none finer than yourself. Nothing would make me happier, but I don't know, you kids. I'm an old fool who doesn't understand the younger generation's relationships any more. It's all changed. There was a time when a couple of good-looking young men like yourselves would be married up and settled down by now. Your father would have loved to bounce a grandchild on his knee. 'Tis a pity, a terrible pity. None of you knows what you're about. Off in England, the pair of you. But we hear plenty about you in the papers, Dan, plenty about you.'

Dan smiles kindly.

'And young Chris,' he says. I sit up. 'How goes life with you? Are you in good health?'

'Yes, thank you,' I say and put on a smile very like Dan's, but I don't wear it so comfortably.

'It's been a while since we've seen you here. 'Tis a pity you could not have come home during your father's illness, but I don't want to interfere. I'm sure you had your reasons.'

He nods to himself. 'Ah, pride's a terrible thing when it comes betwixt a father and a son. I'm not blaming you at all. I don't know the matter of the business and I don't want to interfere. And God knows, Gene could be a stubborn man, God rest his soul. The best I ever knew, but a stubborn, steadfast man. But I'm sure whatever was the heart of the thing he could have set it aside at the last.'

You're *sure*, are you? Don't be.

'Whatever it was – and it's none of my business – I'm sure he forgives everything now. But there's a lesson to be learnt,

Chris, and you might do well to learn by it. Just a few precepts to keep in your memory, if you'll have the patience to attend to a few words of wisdom from a tedious old fool. I don't want to interfere, but – and you'll see what I mean when we take our little look at the matter of your father's will – a young man does himself no favours in life if he's too headstrong. There's no denying it's a mark of strength to choose your own way in life, but neither does it hurt to take a little advice from your elders. Your father was a wise man, Chris, and a good man too. It's never a matter of strength to turn your back on your own father.'

'Thank you,' I say, because I can't think of anything else.

'It's never too late for forgiveness, Chris. He still watches you, Chris. Whatever you two quarrelled about, I'm sure you both had your good reasons, for, as I always say, there was always method in the madness of Gene Putnam. I know what young men can be like and I'm sure you're as impetuous as your brother here. Or your father for that matter, eh, when he was young, God rest him. Ay, like father like son. But, as a general matter of a point of principle, Chris, being impetuous, give matters a little thought, eh? There's naught you can't change, Chris.'

He stops and leans back in his chair as if he expects me to speak, but now he starts again. 'Naught you can't change, Chris, if it's in your nature. To thine own self be true, as I always say. Your father was a good man, Chris, a Christian man. He brought you up well, to honour him and listen to him. I don't know what happened betwixt you, lad, but he brought you up to know you are always free to follow your nature and I'm sure, deep down, you're a good Christian lad, Chris. You're free to make your own choices, but, when all's said and done, at the end of the day, I hope it's in you to make the right ones. To thine own self be true, as I always say.'

My nature? I've had enough of these Calvinist epithets. My father spoonfed them to me. I don't need them from you.

'I say this, son, for your own good, you know. As I've said, I don't want to interfere, but as you'll see, as Dan already knows, your father's will does not favour you. I'm sure he did not mean it to be harsh, Chris, for I know Gene well. Better, perhaps, than any man. He was naught if not fair. I'm sure he

50

meant you to learn from this. I would not interfere otherwise.'

I look at Dan who wears an expressionless face. He is stifling a laugh, I know. He is taking this all seriously: at least he's stifling it.

'But brevity, as I always say, is the soul of wit. So let us now without further ado get down to the heart of the matter of the thing,' and, as he carries on talking, he leans back in his chair and reaches for a black folder from his desk. He pulls out a copy of my father's will and a plain brown puritan sealed envelope. He stops talking and says, 'Oh yes, and there's a letter for you both from your father. You are to read it when you've heard the will.'

*

The last Will and Testament of Eugene Joseph Putnam, being of sound mind, determined that the majority of his estate should be inherited by his younger son Daniel. In spite of, or perhaps because of, his Calvinist belief in predestination, Gene Putnam had always been a cautious man. This had made him averse to risk throughout his years of scrupulous saving for a protracted retirement which, as fate would have it, was never to come. Nevertheless, these investments had accrued what might be considered a generous return. This sum was compounded by the monies paid in insurance against the ultimately inevitable death of the late Mary Putnam six years prior to his own. Certain mortgages on the property herein called Le Noires had been made in respect of school fees and were to be repaid under their terms, leaving, nonetheless, a respectable inheritance for a member of that class at that time.

Gene Putnam's share in the partnership of Putnam, Poulson & Co. (Solicitors) was passed to his partner, Ian Poulson. As was decreed in the agreement establishing the partnership, in the event of the demise of either Partner ownership of the Partnership and all rights pertaining therein shall automatically become the sole property of the remaining Partner.

Other gifts were made by covenant to a number of

charities and causes, not least the Dunmarrick Free Presbyterian Kirk. Small cash sums and certain specified personal possessions were bequeathed to members of the family and friends.

Gene Putnam's other son, Christopher, inherited the sum of £4,514.

Such was the will of Gene Putnam.

*

The sky has cleared a little as we walk up the hill from the village back to Le Noires and all I am thinking about is getting out of these clothes, packing my bag and persuading Dan to give me a lift to the station. Dan lopes along beside me, carrying a file under his arm and the envelope.

'Tell you what, bro, I wouldn't have taken it,' he says.

'What was I supposed to do? I couldn't think of anything to say, so I said nothing.'

'But he was bad-mouthing you something rotten. I'd at least have taken the opportunity to give as good as I got. I would've told him a few home truths. You'll probably never have to see his face again. Could've been a laugh.'

'Dan, you know I wasn't going to do that.' Not while I imagined my father's ghost in the next room.

'I would have.'

'I know *you* would, but I can't come up with things to say quickly enough. Besides, I wasn't about to go into any explanations with him.'

'That's probably what it was all about. Old foolsome-Poulson just wanted to know the great mystery. He couldn't bear to let Gene go underground without knowing the juice. You were his last chance to find out.'

'You don't think he told him, then?' As I say it, I realise how stupid it is to suppose everyone knows everything about me. I'm just being paranoid. It's this place. The place is against me.

'You kidding? Gene would never have owned up to him about having a fruit for a son. That's why Poulson kept spouting such bollocks.' He stops walking, puts a hand on my chest to stop me, looks me in the face and raises an eyebrow sternly. 'Free to follow your nature, young Chris. There's a lesson to be learnt. To thine own self ... what a load of pony.' He starts walking again, leaving me a few steps behind, tucking the file and the envelope under his arm and pulling his rolling gear out of his deep pockets. 'But he was right about one thing, though.'

'What?'

'Gene wanting to see you at the end. The whole deathbed trip.'

'What?'

'The email.'

'What?'

'Wotwotwot. The email. I sent it the week before he choked.'

The email. It is still unopened, unread. 'I didn't get it,' I say. 'I was in Cambridge until the Monday and then, then I didn't, then you phoned and he was dead.' Dan is already licking at the Rizla and pinching it into shape between finger and thumb.

'That's a shame,' he says and stops walking at the gate to the house and hands me the file so he can light the roll-up which, in the wind, requires both hands. Alight, he pushes open the gate leaving me carrying the file. The house looks down, like a frown. My feet crunch in the gravel driveway. Dan's hire car is parked by the front door.

'What,' I begin, 'what did it say?'

'Not much.' He pulls his keys out of his pocket by the long chain clipped to his belt. 'Just sort of last-legs stuff and that he wanted to see you. I thought you'd ignored it. Was a bit surprised at the time. Thought it was a bit heartless – not your style.'

How could you? I want to scream at Dan, at his indifference, but I don't, because Dan wants to get a rise. And anyway, I did. I did ignore it. I feel a growth of regret already churning in my gut, rising as an empty nausea to the back of my throat. He wanted to see me before he died. And I didn't even want to know what the message said. I wouldn't have wanted to see him anyway. I would have said no to this dying man. Would I? I don't know, no one could know, a pointless *what if?* Would I have wanted his deathbed absolution, words of frail forgiveness poured in my ear as I bent over his unrecognisable dying frame shrouded in hospital sheets? Would he have forgiven me anyhow? There was nothing to forgive. I don't want it anyway.

He should have – well, it should have been different in the first place. I'm not going to be made to feel bad about this. If there's any forgiving to be done, it's by me, and would I have wanted to rush to his bedside to grant it? Out of love? Out of pity? Out of guilt?

'Why?' I ask. 'Did he want to see me just to tell me I was forgiven for being me?'

'No, not forgive exactly, it was more to do with making peace, I think.' He pauses just inside the door to see the effect on me, standing still outside. 'He wanted to say that you couldn't help being who you are. In the end, I don't think it was the gay thing. The way he saw things, he couldn't judge what God had chosen to make you suffer – his words, you know. Well, more or less. In the end he might have hoped you'd change, but ... well, he told me he wanted to say he didn't blame you for not being one of the saved, but that it's never too late to show you are. His main objection all along was religious and not, well, homophobic, and, religiously speaking, he wanted you back. I think he thought that part was more of a deliberate smack in the mouth. But he didn't want to leave you thinking he was showing you the shoulder.' He pauses. 'Ironic, really, because instead, he died thinking you'd rejected him. Might even have said he loved you. I mean, I know that wasn't his style, but, hey, he said it to me.'

Dan knows he has me now. I am open like a wound. I am not sure how much of all this to believe. He knows how close I am to breaking now and maybe, at the end, after all, there was a change. But to say he loved me? That's not how my father speaks. Spoke. This doesn't sound like Dan either, he isn't making it up. At least, not deliberately. I don't know what to think. I don't know now whether I have sinned against my father or he has sinned against me. I did not go to see him on his deathbed. That is my fault. And now he is no longer. He is just decay in a box in the ground. It doesn't matter. But it does. He was and is no more than a tide of chemical currents, now oozing into the bottom of a coffin. But he was more.

And I didn't see him at the last. Even when he wanted me

to. Dan holds my gaze and touches my arm and says something but I am not hearing it. He loved me. He fathered me. He loved my mother and yet he loved me so much he could not bear for me to see him cry when she died and so he hid his tears. And I left him alone, to fumble about this house, moving the furniture around to try to make her absence go away. That is what his ghost is now. His absence, not his presence. His absence is here. Here in this house where I left him to get old and ill and be in pain and die and I would not even come when at last he wanted only for me to be there. I did not even want to know. My throat fills with a fist of tears.

Dan steps aside and into the kitchen. I am still standing outside by the front door and the wind is wrapping around the house and whipping around me, sharpening itself against my cheeks and making my eyes water. I step inside and I can see through into the living room and beyond on to the patio where, in my mind's eye, my father's ghost stands by the window. He beckons.

*

Gene Putnam was a cautious man, or, some might say, a coward, because he believed he had control. He believed in inevitability. He built thick walls around his position in life, his home, his beliefs, and he cordoned his emotions against any challenge to that future which he had planned for himself and for his family.

He liked the law, the rectitude it afforded to those who studied it and penetrated it with wisdom, reason and faith; and he disliked the uncertain, the unexpected, the confrontational.

He was proper and even-tempered, shy among strangers, forthright among friends, neighbours and colleagues.

He believed his life would unfold according to divine decree. He accepted his wife's death with grace, equanimity and sorrow. In his modest way, he believed he understood the plan of God the Father, Son and Holy Ghost. He therefore assumed a certain knowledge about how the future should be or, rather, *would* be. To a Calvinist, they are the same.

*

Chris chose to inform his father that he was homosexual on the fourteenth of December 1994 as the two of them sat alone eating dinner in the kitchen at Le Noires. It was the night of Chris's return after his first term at University College London. It was also ten months to the day since Chris's mother, Chris's father's wife, had died of (probably genetically heritable) breast cancer at the age of forty-nine years, on St Valentine's Day. Chris, his mind filled with the thrill and thrall of his novel existence, did not heed the relevance of the date. His father, on the other hand, had taken to investing secret numerological significance in dates and in the counting of days, of weeks, of months.

Chris had been aware of his sexuality for longer than he had been able to define it, but not for as long as he had been aware that it was not a matter for open discussion. He believed, however, that if it were ever to be mentioned, that the Christmas break in question was an appropriate time. He had a new incentive for raising the issue, namely, a boyfriend, Gill Francis, whom he had met in a lecture series on Reproductive Methods. He had reasoned, with growing confidence in, and encouragement from, Gill, that: (a) his father was having to accept many changes in his life; (b) he was now old enough for his father to accept him as an adult and therefore his own adult decisions; and (c) homosexuality was, after all, a common and natural phenomenon. The last point (at least) was informed more by his own change of circumstances (an eighteen-year-old biology student living in London) than by his father's (a Calvinist widower living in east Scotland).

On the whole, he had reasoned, there was never a good time to come out, but, on the whole, he had also reasoned at length, now was as good a time as any and better than most. It is impossible to know whether he had reasoned correctly as there is no alternative to provide a comparison.

Chris and his father ate ready-made steak and kidney pie with instant mash and frozen peas and carrots. Gene Putnam asked his son about college and his son informed him of his academic progress and the structure of his course. Gene

Putnam asked about his financial situation and his son informed him that, in common with all students, it was 'a nightmare'. However, Chris declined offers of further pecuniary assistance from his father.

Gene Putnam asked his son whether he had made any friends. Chris informed him that he had made lots of friends.

Gene Putnam asked his son whether there were any in particular. Chris informed him that he thought he ought to know something. Then he said he didn't like girls. Then he said he did, but not like that. Then he said he liked boys. Then he said he didn't mean that; he liked men. Then he said he had a boyfriend. Then he said his name was Gill. Then he said nothing. Nor did his father.

There was a further week before Dan came home for Christmas from working his way around the world, which he had decided to do for a year, and, in the course of which, he would apply (and be accepted) to study art in New York.

During that week, Chris and his father moved like ghosts through the rooms of Le Noires in different, but overlapping, dimensions of reality, like the stair-climbing monks of Escher's etchings, inhabiting the same space, but apparently unaware of each other's presence. Their lack of awareness was palpable.

The silence was pregnant with noise, with muted fury, with questions the father found too disgusting to frame and with answers to which the son was incapable of giving voice.

In order to break the silence – and, indeed, it is possible to think that it may further have been by way of an explanation, elucidation or justification of his previous statement, although it is more likely that it was an act of sheer and rash desperation – Chris announced to his father, again over an otherwise wordless dinner, that he did not believe in the existence of God.

His perhaps incautious words were: 'I don't think of myself as *a gay*. It's just another thing about me, like being a man, a biology student or ... or an atheist.'

He said it apropos of nothing and it provoked, at first, a well-humoured reaction insofar that his father grinned at him, an uncertain grin which betrayed a suspicion that his son might have been perpetrating a protracted practical joke. The bewildered look, however, that greeted him in return confirmed a sincerity of belief (or lack of belief), at which Gene Putnam ceased smiling, blanched, rouged, purpled, stood up – napkin dropping noiselessly to the floor – and proceeded to shout, to slam his fist upon the wooden table and to rail at his son. Where Chris's declaration of homosexuality had been met with a drought of stubborn silence, this latter declaration was met with a deluge of brute noise. The composure had been punctured, the cordon had been breached. It was evident to Chris that his father considered any denial of God to be a deliberate insult, intended as such and as nothing else. Gene insulted him in his turn. The word 'blasphemy' was employed, in its literal sense and with the full force of its original meaning.

Chris experienced genuine terror at his father's reaction. He shrank, his bladder burning with the fear engendered by the unshakeable childhood belief in his father's omnipotence and in the tide of fury that had always been restrained but which gushed forth. However, having crossed the Rubicon, he stood his ground (or rather, continued to sit) throughout the shouting until it became no more than ridiculous volume, incapable of harm, the flood spent. Gene then grew quiet, apart from the huff of violent breaths. Next, he walked around the table and looked down at his son, who met his gaze, and Gene Putnam spat.

He retired to the living room, closing the door noisily behind him.

Chris regarded with horror the globule of his father's saliva on the stone floor by his chair and realised he was trembling.

Christmas in the Putnam family home was a sombre occasion after the death of Mary Putnam.

*

Afterwards, in corresponding increments, Le Noires felt decreasingly like a home to Chris and his visits became increasingly infrequent and brief. The penultimate stay was in the summer of 1997 after successfully completing his undergraduate degree. He had intended to remain for a fortnight, but after three days, it had become ten days and after five days, he had decided to leave the following morning.

Chris's last visit was for his father's funeral, after which, even until the day of his own inevitable death, Chris never returned.

During the last years of his life, Gene acknowledged to himself that he did little to make his eldest son welcome at Le Noires, but when words passed between them, the absent words sounded louder than those spoken. If Gene asked how long Chris intended to stay, they would both hear, silently appended, a reference to his heathen life of debauchery and debasement of the Lord. Mary Putnam would once have crowded out the silences with uxorial and maternal tendernesses and her absence was as loud as ever. A mother and wife would have healed the wound in the family, but it developed a scab of uneasy silence which finally became a scar of safe distance.

It was easier for Gene, for Chris (like father, like son), not to act, to say nothing, to build thick walls, to cordon their emotions and, in Chris's case, to go home to Gill. Being together was awkward and stilted, but, being apart, the bacteria of resentment bred: distance turned to distrust; distrust turned to bitterness; bitterness to hate, which is, after all, a kind of grievous love.

*

I do not believe in ghosts, but I live with them. They are in my head, no more than memories, or thoughts. I am in my brother's house, Le Noires. He is at the kitchen table, poring over the papers that Poulson gave him. I am standing in the doorway, my bag at my feet.

'Give us a lift to the station?'

'Don't you want to read the letter first?'

'Do you know what it says?'

'No.'

'Really?' He knew about the will and didn't tell me, not that I needed to be told, not that I cared.

'I can guess.'

'What?'

'It probably explains why I got the house and everything

59

and you got nothing.'

'Why?'

'Dunno,' says Dan and he is tearing open the envelope as if the choice of leaving its contents unread forever isn't there or doesn't matter. *'My dear sons ...'* he starts, camping it up as the voice from the crypt, 'blah, blah, blah. I'll cut to the chase, all right? Blah, blah. *It is my profound wish that my legacy should be carried on by you two, the flesh of my flesh. That which I have in life, I render to you in death.* A bit dram, eh? *May you carry forward our name, our legacy, and may the material possessions I leave behind cascade down the generations with our family heritage.* Blah, blah, blah. A bit about what families are all about and ... ah, here you go, bro. *I wish you both to understand that my bequest to each of you personally is the same, but the lion's share of what I own goes to my grandchildren and to their grandchildren and to theirs. The generations will divide it and so I place what I can in the trust of you, Dan. May you be fruitful and multiply* – Jeez, is he writing a letter or a sermon? – *and may my inheritance and that of my fathers live forever in those who live in the knowledge of our Lord.'*

'Yeah, yeah, stop. Enough. I get the idea. You're being paid to reproduce and gay sons don't provide grandsons.'

'And no one's allowed to spend any of it for fear of leaving nothing for the next generation. What a load of bollocks. Enough to make me want to squander my inheritance. Do you want it?' Dan looks at me as if he means it. He does.

'No,' I say, 'I don't want it.' Like it's a weight someone has to carry. 'I don't want anything of his. Nothing. God, I'd give my genes back if I could. I just want to get out of here. Give us a lift.'

'But you're keeping your money, right?'

'What else am I going to do with it? I can't give it back. *He* doesn't want it.'

'I dunno. You could give it to gay whales or something Gene disapproved of.'

'I think the charity he most disapproved of is me. In case you haven't noticed, research assistants don't earn as much as you brat-pack artists. Christ, what's the world coming to? Saatchi pays you more for one canvas than I get in a year.'

'How would you know?'

'Dan. *Everyone* knows.' He looks put out, so I ask him what he's going to do with Le Noires, hoping he'll say he'll sell.

'Might hang on to it. Don't need the readies, the house market's moving up round here and it's one hell of a venue for wild weekends. Shake a few ghosts out of the walls.'

'Just take me to the station, would you? I want to get away from this place.'

*

Dan has made me wait for him to get his own bag together and now we are late. I'm going to miss the connection at Edinburgh and will have to get the overnight train. Dan's going to miss his flight. He doesn't care. He'll get the next one. We are in the hire car and Dan takes the country roads like a speed track with a manic look on his face. A sharp intake of breath as we turn a curve. A truck confronts us in the other direction, the windscreen a ribcage of radiator metal. A swerve and we mount the verge and thud back on to the road, scratching the bottom of the car on something harder than the grass. Dan says by way of reassurance, 'Drive fast, die young.'

'That's *live fast*, you dickhead.'

'Same difference in a hire car.' He doesn't let up on the accelerator. I don't say anything. He changes the subject. 'So, you want to meet him then?'

'This man you've got lined up for me? No,' I say, not meaning it, not wanting to show I'd been wanting him to mention it.

'Come on, do you ever meet anyone? Have you fucked anyone since Gill dumped you?'

I explain to Dan, who knows already, that I don't like the Scene, that I don't cruise clubs or public toilets and that I don't 'fuck' just anyone.

'Surely that's the advantage of being gay? Everyone's shafting everyone.'

'Well, I'm not.'

'Well, wait till you hear who it is. He's coming to my opening. You might want to give him an invitation to yours.'

Chromosome 5
Ante hoc ergo post hoc

'Maybe, just maybe.'
National Lottery slogan

'Or was that only possible which came to pass?'
James Joyce

To lose one parent might be considered a misfortune, or a reason to deny God's existence at the least. To lose two looks like He may be up to something.

Such might have been Chris Putnam's thoughts on the overnight sleeper, but they were not, because it would have been flippant to consider his own situation in those terms, because he did not believe in the existence of God, but, principally, because he slept for most of the journey, albeit fitfully. However, he did not dream.

He might also have thought about those events in his life, in his father's life and in the life of the universe which had brought each of them to their present state at that moment in time and he might have considered how or, more precisely, *whether* he could have played his rôle differently. The Baconian principles underlying his scientific training might well have prompted such *what if*s, but the reality of his daily occupation rarely required any reference to first principles, nor in any case did he regularly apply such protocols to his own life. Like most people, he did not normally think of his life in terms of an experiment. At least, not then.

He presumed that the events in his life had largely been a matter of his own volition. Although, since he was asleep, he was not, during that night, presuming anything actively. If he had, he might, at that moment in his life, have had cause to question his presumptions.

But he did not.

*

Her voice calls 'hiya' from the living room as I open the door to the flat. I drop my keys in the basket by the phone in the hallway and go in to say 'hi' too. In there, the early sun filters through the drawn curtains. It finds its way through the crack between them and traces a stripe across the floor, over the edge of the sofa where Elsi lies, smoking an inevitable joint, and onto the table where she is playing clock patience in what cannot be a comfortable position. Mama Cass is singing that I gotta go where I wanna go, that I should do what I wanna do, with whoever I wanna do it with. At my waist height and above her head the smoke forms complex strata in the air.

'You're up early,' I say and check the timer on the video which flashes '00:00' and now check my watch which tells me it isn't yet 9 a.m., but soon will be.

'Working today, picking holes in Being and Nothingness,' she says, not looking up from the cards. 'Just having a spliff to get the day started.'

I don't see the purpose in clock patience because the outcome is set the moment you've dealt the cards, even before: the moment you've shuffled them. It all depends on the last card you turn being a king and so there's no skill involved. You might as well turn over just one card. I tell Elsi this and she says, 'Patience, my sweet, is a virtue.'

'The joy,' she continues, turning a card, placing it, 'is not in the winning or the losing, but in' – she takes a drag – 'the way the game unfolds.' I point out that the probability of winning is one in thirteen whoever plays and there's only one way of playing it. There are no choices, so what's the point and I immediately feel bad about getting at her as if I'm criticising, but I know that she doesn't see it like that. I'm tired, on edge, and to her, conversations are a game, worth unfolding. 'There's no such thing as probability,' she says, slowly, with minimal movement of her jaw. 'Things turn out the way they do. They could never have been otherwise because there is no otherwise. There's always only' – she takes a drag – 'one way of playing any game and that's the way you play it or, should I say, *will have* played it.' She's not making any sense to me even though she's talking so slowly. She still hasn't looked up from the cards which she still turns steadily, back and forth across the clock, taking drags at apparently random intervals.

She looks up from under heavy eyelids and says, 'So, my sweet, did it put the fun into funeral?'

'I've been to worse.' I have.

'Tell Mama Cass all about it.' She reaches out the joint to me which I look at and refuse.

'Too early for me, thanks. And I'd better go into the lab. I was just going to have a shower. Will there be any hot water?'

'Not so fast, speedy. You don't get out of it like that. I need to hear and you need to tell. Besides, you can't go to work today. They won't even be expecting you to. I prescribe a day of loafing on the sofa with me and watching daytime TV. If you're worried, I'll even write a note to excuse you.'

I remind her she had said she is going to do some work too.

'That, I believe, is already not going to happen. Sartre will be just as wrong tomorrow. C'mon.' She sits up and pats the sofa beside her. A puff of dust rises into the air, colliding with the hanging smoke, recombining and rolling in the shaft of light in fractal swirls, a result or, rather, an instance of the second law of thermodynamics, of mathematical chaos. 'Here, boy. There's a good puppy.'

I flop down beside her, taking the joint, and now lie down with my head on her lap, giving in to the irresistible ruin of the day, drawing in deep.

Janis Joplin sings that freedom's just another word for nothing left to lose as I tell Elsi all about it – about the kirk, about the wake, about Dan, about my father – and she abandons her cards and I return the joint, but maybe she stopped the game because I'm lying on her and she can't lean forward enough. As it is she misses when she reaches to flick into the ashtray and so I sit up so she doesn't keep hanging her breasts in my face and so she can carry on playing, but she doesn't, she tells me to lie back down. I have to ask, 'Don't you want to finish your game?' and she says she doesn't because, as she says I so rightly said, clock patience is without purpose, so, she adds, there's no purpose in resolving the mystery of whether it will come out or not. In fact, refusing to finish the game is the only way to give it a purpose, the purpose being defiance. It is too early for this, conversations like this, and already my legs have become dead weights, remote objects beyond my control. My head is filling with a fog but I take the joint back anyway, now burnt down to the roach.

'I thought you were coming back on Tuesday?'

I need to explain about the will, so I do, and about the letter and about my father wanting to see me and how I feel about it and I don't even want to say it, because it's in there so deep, just to acknowledge it is hurtful and humiliating and so I don't how to describe this – this cancerous guilt – and so I search for another word, a word that will do, which comes close but does not strip bare exactly how I feel and finally now what I say is *embarrassment*. 'You know when there's something you did and it's so abominably bad you just can't believe you were that … were that chronic. It makes you cringe or wish you could go back and just do it differently.' I've escaped. I've escaped even acknowledging my guilt to myself. The fact that so much of the pain of this, of my father's pain, is my fault. But just to think that means that I haven't, somewhere deep, I haven't escaped. 'Or sometimes, you can't believe it happened that way, because you were just too embarrassing, just too stupid to be real.' Now I say suddenly, 'Oh God, shit, like a time I was, must have been six or something and I was supposed to have learnt something at school, um, telling the time, you know, on a clock with, um, a face, and my parents were asking me about it or testing me on it or something and I couldn't do it and I told them that the teacher had told us we didn't need to learn it because the government had decided to ban clocks with faces and replace them all with digital ones. And my parents wouldn't let me get away with lying like that, so they said I must have got it wrong and I dug my heels in and said it was going to be illegal and they'd better watch it and I threw a wobbly and screamed and screamed. And I screamed so much I started to, um, hyperventilate, and they had to stop the car – oh, yes, did I say? Yeah, we were in the car – and I must have been convinced that if I screamed enough they'd believe my lie, even though I knew I was lying, they knew I was lying, I knew that they knew that I was lying, and—' And suddenly I've lost the thread.

'You wish you could have done it differently …' Elsi says, handing me another joint I didn't notice her rolling.

'What?' I say and now realise it's a prompt, something to do with what I was talking about earlier and so now I have to rewind the conversation in my head which is harder than I think and now eventually I pick it up again. I haven't escaped. This guilt is something to be lived with forever. No, that isn't what I was saying. That's what I wasn't saying. I pick up the thread again but now it's been so long since either of us spoke though that it hardly seems like the same conversation, but I take a drag and say anyway, 'It just makes you wish so hard it hadn't happened that you bite your lip or really want to do damage to yourself to make it go away. I don't know. I don't know about my father. It's just so, so *embarrassing* to think about it, about not visiting him then, about whether I even want to have done it now.' I get confused about the words I've just said and in particular the tenses and I say them again in my head or maybe out loud and maybe I'm trying to convince someone and now, 'Yeah, no, that's right. I don't know if I want to have done it. I just want it to not have happened, make it go away by doing something painful like, like, tearing out my own eyes.'

'Cover your bed of shame with a counter pain,' says Elsi, smiling to herself. 'It's what Oedipus did.'

He was the one with the complex, but I don't know what she means or what he did or why and I want to ask, but can't and I'm already talking again about my father and I'm saying how I feel embarrassed, I think, but so embarrassed it's like it hurts and it makes me feel worried but not specifically and the music's ended some time ago.

'Angst,' says Elsi.

I take a drag. I'm heavy all over, I can barely raise my eyeballs over the rim of the lower lids. 'What's in this?' I hold the joint above my head and it is taken.

'Lack of control,' she says, and I don't know whether she means that that's what's in the joint or if she misunderstood me and she means that that's what's in what I feel but it seems too complicated to ask so I don't do it. I can see her hand waving the remote control and the TV comes on. 'So what are you going to do?'

But I don't know and it seems like it just doesn't follow. Does she mean about my father, about the angst, about the joint, about going to the lab?

'Chrissy, my sweet, you are suffering from freedom. I diagnose existential angst. Your father is no longer there to make you feel constantly like you don't measure up. All your life, or at least as long as I've known you, you had this obsession about pleasing your father, getting his love, showing him yours, but hating him too, and now ...'

'No, I haven't.'

'You have, Chris. It's one of the things you don't know about yourself. You think everything you do has nothing to do with him, but it has everything to do with him. In fact, it's precisely the fact that you think it's got nothing to do with him that proves that it does.' She looks at me as if to check I'm following. 'Anyway, that's not my point. As I was saying, now you're suffering from your own freedom about doing whatever you want. Is there abandonment too?'

Maybe. I feel alone. Dan didn't tell me about the email. The TV is a game show, Chance of a Lifetime. She flips channels. Weather forecast. Drag. Hand back the joint.

'Despair?'

I take the control and the joint and change channel. 'Well, yeah. Of course.' The racing form for Ascot on Sunday.

'Classic existential crisis, my sweet. *Angst, Geworfensein* and *Dasein*. You are suffering from existential bad faith, stemming from a refusal to acknowledge your freedom.'

'What?' I think I say. Bad faith? Is she talking about my father?

'You cannot accept the responsibility of your own freedom. Your father's no longer here to tell you what not to do, or, more accurately, to give you an excuse not to do it. Sartre would argue that the absence of your father is like the absence of God and the absence of paternal love is the absence of divine love. Intellectually, you *know* there's no God. It's obviously absurd to you. You're a rational science-y type. It's something you don't even have to debate with yourself – or me for that matter. But emotionally, well, emotionally it's a different matter. Belief is something you've been brought up with. There's a need there, a longing. For love, all patriarchal and perfect.'

'I feel bad about not visiting my father, not about God.'

'If you say so, but either way, now you feel the full weight of the responsibility. The responsibility of being alone. But, don't fret, Chrissy-wissy, Elsi has a simple solution.'

'What's that?'

'Acknowledge your freedom.'

Elsi sometimes is ... what does she mean? 'I *am* free.'

'There you go. That should work. Feel better?'

'No.' But I do: I feel stoned. That has untied the knotted feeling in the pit of my gut.

Click-click-click and there's a business programme that's saying something about financial futures and I don't know about them or what are they and I really should know about them and I watch it for a bit and the man is talking fast and it's really interesting at first until I realise I haven't been listening or understanding anything he's just said and Elsi says, 'It could, of course, just be grief, but' – she takes a drag – 'I prefer the existential explanation. You're a knee-jerk existentialist: a humanist by default. You believe in freedom, but you haven't really given it too much thought—'

I try to protest but it's too much effort and, anyway, I know that what Elsi means by 'thought' is different from the amount of thinking I've ever done.

'—You think you're free, because it feels like you're in control. But you're not, my sweet, you're not. You should take a leaf out of your brother's book. He's a much better existentialist than you – does what he wants, invents himself.' She pauses, takes the joint from me, which I didn't realise I had.

'He's not a better existen—'

But Elsi's finished her drag and now says, 'Of course, *he*'s not free either. With his black polo necks, free love and the rollie cigarettes always hanging from his lip.'

'Those are joints.'

'Christ,' she says to the ceiling, 'he's even an artist. How much more clichéd can you get? He's a typical existentialist. And *that*'s a contradiction in terms if ever there was one.'

What's she talking about? 'What are you talking about, Elsi?' and she explains it to me, over my head and click-click-click as I listen and I've never noticed the remote makes a noise before and there's an Open University programme or something about statistics which makes it easier to listen to her and she's saying that I'm not free, so I try to look round at her, but I can't lying down so I lift myself up on my elbows which is too much effort, so I sit up.

'What?'

'Dan's not free because he needs to copy someone else's version of a free individual. He's a fake. And you're not free any more than he is. You can't help being what you are and what you are decides what you do. Your Calvinist daddy taught you that, surely?'

'But I don't believe in God.'

'My point exactly,' and she's lost me again. Or I've lost her. She takes the control, turns it off and gets up and changes the tape. She waits till Doris Day starts singing and comes back and sits down and says, 'Oedipus again.'

Whatever will be, sings Doris, *will be.*

I am just not following Elsi. I am not keeping up. She tells me things and I feel like I don't know anything.

Elsi tells me about Oedipus. 'Despite anything you might hear to the contrary from the likes of Freud and Aristotle ...'

'I know about Freud.'

She goes on, 'As I was saying, the most important thing is that the story shows how there's only one way it could have turned out. Laius, the dad, *had* to get rid of Oedipus. Oedipus *had* to kill his dad and marry his mum. And it wasn't because of the prophecy, the prophecy is because of it. It's just that by putting the prophecy first, the point about the inevitability of it all is driven home. The effect, in effect, precedes the cause, in this instance. Not logically possible, of course, but that's literary licence.'

'Complex,' I say.

Elsi smiles. 'Not to mention effective,' she adds and I'm not sure if this is another joke. Doris Day has finished and Melanie Safka has been singing. One of Elsi's compilation tapes of female singers. She constantly recombines compilations to make new ones, better ones, she says.

A copy of her book by Sartre is on the table by the cards. I feel nauseous.

Wish I could find a good book to live in. Wish I could find a good book. Oh, if I could find a real good book, I wouldn't have to come out and look ...

'I mean,' she says after a while, 'how can either of us say we're free when we're smoking the proof that we're not? I don't know about you, but I don't feel free to do too much right now other than what I'm doing.' And she takes another drag on another joint.

*

Chris Putnam spent all day on Thursday the twenty-seventh of April in the two thousandth year of his father's Lord in mourning. This resulted in the incineration of a certain quantity of cannabis, the casual observation of daytime television and a preliminary grounding in the theories of Heidegger, Sartre, Kierkegaard *et al.* which Elsi Tarot was eager to provide by way of philosophic counselling under the impression that she was providing consolation. These activities caused Chris to become hungry, to develop a headache and (in the light of Elsi's own personal thesis into which she increasingly digressed) to question his instinctive belief in his own freedom. The repetitiveness of the day also caused both parties to lose track of time; consequently, they consumed apparently random meals at apparently random intervals with no due regard to conventions pertaining to the order of sweet and savoury courses.

Chris returned to work the following day and attempted to minimise the consequences that had been caused by his absence over the last eight (working) days, during which he had marked the birth of his orphanhood. Over the subsequent fortnight, he awaited with eagerness the private viewing of the latest collection of artistic endeavour by Dan Putnam, but his ardour was not a consequence of any aesthetic (nor, indeed, fraternal) sentiment.

*

It is evening. I think – the curtains are closed. I can't lift my head to look at my watch because I don't want to. I can't help it. I didn't sleep properly on the overnight train. I am too tired to get up and go to bed. Elsi is skinning up again. I don't want any more but I lack the control to stop her or refuse when she will pass it to me. Besides, I don't feel ready yet to feel real again.

I have to say now what I've been wanting to tell her all day. My news, the thing that keeps at bay all the feeling, all the absence of feeling, my consolation.

'Guess who Dan's going to introduce me to?'

'Dunno – Prince Edward?'

'No. I'll give you a clue. Movie star.'

'Tom Cruise.'

'British.'

'Er, Leo Martin?'

'Yep.'

'No. Really?'

'Unhunh.'

'Is there anyone your brother *doesn't* know?'

'They're really good friends apparently.'

'Jesus.' She lights up. 'When you say 'introduce', do you mean *introduce*?'

'I think so.'

'Isn't he married, though? I didn't know he was gay.'

'Me neither.'

Chromosome 6
Ars Magna

'To become a work of art is the object of living.'
Oscar Wilde

*'"But he has nothing at all on!" at last cried out all
the people. The emperor was vexed, for he knew that
the people were right; but he thought the procession
must go on now! And the lords of the bedchamber
took greater pains than ever to appear holding up a
train, although, in reality, there was no train to
hold.'*
Hans Christian Andersen

'So, bro,' says Dan who's still in the bedroom, 'how you been
doing?'

I am waiting for him to finish getting ready and we are
waiting for someone called Helen to turn up. The Thames is
sad as I look down on it through the broad window of Dan's
flat, my hand on the bare brickwork. It slouches along,
always the same brown slurry, but never the same. Just
molecules of water, two hydrogen atoms, one oxygen, and
they're all identical. Clones, differentiated only by their
different places in the flow. But what difference does that
make? The river runs past Evendams Warehouse which once
upon a time stored who knows what, but is now flashy flats.
Ignorant, arrogant river.

'Fine, I guess,' but I am not. I was fine, but then my father
died and now, now whatever I do, I do in the light of that,
although Elsi says I always did only I didn't realise it. I want
to curl up in my coat in the corner of the room. 'How about
you?'

As I turn I catch sight of my reflection in the glass. Do I
look that bad? I don't know what you're supposed to wear.
I'm going to stick out like—

'Me?' he says, coming into the open-plan lounge, brushing
a speck off his black polo neck and now looking at me.

'Better than you.'

'What do you mean?' I know what he's doing. Dan sets things up like this date or whatever it is with Leo to show me how nice and brotherly he is and then he always hijacks it by making me feel worthless or by flirting and being more attractive than me even though we're not in competition for the same people. Just to show he can.

'Well, come on. For me, it wasn't so bad, you know. I got to watch the final reel, say the goodbyes. Christ, bro, by the end of the day, it was a fucking relief for me when the old man finally kicked the proverbial. But, for you—'

'Yes, okay, Dan. No need to rub it in.' And there I go. I fall for it again. He knows just where to hit. The guilt resurfaces.

'Oh, I don't mean it like that,' he says, although he does mean it like that, he just doesn't know he does. 'I know you're brooding on it, bro. It's what you do. But you just got to get it straight in your head and move on. It's a beginning, bro, not an end.'

'If it's a beginning, I just wish the story would move a bit quicker, that's all.'

'It is, it is. You just don't know it yet.' He slumps into the low leather sofa and sits up to reach the silver cigarette case on the glass coffee table. It doesn't contain cigarettes. 'Take tonight. You're going to meet the man of your wet dreams, not to mention just about everyone else's on the planet. And you two are so meant to be together.'

'I don't know where you get this idea, Dan. I've only got your word he's even gay. You do know he's married?'

'Yeah, 'course. To Helen, my PR. That's how I know him.'

'The one we're waiting for?' Dan wants me to meet his *wife*?

'But for chrissakes, you must know they're separated. Everyone knows. Besides, he's in love with you already.'

'He's never *met* me. He's never even heard of me.'

'Sure he has. I've told him all about you.' He unwraps a slip of foil from the cigarette case and tips half the contents onto the table and reaches into his back pocket for his wallet. 'Look, he kept saying to me that I'd be irresistible if I weren't such an asshole, so I told him I had a twin brother, just like me in every way except not like me: a nice guy. He didn't believe me at first, but kept bringing it up every time we hung out, so I promised to introduce you.'

I sit down in the armchair too, slumping into it like Dan because it's so low or because my legs won't support me or because we're twins. The air fans the coke across the table.

'For fuck's sake, Chris.' Dan sweeps it back into a little pile with his platinum plastic and continues splicing the lines, recombining them, stretching them out and splicing them again. Click-click-click as the edge of the credit card taps the glass table-top.

'I can't do this, Dan. I really can't. I can't go on a blind date with Leo Martin.'

'Look, bro, he's just an ordinary bloke. Besides, it's not a blind date: one, it's not blind because you both know what each other looks like, and, two, it's not a fucking date because it's my opening and there are going to be about five hundred people there.' He pulls out his wallet again, runs the edge of the card down his tongue, replaces it and selects an unsullied twenty which he rolls into a tube. 'Anyway, Leo is like you, he doesn't get to meet a lot of nice gay guys. Well, except other actors, but he can't risk going out with a screen queen – an unlucky break or a bit of a tiff and he'd be front page. See? That's where you and he differ. The reason Leo doesn't meet people is because he has to be discreet, not because he's a sad fuck. You, on the other hand, are Norman-fucking-no-mates, Chris. I mean, you even let Gill get custody of all your friends. Face it, you've spent the last few months either moping around your little lab cooking up Frankensteins or cooped up at home with your flatmate the witch. And—'

'Our father's just died, Dan,' I say because if he were me, he'd be the same, surely. But he doesn't even skip a beat.

'—and then I bring you an Apollo, a man every woman wants to do unspeakable things to, tell you he already thinks you're irresistible and what do you do? You say, "I can't do it, Danny." For fuck's sake, do a line.' He thrusts the twenty in my face, almost up my nose.

'Look, Dan,' I say, not taking it yet, even though I'm on for it. I want him to tell me I'm looking good, that I'm wearing the right thing, anything. I want to feel like I'm not just trying to escape, that this isn't invented, that I'm really here. 'Thanks and everything, you know, but it's just I'm not as good at this as you …'

He cuts me off. 'That's why you need the charlie, bro. You need to bridge the gap between reality and freedom. Drugs *are* the bridge.' He puts the twenty in my hand. 'Some people say drugs distort your understanding of reality and some people say they enhance it. Then, there are people who say they take away your freedom to act as you want and other people who say they set you free. Do you see what I'm saying, man? You can say it in other ways, too. I mean, you'd probably say something like, do chemicals in the brain control the way you act and perceive? Or is it the other way around? Either way, when the shit comes down, drugs are a spanner in the works of reality and freedom. And taking them puts you in control.'

'You quoting yourself again, Daniel?' says a female voice behind me. 'Weren't you saying something similar in this week's *Time Out*? You were pleased with it, then?' I have turned around and see in the doorway the skinny silhouette of a woman in a tailored suit. 'You must be Christopher,' she steps out of the light and holds out her red-nailed hand, 'I'm delighted to meet you. I've heard so much about you, but don't worry, all good, which isn't something one can usually say about the people one meets through Daniel. But I suppose family's different.'

'Chris,' says Dan with his big grin, 'Helen Bossi.'

I switch the twenty to my left hand to shake hers and she is holding keys – to the flat, I suppose – and I feel guilty about the six thin lines of coke in front of me and the evidence I'm holding. 'Hello,' I say and feel a pulse of red heat up to my hairline as I hear how I sound and think I sound camp. The woman whose husband I'm about to meet smiles at me mainly with her eyes. She's pretty – was bound to be – but even though her mascara's perfect, she has shadows that make it look as though she might have just been crying. Her hand is fragile and bony and I disengage mine and she leans across the table, holding her suit close to her body to stop it from brushing the coke and she kisses Dan on the lips.

'On to the coke so soon? You must be almost ready to go. Marvellous, we have a car downstairs.'

'Sure, sugar. Be right with you.' And he looks at me

expectantly. I hand the twenty back. You first.

Dan casually nestles it in his nostril, the forefinger of his left hand shutting his other nostril, and bends to inhale first one line and now, switching symmetry, another in single clean sweeps.

I try to do the same but I get the angle of the twenty slightly wrong or the strength of my sniff or something else and I only get half a line and blow the rest of it a little out of focus. I try again but have to chase around the little patch of table hoovering up the mess. I feel its chemical gumminess in my sinuses and on the back of throat, cold and tingling like aluminium. I am better with my second line.

'Helen?' offers Dan, taking the twenty, presenting it to her.

'Thank you, boys, but no, not tonight Josephine, as they say. Your prerogative.' She seems sad – she's friendly enough, but there's too much primness mixed in with it. Maybe that's just how she is. I would say something if I knew her better, ask her if she's okay. Dan wouldn't though. He won't even notice. Maybe I'm just trying to connect with her to get closer to Leo, or maybe, as she's his wife, I'm inventing this pity so I can ambush my chances myself.

Dan shrugs and neatly sucks half a line into each nostril, handing me back the twenty. I didn't plan to have so much – Sir Hugo has called one of his pep talks in the lab tomorrow so I shouldn't be up too late – but I only think about this now as I'm finishing the last line anyway, leaving white trails on the table, most of which Dan gingerly mops up with wetted forefingers and rubs into his gum. 'There you go,' he says, leaving me the rest and I copy him.

It is sharp like lemon or more like lemon detergent on my gums and as we leave the flat I feel them expand numbly and my tongue becomes a useless rubber strap in my mouth. I sniff and am sure I have nostril hairs poking out everywhere coated in snow. Oh, well, here goes. Maybe, just maybe, there's a realistic chance.

*

Some indefinable element in the nature or nurture of Dan Putnam caused him to covet fame and, during the summer of

1998, serendipity occasioned that it was him and not some other person who did indeed acquire it. Just as a species develops because it happens to own those characteristics most fitting to the circumstances in which it finds itself, Dan Putnam chanced, not entirely through his own deliberate contrivance, upon the exact combination of style, approach and substance most fitting to the acquisition of renown at that moment in time. He provided what the *zeitgeist* demanded.

The situation associated most closely with the incipience of his celebrity, although not necessarily the sole or direct cause of it, was the series of events before, during and after the degree show which had been the culmination of his studies at the New York College of Art.

Ray L. Tod, writing an appreciation of Jackson Pollock in the *New York Times*, chose, from among so many he could have selected, Dan as the appropriate object for a denunciation: 'a depressing exemplar of cynicism,' he wrote, 'an epitome of today's ignorance of the true values of art'. Soon he was not alone. Other critics chimed in, dismissing Dan with the claim that his ideas were thirty-five years out of date and, in any case, they had been done far better by the likes of Klein and Judd.

However, in such claims, it tended to be the comparison and not the dismissal which counted. It became respectable for other critics to attack the dismissals. Dan Putnam was referred to as 'the next Rothko'[3] and then as 'the next Warhol' (which had more popular appeal). Rudi Ballard, critic, chose to defend Dan by granting his considered endorsement in the *New Yorker*: 'So early in his career, yes, even as early as his degree show, 22-year-old British artist Daniel Putnam has already recognised the only way to draw together everything art has been doing since Cezanne, Matisse and Mondrian. He takes that extra step post-modernism never dared take before. And that is by defying, yes, even *denying* art itself.'

Attentions subsequently spread and bifurcated, infecting both the more academic and the more popular spheres. Dr.

---

3 See Maya Kufu in the *Washington Post*, 1 June 1998, subsequently quoted out of context most liberally.

A. Reid expanded on Ballard in the conclusion to a seminal contribution to the *Po Mo Quarterly*: 'As we have seen, the canvasses of Putnam's "The Emperor's New Art" exhibition constitute the teleological response to many of the crucial issues in visual art of the twentieth century. It absolves the crisis of representation which, since Picasso, is beyond ignoring ... It incorporates the ready-mades of Duchamp. It is the nihilist protest to the mechanistic assembly-line that was Dada ... In the public outrage it has provoked, it even adopts and adapts the Pop Art "happening". It is the marriage of structuralism, deconstruction and post-structuralism. It is quintessential minimalism in a constructivist mode. Shamelessly, it appropriates everything without using any of it. It is the ultimate meta-epistemic simulacrum. And, yet, it is hyperreal, virtual, Nothing.'

Meanwhile, for almost a fortnight, no tabloid television programme or newspaper was without its commentary, discussion and counter-commentary on the phenomenon. Tom 'Chief' Aucull on *Sixty Minutes* inveighed against it: 'How does this limey think he'll get away with it? There's nothing clever about it, in fact, there's just plain nothing.' Al Can countered on *Hard News*: 'Enough of pickled sharks, this dashing young Brit has said something about modern art we can all understand. It's a whitewash for the establishment.'

The exhibition itself, 'The Emperor's New Art', consisted of sixty canvasses of varying size, hanging on starkly lit white walls in the Chelsea Gallery of Twentieth-Century Art (TCGTCA). The canvasses were mostly unframed and, moreover, they were entirely blank. They featured no paint nor charcoal nor other markings whatsoever.

Each canvas boasted a small plastic plaque below the bottom-right corner which provided for each a title as follows: 'Canvas'; 'Picture'; 'Untitled'; 'Titled'; 'Composition in Transparent and Clear'; 'Framed' (on a framed canvas); 'Unframed' (unframed); 'Picture of *Unframed*' (on a framed canvas); 'Blank'; 'Void'; 'Being and Nothingness'; 'A Picture of a Canvas'; 'Embryo'; 'The Self'; 'Postmodernism is up its own ass'; 'A Picture of a Window (unframed)'; 'Signed' (unsigned); 'Unsigned' (also unsigned); 'A Forgery'; 'Virtual Painting'; 'Relativity', 'Uncertainty' and

'Complementarity' (which were displayed as a triptych); 'The Cubist Atom'; 'A Pointillist Dot'; 'Signifier' and 'Signified' (exhibited together); 'The Same'; 'The Same but Better'; 'The Same but Worse'; 'I Can't Believe It's Not Better! Light!'; '*sic*'; '*ibid.*'; 'Representation'; 'Truth'; 'Beauty'; 'All ye need to know'; 'Metaphor'; 'Ready-made'; 'Deinstallation'; 'Unfinished'; 'Sketch for *Unfinished*'; 'WYSIWYG'; '®'; '""'; 'Copy this, Walter Benjamin'; 'The Sublime'; 'In Memoriam: Bauhaus'; 'The Death of the Artist'; 'Neo-Prehistoric'; 'Dada was my Daddy'; 'Watch this Space'; 'Palimpsest'; 'Memory after Death'; 'The Original'; '$1,000,000'; 'Priceless'; 'History'; and 'The End of History'.

According, however, to Dan Putnam in his presentation to the examination panel, the artwork did not consist solely of the exhibition itself, which was, he argued, no more important than the canvas is to the painting. He further argued that the media campaign and the artifice involved in stimulating public attention was the true object. He offered, he claimed, PR as art form. It wasn't original, but that was his point.

He produced press releases (peppered with testimonials from critics, usually quoted out of context) and taped telephone conversations with arts editors and rant-columnists. He showed them videotape of himself committing acts of self-violence and informing news crews that he had been assaulted by a marauding mob of irate art historians.

He brought forth spreadsheets indicating ticket sales to TCGTCA and copies of receipts for sales of the canvasses. To convince people to see blank canvasses is an art, he maintained, therefore to persuade them to part with considerable sums of money for the same must surely be a work of genus. This was, he suggested, a quantifiable artwork and, he ventured, a masterpiece.

The college authorities were presented with two alternatives: to disown Dan Putnam and his ostentations or to lionise him and bask beside him in the glory. Despite aesthetic sensibilities amongst almost all concerned which had urged the former course, all had to acknowledge the good sense of the latter for the reputation of the college: they, if anyone, should champion the cause of their graduand. Therefore they granted Dan his degree *cum laude* and awarded him the college's discretionary prize for excellence.

And thus Dan Putnam's conquest of the United States was secured.

*

On his return to London, Dan was alert to the added value in America that had been associated with his standing as an eccentric Briton and he recognised that it might prove harder to translate his success to the kingdom of his birth.

To this end, he invested some of the revenue from the New York show in the engagement of the professional services of Helen Bossi, the erstwhile paramour of a fellow student who was at that time employed in an arts and entertainments public relations agency in Covent Garden. He also expended additional reserves on the acquisition of sixty new canvasses to replace the originals, most of which had been sold and the remainder of which would have been prohibitively expensive to transport to the UK and to insure in transit.

He contended that what he was creating in London by recreating his New York show was a copy of the original work, a fake. Nevertheless, it was a reproduction which would be different in its very nature (not least because its own nature was that of a reproduction) and which would therefore have to be cultivated differently. Yet, under extravagantly disparate conditions, given a different approach, it would be possible to realise an identical outcome, a simulacrum of the original show. It would therefore be both an identical work of art only by virtue of its difference. The same but different, he suggested, like twins.

The plastic plaques he transported in a used A4 padded manila envelope.

Of course, the success of the venture in America had provided a promotional premise, but Dan Putnam and Helen

Bossi predicted, correctly as it later turned out[4] that the British art establishment's reaction would prove more contemptuous than the response of either the American establishment or the public. The British establishment would be likely to argue that 'The Emperor's New Art' constituted nothing different from the grand, but essentially simplistic and ultimately vacuous, statements on aesthetics posited at some point during their studies by almost every art student.

Dan counselled against the perils of pessimism, explaining to Helen that the method he had employed in New York had been to turn any adversity to his own ends. Indeed, he had courted it, writing to newspapers himself in order to voice exactly such opinions. Then he had demanded a right of reply as the artist (a reply which would be deliberately and inevitably directed to the conflation of further controversy rather than any genuine self-justification). The fact that he would not have to invent any arguments against himself would merely save them both time and effort.

Helen explained to Dan that he had been fortunate to avoid arraignment.

He, he said, would have craved clemency on grounds of reasonable artistic licence. Indeed, he claimed, had he not already convincingly argued that the artwork was not the exhibition itself nor anything in it, but the media campaign? And did he not have no less an authority to ratify this claim than the New York College of Art?

As it turned out (because Britain lacks the wide open space of the USA), Dan's minimalism did not appeal to the British art establishment, nevertheless, they proved unequal to the task of presenting any reasonable grounds on which to attack it.

Some tried to argue it was 'unoriginal' or 'plagiarism', but did so awkwardly and without conviction, undermined by their own suspicions that such concepts are redundant in postmodern art.

Some tried to construct an analytic deconstruction which

---

4 See, for example, B— S— in the *Evening Standard,* 'Canvas opinion', 11 August 1998, and 'Nothing to write home about' by gossip diarist Bill MacRake (*Daily Mirror*, 13 August 1998).

merely served to provoke further public support for Dan, because more even than they adore pomposity, the British adore those who puncture it.

Others tried to say it was simply uninteresting, but the more they protested it, the more patently interesting it was.

And so it came to pass that, during the media's late-summer 'silly season', the ardent duo repeated and enlarged on Dan's successes in New York and, intermittently, had sexual intercourse, notwithstanding Helen's marriage two years previously to the as-yet-unknown young British actor Leo Martin, with whom Dan developed a close, but nonetheless platonic (or rather, non-sexual), acquaintance. Over the subsequent two years, Dan consolidated his position as a celebrity artist, on the one hand, by displaying sufficient conventional talent by painting (and selling at inflated prices) what he termed 'fake forgeries' (identical duplicates of the work of the grand masters, save for the signature which he would replace with his own in their style), and, on the other, by being fêted in *A South Bank Show Special* and appearing in the pages of, among many others, the *Guardian*, *Loaded* and *For Women*.

His popularity was in part the product of his photogenic and telegenic appearance. Dan Putnam, it should be noted, was considered, by common consent, very good-looking and, by extension, one might suppose the same of Chris Putnam even though the two brothers carried their looks differently. For example, whilst Dan managed to effect rakish charm through the curl of lip or kink of eyebrow, Chris's face, on the other hand, always expressed mournful hopefulness in his furrowed brow, his upturned eyes and his anxious, tentative smile. Nevertheless, in what would come to pass, Chris's prepossessing appearance would prove of considerable importance as an apparently significant cause.

During those two years, Dan did not mount another exhibition, a state of affairs which was brought to a close on the May Day Bank Holiday (Monday the first of May 2000) with the opening of his new show, entitled 'I Could Do That!'

*

Clerkenwell and by the time we get to the gallery and the car draws up – the car, a flash black limo – I want to get inside, I am excited, I want to see Dan's pictures, but more, I'm going to meet, about to meet, Leo. SuperLeo. MegaLeo. ÜberLeo. I'm not excited though, I tell myself. He probably won't notice me. Probably not. But he might. I look at Dan and Dan looks smug but excited. Dan's grinning at me and talking to Helen. Talking to Helen and being told about the people he's going to talk to, got to talk to. Now Helen's telling him other stuff and he's nodding at it all and looking over at me and grinning and nodding and Dan's good-looking when he smiles and I can see that and I'm smiling too and I must look good too. Maybe Leo will … and then we'll talk and I'm going to be so relaxed, so free and easy, so in control.

*

Okay, where are the drinks? Cool, thank you.

*

Dan is over by that far wall. Who do I know? No one, he's not here yet. Never mind. Champagne. Great with coke. I'll have another, don't go away, thank you.

'... *Sad thing about our poor friend Paddy* ...'

No, I'm his brother. No thanks, nothing to eat.

'... *speak in French when you can't think of the English for a thing* ...'

I can't face the prospect, I haven't eaten all day what with tonight and everything. No appetite.

'... *it's all to do with Lotus-Eaters and Red Kings* ...'

Thanks, yeah. No, no orange juice, I'll have mine straight.

Cute waiter, too muscly perhaps, underneath the white jacket, bum's too square.

Good-looking guys everywhere with shaved heads or ponytails.

'... *what does one mean by "real" anyway?*...'

*

It's a big room, isn't it? Big and white, with cool people in black, but the pictures are colourful. The room is full of pictures, hundreds of them and there are still corners partitioned by white screens I haven't explored yet, like over here.

'... *vanished quite slowly, beginning with the end* ...'

Yep, more pictures. Loads and loads and loads of paintings. Poster paints on paper, primary colours, round heads, triangular bodies, flat strips of blue for sky. But Dan has signed them all and given them names. This one says it's called 'Child's Play' and this is ... 'Insult'. Don't get it.

Not here yet.

*

Me? No, I'm his brother.

Thanks. Here, would you mind taking the empty one? Thanks.

'... *I called you naughty boy because I do not like that other world* ...'

Not here yet.

*

Feeling a bit out on my own here. Don't know anyone. Dan is over there doing his talking to the right people, in his element. He just has no idea how obvious it is how coked up he is, but no one seems to care. Or maybe they just don't notice. Maybe they're all on it! We're all on something! Thanks. He is and him. And him, definitely. Her too, but he's probably just pissed.

'... *Là ci darem la mano* ...'

Not here.

I think I'll talk to someone and—

'... *must have two you know – to come and go. One to come, and one to* ...'

—and so I am moving through the people, excuse me, and none of them, excuse, none of them is looking at the pictures. Excu— Thanks. This one will do, hi.

No, I'm his brother. He's over there with the—
All right, suit yourself.
'... *large as life and twice as natural* ...'
Hi, yeah. The time. Have you got the ... ? Thanks. Quarter past nine. Nine fifteen. Twenty-one fifteen. Thanks. No, his brother. Oh thanks, yes. No I must have left my glass over there somewhere. Thank you, yeah. I'll guard it with my life. Yeah, thanks. What were you saying? Yeah, twins. Obviously. He hasn't? Well, you know, we've not seen so much of each other lately, he's always and I'm usually ... anyway, I'm the one they keep in the attic, only let out on special occasions. Hahaha. Okay. Yeah, no, that's fine. I'll speak to you later.

Not yet.

*

Hi, yeah. Don't know anyone. What? Oh no, I'm his brother. Hmm, yeah, so, do you know anyone. It's so hard to meet people these days don't you think. Where do you go, I mean, I don't like the Scene, you know, clubs and, well no actually, it's stronger than that, I mean I *hate* the Scene. Really hate it, you know. So I mean I don't get to meet many gay men you see and when I do, do meet a man, any man that is, like you for instance but, hey, by the way, honestly, I'm not hitting on you or anything, although you look great, honestly, I mean that, it's just this is really interesting, because I always tend to presume they're straight, you see. Why do you suppose that is. I think it's because I never meet them in a gay context and I just can't tell, you know. My queer antennae just don't work or something, I don't know, so it never comes to anything anyway. The only time I find out is if they mention they have a boyfriend, by which time there's no point, because that means they're not going to be interested anyway or I presume that's what it means. Or sometimes, very occasionally, I'll drop a hint to find out like, um, like, a reference to interior decorating or something. Yeah, I know, but that's the point. But then, if it turns out he's straight, he might get really embarrassed or I'm always afraid he might get abusive. Sometimes even the straight guys go along with it and they'll flirt anyway, but they're the worst you know

85

because they're just teasing you or it's even worse if they're not, because then they're just day-trippers who want to hump you and dump you.

Anyway, so I never usually tell anyone I'm gay and I've no idea why I'm telling you all this, I don't even know you and I must be boring you silly, I'm a bit coked up to be honest with you. Sorry, but what can you do. Generally, I hate to shove it down anyone's throat, you know – oh shit, no pun intended – because, you know, sometimes it makes people a bit awkward. I'm not making you feel awkward, am I.

I don't know, maybe I'm ... maybe there's some guilt at work here about how my father took it, you know.

Maybe the whole thing's all about my father.

I know that's what Dan thinks, but he believes that it doesn't matter what other people think and that's all right for him. Because he can live like that, but I can't. It's just not the way I am. Sometimes I wonder why I can't be more like him, why I'm not.

Especially if they're bigots, Dan says – doesn't matter what they think. And I asked him if that includes Dad. And he said that it's different. It's different to discover one of your kids is gay. But that's not good enough, Dan, you're just protecting him.

What? Yeah, I'm sorry, no sure. See you later. Maybe.

Maybe he's stood me up.

Thanks. Just a drop.

*

Ah no, there he is. At last. Keeps me waiting all this time. But there he is.

I can't talk to him now.

*

Flash, flash. Jesus, look at them. Vultures round him instantly. He can't even get away from the doorway. *And* this is a private party. They're not even fans, they're, they're psychofants.

Leave him alone, he's mine.

He looks more ... more *real* in real life and that's better, I think, yes, better. Better to be real. He has a height and dimensions and exists from one moment to the next without a break. Is this weird that he's now in front of me? Is it weird he's not someone who, for all I know, is a figment of someone's imagination? No, it's not weird, it's reassuring. Puts my life in touch with a dream world, like I'm going through the looking glass, entering a make-believe. But it's strange to think that the circles of so many people's lives are directed on the circle of his, and yet his daily, twenty-four-hour existence, is something so far away. But now so close. Like a Venn diagram. A circle made up entirely of intersecting subsets. Overlapping mine, but not yet interacting.

Until now, I didn't really know he was real. Could have been an invention, like a character he's acting, or a conspiracy. I could touch him. If I were close enough.

Yes, he is better in reality. Being real is better than being imaginary. I mean, it's not that he was ever not real, just that I didn't know. He's like an ideal out there, but it's not really as good as somebody right next to you. For someone to be perfect, they must be real, however imperfect they are. He's as tall as he looks. Being imaginary is the biggest imperfection possible. Is he perfect? He might be. Leo Martin might be perfect. I need to smell him to know, to feel the cradle of his shoulder, to—

'... *Do tell me what kind of perfume does your wife use?...*'

I can't talk to him. This isn't right. Not here. Leave him alone. This isn't how I thought ... a crowded room and he walks up to me and says ...

—but I'll go home in a bit and I'll be going on my own and I'll come down with Elsi and a joint. It's wearing off already. Tonight's not going to happen.

'*Watch out, fella.*'

Hmm?

'I said *watch out.*' A man in red. 'You're spilling your drink.'

Oh, yeah. Yeah, I am. I'm sorry. I'll get another one. I'm sorry.

'All right, you do that.'

I move through people and roll my shoulders to edge between them and get into the roll and they're now moving apart for me and I'm drifting through steadily but fast and faces appear on my left and right like cars zooming by and I am smiling at some of them and some of them smile back and some of them carry on talking and some of them do both. I am not bothered where I'm going but end up by the buffet, but I still can't eat anything, but I ask for another glass of champagne, but they've run out, but they've got wine and beer left, so I'll have one of those thank you.

'Which, sir?'

Hmm?

'Which would you like, sir? Wine or beer.'

Hmm, yeah, either. Err, the beer. Thank you. Thank you very much.

And sway away and roll shoulders through the crowd.

*

And suddenly, Dan. 'Where you been, bro? The pictures grab you?'

I am looking at one, but there are two next to each other and they look the same, they all look the same and there's nothing to look at even though I look at the figures and now the boxy house and now the lollipop tree and now the figures again.

'They're not very good.'

'Well, the kids who did them are only young.'

'You mean they're not real?'

'Sure they are. Real, genuine children's paintings by real, genuine children. That's the idea.'

Still don't get it.

'Don't look at me like that. Jesus, let's go meet Leo.'

No. I back off, but stepping back I'm not steady because, because something's holding on to me, holding my, my arm and it's Dan's arm which is on mine and he wants to take me through the crowd to Leo but I can't, but we're moving anyway. 'Dan, I can't,' but faces are moving past me again looking and I look down at my feet moving, one in front of the other, in front of the other, in front of the other.

And Dan stops and I nearly bump him from behind but stop and crouch down, rest on my haunches on the floor, rock and look into my drink. Red wine? Wasn't I drinking beer a minute ago? Crouched behind Dan and a glade has opened up in the forest of people and skinny Helen's there and Dan and the beautiful Leo, SuperLeo, slap their arms around each other and now I'm looking up from my drink, up at them, but that angle's a bit unstable, and they're not noticing me.

'... *oh man, how you been ... days and nights ... hunh, pear-shaped shit ... god, man ... wo, unreal ... in London, then ... yeah, my brother Chris.* Where's ... what you doing down there, bro?'

Look up. He's looking down. Leo is looking down. Leo is looking down and his eyes and skin and hair like dark melted chocolate and he's saying to me, 'Hello.' He is saying hello and I am looking up and rocking back and, oop, sit down on the ground because it's easier and now he's saying, even though his amber voice is far away, 'You must be the hero. The good twin, right?' He's holding out his hand to shake mine or help me up. 'Where there are twins, one of them is always evil. We all know which one Dan is, so that must make you the good guy.' And lots of people laugh.

And I want to lie down for a bit, but Leo's hand is still there and I want to take it and I grab at it and it's okay, he catches mine and helps me stand and my shirt is wet and my glass is empty. And Leo looks at me like a little boy and he smiles. Leo smiles.

I'm not the good guy. I'm not the good guy at all. I'm the mad one in the attic. I'm the family's filthy little secret. I'm the. Excuse me, I have to—

*

A breath. And another. And listen to them steadier now. Cold, firm mirror to lean on. Steady. Lemon disinfectant and cologne. A breath. And heartbeats, lots of little heartbeats.

Out of rhythm with the breaths. Won't slow down. Please no, a heart attack. But no, just exertion, standing, leaning against the soothing mirror. No people now. Just my breaths. Loud and hollow in here. Cooler in here too and air to breathe.

Fuck, I am very, very pissed.

Let myself slide down the wall. Hand in front of hand crawl across the cool tiles. My knee's in something wet. Push up the seat and cling to the rim. The water inside. Bleach and urine.

Gag like a punch in the chest.

Gag again.

Spit a sticky thread. Spit again – it won't drop off. Oh god, I want to throw up, but there's nothing in my stomach. Spit. Spit. Rest my head on the cool, cool porcelai—

*

'... *rymay, yullrymay* ...'

Hunh?

'You all right, mate?'

What? Yeah, yeah, I'm fine.

'Jesus, don't look it. *Looklykyejztadafywi*—

*

Ow. What? Hard. What? Where? Oh.

Okay.

*

Stand up. To the sink. Water on face. Splash everywhere. Face and hair. Drink it. Gargle. Drink. Swallow.

Door behind me.

'Sorry, didn't mean to startle you.' An American in a suit. 'Just came in to do a line. Don't mind, do you?'

No, I say, but not loud enough. 'No.' Maybe too loud that time.

'Look like you could use some yourself. Wanna join me?'

'Better not.' Erm. 'But thank you very much indeed for your most kind offer.'

*

Heat, back in the gallery.

'... *a duller spectacle this earth of ours has not to show than a rainy Sunday in London ...*'

No, I don't think I will, thank you.

*

Dan. 'Chris, I'll get some—

*

Raining outside. Cold fresh rain in the dark. Look up at the streetlights. The rain comes down at me like white lasers in the lamplight. Gets in my eyes. Footsteps in the alley down the side of the gallery.

*

'... *lies, you know it's all lies, don't you? You worthless fucking piece of crap, all lies. You're nothing you know, nothing. You cunt, you little shit ...*'

Hunh?

*

Thud in the ribs. And another thud in the ribs. The pavement's by my face. And the wet's all over me, my clothes and my face. And thud in the ribs again. And he runs off, splashing. Click-click-click.

*

Open eye. Car. Rain.

*

A ceiling in darkness. My ceiling. My ribs hurt. My head hurts. Bed. Snuggle into the warmth. There's breathing. Not my own. Just close my eyes for a bit.

Chromosome 7
Improbability

'Among the things Billy Pilgrim could not change were the past, the present and the future.'
Kurt Vonnegut

'Der Mensch kann tun was er will; er kann aber nicht wollen was er will.'
(Man can do what he wills; but he cannot will what he wills.)
Arthur Schopenhauer

Any possible chain of events which might have resulted in a relationship developing between research assistant Chris Putnam and the latest great hope of the British film industry Leo Martin was always unlikely.

Furthermore, even despite the fact that, by the morning of Tuesday the second of May 2000, the two had met (which might usually be supposed to shorten the odds), the probability of a relationship had, it must be supposed, reduced still further.

Based on the probability, it might well be safe to state categorically that no relationship later took place, thereby rendering inaccurate the horoscope Chris had read barely a fortnight previously and demonstrating the impossibility in real life of effects preceding their cause.

However, it must be considered what is meant by 'probability'. What had happened had happened and could not be changed. What was currently happening was the necessary outcome of those prior events. What was yet to happen would, in turn, be the necessary outcome of current events. Wherefore chance? To talk of probability is to suggest that events might happen differently from the way they do, whereas events themselves will unfold according to an inevitable path. It is simply that the future course of that path cannot be known in the present any more than the present could be known in the past. The future is certain. It is just not known.

One element of the future, however, is known: death. Chris Putnam would be dead eventually (just as his father died before him) and a relationship with Leo Martin before his death was not likely. (It would, naturally, be impossible afterwards.) It should not be supposed that the likelihood or otherwise of such a relationship provides any information whatsoever whether such a relationship did or did not later occur. Without knowing either way, it would be wrong to make any assumptions. It would, for example, be wrong to make the assumption that Chris and Leo ever so much as saw one another again, let alone engaged in a romance. One might expect as much in a storybook, but not in real life.

Nevertheless, unlikely events, however unlikely, given sufficient opportunity, are bound to happen sometimes. What to some people is supernatural, is mere coincidence to others. And to determinists, whatever happens is inevitable. For example, the probability of the existence of Life itself cannot be estimated, because, given random chemical stews and sufficient time, Life was, ultimately, inevitable, as is demonstrated by its existence. If there were no Life, then one might call it unlikely. As it is, it is certain.

*

All life is preoccupied with death. Death is the only certain future. Yet the one thing that is certain is the one thing that no one wishes to accept. In the face of reason, everyone holds out hope for the highly improbable.

*

I think I'm awake, but I'm not even sure I'm alive. I do not dare open my eyes. Even the light that infiltrates my eyelids is painful. My skull is overfull of swollen matter and a shaft of agony has gathered in the right side of my neck and I know it will erupt if I move. Let me be dead.

I am going to have to shift, even slightly, to get this pain under control, but I feel sure it will release a whole new battalion of aches from those reaches of body still numbed by sleep. Now I move, under tortuous control, but that triggers a booming at my temples and, now, ow, an unexpected pulse of violence from my ribs and I cry out aloud.

There's a snuffle of sound in the bed and a shift of warmth. Leo?

In surprise I open my eyes, instantly gouged by the light, but I have to sit up despite the gruesome reminders of pain all over and I have to speak. I speak to the sleeping form presenting through the fug of my vision a naked back to me and my throat won't work and when the sound breaks through my head resounds and my voice is loud enough to make me want to throw up.

I can't help it.

'Leo? How did you get here?'

*

There are many reasons that a reasonable observer might cite as to why a romance between Leo Martin and Chris Putnam was not going to happen. Such a romance would clearly be too good to be true.

Even supposing that the observer had made such a judgement on *that* morning rather than later when more information might be known, the reasons they might have chosen would have depended on the privileges extended to them in terms of their knowledge of circumstances and past events.

For example, knowing nothing more than the names, genders and social positions of the two people in question, they might have judged a relationship improbable on the basis of these factors alone.

It is, however, more likely, that such an observer would know more. They would, for example, have been cognisant of various well-known details relating to the life of Leo Martin which were matters of public record. The reasons they might have given would, therefore, have been plentiful.

*

The publicly (extremely publicly) acknowledged account of Leo's past was based largely on media interviews with him and other details gleaned by journalists from, among others, Helen Bossi in the rôle of Leo's public relations representative. Leo's past, and, indeed Leo himself, were clearly too good to be true. Nonetheless, the unreliable truth was as follows.

Leo Martin came into this world on the fourteenth of February 1975, in Chester, the son of Peg Martin and an uncertain father. He made his television debut on the twenty-first of June 1977 at the age of two, the apogee of infancy asleep on a cloud in an advertisement for Perfect Pillows™ and trod the boards (albeit in Titania's arms) one month later as the changeling in *A Midsummer Night's Dream*. His professional acting career was, however, thereafter woefully deferred for a further nineteen years. Those early appearances had merely been one of many, usually fruitless, schemes by his mother to supplement her income, an income ever insufficient to keep together simultaneously the bodies and souls of them both. Nevertheless, perhaps, even at that tender age, Leo, bedazzled by the limelight, was ever after destined to pursue its glow.

He graced the stage again in school productions where he displayed uncommon acting ability and a bewitching singing voice. But, most of all, he was objectively, quantifiably handsome, or perhaps beautiful, but in any case, supremely pulchritudinous. Empirically so.

His talents and virtues, it seemed, emerged *ex nihilo*. Certainly, his mother was blessed with no particular adequacies.

At eighteen, Leo was admitted on a scholarship as a drama student by the Bristol Old Vic Company, after which he moved to London to perform above pubs in fringe productions without pay. He shared digs in Tufnell Park with the woman who was to become the one true love of his life, three years his senior and a graduate from Cambridge, who was at that moment employed in an arts and entertainments public relations agency in Covent Garden. The slim and elegant Helen Bossi was no more able to resist his tremendous looks, his innate wit and intelligence and his famously good nature than anyone who crossed his path. The young lovers, poor though they were, married the following year just two weeks after Leo was cast as Ariel in an all-male production of *The Tempest* at the Globe Theatre.

For the next eighteen months, acting jobs came haltingly. Leo peppered his bank balance with work as a photographic model (usually for catalogue and magazine advertisements) and occasional appearances in small television rôles including an appearance in *The Bill* as a good Samaritan. In early 1998, whilst strutting and fretting his hour upon the stage of the Theatre Royal, Guildford, in a production of *The Boyfriend*, he was spotted by Cameron Mackintosh. The impresario marched backstage during the interval and immediately cast Leo as the new Marius in *Les Misérables*.

Meanwhile, his wife began working with the up-and-coming art phenomenon Dan Putnam, with whom Leo also became best of friends. She set up Heaven Ltd, her own PR agency, off St Martin's Lane and, among her list of more promising celebrities, she assumed the management of the growing public interest in her husband.

Later that year, he started to cause stares in the streets after landing the leading rôle in a highly successful three-part serialisation of *An Ideal Husband* for BBC Television. He began to receive offers for film parts, some of which he took. His range as an actor was broad, but with his looks and charm, he was nothing if not a romantic lead. Most notably, of course, there was the part of Adam in *Utopia*, which, to the surprise of many, over the summer of 1999 raced to the top of the film charts[5] and stayed there. Its runaway success was attributed to the triumph of genuine talent over hype[6] and (ousting Ewan McGregor, Robert Carlyle and others of their ilk) it propelled Leo to the status of the UK's most promising international star at the dawn of the new millennium.

---

[5] *Utopia* grossed $78 million in the US box offices in its first fortnight and £22 million in the UK in the same period, making it the most successful British feature film ever (although it was part-financed by the American-owned DreamWorks Corp.).

[6] This was in the same season that, among others, *Star Wars: The Phantom Menace* had been expected to break box office records. *Utopia* was among the reasons it did not.

The multi-million-dollar offers flooded in from Hollywood. Comparisons were made, praising not merely Leo's star quality but also his genuine ability to act, not to mention his tremendous looks, his innate wit and intelligence and his famously good nature. He was the embodiment of the man's perfect Englishman and the woman's also. It seemed only natural that he could be James Bond as soon as he was old enough, but he and his career had already surpassed 007.

In January, the rumours began. Helen was having an affair. How could she do it? Every woman from five to a hundred-and-five wanted him as her father, husband, son or grandson. He had tremendous looks, innate wit and intelligence and a famously good nature. Leo was universally acknowledged as the ideal husband. And yet she was cheating on him.

No one trusted her. A PR woman. All glitz and gloss. A cold, calculating bitch who had used poor Leo to build up her business and cast him aside in favour of ... in favour of, what? An accountant from LA named Vic Hemitt.

Poor Leo the victim. For once, there was scarce criticism of the tabloids who had exposed his betraying wife and her lover. Leo had a right to know and the public shared his grief and loved him all the more.

Leo's reaction was noble. He announced that he held no grudge against his wife. Indeed, although they had formally separated, they would remain close friends and, unlike some of her clients who had walked out in disgust at her treatment of Leo, he himself stood by and publicly announced that he intended that she should continue to represent him. (After much speculation about whether they would go together to the Oscars ceremony in March or with which other beautiful woman he would choose to attend, Leo arrived on his own and had no one to kiss as he stood up from his seat in the gaze of billions.) It was also announced that, in spite of the wreckage of his marriage, he was to bravely start work in August in his first major Hollywood rôle. He would star in *Odysseus*, a $160 million blockbuster (with a prequel already in script development). Before then, however, his British fans would have the chance to see him as Hamlet, for a strictly limited period, at the Lyceum Theatre in London's West End.

The public mask of Leo Martin bore only a resemblance to the private life of the real man, insofar that there was a real man behind the unreal mask. The two were like twins.

For Leo Martin had a fatal flaw, as anyone of such heroic stature must, and that flaw was cowardice. He was afraid to climb ladders, afraid of swimming in the sea, afraid of confrontation. He was not the sort to perform his own stunts, but nor could he watch as his double assumed the risks. Yet more importantly, he was afraid to be unknown and afraid of fame, afraid of putting all that he had gained in jeopardy and afraid of standing still, afraid of acting and afraid of not acting.

It was easier not to act, to do nothing, to build thick walls, to cordon his emotions. Yet, that was not what he needed. He needed to exert control, free will. Unfortunately, his will feared to do other than to let life happen to him. Cowardice.

*

An observer privileged to know almost every level of truth about Leo Martin would have cited many reasons why a romance between him and Chris Putnam would not happen. They too would have found it almost unthinkable.

*

The naked back unfurls and stretches out a head from under the covers, a head with short blond hair. The person raises its arms to its face as it turns towards me and rubs its eyes moaning contentedly. 'Morning,' it yawns.

'Yes, morning,' I say because I cannot say anything else. I am too shocked by the pain all over and by the beating that's especially in my head and by the first thing it said.

It takes the hands away from its face and it looks like a girl. It reaches behind its head and takes a pillow and puffs it up and props itself upright. The duvet falls from its chest – it is a girl, a woman, naked. In my bed. I mustn't show horror. I scout my senses: I am still wearing my jockey shorts, but that doesn't mean much.

'How you feeling?' she says and rubs her hands across her head, ruffling her scalp. Her hair is short enough that this will probably do instead of brushing. With her arms above her head, the fleshy lumps of her breasts stand up at me and I let myself collapse on to my back, but she's got my pillow and so I go down further and harder than I had thought I would and get a stab of pain all around my ribs. Trying to look down without moving, I glimpse at the marblework of mauves and blacks and yellows. It is bad but it doesn't account for the pain I feel all over.

'Shit,' I say and there are so many things bad and hurting and confusing, I am just going to lie here for now and let them explain themselves as they must, in their own time. I close my eyes to keep out the light and the noise, but the pressure of my eyeballs only creates a throb in my forehead.

The girl budges about beside me and says, 'Angel.'

'Hunh?' I say back, but don't open my eyes.

'My name.' More moving around and rustling and now the scrape and flare of a match being struck. I am keeping my eyes shut, but I can't block out the noises. 'My name's Angel.' I hear her suck on a cigarette. 'So, you don't remember much about last night then?' Her accent is chirpy and Liverpudlian, too chirpy. I don't feel the need, or cannot bring myself, to voice an answer. 'What's the time?' she now asks and I feel her press her sweaty skin against mine as she reaches across to pick up my alarm clock. I smell her ash breath and other stale souvenirs of a night of alcohol and cigarettes. I let out a groan.

'Your ribs hurting you? Or is it your head? I got some painkillers in me bag. I'll get you some water and fix us some coffee after I've had me shower, but I've got to get a move on – I got to be in work by lunchtime.' The words barely register and after she stops talking, a seasickness of waves bounces through the bed as she gets out. The motion makes me open my eyes again briefly, long enough to see a small butterfly tattoo on her buttock as she reaches for my towel which she starts to wrap around her, a puff of smoke from her cigarette, but I close my eyes again and again wish to die.

I want to return to sleep, to non-existence. I want

emptiness in my head, but it is full of questions and thoughts that have already clawed too far into consciousness and need to be settled. It is also full of a giant with a hammer. I will lie motionless and wait for them all, the thoughts, the questions, the giant, to go away. What happened last night? Was it even last night? How many lives might I have lived, must I have lived, to wake up with, with her? There is no conceivable chain of events that could possibly have led to her being here, naked, in my bed in the space of just one night. I can't imagine any ... I don't even want the effort of trying. No, I just want my brain to be blank.

Angel. Am I dead? The pain, the bruises, the ... Ridiculous. I am alive in my own bed. With a girl called Angel. Did we have sex? I have never had sex with a woman in my life. Did she rape me? Did I want to? Perhaps if I was drunk, some deep repressed urges emerged and I couldn't help myself. Maybe I'm really straight deep down? Or bi? No. More likely I'm dead. Let me be dead. Stop thinking about it, just for a moment.

Perhaps the primal urge, the Darwinian imperative? I couldn't help it. My genes' demand for reproduction got the better of my natural sexuality. Then that would mean my sexuality is only what I was brought up to be. This is too much for my head right now. I shall try to picture blackness. But, no, I know I can't choose what thoughts may come. Would I be straight if all else were equal? What does that mean, if? Under different circumstances? What different circumstances could there possibly be? In order for things to have a different outcome, they would have to have a different set of causes. And those causes would have to have different causes of their own. You would have to go right back to square one, the Big Bang. Probably beyond. No, just stop. I'm not going to think about it.

I know the coils of my DNA do not prescribe my sexuality, they do not make me gay, I just know it – it's not that simple – but I have always been gay. Surely I have, but maybe, last night ... Stop.

The coke and all those drinks. What was it Dan was saying about making you do what you really wanted to? Did I really want to or was it just the alcohol and drugs? Was it the real me or ... or ... who?

Drugs are chemicals in the body and brain, so are hormones, neuropeptides, proteins. If ecstasy can make you love everyone, why should I be worried that I had sex with a woman? Just a balance of chemicals. That's all. But then, what's real? What's the balance that makes me gay in the first place? How did I come to be gay? Who am I if I'm not gay? Think of something else. Blank space.

But what happened? I can't ask her. It's obvious what happened. To be naked in bed and for it to mean nothing? And who the hell is she anyway? What time did she say it is? The lab! Sir Hugo. Jesus, I feel dizzy. The bed's unstable. Open my eyes. Hold the blank ceiling steady. But that doesn't help. I think I'm going to be sick.

I can't help it.

I can still hear the shower. The girl is in the bathroom. The kitchen sink.

*

My head is in my hands and I am sat at the kitchen table panting like a mother in labour. Nothing. For ten minutes I have retched and burped and gurgled and prodded my throat with my fingers and I can't, I can't any more. I have made my chest jerk so much I now cannot tell whether perhaps I am sobbing. One thing I know about last night. I didn't eat anything.

I will sit here till my breathing calms. I will feel better soon. Somebody comes in, I cannot look up, but it is Angel or Elsi. I hope it's Elsi, but I think it won't be.

'Not feeling better, then?' chirps the Liverpudlian voice. 'Here, try these,' and moving my head minimally I can see at the edge of my vision paracetamol, Alka-Seltzer, glass of water.

'I'm sorry,' I say without looking up, 'I'm really sorry, but I'm afraid I really can't remember anything. Please, can you just tell me what we ... What happened?' I take the paracetamol.

'When?'

'Last night.'

'Which part?'

'Any of it.'

'You were at your brother's private viewing.'

'I know that bit. Can you just ...'

'You got a little bit rat-arsed. In fact, you got totally ...'

'Yeah, yeah, I guessed. I had some coke, you see, and nothing to eat all day.' I am mouthing the words as much as saying them. 'Then I drank a lot – I guess I didn't realise how much 'cause of the coke, but when it wore off ... Later. I'm sorry. Please, tell me what happened later.'

'Don't worry, we didn't do it, if that's what you're thinking.'

I pause. I can look up now. She is dressed in a tight white dress, from last night presumably, and eating bread as she stands by the kettle humming slowly to itself. She continues, 'Dan asked me to bring you home. You went out on your own and then came back with your clothes all damp and dirty, like you'd fallen in a drain or something, and Leo looked after you and I said I thought you'd been beaten up, but they didn't take your wallet. That was still in your pocket. Did you have a watch?'

'A what?'

'A watch. Did you have a watch, because you didn't when I undressed you. Did they take that?'

'No. No watch.'

'Why'd anyone want to beat you up then? Seems a bit unreasonable, a bit pointless. I mean, did you piss anyone off at the party? Well, no point asking you really, is there? Still, it's not the kind of party where people get into fights, but you never know. I dunno, sometimes it seems some things happen and there's just no reason for them at all.' She has found muesli in the cupboard and empties some into a bowl with milk. 'Here, eat. It'll make you feel better.'

'Thank you, I don't think I can. Erm, why were you in my bed?'

'Well, Leo gave me cash for a cab to get home after I'd dropped you off, but the driver wouldn't take you, so I had to give it all to him and then he did, so it was either crash here or the night bus across the river. And, well, you were well out of it and not likely to mind, so ...'

'But you were naked.' I drop three Alka-Seltzer in the muesli. I must show willing.

'Oh, sorry. Did it upset you? I always sleep in the buff, can't sleep with clothes on and, well, you being gay and everything, I didn't think it would ...'

'How do you know about ...'

'Chris,' she interrupts, '*Everyone* knows.' The kettle clicks and the noise reverberates in my head. Click-click-click. The milk in the muesli froths at the rim of the bowl.

'Oh,' I say, and I pause and now I say, 'how? No. Never mind. Thank you. I mean thank you for everything.' She smiles and shrugs it off like it's all part of the service, an entertainment for her. I feel so much gratitude, but feel incapable of expressing anything in more than single syllables. 'What did you say about Leo?'

'When?'

'Just now.'

'Nothing.'

'No, you did. Something about he looked after me.'

'Oh, yeah, sure,' and she is turned away towards the kettle making instant coffees. 'I don't quite know, but he carried you into the office at the gallery and got Dan to make arrangements to get you home – I'm sorry, but your brother can be such an arsehole sometimes – and he waited with you until the taxi came and then I took you home. I promised I'd give him a call and let him know you were okay as soon as I got into work. Fucking hell. Is the clock on your oven right? Fuck. I must drink this and get going. I want to go home and change before ...'

But I am not listening anymore, I am looking at the clock which says '10:09' and changes as I am looking at it to '10:10' and I am taking a few seconds to compute the meaning of the number and now I understand it and the panic hits.

Sir Hugo. Shit.

'Shit,' I say, 'oh, christ, look, god, I've got to go too. I didn't realise it was so late. My boss. Sorry. Thanks, really. His pep talks. If I'm not there ...' and I'm already out of the kitchen door and heading into the bathroom before I feel dizzy again.

*

'I'm off then,' says the girl, as I am grappling with my jeans and a white shirt and I look round and see her head poking round my bedroom door .

'What? Oh, dear. Oh, I'm sorry. Look, thanks. Thanks a lot. So much. And erm, Leo ...'

'Yeah, don't worry,' she says, 'I'll call him. Gotta go. See ya. Give me a call, okay? Or I'll call you.'

And she's gone. The front door clicks behind her.

I don't even know who she is. Her first name, that's all. *Or I'll call you*. Does that mean she will? Or *maybe* she will? Or is it just one of those things you say? She doesn't have my number. Does she? I don't have hers. That's the end of that. I can't thank Leo. He looked after me. I know I'm fantasising, but still, it's a chance with him. A realistic chance. It's like a chance. She's my connection. But she doesn't even know I want to talk to him. I don't think I made it clear. Do I anyway? What I know of last night does not sound good and I don't even want to know the rest. I don't think I thanked her enough. Maybe I thanked her too much.

He looked after me.

'So who was *she*, then?' says Elsi pushing my door and letting it swing open accusingly. 'If I didn't know better ...' She leans against the door-jamb in her paisley kimono and cradles a mug of herbal tea, presumably, in her hands.

'What? Sorry, not right now, I'm late. We'll talk later.'

Chromosome 8
A Question of Identity

'Twins' history affords a means of distinguishing between the effects of tendencies received at birth, or those that were imposed by the circumstances of their after-lives; in other words, between the effects of nature and of nurture.'
Francis Galton

'"To this end I was born, and for this cause came I into the world, that I should bear witness unto the truth. Everyone that heareth the truth is of my voice."

Pilate saith unto him, "What is truth?"'
John XVIII, 37–8

'Ah, here's the man, Mr Putnam. Thank you so much for taking time out of your busy day to join us. I realise these early meetings must play havoc with your schedule.' Sir Hugo is sitting up on one of the workbenches in what I have always supposed is an effort to look casual, but just looks uncomfortable. He is too formal to dangle his legs like a kid and it makes his purple waistcoat bunch up and the shirt shows between the buttons. Everybody is standing around looking bored and twelve pairs of eyes stare at me as I come in. I glance at the clock. Only just after eleven. I thought it would all be over by now. I hoped so.

'Yes, sorry I'm late.' The rebellion in my stomach has quelled for the time being, but my head still feels like thorns. 'I'm not feeling very well.'

'Out on the razzle were we?' Immediately I want to deny it, but since it's true, I am panicked and wonder if someone told him, so I try to look ill, but probably just look sheepish. I take up a position next to Eve by the centrifuges. 'Never mind. You have missed our round of congratulations to your colleague *Doctor* Babb and I was just starting a debrief on an exciting new chapter in all our lives.'

He pauses as if starting a new paragraph. 'I don't need to tell you the implications of the completion of this first draft of the human genome. We have at most two years during which the G-5 labs and people like Craig Venter are going to pad out the detail and then they're going to turn their focus from the sequencing to the biology. We, I am delighted to say, have a head start on our competitors and the future looks bright for all of us, indeed, for the entire field. Government is beginning to appreciate that, just because we've got the genome, that's no reason for the funding streams to run dry any time soon. On the contrary, now that we have the genome – or near enough – we want to know what it is that the genes do. It is my belief that the money will continue to flow. We already have considerable commitments from Wellcome and, with a few words in a few friendly ears, I'm sure I can get government on side too.

'However, the money is going to start shifting and we must all stay one step ahead of the game. We've got to be seen to be doing something useful, something practical with all the information we've gathered so far. The genome's taken us, what, a dozen years? There's a hundred years' work involved in making sense of it and, if we play our cards right, we're the ones who are going to be doing it.'

I edge in closer to Eve and whisper, 'What's he on about?'

'Sara Babb's got her doctorate.'

'Good for her. What's this about the first draft?'

'Haven't you heard? Finished, apparently. There was a joint statement this morning from the Sanger Centre people and Celera. And Clinton and Blair have been on the telly doing the all-hail-the-new-dawn fanfare. That's why we were late starting – he's been off doing the media rounds.'

'This is the world's most exciting, challenging and innovative field of science today, not to mention the best funded,' continues Sir Hugo, looking at each of us in turn as if he's making a big point, something we didn't already know. 'But, ladies and gentlemen, ours is a very specific challenge and, as you know, it is always my practice to share the Laboratory's plans with you. I think of it not as my laboratory, but as ours. As you know, we have our Grand Plan and I want you all to be a part of it, because you,' he pauses for effect, 'are our number one resource. I know I don't see as much of you all as I'd like, but that is because I'm out there working for us, for our little lab, bringing home the bacon, as it were. And what do I tell them? Queen's HGL has the best team in the business. Productivity is our raison d'être. Productivity and results. Lean efficiency, eh?' I feel dizzy again. I want to sit down. There's no stool nearby. I lean on one of the centrifuges. It whirrs. Everyone looks at me. I move my elbow and with a click-click-click, it stops. 'And I'm delighted to announce that I have pulled off what I think we can claim is something of a coup. Last week on my way back from Mount Vernon, I came via Toronto and, together with a contribution from BBSRC, I have now finalised funding for the largest study yet on sexual orientation. We're going after the gay gene.'

He pauses again and surveys the room, as if awaiting something. He is more used to conference audiences. The something doesn't happen. He continues, 'We're going to take this thing back to basics: establish maternal inheritance patterns, have a stab at heritability, explore X linkages – especially Xq28, obviously – sequence the locus or loci, as the case may be, identify the gene – or genes – and determine the biology.' He counts off the objectives on his fingers.

'Is that all?' says Lee sarcastically and I guess he didn't mean to say it so loud.

'I know it sounds ambitious, Dr Sall, but, come on, let's all have a little vision. We're going to form a centre of excellence here, the UK Institute of Sexuality Studies. The acronym's rather neat, eh? Something like that, anyway. Besides, in the first instance, we've got three years before we need to show any results at all.'

A groan of exasperation from everyone.

'It's *only* a target and we all need targets or we don't know where we're heading. And may I remind you, ladies and gentlemen, that in this game, three years is a long time. Hamer's team in Washington are already way ahead of us, but they haven't got the funds we have and their project's tiny by comparison. Besides, everyone dismisses him as a gay crusader these days. No one's going to pay attention to anything he comes up with now. Not since Rice and Ebers put paid to Xq28's credibility.'

'So why are we still bothering with it?' says someone by the window, Lee again, I think.

'Because,' Sir Hugo addresses all his troops, 'I believe Hamer may have been right anyway and, if no one's going to believe *him* ... well, put it this way, people are hardly going to say *I* have a gay agenda.' He chuckles. 'Furthermore, ladies and gentlemen, this subject is right up there with alcoholism, intelligence and criminal tendencies. Remember the big picture. If we can find anything the hacks can call a gay gene, we, my dear friends, will have established ourselves as the miracle workers of Neo-Darwinism. We will be set up for life.' Again, he looks at us each in turn, and now into mid-air. He is transparent – in his head he is announcing findings in packed lecture halls, appearing on chat shows, being awarded fellowships, honorariums, prizes.

'And if we don't?'

He snaps his gaze onto Lee but pauses, considers. 'If we don't, then we publish whatever we find. Of course. But our funders and I have discussed it. We all feel there's something there – it is on the basis of that hypothesis that I have convinced them to back us – and assuming there is, we're prepared to do what it takes to find it.' He senses remaining scepticism in his small audience and purses his lips impatiently. 'For goodness' sakes, just think about it. I can't find anything wrong with it. The evidence all points to at least some genetic influence: the twin studies, the pedigrees, the endocrinology. It's more obvious than left-handedness and no one has a problem with that. If there is no gay gene, or genes, what is it? Ask any queer when they thought they became gay, they'll tell you: always have been. Classic genetic phenotype. Ask our colleague Mr Putnam here.' And he gestures at me with an outstretched arm and an upturned palm. I am to be made an example of. Everyone turns to look at me and nails me with their eyes. I feel my skin bristle with the heat of it all and the boom in my forehead drowns their look and the pain in my ribs stabs me and I go cold and want to puke.

Sir Hugo continues, but I am hardly paying attention now, just aware of his voice and his plumpness, dropping inelegantly from the workbench. 'Anyway, ladies and gentlemen,' he tugs his jacket straight but not his waistcoat,

'Dr Ng is taking charge of the project for the time being and will be putting together the team. We'll be getting some new people in, but you chaps are the real key, remember. In the meantime, I'll get Nicole to post some references on the board – Hamer's papers, Rice's, Byne, Bailey, and so on – I'll expect you to look them over. I'd like you all to do so, even those of you who aren't going to be working directly on this – we want ideas and input from everyone. Remember, we're a team.' People start to shift and move away – Sir Hugo is rounding off now and they don't have to listen anymore. 'That'll do for now. Back to work everyone and keep it up. That's the spirit. Good work, everybody, I'm very pleased with everything. Well done. Oh, and Mr Putnam, Chris ...'

I straighten, flush.

'... I'd like a brief chin-wag this p.m. I've got to be at ITN shortly, then I have a lunch, but can we say four-ish? Jolly good, see you then.' And he turns on his heel and goes into his side office closing the door behind him.

I turn and Lee is standing beside me. '*He* believes Hamer may be right. What the hell does he know about it?' he confides to me, thinking I am his ally, probably for no other reason than I am standing nearest. 'Last time he touched a fucking test-tube, people were trying to make gold out of lead. But he sends us off anyway on some wild goose chase just so he can ponce about as if he's done any of the work himself. Well, I'll tell you one thing for free, if Colin asks me to work on it, he can stuff it. I'm outta here. The funding will be taking the piss. This "institute" thing's clearly a joke. And there's no way we can fit anyone else in here, there aren't enough workspaces as it is. The whole thing's going nowhere – it's going to be three years of nothing but number crunching and coming up with sweet fuck-all.'

*

Dan Putnam was right-handed. On the other hand, Chris Putnam, was left-handed. Or so they both said. And who else would know? Nevertheless, such a difference between monozygotic – so-called 'identical' – twins is not unusual. Indeed, if one twin is left-handed, the probability that the second will also be left-handed is improved by only fifty per cent.

Dan Putnam was born shortly after midnight on June the twenty-second 1976. Chris Putnam, on the other hand, was almost twelve minutes older, born shortly before midnight on June the twenty-first. *Ergo*, Dan was born under the sign of Cancer and Chris, on the other hand, under Gemini. Again, such a coincidence is not unusual: more births take place during the night than during the day and therefore the probability that twins will be born astride midnight is greater than at another time of day picked at random. Furthermore, there is a zodiacal cusp approximately every thirty days; twins born astride one such midnight should not give cause for greater surprise than twins born at any other time in particular.

Chris Putnam was homosexual. Dan Putnam, on the other hand, was heterosexual. Or so they both said. And who else would know? And again, such a difference is not unusual: amongst male monozygotic twins, if one is homosexual, the probability of his brother sharing his sexual orientation is only fifty per cent.

*

There is no such thing as a gene which makes an individual homosexual. Nor, for that matter, is there a gene which makes an individual short or tall or blond or blue-eyed or colour-blind or sickle-cell anaemic. Genes do not make an individual anything, any more than brain chemistry makes you hungry, food makes you breathe, breathing makes you die. Genes make ribonucleic acid. That is all. Amen.

Genes are made of DNA and DNA is not a mystery. It is a chemical. DNA makes mRNA. mRNA makes tRNA. tRNA makes amino acids. Amino acids make proteins. Proteins make hormones, cells and all the chemistry and biology of the body. And in every new cell that is made is the same DNA to make more mRNA. The chain replicates. Amen.

But genes make nothing on their own. DNA is just an acid. Genes make nothing without the ingredients with which to make them, without the cell nucleus in which the chemical reactions take place and without the conditions for those reactions to happen.

What makes the ingredients? Food? Air? Proteins?

What makes the cell nucleus? Biology? Chemistry? Physics?

What makes the conditions? The womb? The body? The environment?

What makes a book? The words? The paper? The printing press?

Or the writer? The reader? The language?

What makes a homosexual? Nature? Nurture?

Or neither? Both?

Genes do not make an individual homosexual. They play their part, but so does the rest of the universe. Amen.

*

Chris Putnam and Dan Putnam were clones and yet they were not the same. What was the cause?

If their genes were the same, the cause must have been differences in their environment.

Identical twins have identical genes except for minor differences owing to mutations taking place after division of the fertilised ovum. Was this the cause? All else being equal, this must have been the cause.

But all else was not equal. Chris was nurtured in his mother Mary's womb on one side. Dan was on the other. Chris was born twelve minutes earlier, under a different sign. Then Dan was born, to Mary's greater relief, to the sound of Chris's indignant howls. Chris slept in a room shaded by a yew tree. Dan awoke every morning to the rising sun through his window. Which of these differences was the cause?

*

Eugene Putnam believed the cause was neither in his son's genes nor in his upbringing, but in his soul. Whatever that may be.

*

Sir Hugo Huttenton believed in himself. Because he believed in himself, he believed what he did was important. Or maybe he believed what he did was important because he believed in himself.

He believed what he did was important because he believed genetics to be the cause of every human trait. Or maybe he believed genetics to be the cause of every human trait because he believed what he did was important.

A cause is always an effect and an effect is always a cause.

*

It is past four and Sir Hugo is not back yet and I am drinking my eighth or ninth or tenth coffee of the day and I am tired and I am thirsty, but I might as well be downing vinegar. I'm staring at an egg and tuna sandwich and it is staring back at me and it is all that was left in the cafeteria, but I can't eat it. I feel better but I can't risk the sandwich. Today I am grateful my job requires me only to move chemicals from place to place and to watch letters scroll endlessly across my computer screen. I don't think I could handle anything else.

What does he want to see me for anyway?

*

It is four forty-two and still no sign of Sir Hugo. I want to give up the ghost. If he didn't already know I'd got in late, I could leave at five and I wouldn't have to wait for him, but as it is, I don't think I can leave before six at the earliest and even then, I should wait for him really. I shift in my seat and get a reminder of the pain like my side is pierced.

Why would anyone do that to me? Why me? I haven't done anything wrong to anyone. Was it for no reason at all? It's not fair. It's, it's knotted into a ball of frustration now. It makes me feel miserably sorry for myself. Along everything else. It stirs again that cancerous guilt and I just want go back and find out who it was and ask them why, why they'd pick on me? It doesn't make sense. It just doesn't make sense. I'm senselessly, powerlessly angry about it now.

Now I think about it. There must have been a reason. There can't have been no reason at all.

*

Five sixteen. I remember that horoscope. Only just over a fortnight ago, but it feels like forever. Important changes. My daddy died. A cruel joke, no, a cruel irony. Whoever wrote it didn't know. I was happy that morning, but it wasn't the horoscope that made me happy. The fact that it might have been a catalyst is irrelevant to the reason why. It wasn't the reason any more than it was the reason why my father died. Prophecies aren't reasons why. Even if it did say *important changes*. Even though it did.

Happy because I'd had a good night's sleep, because I'd talked to Elsi, because, because, because. The reasons don't matter. We could only talk the way we did because that was the point I'd reached, I was prepared to get over Gill, prepared for the next thing. If it hadn't been that morning, it would have been another. But it was a long time coming.

Maybe I was already waiting for the next thing. My father. I could not grieve them both, so I gave up grieving Gill just in time. There wasn't room in me to want them both back. But I didn't want either of them. I must keep telling myself that. It's how it will make sense in the end. It's how I'll fill the gap. It's how I'll see there is no gap. I don't need them. Never did.

No, the logic doesn't work. I couldn't have given up Gill deliberately. I didn't know, not until that morning. The effect must follow the cause.

I must stop my mind from asking these questions. But I can't. Science is all about asking questions and that is what I do. That is who I am. I am a scientist, for God's sake, even if I just clone and sequence DNA.

But maybe I went out with Gill to stop me grieving for my mother. Am I gay because my mother died? No, Sir Hugo's right, I have always been gay. The effect must follow. Am I gay because my mother was always going to die?

I am gay because I choose to be. But no, it's not my choice. I like to think I choose to sleep with men, but I have only ever slept with a man, one man. I don't *choose* anything.

But that's because men don't choose to sleep with me. Elsi tells me they would if I wanted them, but I'm too choosy, so what does that tell me? This morning I thought deep down I might be straight – if I'd had sex with that girl would I be any more gay than straight? One each way.

Being gay is about more than that. It's not just what I do, but who I am. It is a thing about my whole life. It can't be bottled up separately. It is part of how I choose to live my life even if I never made the choice.

There's no point to asking why.

I choose to prefer men. Or more accurately, I choose men because I prefer men. Men are what I like. I see someone. I do not stop and ask myself the question, do I like them? Sometimes I like them. Sometimes I don't. Sometimes I think maybe. But the fact is *I decide*. I decide automatically who I like and it just so happens that, if I like them, it's always a man. I choose men because I prefer them. And I prefer them because I like them more. No, the logic doesn't work. Circles. I am gay, because I am. That's all there is to it.

Why do I care? I don't mind. I'm happy with it. It's my father who minded. He minded and, okay, it must have hurt. He couldn't help that. He didn't choose for it to hurt.

I never thought about how much it must have hurt. I only blamed him for it. Now, he is dead. So why do I care now? Why do I want to know why? Why does Sir Hugo?

Because of Science.

I want to know because my father died and while he was alive I could blame him instead of wanting to find reasons or excuses for myself as if I'm guilty of something.

I want to know because a horoscope can't make me happy and never could. If I had faith in horoscopes, I'd never ask any whys. And if I never asked whys, I'd be able to believe in anything, even horoscopes.

What else did it say? Don't let the past decide the future. Love life to hot up. See? Wrong. A cruel joke. Especially after last night.

*

'Hey, gorgeous, do you want to come to the pub?' I look up from the screen and it is Eve. 'We're going to have a drink to celebrate Sara's PhD.'

'I can't. I'm waiting to see Sir Hugo.' And I can never drink again.

'All right then, but come and join us when you're through. We're going to the Prince and the Pauper. Then some of us may be going for a meal in King's Cross.'

'Yeah, okay, maybe.' Five thirty-nine.

*

What am I doing here?

Waiting. Is it worth it? Is this what I want to do with my life anyhow? Jesus, I don't know. I don't even know how I got into this.

I remember the miniature garden. Up against the south wall at Le Noires, Daddy made a space for Dan and me. Dan couldn't be bothered to water his regularly, so he swamped it all at once. Everything died and smelled. But I planted seeds and got little flowers and carrots and Daddy showed me how to dibble properly so the soil is oxygenated. I collected worms too. He even helped me write a letter to *Gardeners' Question Time* once. And I grew peas too, I remember that now. I remember understanding about Mendel and genetics at school because of my peas.

I suppose it's possible that's where I started. It was all his fault in the first place. Shouldn't have given me a garden to look after. I never would have got into science.

I don't even have a houseplant now.

Five-forty-nine.

*

The phone. I'll leave it, almost everyone's left already anyway and it's not likely to be for me. Five-fifty-four. Irritating. Where's Sir Hugo got to? Oh sod it. 'Hello, Human Genome Lab.'

'Hey there, asshole.'

'Dan? How you doing?'

116

'I'm pissed off, but, on the other hand, *I* didn't humiliate myself last night.'

'I was that bad?'

'Bro,' Dan says, 'you were worse.'

'What did Leo say?'

'I didn't ask, but, listen, you've blown it there. Well and truly.'

'But he looked after me.'

'What makes you say that? *I* was the one who sorted you out, got you home. Jesus, as if I didn't have enough to do. Did you see the papers?'

'But that girl said ...'

'What girl?'

'Angel?'

'Oh yeah. Anyway, did you read the papers?'

'What papers?'

'The reviews. Hah! Both of them. Critics. Wankers. Every single fucking one.'

'Does it matter? I thought that was the point. I thought you use the bad reviews to ...'

'Yeah, yeah, yeah. Bad reviews, hunh, could've done with more bad reviews. Anyway, it's fine, don't you worry about it' he says and he pauses for a moment and I want to ask him more about last night. I want to know what happened. I want to say something to Leo, about how I'm not like that, to get in touch with him again, but I don't want to do it through Dan. Dan says he didn't do anything, but Dan's probably not telling the whole story, but if he is, then Angel might thank him for me for nothing. It's going to be even more embarrassing than it is already. I want to get in touch with Angel, she said I should call, but I don't have her number. And I don't think she meant it anyway. I want to see Leo again, but there's no way it will ever happen without Dan and I don't want him involved. It's all his fault I was pissed. Okay, it's not, but I don't want him to be a part of it. He can't be serious. He'll ruin everything. Angel's my only link and I don't even know who she is or how to get in touch. 'It's fine,' Dan repeats sadly, 'but, Jesus, what the fuck are they writing about instead? If there'd been one juicy one, just one, we'd have something to work with.'

The double doors swing behind me and Sir Hugo strides

in. 'Be right with you, Chris. Soon as you're off the phone.'

'Dan, I've got to go.' But I realise Sir Hugo isn't in his office yet. He will have heard me. He will know it's a personal call and he doesn't know Dan called me, not the other way around. I feel like a slacker today. No, I feel Sir Hugo feels I'm a slacker today. Whatever I try to do comes out wrong. He's convinced I'm crap. Why does he want to see me? Is he going to fire me?

'Listen to this,' Dan starts quoting, 'the *Guardian*: "Art has moved on, but Dan Putnam seems stuck—"'

'Dan. I really have to go.' He's going to fire me.

'"—His latest exhibition at the—"'

'Dan. I'll talk to you later. Bye.'

'Thanks, bro. Thanks a fuck.' And he hangs up.

I replace the receiver and shut down my computer and find a pen and take a piece of paper from the printer tray and go to Sir Hugo's door. He's about to sack me. Why? I don't want to knock. I knock.

'Come.'

I enter and he's on the phone with his chair spun towards the window and with his pen in his hand, he flicks a gesture at the chair. I sit down in it and wait.

I try not to listen.

'Can't we split the new Tetrad machines with another cost centre and depreciate them over a longer time?'

I used to swivel on the chair in my father's office after school when Mummy was first ill. He'd get cross and I'd do it more. I try not to listen.

'What about the overheads budget?'

I look at the framed articles behind his desk, the ones I always look at when I'm waiting in here or unable to meet his eyes. They are by Sir Hugo or about Sir Hugo or for Sir Hugo. There is a little purple china pig on the desk. I wait.

I read every headline and caption. I have read them all before. I read them again. I cannot read the articles, the type is too small. One frame has a certificate with a laurel wreath and writing in Latin.

I wait.

I try not to listen.

Now it sounds as if he's winding up the conversation. I can't see the clock from here. How long's he been talking and have I been here? I wait. Must have been ten minutes. Fifteen? Maybe twenty. I need to piss.

I stare at the articles and the headlines lose their meaning. The words stop representing anything, they're just letters collected and spaced out in a stream. I have been watching scrolling DNA bases too long today. The As, Cs, Ts and Gs start to highlight themselves and stand out in the flow. It sounds as if he's getting on to a new topic. Opera tickets for Gabbatha or something. I try not listen. I wonder if I can leave, go to the loo, come back. I jiggle my legs a bit. It helps.

'Bye then, J—, must go. Got someone waiting to see me. See you at the weekend. Cheerio.' And he puts down the phone. He always does that if you're talking to him, finishes abruptly, to let you know his time is more important than yours. He swings his chair round, leans forward and says, 'Sorry about that, old chap, it was ...' and he tells me and I think I'm supposed to know who they are and be impressed, but I don't hear properly or instantly forget or I don't know them anyway. 'Terrible old bore. Anyway, thanks for hanging around. Won't keep you long anyhow, I've got an early plane in the morning. Ten minutes, okay?'

I say nothing. I know it won't be, it never is. He always tells you how long you're going to talk and never sticks to it. But maybe, if he's going to fire me ...

'Great,' he says and takes a serious breath. 'I wanted to chat about your future here, Chris.'

Here it comes. I want him to shout it at me. I don't want him to be calm. I want him to get angry and spit on the floor ... That I could stand. Just sit. But I need the loo. Say nothing.

'You've been a part of our little family for' – he looks at his desk and I realise he has my employment file open there – my CV, my job application letter, a few other papers, not much else – 'it's just over a year and a half now, isn't it?'

'If you say so,' I say or whisper, I think.

'Right, good. Anyway, Chris, as you know, I like to see all the members of our family get along.'

'I get along with everyone,' I say quickly. I thought I did. Does someone not like me?

'No, no, no. *Get along*. Move on up. Progress, Chris.

That's how we manage to be a centre of excellence. We train our own, breed our own loyalty. Like Man United.'

He's not going to fire me. He's not. I think he's not. I breathe out and sit back. My ribs hurt. I sit forward. My bladder stings.

'So, Chris, what do you want from life?'

I don't know. He wants me to decide this now? I say, 'Well, I'd like to, um ... progress.'

'Good, good. Because you're a high-flyer, Chris. I could say the same of anyone here, of course, but I've always taken a special interest in your success, my boy. I was thinking it's about time we got you a doctorate, don't you think? And this new project is just the thing for you. Plenty of scope there, eh? Plenty of scope for you and directly in your field of interest, I should imagine.'

'The gay gene project?'

'Yes, there's quite a lot of work involved and plenty of scope for a high-profile paper. A good opportunity I should think. You know, give it some thought and come up with some appropriate ideas. I'll see what I can do about clearing the way with some funding. I'll supervise, obviously.'

'What sort of ideas?' I don't know if I want to do a PhD.

'Oh, you know. Doesn't matter too much. There's a few things specifically I'd like you to pitch in on with the project. They might inspire you.'

'Such as?' Three years and then writing up my thesis and then, what am I good for? An academic career. More of the same. I don't think I want to commit to that. Not yet.

'Well, for starters, we're going to need lots of help finding suitable study subjects. We're planning on finding at least a hundred gay sibling pairs – twice as many as George Rice – more if we can. I'm sure you can help us there, work out where we should be looking, where to advertise, that sort of thing. You've probably even got some friends we could enlist, eh?'

'Not really.' But if I say no to this, he'll get rid of me. He doesn't want me sequencing forever. And I don't want to do it any more. But don't make me do this. I don't want to feel fenced in, all my options down the line laid out in some grand career plan dreamt up by someone else. I want to be free to make it up for myself as I go along.

'Oh, surely. Perhaps your boyfriend knows some people?'

'We split up.'

'Okay, sorry to hear that. But anyway, I trust *you*'ll volunteer at least. You've got a brother, haven't you?'

'Yes,' and I add, 'we're twins, but he's not gay.'

'Never mind, control group material. But twins, eh? Monozygotic?'

'Yes.'

'Marvellous. Then it doesn't matter. We can use you both anyway.'

'I'm not sure whether he ...'

'And uncles. Do you have any gay uncles? Or great uncles? Particularly on your mother's side?'

'I don't know. I mean, I have one uncle on that side, but I really don't think, I mean, I don't know if he's ...' Leave my family out of this.

'What about your mother? Why don't you ask her.'

'She died when I was—'

'Oh, shame. Shame.' He pauses and says, 'Still, you could ask the rest of your family. Do a bit of pedigree research, eh?'

I say nothing. I have nothing to say. I am not sure about a PhD, but I am not sure about anything else instead. I don't want to be told what to do. I know if I don't choose one future or another, one will be chosen for me by default. I want it to be my choice what I do with my life. My options are already limited by what's past, by what the situation demands. I have to live. I have to earn money. Everyone has to get by. Why ask why?

I'm not free to refuse unless I want to be sacked, but any power he has over me isn't his either. He's no more free than I am. I have him to face but he has the university and his backers and his wife and his kids and whatever. His freedom, his power over me, is conditional. But knowing that doesn't help either of us.

'Actually, Chris, I'm sure you can help me out on all of this. I'm going to have to do quite a bit of media on this whole area. It would be useful to get the, erm, *community*'s angle on the gay gene.' He looks at me with his paternal eyebrows raised over his glasses, waiting for me to speak. 'Well, not the gay community as such, more the gay-on-the-street. What's the general reaction? How should I play it? What am I facing here?'

'I don't really know.'

'Okay. Well, put it this way, is it talked about?'

'I don't know. I really don't know that many gays.' What does he think? We all know each other because we're gay? I don't understand what he wants to hear.

'Okay, okay, well, what do you think?'

I look at the articles on the wall as if they hold answers. 'I think some people are worried about testing and abortions.'

'Yes, yes. Look, I don't need the pressure-group hogwash. I've read the articles. What do *you* think about the gay gene?'

I don't know what to say. I haven't thought about it. Or, rather, I have, but I just haven't got anything to say, nothing that *sounds* as though I've thought about it. It just *feels* wrong, like there's no such thing, but I know I can't say that. I must be scientific. I try to look like I'm thinking. I know Sir Hugo is a reductionist, everything's genes and genes are everything. I want to please him, to get his approval, emotionally, no, professionally. 'I really don't know much about it.'

'For goodness' sake, lad, just a knee-jerk reaction. Gut feeling. What do you *believe*?'

And, at last, I see he doesn't want the truth. He doesn't want what I know. He wants belief. But I'm uncertain how to say it, whether to say it. 'I don't think I believe it.' Sir Hugo sighs and purses his lips and looks like he's about to launch into an argument and I've got it wrong, so, quickly, I add, 'I mean, to me it's not that kind of a question. Being gay is about how I feel and who I feel it about. It doesn't feel like a scientific issue?' I try to say it so it sounds like a question.

'What do you mean "not scientific"?' he says impatiently.

That wasn't what I wanted to say or maybe just not how I wanted to say it. 'I mean, I don't feel like that's the reason I'm gay,' I say quickly. I need the loo. 'I don't know, it's probably just that I don't want it to be true,' I add, but it doesn't sound any better once the words are out there.

'*Want* it to be true – Christ almighty, what's that got to with it?'

'I want to feel I've got more choice in the matter, that it's more something I own than something that was there before I was.'

'Come on, you know perfectly well genetics doesn't work like that. Or you bloody well should.' He slumps back into his chair, exasperated.

'Yes, I do, it's just, you know, from the inside it feels more complex than—'

'I'm not saying it's not complex, lad. For God's sake, don't be so defensive.'

'Please, I'm not, it's just you asked me what I believe and I—'

'But, look, if it's not your genes, are you saying it's your upbringing or are you saying it's completely random and there's no reason behind it whatsoever? Eh?' He gets up and paces to the window. 'Or God made you gay? Eh? Eh?'

'I don't know.'

He walks back fast and stands over me. 'Well, for God's sake, Chris, you must have given it some thought.' I really need to piss.

'Can we get the subject away from me, make it less personal?'

'Look, I'm not being personal. I just want you to justify what you said.' He has raised his voice but it is controlled. I was wrong. I am afraid of his anger. I want to make it go away. What can I say to make it go away?

'I—' I have to look down, look away, look at the articles on the wall, look at him.

'You're an intelligent young man—'

'I—' I don't know what to say, what to say to make his fury go away.

'But if you're going to be so bloody stupid about this—'

'I—' and I'm thinking about this morning and about Angel and about the butterfly tattoo and about Leo and Gill and Dan on the phone and who I am and not what I do and reasons and theories and anything to say and my bladder and Daddy—

'Stop blithering. Come on, simple question, simple answer. What's the matter with you?' I look up into his frown and say nothing. 'If you don't want to help then, Jesus, Chris, I'll wash my hands of you—'

'Daddy, I—'

I hear my own voice and my eyes mist immediately and I can't believe what just came out of my mouth and I think nothing, nothing will be the same now and so I run, run from the room, get out. Out. Out.

Chromosome 9
Relief, Grief, Belief

'To do is to be.'
Jean-Paul Sartre

'Thus conscience doth make cowards of us all;
And thus the native hue of resolution
Is sicklied o'er with the pale cast of thought,
And enterprises of great pith and moment
With this regard their currents run awry,
And lose the name of action.'
Hamlet, III, i

I wake up in my own time to the sound of no alarm and watch the calm sunlight on the ceiling. I wonder what time it is but I don't want to look at the clock. In the relief of Saturday morning, the time is unnecessary.

Whenever I wake up, it is always as if I have emerged from a blackness, from a lapse in being. I don't know if it is like that for other people. I never dream. I cannot remember a single one ever, but I know what people mean when they talk about it, so I suppose I must have dreamt sometime. But I don't remember any.

The bed's too big for one. It is lonely. A rainy afternoon on the Holloway Road, Gill and I were buying it, he chose it, although I paid for it. I want someone here with me. I want Mummy. I want Leo, Leo who was kind to me when I was drunk and broken. I have a feeling we connected somehow that night but I know I'm just making up fantasies. It's been a week now and Angel's clearly not going to call me. She doesn't have my number anyway. She's probably forgotten all about it. I just want to know what she's thinking and I want to know what she knows because she knows what happened that night. But she's probably not even thought about it once since then. And I don't know how to get in touch with her. I just pray she'll call. Well, I could call Dan.

But I don't want to ask him because he'll want to know why I want to talk to her and he'll know if I make up some story. I don't want to involve him if I'm going to get rejected. Dan never gets rejected. Besides, he won't return my calls.

I might call him again later when I get up.

The door opens and it is Elsi in her dressing gown with two mugs. 'Hello, stranger,' she says.

I prop myself up on a pillow. 'Good morning.'

'Long time no see,' she says, 'What you been up to all week?' As it happens, it's her who's not been around all week. I've stayed in every night with the telly and cheese on toast while she works nights in the library I guess and doesn't get up till after I've gone out, but Elsi doesn't think in terms of it being *her* who's not been around. She hands me a coffee and places her mug on the bedside table and now climbs under the duvet beside me. I snuggle up close and her warmth comforts me. 'I've been dying to hear what happened with your movie star. And just what, exactly, were you doing with *a girl* in your bed?'

'Oh, Elsi, I don't know. I fucked it all up.'

'We're not talking heterosexual sex, I trust?' She buries her face in her herbal tea.

'What? No, no, nothing like that. With Leo Martin. It's just not going to happen and Dan was crazy to think it ever would. I was even crazier to believe him. I think he was probably just stringing me along to impress me. I just wanted it to be true. And I've fucked up at work. Everything's a mess. I don't know what I'm doing with my life. I can't decide on anything and I can't find anyone to love me.'

'*I* love you, Chrissy.' We do not look at each other as we talk, just sip from our mugs from time to time and stare down the bed.

'Thanks, but it doesn't help.' I want to tell her about what I said to Sir Hugo, about what I called him, and about running out, but I can't because it's all too humiliating, even to tell Elsi. I spent all Wednesday, Thursday and Friday expecting the fallout, but nothing. And I am not sure that nothing isn't worse. Waiting for the delayed effects, never knowing when they'll come or what they'll be, but knowing that it can't be that nothing happens as a result. He's not been in the office since and I don't know when he's back. I don't want to ask anyone else because there's some part of me that thinks they'll know what I said, that they've all been laughing about it together. I don't even know that Sir Hugo heard me, but I think he must have and, anyway, I ran out all the same, so it can't be good. I've been swotting up on the gay gene work, just in case. The repercussions are inevitable, eventually. But I didn't want to start phoning aunts and uncles in Scotland to find out about pedigrees, so I emailed Dan and asked him what he knows about our background, skeleton poofs in the closet and so on.

'I don't know what you're complaining about,' says Elsi. 'It's worse for me: it's a well-known fact that all straight guys are bastards.'

'Yeah, but let's say one in ten guys is good-looking, one in twenty is gay and one in a hundred is nice. That means I'm facing odds of twenty-thousand to one, whereas for you they're—'

'They're still a thousand to one,' says Elsi.

'One thousand and fifty to one,' I correct her and even though I'm not looking I know she's smiling to herself, because she knows the principle's the same but that when it comes to maths, I like to get it right.

Now she counters, 'Not really. Remember, nine out of ten good-looking men are gay and *all* the nice ones are.'

'But it doesn't follow that because they're gay they're either good-looking or nice, let alone both.'

'Nice syllogism, Chrissy. I've taught you some logic after all,' says Elsi, finishing the discussion.

We both sip.

'So,' she starts us off again, 'your movie star. In what way, shape or form did you "fuck it all up"?' So I tell her the story or as much as I know and tell her I was beaten up, but I don't know who by or why, but that someone had it in for me for some reason. 'Or for no reason,' she interjects.

'I don't know. On one level, it seems fair. I'm a useless git who behaved like a twat and I got beaten up. It may not have been why, but I can't complain.' No cause for that and no effect from the Sir Hugo situation. Perhaps being beaten up was the punishment for that. But it can't have been. They're not connected and they're the wrong way round.

'You, my sweet, are developing a streak of self-loathing.

It's very endearing, but I shouldn't cultivate it.'

I tell her Leo is beautiful.

'Oh, I know,' she says.

'Yes but, I mean, he *helped* me. He helped a stranger, for no reason. Him, a celebrity.'

She looks sceptical. 'I think perhaps you may be over-romanticising this, Chrissy.'

'It's not a lot, I know, and maybe I'm clutching at straws, but, I don't know, even the thought of it is comforting.' And now I tell her about waking up with Angel and being lost all week and Sir Hugo saying I should do a doctorate, but that I don't know, but that when he says *should*, it means sooner or later I must.

'Cool,' she says. '*Doctor* Chrissy-wissy Putnam. What would you do it on?'

'It's all right for you. You know what you want to study and you know you want to study it. He wants me to get involved in a project they're doing to identify a gay gene.'

'And the problem is?'

'I'm just not sure about it, about the whole idea. Biological determinism seems so rigid. If I thought one thing or the other about it, I might be able to decide. My gut reaction is to reject it but, but, my brain tells me it makes sense—'

'Tell me then. Background. Case for.'

I sigh. I don't want to talk about it, it's Saturday and I've only just woken up, but Elsi's going to pester me otherwise. She won't let me not have an opinion on this, even if she hasn't got one herself. 'A few years ago, this guy called LeVay published a study claiming to have found differences in the hypothalamus, um, the brain structure of gay men as opposed to straight men. Some nucleus is bigger or smaller, I forget which, but more like women's. He argued that this showed a biological difference between gays and straights.'

'Could be a result of the sexuality rather than the reason *for* it,' says Elsi. 'I have a scar here,' she folds down the duvet and pulls her dressing gown open just enough to reveal a fleshy white track above her hip. She does not care that she's showing me the outskirts of her pubic hair although it's more than I want to see. 'So do many people, but that's not *why* none of us has got an appendix.' She pulls the duvet back.

'Well, exactly, and in order to look at the brains, they had to be dead and it turns out they'd all died of AIDS so it could have been a result of the disease anyway.'

'Okay, but carry on with the case for. Leave the critique to me.'

'Various others tried to replicate the results, but they couldn't—'

'Case *for*, my sweet. And get on to the gene.'

'Okay. Then there was this other study by Dean Hamer which is the really important one. They'd worked out – I can't remember who, but that's not important – that five per cent of men are gay and that, among identical twins, if one's gay, there's a fifty-fifty chance the other is too.'

'Dan must be in the other fifty.'

'Right. Anyway, because it's so common for twins to share their sexual orientation, the twin study provided a good basis for believing there's a genetic element in the phenotype, that's the trait – homosexuality. They'd also found that being gay runs in the family, especially on the mother's side, which also implied a genetic cause. And because it was on the mother's side, the best place to look was the X chromosome.'

'Why?'

'Because men only have one X and it always comes from their mother.'

'Okay, carry on.'

'Basically, Hamer studied the X chromosome of a whole load of gay men with gay relations on their mother's side of the family and compared the results to their straight brothers and looked for the difference.'

'But if they're twins, aren't their Xs the same?'

'No, these aren't twins, they're just brothers.'

'Okay, so?'

'Well, being male, they only have one X, but their mother has two and her two Xs aren't necessarily the same as each other. So one brother might have inherited one version and the other brother might have got the other one. If that's the case, then, well, let's say there's a gay gene in one, but not the other, that would explain why only one of the brothers was gay. So, look for the difference in the brothers' Xs and you've found the gene. Or you've found where it is.'

'And they did?'

'Well, Hamer said that the certain pattern of DNA at a

certain place on the chromosome cropped up significantly often. Xq28.'

'What?'

'That's the locus, the place in the genome where he argued the gene is – the page and line reference, if you like – but they weren't able to home in on the gene itself. I mean, that wasn't the point of the study. Then they repeated the study a couple of years later with a larger group ...'

'How many did they take?'

'In the first instance? About thirty-five, I think. Then around fifty the next time.'

'Not many, but anyway ...'

'Well, statistically, it was enough. Supposedly. Anyway, they got the same result. But then, another group, in Canada – Rice and Ebers – did another study and they didn't get anything significant at Xq28, but their subjects didn't have the same background of maternally inherited homosexuality. Hamer only ever suggested that he thought he'd found the locus of one X-linked gene which was related to sexual orientation. It wasn't him who called it *the* gay gene and he never said it was the only gene involved or that it would always be expressed or that upbringing didn't have anything to do with it.'

'That's the case for?' Elsi asks.

'Well, more or less.'

'Okay, give me a minute,' she says and gets up, taking our empty mugs and going into the kitchen.

Elsi will sort me out, will resolve things for me. Whoever said philosophers are good for nothing? We always talk about everything. Almost everything. Not quite. I can't tell her about what I said to Sir Hugo, for instance. Even though she might understand. I mean, I think Sir Hugo must know why I wasn't in work for a fortnight – about my father – but I think that only makes it worse.

I'm not sure myself why I said it. Well, I've got an idea, but I don't want to think about it. I don't want to think about any of it.

There are things I can't tell her even though I want to. I can't tell her how I feel. I try, but it doesn't ever come out quite right or she doesn't understand. She always wants to rationalise it, to turn feelings into ideas, like she's afraid of them. There are things we don't talk about and there are times it seems we're talking about something else. She thought I'd had sex with Angel.

And now, Leo again. I'm picturing him and maybe recalling or inventing a memory of him that night, a feeling of body, of warmth, of comfort, of him cradling my head on his shoulder and holding me close to him in the office at the gallery. I sink into the bed and stare at the ceiling. The patterns of light and dark combine as the sun goes behind a cloud.

Now I realise again, I won't see him again. Except everywhere. On magazines, on TV, on cereal packets, for chrissakes. My life is in ruins. I am infatuated with a man everyone is infatuated with. I am no better than a hundred million teenage girls. But to me he is a man who is real, whereas he's just an invention to them. Maybe that's all he is to me? Who am I trying to kid? I met him once and I was too pissed to remember it.

I don't know what to do with my life since my father died. Is this my version of grief? Because I don't feel anything. I think I don't. Because there's a part of me that's glad. Maybe that's it. I have no opposition now, so I don't know what to do.

I have a guilty conscience and I'm afraid to do anything in case I heap on more of it. I'm incapable of deciding anything because I'm afraid of the outcome. I overanalyse and then feel sick with fear or doubt or pre-emptive guilt and my resolution pales instantly. There are so many things I should do, but they all seem to get washed away. I can't *do* anything. I've lost the name of action.

I'm just doing what I have to in the course of things. I'm not living. Life is just something that's happening to me. I am afraid that is the way things are.

Click-click-click. What *is* that noise?

Elsi pushes open the door again and leans against the door-jamb with a spliff half-raised. 'Okay,' she says, 'three points for starters. One: on the twins study. Identical twins have identical genes and half of them have the same sexuality, right? And that's taken as evidence that there's something biological going on here?'

'Not quite. In half the cases where one twin is gay, the

other one is too.'

'Same difference. My point remains: what about the other fifty per cent? If sexuality were genetic, then if they have the same genes, they should have the same sexuality. Therefore it is not one hundred per cent genetic. So it's not purely down to nature.'

'No one's saying it is.'

'Which brings me to point number two.' She takes a drag. She has claimed before it helps her think and sometimes I even believe it does. 'Two: if it's not nature, is it nurture? Okay, identical twins are usually brought up together and therefore they share, let's say, at least fifty per cent of the same upbringing, so we could argue it's one hundred per cent nurture and, furthermore, it's surprising that as few as half the gay twins have gay brothers. The fact that they have the same genes too makes it even more surprising the percentage is so low. Upbringing alone explains it perfectly sufficiently. Furthermore, point three: this is why it runs in families. Parents bring up their kids like they were brought up themselves. You inherit your environment just as much as your genes. Want some?' She holds out the joint.

'No thanks. Too early for me.' Although I am tempted and I know I won't be able to say no next time she offers. 'But the inheritance is stronger down the female line. How do you explain that?'

'Come on, that's obvious. Firstly, women do most of the nurturing, so, whatever the element is in that upbringing which causes homosexuality, it's more likely to get handed down by her. And secondly, you're supposed to be the one who knows about evolution. If there were too many males handing on a trait like homosexuality, the species wouldn't have lasted long.'

'But that's an argument for it being genetic.'

'Either. But, anyhow, it explains why it's more common in mum's family without needing to worry about ex-queue-whatever.' She exhales smoke into the corridor and now says, 'You don't mind if I bring this in with me?' and she holds up the joint.

I'd rather she didn't smoke in the bedroom, but not so much because of the smell or the smoke. Mainly, because I'm afraid I won't be able to do anything all day and I won't even get out of bed. I say 'No, sure' anyhow and watch as she picks up the bin as an ashtray which she puts down by the side of the bed as she gets back in and I take the joint from her as she does and I take a toke. Just one. For now.

Now she's here she starts to think again and she says, 'Let's suppose the Freudian model. Homosexuality is down to an overprotective mother and an emotionally distant father.' She takes the joint back and flicks the ash down by the side of the bed, into the bin, I hope. 'There's nothing to say that your scientist's gene in the X chromosome isn't a gene for maternal overprotectiveness and that being emotionally distant isn't genetic too. It's no more ludicrous than it is to say that *being gay* is down to chemistry. If the Freudian model is right, but is genetic, that would make homosexuality causally contingent – *indirectly* genetic. However, can we say, in this case, that the cause of a cause is the relevant cause?'

The question is rhetorical. I leave her to go on which she will do after another drag. This is no longer about me, but about Elsi's thoughts and, for all I know, about her own doctorate. The names she has talked to me about, talked *at* me about, always hang around in my head – in Hegel, Hume and Heidegger, hurricanes hardly ever happen – but I never remember what ideas went with which person and now I can't remember even any of the ideas.

'Of course, even if it's not directly genetic, it may nevertheless be biological. A certain diet or a virus may affect one person one way and somebody else completely differently. Like an allergy. Or if it got them at just the right moment in their development. Chrissy, would it be possible being gay might be triggered by something like that, a virus, say?

'I guess so. There are plenty of genes that don't get expressed unless there are the right biological conditions.'

'There you go then, my sweet. Neither nature nor nurture. The interplay of both. Some causes might be environmental, like the right upbringing or diet or seeing a Judy Garland movie at the age of two, but you've got to have the right biology in place for the causes to have the right effect and that might mean genes, or it might just mean having a body to express your sexual preference with – whatever.' And with that, she extinguishes the smouldering roach on the side of the bin which is wicker and I hear it burning and then its woodsmoke smell reaches me.

'That's what I should have said to Sir Hugo.' Maybe I still should. Maybe I could get out of it. I really don't want to do this PhD. It would be wrong if I don't agree with it. I don't want to *have* to do anything. I want to decide for myself, which means deciding not to decide, deciding to do nothing. Yet.

'The real question – now that we've worked out being gay isn't nature *or* nurture, but the interaction of both – is what do we do with the knowledge? That's the moral issue.' She nestles down further into the bed and crosses her arms behind her head. 'If it had been genetic, then it's natural, it can't be changed and that should teach everyone to accept gays.'

'But the gay gene could be used for screening,' I say, 'and, anyway, people say that if it's genetic, then it's because of a mutation because it can't possibly help species survival. So, it's like haemophilia or muscular dystrophy.'

'But, in that case, aren't beauty and intelligence mutations too? Evolution doesn't make value judgements, you know that. There is nothing either good or bad, but thinking makes it so.'

We lie there quiet and I don't know what Elsi's thinking, but I am thinking about what she said and it makes sense. 'But, as I'm sure you appreciate,' she says suddenly, 'the logical extension of what I'm saying is that *everything* is down to the interaction of nature and nurture. Everything. The question isn't which, because the answer's *always* both. If it weren't, then it would have to be because of either, a) God or, b) randomness, and I think you'll agree, Chrissy, they're both a bit far-fetched. God? Well, that idea went out even before *The X Files* became passé. And randomness? Well, what that means is things that happen for no reason, no reason at all, as opposed to *some* reason, and, I'm sorry, I just have to say, if they have no cause, *how* do they happen? Nothing's random. Even if it looks that way, it's just because you don't *know* the causes.' She pauses. 'Predetermined, Chrissy, that's what we are. I've told you before.' The phone rings and Elsi leaps up, out of the bed. 'Think about it,' she says as she disappears.

I am lying here and thinking about it and trying to think of something that happens for no reason at all. But everything has reasons, even if they're not good ones. And the reasons have reasons. And those reasons too.

'It's for you,' Elsi says passing by the doorway going into the living room and I jump out of bed and get a head rush and the door seems to slide away on a slant and I put out my hand and put my foot forward to stop myself from falling. Extreme pain, extreme, in my toe as I stub it on the bed leg and tears rise to the back of my eyes and I hop out of the room to the phone, still with the pain. I pick up the receiver.

'Dan?' I say.

'No, we met at his viewing.'

Shit, ouch, ouch. I want to say it out loud as if that will make it hurt less, but I manage to say, 'Sorry, who is it?'

'Leo,' he says, 'Leo Martin. I hope you don't mind ...' And the pain goes away.

*

'You'll never guess who that was,' I say to Elsi. I leap on the sofa beside her and clutch her arm. 'Guess, guess, guess.'

'Stop bouncing.' She doesn't turn the TV down. I don't care. 'I don't know. Tell me.'

'Leo.' I wait to see her reaction, but there isn't one. 'I'm seeing him next week.'

She nods and smiles, 'That's nice.'

'It is, isn't it? Angel phoned him and he asked her for my number and she gave it to him and I didn't even know she had it—'

'Oh yeah, I gave it to her.'

'What? Really?'

'Yeah. That morning she was here. She asked me for it, and at first I thought you may not want her to have it, but then I thought, who you sleep with is *your* business, but if you're going to be straight, I'm not going to be an accessory to you being just another straight bastard male.'

'Oh, Elsi. Don't tease. You knew I didn't sleep with her.'

'Well, whatever,' she says. 'I thought that's why you'd just left her number there.'

'What? Where?'

'On the mantelpiece. It's been there all week.' And I look and it is. 'Angel' it says in big curly letters.

'Elsi, I love you,' I say and hug her like I want her to pop.

'Thanks, Chris. But not as much as Leo, right?'

*

Nothing happens without a reason, a cause, a motive. Take, *exempli gratia*, the assault perpetrated against Chris: he was aware of neither the identity of his assailant nor the nature of his motive, but surely that does not mean that neither assailant nor motive existed.

Conversely, everything is a reason, a cause of something else. Hence Chris's concern about the absence of effects pursuant to the somewhat untoward denouement to his colloquy with Sir Hugo. Again, the absence of perceivable effects does not mean that they do not exist. Surely, in real life, something like that does not simply dissipate? After a storm, the ground is damp. After a wound, there is a scar. After a death, there is grief. Grief might not show itself, but it will out; denied, it will surface in borrowed rags, the mad, sad clothes of paranoia, fear or loneliness.

How grievous was the bodily harm committed against Chris's person? Perhaps the grieving was already there and, like his bruises, in order for him to be cured, events would ultimately have to run their course.

Chromosome 10
Chaos and Strange Attraction

'For want of a nail, the shoe was lost;
For want of a shoe, the horse was lost;
For want of a horse, the rider was lost;
For want of a rider, the battle was lost;
For want of a battle, the kingdom was lost.'

Traditional

'An intellect which at any given moment knew all the forces that animate Nature and the mutual positions of the beings that comprise it, if this intellect were vast enough to submit its data to analysis, could condense into a single formula the movement of the greatest bodies of the universe and that of the lightest atom: for such an intellect nothing could be uncertain, and the future just like the past would be present before its eyes.'

Pierre-Simon de Laplace

Why would he want to see me again, I am wondering as the 29 bus farts and opens its doors on to Charing Cross Road and the pavement steadies itself. Elsi said it was because I'm good-looking and I denied it and she accused me of fishing and I do know that some people think so and then she said if I don't want to believe that it's my looks then how about because I'm vulnerable. She thinks I'm being self-indulgent, but she calls it self-loathing – she won't discuss it any more. I still feel the need to ask why, but, under the circumstances, I'm willing to put my questions aside. I am going to see him though, that much is certain.

I'm dodging the people on the pavement and I'm still limping slightly and I'm scouring my brain again, trying to recall our conversation, but all I remember is stubbing my toe and picking up the phone and it being him. Then it was all over so quickly and I hardly remember what he said at all. I remember what *I* said even less, but I'm sure it was crass. I wouldn't be surprised if I've got the wrong day or the wrong time.

But maybe I have? I stop, stock still on the pavement, and am shouldered from behind as a body pushes past whispering *dickhead fuckin' tourist* and I'm looking to see his face, but he has been slowed in the flow enough already and has settled the score under his breath, now he's moving on to argue with more pavement traffic.

Am I sure he said Thursday? Am I sure he said twelve thirty? At Heaven? I'm not sure about any of it. I have trawled our conversation so many times for detail, rereading, rewriting every sign, every word, every phoneme, to draw out things he never said, but hearing them all the same the one-hundredth time I repeat it to myself. I may have invented any of the details and maybe now I'm remembering my last inaccurate memory rather than the original facts. I may have invented the entire conversation. Did I dream it? But I don't have dreams. Unless it's all a dream.

*

Del Bortman, thirty-three, telesales, had an hour for lunch officially, but preferred to get a sandwich and take it back to his desk – with a Pepsi Max, always a Pepsi Max, if he doesn't get his Pepsi Max, then a little thing like that can jinx his whole afternoon. He'd take a Coke and think no more about it, but something back there would niggle him. At his desk, he never made calls as he ate and glugged – no point calling when everyone you're trying to call is out to lunch – but he would receive them, nonetheless. On commission only, you can't afford not to be there to take the calls. There were those in the office who'd stiff a lead soon as your back was turned given half a chance. And if you were there, you might get a chance to do it to them.

That day there was no Pepsi Max and the cement-mixer people hadn't called all morning like they said they would and that would be a six-month ad series if they book. *When* they book, assume the sale. Bortman was worrying that Chok would stiff the cement-mixer people, but Cecil Court was full of slow movers, so he was weaving with a sigh as he passed all the people with nothing better to do with their lives than stare in bookshop windows. The books weren't even new. And no one gave a thought for the fact that some people had work to do and then some dickhead fucking tourist stopped slap-bang in his path. Had to pull up sharpish not to slam straight into him from behind.

Had Chris Putnam not looked at Del Bortman for a moment, he might have seen the man who stopped to talk to the teenage girl, but when he looked up, she was standing between them and neither noticed the other.

*

Amy Fenn, seventeen, GNVQ student, was about to have an experience she would tell everyone about for a week. Indeed, she would still be mentioning it decades later as her claim to fame (whenever such a subject came up, as it does) and others would cite their brush with a soap star or the time they appeared in the background of a TV news report when there was that kid stabbed.

The funny thing was she had just been reading about him in the paper while she waited for her friend Melsa on the corner just down from the tube, because the Leicester Square Tube exit itself is a nightmare place to meet, and she wouldn't have bought it if the man hadn't been right there selling them and if Melsa hadn't been late and if the masthead hadn't mentioned an interview with him. And she wouldn't have looked up if it hadn't been for the burst of a siren, out east somewhere, an ambulance arguing with the traffic at the junction of St Martin's Lane and Long Acre, where it wouldn't have been if Roz Len, fifty-two, tea lady, hadn't been by the scalding urn on the trolley on the thirteenth floor of Centrepoint when the door swung the other way and after which she never returned to work but took early retirement instead.

And there he was, looking gorgeous and, if it's possible, so much better in the flesh, about to go into a restaurant, just an ordinary restaurant, not posh. It was really an intimate moment, because he wasn't acting, he was just him, with this hassled look on his face. She wouldn't have asked him for his autograph if she hadn't had the courage, but she had always been a brassy lass according to her nan, and so she didn't think twice. She just rushed up and asked him to sign the interview in the paper and it took a few moments while he fumbled for a pen in his jacket and all that time she stood right by him, close as anything, and partly she was wanting to shield him so other people wouldn't see him. She didn't want a stampede. He wouldn't want that. It was important not to invade these people's privacy.

*

And now I'm *sure* I'm half an hour late and he had said twelve not twelve thirty and also I'm equally sure I'm half an hour early on the wrong day at the wrong place, and even though this is Greek Yard it's littered with the homes of the homeless and with litter. On the step of number two, there's a man with a can of Tennent's who doesn't shift as I find the brass plaque and scan it to the top. '7th Floor Heaven Ltd'. So I press the buzzer and the door buzzes right back and click-click-clicks to say it's unlocked. I say 'excuse me' to the guy on the step who still doesn't budge, I think he may be asleep even though he's sitting up, and I push the door. It's an old building, the stairwell's almost derelict – I had expected something swisher – and I press the button for the lift. I hear it start to descend and my heart rises to my throat.

*

Angel, twenty-three, personal assistant to Ms Helen Bossi, holding her Filofax and her purse, heard the lift chunder into activity heading down just as she was about to press the button. There was no point waiting for it to go all the way down and come all the way back up and she was in a hurry so she took the stairs.

*

Through the diagonals of the old concertina lift gate, I see the building climbing. The 'model' on the first floor, then a small ad agency. Magazine publishers. Book publishers on fourth. A TV and film production company on five and six. I tug open the lift on the seventh floor and I am in a different place, a different era. The space expands to widescreen, open-plan designer offices. The carpet cushions your feet. Heaven Ltd can't possibly just be the top floor of this building. It must be the buildings on both sides as well. Everyone is good-looking and well-dressed and, well, clean. Everything is washed in whiteness and warmth. Light streams in through rows of large skylights. They've replaced the roof and the blue sunshine above just goes on forever. The sun seems closer here and I feel sure, at night, so do the stars.

*

Bill MacRake, thirty-three, tabloid journalist, was not happy. The Leo Martin interview should have been big for him (he did gossip and diary pieces usually, not big celeb interviews), but he'd been messed about and had only ended up with twenty minutes.

The plan had been they were going to do lunch. Exclusive. Then, apparently Martin had another lunch come up, so he got bounced to eleven thirty and just three-quarters of an hour. Then it turns out Martin's done another interview before him which Bill only finds out when Martin turned up nearly twenty minutes late and spent five minutes apologising because now he had to leave early because his publicity had scheduled him with someone else right after the lunch which had bounced Bill in the first place and which had then been moved forward to twelve fifteen. On top of all that, the *Standard* had already got an exclusive interview in that day's paper.

In twenty minutes at the Groucho, the only thing that Bill MacRake found out about Leo Martin which he couldn't have read in the *Standard* was that he was extremely anxious not to be late for his lunch appointment at twelve fifteen.

'Can I help you?' says someone clean and pretty and posh who walks towards me, smiling.

'I'm supposed to be meeting Leo Martin here at twelve thirty?' I make it sound like a question because she's so polite and I don't want to put her to any trouble and because I'm not in control of the sounds my voice is making.

She smiles and says, 'Would you care to take a seat and I'll find out the scenario for you? Can I get you anything in the meantime at all? Tea? Coffee? Sparkling or still water?'

'Nothing, thanks. Thank you. Oh, uh, where's the loo, please?'

*

Julio Stanga was a waiting actor or an actor waiting. The part was more demanding than most. Not vocally, since he really was Italian and he still spoke it with his mother and, although his English was more Peckham than Perugia, he could camp it up for the table trade. It was more demanding because the performance lasted maybe nine or ten hours a day.

Julio greeted him with hugs and hands clapping one another's backs. They had worked together three times: when Julio had done Stephano at the Globe, when he'd done Italian Waiter in *The Bill* and when they'd both done outdoor wear for BHS. They were friends, insofar as a major star and a waiting actor can be. Most recently, Julio had played Iago above a pub in Birmingham, nineteen months ago.

'Leee-oh, my friend!' He kept the accent for the benefit of the other diners who stared as the star entered. Leo was good for business and Julio had retained few enough theatrical ambitions that the state of the restaurant business did genuinely concern him. He led Leo downstairs. 'How yoo beeen, ey?' When they were out of earshot he added, 'Like I need to ask.'

They exchanged pleasantries without discussing acting. Leo Martin had always liked Julio and made a point of eating where his old friend worked. He didn't see enough of Julio these days. He smiled broadly to show he thought so.

Among the other reasons for eating at La Farfalla was that it was between the Groucho Club and Heaven Ltd and had a basement which was candlelit and many-cornered.

'Sorry I'm so late,' said Leo, 'Is my, erm, guest here yet?' The romance of the setting was not his prime consideration, more its discretion. They stood in the restaurant cellar where there were just a few tables, all vacant. It was cosy nonetheless.

'Not yet,' said Julio.

'What time is it?'

'Nearly twenty-five past.'

'He probably didn't get the message about the change of plan.' He paused and looked around him as if Julio had secreted his guest in some nook, but did not go so far as to explore. 'I guess I'll head up to Helen's office and see if he's gone up there. Keep him here, if he turns up.'

Julio had already read the *Standard* interview. It contained the following words: 'There are a lot of out-of-work actors out there who're really dross'. These words were the effect of a simple transposition of adjacent letters on a keyboard. In fact, Leo had said, 'There are a lot of out-of-work actors out there who're really cross'.

*

There was a man who looked familiar to Angel poking his head through the doorway of La Farfalla when she got there. 'Excuse me,' she said so she could get past and he looked up and looked embarrassed and then stood out of the way and looked at the menu board nonchalantly.

Angel found a waiter and asked if Mr Martin had arrived. He discreetly denied all knowledge. She insisted she knew he was eating there because she had made the booking herself and the waiter referred her to another waiter.

The other waiter, Julio, said Leo had come but had just left through the kitchen because he didn't want to walk past the other diners again. Julio added, 'He thinks hees friend has maybe stood him up.'

He denied knowing any more on the matter, but Angel supposed Leo must have gone back to Heaven.

*

'It appears there's been a slight change of plan. We tried to contact you, but all we got was your answerphone,' the polite girl says and I am about to tell her it's okay and just run away, when she says, 'You're to meet him at the restaurant instead and we had to move you forward to twelve fifteen, so he's probably waiting for you. Don't worry, it's just round the corner. La Farfalla on the corner of Cecil Court.'

I picture him waiting there for me.

'Right. Right, thank you. Um, okay, I'd better run.' And I go back to the lift just as I hear it start to go down to someone on another floor. I won't wait. I'll take the stairs.

*

Leo tugged open the concertina lift gates. Maybe Chris had come to the restaurant and gone already. No, he thought, he would have asked for me. But if Julio hadn't been there, he might not have asked for the right name and they would have denied any booking. Still, he would have waited ten minutes.

If, like any other celebrity, he had been willing to have a publicity chaperone at interviews, he would have known what was happening. Furthermore, if he had been willing to have a publicity chaperone, his PR agency would not have felt it necessary to call him on his mobile eleven times before 10.26 that morning. If the agency had not felt it necessary to call him so many times, the battery might have lasted beyond 10.26 that morning.

Leo, however, did not agree that being pampered need be the necessary effect of being famous and declined the attendance of flunkies even to the point of his own inconvenience. To him, it was about maintaining a corner of himself, of the real him. Whatever that was.

Leo Martin did not need to be looked after. It was more the other way around.

Bill MacRake did not have to file his interview until at least four thirty and so far, he did not have much to write up. He reasoned that he should not go into the restaurant as that would be too obvious. Martin had mentioned that the *Sunday Telegraph* interview was at two. Therefore, he reasoned, he could hang around till then.

The slightly boyish girl from Helen Bossi's office came back out of the restaurant. He carried on reading the menu in the window. He thought she probably hadn't recognised him.

*

Ian Coper, forty-one, delivery truck driver, did not like the West End. He had been lost in an argument of traffic for the best part of an hour and was not about to waste any more time finding a better place to park. He pulled the handbrake and hit the hazard lights. It was only going to take him ten minutes to unload from right outside the model shop, but if he'd had to find somewhere else, then he would've been expected to lug the stuff a couple of hundred yards. It would have probably taken twice as long and would have caused just as much bother for the other traffic. So, if cars couldn't get past, they could just wait.

The delivery was necessitated by an order automatically printed last week by the model shop's automatic EPOS stock-control system. An uncle had bought an eighteen-centimetre E-Type Jaguar for his nephew's birthday (on Sunday) which had reduced stocks from that supplier below the critical level. The nephew's birthday was on that day because his parents had holidayed in Spain in August 1986 and there had been a national holiday on the fifteenth and fireworks had always stimulated her sexually ever since a public display and a teenage encounter in Finsbury Park on Bonfire Night 1977.

*

I run around the front of an illegally parked delivery truck and into the restaurant which I'd walked straight past on my way to Heaven.

I ask the waiter if Leo is there. He denies all knowledge. I say that I was supposed to meet him there at twelve fifteen. He refers me to another waiter who shrugs unhelpfully and says Leo came and has already gone.

I am not going to see him. I should be at work, but I phoned in sick. I put on a cough all yesterday afternoon so it would be more convincing when I phoned in this morning. And now I'm not going to see him.

*

Angel ran round the back of an illegally parked delivery truck across the road and into Greek Yard. 'Excuse me,' she said to the man drinking Tennent's who looked up and waved his can in salute.

'Gi' us a quid for another of these,' he said and she stopped and opened her purse and gave him fifty pee and he shifted to one side to let her pass and raised his can in another salute.

*

Leo tugged open the concertina gates and got back in the lift, glad that he had caught it this time.

*

Angel did not bother to press the lift button because she saw it had just started to come down. Had she not given money to the man with the can, she might have arrived in time to witness the lift still ascending and might have decided to take the stairs.

The lift arrived and behind the concertina gates was Leo.

'Angel,' said Leo.

'Leo,' said Angel. 'Where's Chris?'

'He's not with you?'

145

I don't know what to do with myself now. I can't go to work and I don't want to go home and have to explain this to Elsi. I must have bored her rigid going on about it all week and now I feel humiliated and I need to think about it on my own, turn the feelings into thoughts, before I can explain it to her.

Slowly I limp out of the restaurant, but do not move off yet, considering seeing Leo anyway. On a cinema screen. *Utopia*'s probably still playing somewhere.

A man in a flak jacket which is too big for him stands opposite looking at me and smoking. He looks away. I wander off slowly down Cecil Court.

There is a siren sound behind me and now some shouting and I turn around to look.

*

Leo and Angel arrived at La Farfalla and could not see Chris. They asked Julio what had happened to Leo's guest, who said that he thought he was going to wait, but maybe he had given up. They left the restaurant.

Outside there was chaos.

*

I walk back to St Martin's Lane to see what's going on and it is chaos. There are two ambulance men around a beggar lying in the middle of the road behind the ambulance. A crowd of people are standing and staring and two teenagers are shrieking at a big man and following him about as he tries to walk away.

'Chris,' says someone behind me and I feel a hand rest on my shoulder. 'That's lucky. I almost missed you.'

*

An ambulance carrying Roz Len, fifty-two, tea lady, from Centrepoint to St Thomas's, was unable to pass a delivery truck illegally parked at the narrowest stretch of St Martin's Lane. Despite the ambulance's sirens, the truck did not move because Ian Coper, forty-one, the driver, was downstairs in the stockroom of a model shop getting a signature for a delivery.

To avoid becoming jammed by advancing traffic, the ambulance reversed urgently, knocking down Big Man Ufee, circa fifty-five, of no fixed abode, crossing the road, who having recently accumulated just enough cash, was unsteadily returning to an off-licence in Lisle Street which would sell him a can of Tennent's.

Amy and Melsa, both seventeen, leaving McDonald's, witnessed the incident and, as the ambulance men were more concerned with tending to Big Man Ufee, they took it upon themselves to chastise Ian Coper on his return to the delivery truck.

The incident was also witnessed by, among others, Bill MacRake of the *Mirror* and Del Bortman, who had just come out for a cigarette to calm down having been stiffed by Chok over the cement-mixer people and who was regretting those few moments he'd spent choosing Coke when they'd had no Pepsi Max in the sandwich bar earlier, because if he hadn't, he might have got back to the office before they rang. Neither MacRake nor Bortman, however, offered their testimony to the police who turned up shortly after.

The turbulence of other events resulted in almost everyone in the vicinity failing to spot the presence of a famous actor. Almost everyone also failed to notice the man with whom he retired to a nearby restaurant.

*

'Why are you limping? Are you still hurt from the night at the gallery?' he says.

'Oh, it's nothing. I stubbed my toe the other day.'

He looks in my face and smiles a smile that tells me, no, you invented nothing, all of this is real, even me. 'Honestly, Chris, you need looking after.' And he laughs.

*

Meaning is sought. Scientists read the human genome like a book as if its meaning were in the words, but meaning slips through the gaps and spreads from spaces between. They chase genes in isolation and read great import into the transposition of a single letter. Opinions divide and divide like the bifurcating tendrils of Mandelbrot. They feed back their assumptions into their assumptions and overinterpret *ad ridiculum, ad absurdum, ad nauseam.* They scrutinise the endless rearrangements of A, C, T and G like anagrams or quotations which they recognise but cannot quite place. And why should they not? Some are holy grails, some are red herrings.

Meaning resides, they believe, in things just beyond what they understand. That is what draws them on.

To search for meaning is to suppose simple truths, but the only simple truth is that there is nothing simple in this complex universe. Everything relates. Everything connects.

Sometimes a butterfly flaps its wings and the weather turns out fine. But in such cases, it's hard to say whether it was destined to be fine anyway or, perhaps, after all the hurricanes, the butterfly should get some credit.

Chromosome 11
Superreality

(i) God is something than which nothing greater can be conceived.
(ii) Something that exists in reality must be greater than something that exists in the mind only.
Therefore, (iii) God must exist outside as well as in the mind, for if he existed in the mind only and not in reality he would not be something than which nothing greater can be conceived.

St Anselm

'They loved one another as one can only love something that does not really exist.'

Fanny Burney

I don't believe I'm really here. It's no more likely than that he is here with me. I am staring at my menu, but not because I'm reading it. The words on it swim like pasta swimming in minestrone, meaningless symbols that represent nothing, shapes like a veil or a mask between me and what I see. I'm too full of the situation to make sense of them and must calm down. Deep breath.

'What's the matter?' says Leo.

'What? I'm sorry. Nothing. Why?' I say too hurriedly looking up at him. He has grown a goatee since Dan's opening. For Hamlet, presumably. It makes him look piratical and romantic. It is only in the changing forms of candlelight that he is visible in this cellar, casting shadows on the cave-like walls. It doesn't seem like it can be day out there in the real world.

'You sighed.'

'I did? Did I? I'm sorry.'

'Don't worry. It's my fault. This must be as awkward for you as it is for me.' He puts his menu on the table and leans towards me. Everything is okay, he's saying. *'I* should be sorry. I guess you're wondering what's going on here—'

*

There are many possible reasons why Leo Martin would have chosen to have lunch with Chris Putnam.

For example, the Hedonistic: because he wanted to and he could. This reason would be consistent with his status as a celebrity, if not with his reputation.

Alternatively, there is the Sympathetic: because he was lonely in his celebrity and covert homosexuality. This reason is plausible, if trite.

The Metabolic: because he was hungry.

The Sexual: because Leo wanted Chris physically. After all, Chris was regarded as good-looking by everyone but himself (although even he acknowledged both that he looked very like Dan and that Dan was indisputably fine-featured).

The Romantic: because Leo had fallen in love with Chris at first sight. However, given the first impression Chris presented of himself, this is not likely.

The Endocrinological: because he had produced abnormal levels of adrenaline and endorphins on first seeing Chris.

The Psychoanalytic: because he had had no father, he felt protective towards the hapless, the helpless, the hopeless.

The Theistic: because God the Father – or some other Creator – had ordained it.

The Conspiracy Theory: because he was doing a favour to Dan, or indeed, because Dan had, in some underhand way, contrived the situation.

Or the Deterministic: because he could not help himself, which indeed explains everything and nothing.

Throughout the six days between appointing the time and date of this lunch and the appointed time and date itself, Chris had considered, dismissed and considered again most of the aforementioned reasons and many others besides without formulating any single testable (that is to say, falsifiable) hypothesis. How it should come to be that he was in such intimate circumstances with Leo Martin, of all people, a celebrity of considerable stature, was beyond his reasoning. There was, in the first instance, a question relating to the reality of the situation and whether that reality could be trusted or believed.

In fact, Chris should have wasted no effort trying to believe; not least because celebrities are not real. That quality called 'celebrity' exists only in the collective mind. A celebrity is invented by people – by audiences, by agents, by promotions personnel, by advertisers, by broadcasters, by movie companies, by the celebrities themselves, by writers – and by circumstance.

It is a matter of mere coincidence that there *is* often a real individual who corresponds with the notional celebrity, signifies them.[7] The two, however, the real and the invented, the mask and the face underneath, should not be confused.

Chris began to recognise this as he had lunch with Leo, that there are many levels on which a person may be real: there was the Leo who sat before him; there was the Leo about whom he had read and heard much; there was Adam whom Leo had played; and there were other levels too. All were represented by the data his senses received at lunch. Who was to say that any of them existed, except the one who appeared before him? Even he, especially he, seemed too good to be true.

Indeed, because Leo seemed too good to be true, Chris had not considered another reason why he might wish to have lunch with him.

The Symbiotic: because Leo had experienced something in Chris that promised him refuge from his cowardice, something that granted him endorsement. If he could take the upper hand with fate, if he could dare to let loose his feelings and share his fears, if he could take responsibility for another person, a person who needed his care, then he could take responsibility for himself, feel brave, feel free. He needed to be able to remove the actor's mask.

Chris had not considered the Symbiotic reason not only

[7] A real individual is not always signified by a celebrity, or, sometimes, the level of reality of the individual is different to the level of reality of the celebrity they signify. Consider, for example: Kermit the Frog; King Arthur; Lara Croft; the 'Boys from Brazil'; Ziggy Stardust; Princess Diana; Da Vinci's Mona Lisa; The Real Inspector Hound; the ghost of Hamlet's father; Bart Simpson; a hologram; Jesus Christ; God; indeed, even me. We all exist, but not all at an equivalent level of reality and sometimes on one level and not another and sometimes on several levels all at once. Reality, it seems, is not a flat plane, but has as many layers as an onion has skins.

because the intelligence of certain aspects of reality, certain facts and flaws, were not presently at his disposal, but also because it is all too easy for a rejected son to lack faith in what he might have to offer to a man he admires.

However, in all probability, this reason was no more true than any other. In a deterministic world, everything that is past is part of the reason for the present.

*

'—Can I just say I'm so sorry about that night?' I interrupt. His eyes relax as I go on: 'I mean I'm not normally like that – I mean pissed – Dan gave me some coke you see and I hadn't eaten and I guess I was nervous because, um, because I didn't know anybody there.' What am I saying? Why am I reminding him of all this? It was bad enough first time around. And he was going to tell me something, why he wanted to see me.

'Look, honestly, really, that's all okay.' His words sound timid. I never expected him to seem so shy. But his voice is quiet, like rich dark chocolate eaten in secret or like black coffee in a French café. 'I was worried. Someone attacked you. Do you know who it was?'

'No. Do you?'

'Me? No.'

We pause, awkwardly. So now I say, 'It's a mystery, just something I think I'll have to live without knowing.'

'Did you report it?' he asks.

'Not much point. I can't even remember it happening. I can only be sure it did because of the after-effects.'

'You don't remember much about it, then?'

He's looking at my face and I'm looking back, exploring his. I shake my head. We are not comfortable with each other yet, but I don't know if it is because we never will be or because we are too afraid.

He looks at the menu and says, 'What are you going to have?'

'I don't know. I can't decide.'

'I'm starving. Today, I've been given the day off rehearsals, but the price is to spend it doing PR for the show.

I've been interviewed all morning and, I'm sorry about this, but I'm going to have to scurry away for further interrogation at two.'

'That's okay.'

'And I'm sorry I messed you about on the arrangements. What time do you have to get back to work?'

'Erm, I don't. I took the day off.' The brown of his eyebrows knots. 'It's fine. It's pretty casual where I work.' Sir Hugo is in Palo Alto, but maybe I shouldn't have said that anyway.

Leo asks about what I do even though it seems he knows already and now the waiter who was unhelpful before, who Leo seems to know, comes and asks what we'd like and we both realise we haven't chosen yet, so we stop talking and look back at the menu.

The waiter waits.

'Sorry, Julio,' says Leo and orders penne al truffati and a steak. I want the waiter to go away, but I haven't made a decision yet, so I say I'll have the same. It sounds corny, so I don't meet Leo's eye but look at the menu instead which I fold shut and give to the waiter who asks how we want our steaks. And now, if we want wine. Leo looks at me questioningly. I look back questioningly. I don't want him to get all pretentious about this.

'Red?' he asks me.

'Why not?' I ask him.

'Please, whatever you think's good.' he tells the waiter, who goes away.

We both lean forward and then I lean back. 'Go on,' he says and now we have no menus to hide behind, to look at instead of each other, so I go on talking about the lab and about the human genome project and he asks me interested questions and I am trying not to make it sound interesting because it isn't, but trying not to be boring either. I am not mentioning the gay gene project. And he asks about Dan and the wine comes and the waiter doesn't bother to ask us to taste it, so he just pours and we just drink and I tell him about Dan. I complain about Dan really, about how he is being all holier-than-thou about our father, about how if I wanted to know anything when our father was dying, he was the only person who could keep me up to speed.

'Did you feel Dan was keeping your father to himself?

'Oh no, I mean, my father and I, we weren't ... we didn't get on that well. I didn't mind at the time. I mean I wanted to know what was going on, but I felt pretty clear about the fact I didn't want to see him.'

'And he didn't want to see you?'

'Well, I thought not, but ... now I think perhaps he did, but he was so scared to come out from behind this mask he puts up, you know, straight-laced God-fearing man. He was a strict Calvinist, you see, and so he believed in preordination, that God's got your destiny all mapped and plotted. That gave him a permanent way of absolving himself from any responsibility. So when it came to seeing me before he died, I suspect he didn't want what he thought would be a big confrontation – you know, uncomfortable truths he'd rather not know about and all that – so he put the responsibility back on me to decide to see him. Or he meant to, but it was a bit too late. And so now that's all my fault.'

'Why?' he says and so I tell him and I tell him how Dan was stirring it up and now I'm talking about the last time I spoke to Dan which was the day after the opening.

'The critics were pretty savage,' says Leo. 'Those that bothered to cover it at all. There's only one thing worse than being talked about—'

'You must know what it's like,' I say and realise how rude that is. I bite my inner lip to feel pain. But he just laughs.

'I'm lucky. I've often been criticised, but never critically wounded,' he says and I laugh too loud, but it doesn't matter because it's only us here and Leo smiles and now smiles more broadly, as if everything was uncertain to him, but now I laugh, he can be pleased.

Now I feel guilty about moaning about poor Dan. 'Dan is so full of himself most of the time, but you know if you pop it, he deflates completely. It's just a front. It's not real.'

'I know.'

'He puts up this arrogant show to protect himself. He comes across as really close-minded sometimes.'

'But why should he be open-minded when he thinks he's right?'

'Good point,' I say. It's not just the way he sounds, but what he says. It all sounds witty and clever, like he's had time to think about it and this is what I would say and how I would say it if only I could think that fast. But he doesn't sound smug or too-smart-by-half. He just offers his comments, like a gift, a suggestion, an appeal for advice. And at the same time we raise our glasses and I realise I was telling him about my father and it doesn't humiliate me to talk to him about it, so I tell him more and he nods and smiles and listens like he cares.

*

Leo uses his bread to mop up his pasta sauce and it makes me think of Gauloises and movies and sensuous tastes and I do the same, clearing the specks of black truffle whose smell lingers pungently, almost like urine, while their taste cloys to the roof and the sides and the back of my mouth. The cream of the sauce still lathers my tongue. We are laughing about the same thing that he said or I said five minutes ago, but it still seems funny and we keep feeding it, stoking the joke and laughing more. I look into my glass and see only its surface, little golden candlelights and whites and blues and purples and reds. I cup my palm around it and sense its tulip shape and imagine that even its smoothness is made of patches of colour, like petals, only a tulip is soft and warm. Tulips at the altar. I lean forward.

'What's it like, being you? Well, being famous, I mean.'

'Surely you've heard how simply *ghastly* all that glamour is?' His face is serious, but not seriously serious. 'How it becomes tiresome and shallow? How it becomes a trial simply to cross the road?'

'All true, then?' I say, responding to the tease.

'No,' he answers flatly and the seriousness shifts into a smile on his lips and in his eyes. He shrugs, showing me his palms. 'Being famous is fabulous. Almost every minute I thank fortune or fate or whoever for the chances I've had and for everything in my life. You know, sometimes I even envy myself.' The way he talks, I don't think he could be further from smugness – it is humility, it is contentment. But then his face closes up. 'I mean, naturally fame has a fallout, but, it's not so much the fame as the famous that upset me.'

'Such as?'

'Well, the way they complain, for a start. Most people go to work day in, day out and it's worth it because they have weekends and a fortnight a year on the Costa. Meanwhile, what are celebrities doing? Moaning about the emotional trauma they suffer for their art. Anyone else would call it a good day's work and be grateful they're chauffeur-driven home to a five-star hotel. They tell some hack that they never wanted the fortune, all they wanted was recognition, but then they whinge when recognition bothers them in the street. Most of them lose what made them famous in the first place. Did I say "lose"? I should say abandon. If you ever catch me acting like that, please, put me out of my so-called misery.' I like the idea that I'll be around him long enough for that.

'I thought being superficial was part of being an actor.' I raise a jaunty, only-joking eyebrow.

'Actors,' he says, 'should only be superficial on the surface.' He continues, 'We strike a pact. We say to fame, I want you. We beg it, implore it. And many do a damn sight more. But, in the end, life is fair to everyone – more or less and in its own way – fame has its crowns and its thorns. People just feel life is unfair because they envy what other people have, but they never think what they go through as a result. It's just like a doctor who gets to save people's lives – they have to watch others die. To be famous is to have a public life. A public life means just that, your life is public, it means not having a private life. What's so bad about that if that's what you chose?'

'But, erm, you have a private life,' I say and immediately wish I hadn't. It will take us on to different territory. I want to be there, I just don't want to risk going.

'Sure, I have private things, things the public don't know, but not really, not a real private life,' Leo says, quietly, but not distant.

'What do you mean?'

'Chris,' he says and I like the sound of my name in his mouth, it's like a flake of air between us, 'I'll tell you about it, because I want you to know. I can trust you, can't I? I've made a deal of my own, you see.' His face is serious again, but it is real this time, I know it is, because it is uncertain too. 'I know I can trust you because, well, because of what happened that night.'

I nod knowingly, but then I admit it, 'Leo, I'm afraid I really don't remember what went on. I—'

'No, I know you don't. The thing is ... well, I guess this is why I waited a week to call you.'

'Five days,' I correct him.

He smiles. 'I was a bit anxious about how you'd react to how I behaved. I mean I was afraid you'd think I'd been strange. I mean I can handle people having a go at me as an actor, but I'm a wimp when it comes to being judged more personally.' He pauses like he's summoning courage. Him? 'You know when you cried? We were in the office ... and I, I comforted you?'

I don't. No. I don't know any of this. But it is like he knows secret things from inside my head. I remember imagining it, but I don't know if what I imagined was also real.

'It seemed like something more than tears was pouring out of you, so I held you close and then – do you remember? – I held you closer still, clung on, tight.' Leo stops speaking and our faces are close. I am examining the curve of his mouth, the individual hairs of his short beard, the shapes and shades and shallows of each feature's details. I am relaxed again because he is giving me a secret in return for my embarrassment. I think about kissing him – I could, our mouths are just inches apart, I could make that move, but, but that would be too much to bear. I do not move. I wait for him and now his garnet voice begins again, slowly. 'That was because I started crying too. It just started. Really. This sounds so foolish and you must think I'm crazy. It's a cliché, but I felt like years of tears were all backed up and, well, holding you,' he pauses for a decade, an aeon, a moment, 'that human touch, solid realness – warmth – the dam just burst. It reminded me what I ... well, of the downside of my life. It gave me perspective, a sense of self. For a moment, it took away a lot of things I'm afraid of.' His eyes look into me. 'You don't remember?'

'I'm sorry.' He nods, minutely. 'But, honestly, I do know what you're talking about.'

'Your father?'

'Yes, there's that and, I don't know, just my whole life since, well, since my mother died. Even today, I could weep rivers for her but she died more than six years ago. I guess I love, *loved* my father too, but I haven't cried at all. Except that night. That was it. I had to get drunk that night, because I had to let it all out. You see, I think I know what you mean about getting to *that point*, the place where it all spills over the edge.'

Only now, as he tells me that I got there that night, do I know it's true. But now I know, I also understand, that *is* what happened that night. Grief happened that night. And to know this makes me feel better. It eases the guilt. It explains why I've been so infatuated with Leo. He was there to displace it all, to take over my thoughts from my father – one who didn't want me for one I couldn't have. And what did I give him? Touch? Can it be as simple as that? I think of my father's warm dry hand and—

'So, you liked the pasta?' says the waiter and we sit back suddenly to let him clear the plates and Leo says something croakily about it being good.

And when the waiter is gone, he says, 'I guess I'm just a sucker for a tragedy.'

'Does that make me a tragedy?' I reply.

'A tragic *hero*,' he says.

I laugh. But the thickness of the air in the darkness is not dispelled and so my voice drops and I say, 'You said you'd made a kind of deal. Can I ... what kind of deal?'

He tries to laugh it off, but doesn't laugh. 'It's nothing Faustian.' He looks into his glass. 'Well, maybe it is. I've made certain sacrifices. Or, other people have made sacrifices for me.' He drinks the rest of the wine from his glass and looks at me. '*I've* sacrificed them. I didn't want to, but the way things turned out, every step required just a little more and the deal evolved. I guess I'm a coward. I'm not making myself very clear, am I?' I refill his glass. 'As I said, I have no real private life. My private life is all a lie. Beyond what you see is a vacuum, like flats on a stage or a film set. I'm not shallow – I'm just empty. And the deal is, the deal is that I let this go on, I carry on delivering sacrifices to the altar, and I just go on getting more and more famous.'

'Is it worth it?'

'I don't know. Really I don't, but it's not a choice for me.' He fidgets with his glass. 'I remember my mother used to test me on the names of famous people with their pictures in the *Radio Times* and I can't get rid of the idea that being remembered is important. Being an actor is more than what I want, it's what I am. And you measure actors with fame. I can't risk throwing it away, I'm too frightened or maybe too intoxicated by it – I'm addicted. There's that one step right in front of me, that one decisive moment where everything would change, and I can't take that step, because I don't know what's out there. The deal I've made with life works. It does. Can I say as much if I broke it?'

'Would it make that much difference? If you ... came out?' I am not sure whether I should have even said the words, as if I have outed us both and the reason why we are here, why *I* am here at least.

'That's only part of it, it's only part of the deal. I might as well not be gay or straight or anything, because I've cut myself off from everything I feel. Except when I'm acting. Then I let it out. Then I'm real. And ... well, that night.'

The waiter comes back and we sit in silence as he places our plates in front of us. We both thank him, almost in whispers.

When we are sure he is gone, Leo speaks again. 'I'm not unhappy with my situation, don't get me wrong. It's just it seems it's the only way it *can* be. And therefore I have no private life – I have guilt, that is all. Guilt because ... because there are people who've had to go through hell for me, Helen mainly. Chris, everything that's happened, all that's gone wrong for the people around me, it has all been because of me, but I want you to understand, that doesn't make any of it my fault. Or, rather, it *is* my fault because I know there were chances to do or say something different at the time, but when I'm afraid like that, I just freeze up and surrender. I get swept along, which makes me all the more scared because I'm not in control.' He seems anxious to convince me of his guilt, but I acquit him of everything. He's a victim of circumstance, like me. 'I said I envy myself sometimes – that's because the charmed life I lead is at other people's expense, no matter what I do. I can't believe what she's put up with. And it's not as if I've behaved wonderfully or deserve it – quite the opposite – and the past six months—'

'I don't know much about it, I'm afraid. I don't really read the tabloids, well, any newspapers really.'

'Don't worry, I'm glad. They've got the story all wrong anyway, but Helen thinks it's better than telling them the truth and I've been too willing to go along with what's easiest to do anything else.' He sips his wine and as he puts down his glass his knuckle brushes my wrist. The sensation runs up my arm like someone stroking a buttercup under my chin as I lie in the sun. I wonder if it was deliberate, but then even accidents are subconsciously deliberate. 'I married Helen when I was twenty-one. Nothing was happening in my life and it seemed like the next thing, you know, go to school, rent a flat, get married. I didn't know quite what I was doing. She loved me and I loved her back, but not ... well, you know. I honestly thought it would work because we were such good friends.'

'Did *she* know?'

'That's the thing, you see. Sort of. She says she thinks she did, but that she didn't want to admit it because she loved me and *wanted* everything to be okay. I didn't know either, not entirely.' I want to ask him what that was like, not to *know*, but I know that if he could tell me, I wouldn't need to ask. He continues, 'I was in a production of *The Tempest* – all-male. I had to kiss this guy playing Miranda and the production made a really big thing of it, Hollywood-style, to get a laugh, because it was two guys. Well, I'd always felt ...' Leo pauses looking for the right word and, finding it, he looks straight into my eyes, '*sensual* about men. I'd even messed around a little with the other boys when I was a teenager, you know, experimenting, but you have to remember where I was coming from. I don't want to make a big thing of my Northern working-class roots or anything, but it's not exactly a nurturing environment for discovering your sexuality. I had always somehow blanked it out, like it was something I couldn't see even when I stared straight at it. But kissing Miranda ... frankly, I just fancied him, the actor, and I understood why I'd always felt a certain way about things.'

'Such as?'

'Such as being afraid to sleep with my wife.'

'Did you get it together with Miranda then?' I ask and

silently I hope he didn't.

'What? No. Oh no, I panicked. As soon as I realised how I felt, I cold-shouldered him for the rest of the run. It wasn't a nice thing to do, but I was scared. But I did tell Helen about it. I had to, out of respect. She was great about it, which makes me feel all the worse now. Although one morning I found her crying in the living room, hunched over a wedding photo. At first I think she'd thought I'd come round eventually, that ultimately I'd get over it and it would be moonlight and roses all over again. But the thing is, it never was. Even the picture she was crying over was just a performance. A registry office. I wasn't even wearing a shirt – the collar and front and the tie were just sewn on to the waistcoat. It was a quick-change costume I'd borrowed.' He sighs and pushes at his food with his fork. 'We stayed together, though, because it was easier. As I began to get a name, it stopped the press from speculating. I could play the loyal husband. Meanwhile, we settled into an arrangement where, theoretically, we both could see other men, but in fact, neither of us did much. I felt like I was betraying her even to contemplate it and it simply wasn't worth it for a one-night stand. And she, well, she had a few short flings, but I think it was years before she gave up on the possibility that I would change. She believes people can be whoever or whatever they want. I know it sounds insufferably arrogant for me to say it, but the truth is she just loved me. I don't know, maybe she still hasn't given up on me, but at least she's moved on.' His lips part as he dampens his mouth before he goes on. 'The fact that she has loved me all along should make me pleased or proud, but instead, it's a source of shame. I know she's loved me because she has said so and because of what she's done for me and because I know that, even in spite of everything, *she* feels guilty about leaving me. Can you believe that?'

'Isn't there another man though?' Elsi has given me more background than I want to admit.

'Yes, Vic. He's okay, he's great.'

'She couldn't wait for you any longer and decided to settle for less than she really wanted?'

'That's not for me to say, but if she did, it was so that I didn't have to. She says she's *happy with him*. Her words, not mine, and I *know* he's devoted to her. She met him in the States a couple of years ago and he moved over here at the end of last year. She moved in with him in January and that's when the media got hold of it all. They made out that she'd left me, which she had, but they didn't know why. They didn't know that, in a way, I'd left her years before and, after all she'd been through with me – I mean that woman virtually constructed me, not just my public image, but *me* – she has a right to a little private happiness. I made the deal, she didn't, but she's taken the clouds so that I can have the silver lining.'

'Why didn't you just explain it all to the media? People are pretty broad-minded these days. I don't think they'd mind you being gay. And those that do, well, bollocks to them.'

'You're right, absolutely right. The public wouldn't mind, not consciously anyway, but I'm a romantic lead. There are no *out* gay romantic leads and there's a reason for that. The public, however broad-minded they might think they are, are prepared to believe a hero can walk through fire and leap out of planes without a parachute, but they won't believe he's manly and straight – they won't fancy him or admire him – if they think the actor who plays him would rather be buggered by the villain than be kissed by the heroine.'

'Surely it's not like that anymore?'

'Think of Tom Cruise or Richard Gere. I mean, I don't know them personally and I'm sure they're as straight as Roman roads, but think about how hard they stamped on any rumours to the contrary. I'm sure it's not because they're homophobic or anything. It's just because they have to protect their image or else the public won't find them credible. The movie companies know the public thinks like that and so, for certain parts, they won't touch out gay actors with someone else's barge pole. Those certain parts are the ones I'm offered. It doesn't matter how good I am. There are plenty of good actors out there. It's a matter of credibility. If I don't have that, they'll just hire someone else.'

'But no one *knows* that it would damage your credibility. Maybe the public wouldn't mind after all?'

'Maybe so. But who's going to risk it? It doesn't even matter if the threat is real. Just to think it is, to imagine it, has the same effect. It's not worth the risk. Think of Rupert

Everett – one of the best actors of his generation and total movie-star looks, but does he get romantic leads? No, he's always the bad guy or the best friend or, usually, the *gay* best friend. Anything else just wouldn't wash 'cause the audience knows which way he really swings. The next film I'm doing, my contract actually states that they can dump me, no penalties, if I get adverse publicity before the release, and in the definitions, along with drug-dealing, gun-running and pederasty, they specifically mention being outed. Believe me, that's not because they know; that's standard in Hollywood.'

'Are you serious?'

'I'm afraid so. It's not intolerance, Chris. It's business. Money's more homophobic than people.'

Neither of us have touched our food and looking at it and thinking about what Leo can do, his lack of options, I feel sickened. 'It's so unfair.'

'Only because Helen took all the crap. By rights I shouldn't have survived it, but Helen took it all on herself. It's unfair on her. She let the world believe that she was the adulteress and I was the wronged husband.'

'But why?'

Leo sighs and shakes his head, projecting clouds of shadows behind him on the cave-like wall. 'So many reasons. She'd invested so much in building my image, even accidentally casting herself as proof of my heterosexuality, maybe she just couldn't let it go. And I don't believe even she could guess how much the media would make of it or how it would be. She's used to being in control. Not just news stories, her whole life, but this one crept up on us all. Vic had only been in the country a month and then he found himself branded a love-rat by some papers and an unattractive bore by others who wanted to make Helen seem all the worse for moving out. Every day we thought, that's got to be it, they'll have to write about something else tomorrow. So we all stuck to Helen's version of the story for one more day. But every day they found a new way to keep the story alive. They found someone Helen had slept with a couple of years ago, then Vic's ex, then Helen's clients started to leave the agency, so they splashed that across the front page. And me? It was all my fault, but that didn't matter, every story was full of sympathy for me. And every word made me feel guiltier and guiltier.' He swallows although there is nothing in his mouth.

'Back in February,' he goes on, 'I tried to persuade Helen we should own up. I really did. I was prepared to take what was coming, but she said it wouldn't do any good. I wasn't hard to convince. She said it was all too late. The media had already written their story and they had cast me as the good guy and Helen and Vic as the baddies. If we tried to rewrite it, they would only attack her more – they would say she had persuaded me to say it, to save herself, or, if they believed it, they'd say she'd always known, that she had deliberately acted as my "beard" and used my fame to boost her business. And now she no longer needed me, she had dumped me and blackened my name. Knowing the media is her business, Chris. What could I do? So I did nothing. It was easier. None of us have been players in this, we just let the events decide for themselves. I don't think even Helen believes she's in control any more. And I, I am just a coward. What good are choices anyway if you're too afraid to make them?'

Glassy beads assemble in the corners of his eyes and my hand moves over his, it is warm. I close my hand around his and his closes up tightly. A tear breaks away and starts to etch its track down his face. His does not wipe it away, but says, 'I'm sorry, Chris. Jesus, every time we meet, I start blubbing,' and he smiles and sniffs and removes his hand to wipe away the tear, but then replaces it on top of mine.

Now I realise something, something obvious, too obvious to see. He is lonely. Leo Martin is all alone. Lonely, scared and out of control. Like me. Who'd have thought it? 'It's okay, Leo,' I say. 'Everything's okay.'

*

Leo is late for his next interview but lunch has been a fairly emotional affair and he doesn't seem too bothered that we took time over it. We have come out the other side in laughs and smiles and closeness. 'Popularity breeds contempt,' he said to sum it up and I laughed. We are in the same boat. Our shameful secrets. My father and Helen. I can be something stable in his life, something controlled, if he'll let me. He can call the shots. Now he pays and leaves an enormous tip but it doesn't seem to make the waiter any happier. He and Leo exchange a few words and then he leaves us alone together at the foot of the stairs, looking up from the basement back into the light of day.

'Thank you for ... well, just thanks,' he says. 'Let's get together again, soon.' He pauses and looks frustrated. 'The thing is we can't hang around in public too much. And I'm rehearsing constantly at the moment and when I'm not rehearsing I'm on promotional duty.'

'That's fine, I understand.' Perhaps I have served my purpose. I don't like it but I understand.

But now he says, 'Would you like to come to dinner on Sunday? At my place?'

'Yes. Yes, please. Great. I'd love to.' And he writes his address and phone number on the back of his Amex receipt and gives it to me.

'Lovely. Well, I'll see you on Sunday. Eight-ish?' he says smiling broadly, beautifully, and now he rubs my arm affectionately and so I hold his other arm and we move together into a parting hug, an embrace, a tight embrace, and he is taller than me and wraps me in his arms protectively and I feel his chin against my cheek, the tickling of stubble, and we move our faces apart slowly, sliding apart, but not parting, and our mouths are so close that I can smell and taste and feel the warmth of his breath on my lips. And we kiss. Lightly. Once.

It is enough. I feel unstable and step back. The stairs seem precipitous for a moment and there is a figure at the top or I think there is, but, no, I'm steadier now. There's no one there. Too much chianti, I can tell myself, but no, I know. We climb the stairs together. I follow Leo and with just the word 'bye', we part outside. He walks west and I watch as heads turn and some whisper or point. I head back to the 29, not limping, but striding.

*

An individual may seem too good to be true and that may be because they are either not good or not true or both or neither.

165

Therefore, it may be postulated (i) that Chris did not and could not know whether his altogether favourable perception of Leo was real. His beliefs about celebrities might have made him distrust his perceptions. However, he believed his senses to be more reliable than his beliefs and so he trusted his perception.

Therefore, the postulate should be (ii) that Chris *did* indeed know that his perception of Leo was real, but what he did *not* know was whether or not Leo himself was real.

Let the truth be known: the perceiver exists, the perceived exists and the perception exists, but the three do not share the same order of existence. The perception is a *relationship* between two real objects, the perceived and the perceiver. The perception is not a third object itself (just as *distance* is a relationship between two points – as opposed to a line). The importance of relationships cannot be underestimated.

As he journeyed home, (iii) Chris sensed there was a relationship between himself and Leo and that this was very important indeed.

Chromosome 12
Calmer Stupor

'Free will is a delusion caused by our failure to analyse our own motives.'
Charles Darwin

'Love is a striking example of how little reality means to us.'
Marcel Proust

'Wracked with indecision, he ponders his choices, demands certainty and, ultimately, cannot avoid his destiny anyway. Until the very end, he spends his time failing to decide what to do,' explained Tom Petin, director, to Leo Martin at the start of rehearsals, 'and then, finally, he gets killed. Make it interesting that he does nothing much and you've cracked it. Hamlet is unable to act.'

Leo, on the other hand, was able to act. Indeed his acting ability as the man who is unable to act was lauded and applauded. It is not common for schoolgirls to flock to a production of *Hamlet* with as much, nay, greater enthusiasm than more regular theatregoers. It is rarer yet for schoolboys. Nevertheless, such flocking was the effect of casting Leo Martin in the rôle of the Dane.

After a week's previews, the curtain rose on Ascension Day, the first of June, 2000. Chris Putnam attended the first night, having spent his own first night with Leo eighteen days previously. He went backstage afterwards having agreed to accompany Leo to the party at the Savoy. They had not yet been out together in 'public' (albeit, in this case, an exclusive gathering), but had decided that, so long as they assumed a mask of mere friendship, they might risk it. They judged that Chris's presence would raise no suspicions: no one notices people they do not recognise at such functions. Indeed, even if Chris were noticed, they could rely on his identity being mistaken. It was, after all, common knowledge that Leo and Dan were frequent confréres. Furthermore, they were confident of Dan's absence, because, since neither Chris nor Leo had particularly wanted him there, he had not been invited.

Indeed, Chris did not want to talk to his brother at all at that time.

Firstly, as he was becoming increasingly resentful of the lack of choice presented by Sir Hugo's decree that he should apply himself to a doctorate, he did not particularly want Dan to reply to his enquiry about their family history. Fortunately, it appeared there was little chance of that.

Secondly, his brother's very existence jerked the noose of guilt Chris still wore regarding his father. Chris believed he had moved on. (After all, how much could he feel for a man he had not seen for years? He could forget, surely.) Even so, he was not yet willing to expose himself to reminders, not readily.

Thirdly, he did not wish to play the audience for Dan's tirades; all he *had* heard from him for the past month was a couple of emails which fulminated against the four and a half critics who had criticised his show and fulminated still more vehemently against those who had not even chosen to do so. Chris had responded to the messages swiftly and glibly and Dan, it seemed, had refrained thereafter.

Finally, Chris was anxious that Dan would somehow and destructively insinuate himself into his relationship with Leo. This was an uncharitable thought on Chris's part, borne out of his own insecurities, but such fears waned as the affair waxed.

Chris had doubts about the first-night party, not least because of the pretences it would necessitate on his part. He would have to hide his affections, affections that wanted to cry freedom from rooftops, that wanted to run up to strangers and challenge them to believe it. When alone he and Leo would touch each other all the time, accidentally, incidentally, deliberately; to not do so would feel tantamount to shunning one another. Furthermore, he would have to play the rôle of his twin which would be difficult, given that Dan was something of a celebrity in his own right and they had not switched identities since school. This was not quite true, he realised, not *wilfully*; there had been his father's wake, for example.

Chris did not want to go. He did not think he would enjoy it but he did not want Leo to know.

The two of them sat in Leo's dressing room, relentlessly interrupted by congratulatory heads poking round the door. Leo, at the mirror, surrounded by flowers, recognised Chris's anxiety about the party and was immediately plunged into anxiety of his own. He was aware that he was in breach of his contract with success and, his cowardice having become almost a matter of sacred rite, ever present in his mind was the danger of infecting Chris with the plague he had brought upon Helen. However, the danger only filled his veins with a sense of belief in himself, in Chris, in the two of them. He felt powerful, brave, in control of his life. Most of the time, his fears were kept smothered, but even then, it was an effort; a moment's distraction and they would fly in his face. He felt protective of his vulnerable lover. He felt fatherly.

He did not want Chris to come to the party. He did not think either of them would enjoy it but he did not want Chris to know.

Neither of them wanted to be the first to express their concerns, however, and the matter was brought to a head by the arrival with a flourish of Tom Petin, who announced that the limo was ready to take himself, Leo, the producers, the sponsors and 'Gertrude' (*cette Grande Dame de la Théatre*, Jocasta Rickes) to the Savoy. Leo insisted he could walk. Tom insisted the sponsors expected him to travel with them and, in any case, walking would take him hours. Leo pointed out it was barely 300 yards. Tom pointed out that there were crowds not only outside the stage door, but most of the way down The Strand.

There would not be room in the limo for Chris, who took the opportunity to whisper the suggestion that maybe he should miss the party and instead return directly to Leo's apartment. Leo smiled a relieved smile which Chris understood and, with a make-up stick, Leo wrote a number on a paper tissue, handed it to Chris and whispered in his ear. Chris felt the warm brush of breath on his ear, the tickle of lips, and heard the words, 'The entrance code. And by the way, I love you.'

He said it almost without saying it, getting away with it by surprise, stealth and supposed simplicity. Leo had chosen a moment when Chris could say nothing in return, and so he said nothing in return but left the theatre and crushed through the happy crowds, pressing in the other direction, feeling the comfort of strangers around him and then, having received that very morning a cheque from Ian Poulson in his rôle as executor of Eugene Putnam's will, and, despite the fact it would do little more than eradicate the debts of Chris's protracted studenthood, he caught a cab to Holland Park.

*

The tidy, tasteful rooms are Leo if Leo were a place. I wander through them silently with dimmers turned down low and am glad to be alone in his space. Incredulous. I should like to tell anyone, everyone, that I'm bubbling over with contentment, but being alone is part of my joy, so I cannot and so I keep his love to myself. I repeat it and repeat it and it makes me laugh out loud, the noise a pleasant presence in the half-light – *by the way … And by the way … And by the way …*

In the living room, I find a video to watch and sink into the sofa that gobbles me in an embrace and I stare at the wall that passes as a TV screen. I want no sound, just the pictures, just Leo in *The Ideal Husband.* Hidden, as if it were just another tape. He is better in the flesh. The touchable reality of him. Idealer.

This silence and this man who barely an hour ago just said, *And by the way, I love you,* ten foot tall before my eyes. And I am waiting for him. I will be here when he returns. In his bed. Ours. Hours. He will be hours. I would wait for years, wait in this place, full of him. So intimate to be here alone, with the little ghosts of him. Like the half-finished crossword on the coffee table. Cryptic. It is secure. It is trust. It is … the word he used about me. I cannot sit still. I want to move about inside his space, discover its secrets that he has left me here to uncover, that he has left here for me.

The bathroom is full of his scents, some bottled, some basketed in his laundry. The shirt he wore last night which his cleaner has not yet whisked away and which I took off him button by button, kiss by kiss.

There's no food in the kitchen cupboards, none to speak of. Fully equipped with pots, pans and everything and all of it spotless. Lots of designer jars too, but all of them empty. Some tinned olives and some baked beans with little sausages. Sugar Puffs. It's so sweet. Once I would have thought it strange that such a man had such everyday things. Now, it makes him real to me. His tidy, meagre needs.

On the nightstand stands his mother, cheaply, anciently framed. His forehead and the bridge of his nose. In the bedside-table drawer, there are hotel matchbooks, cufflinks, pens, cotton buds, a novelty key chain from Universal Studios, condoms, a cotton reel, his little nail clippers. And, in an envelope, his wedding ring. Somehow, they all came to be here, the accretions of time. Events, chains of circumstance brought each of them here, to this place and no other. *His* things. A key chain. He kept it. By chance or intention. And *here*, not in the living room or in the study or in the bureau in the hall. It is for him here. All the things that belong to him, we all are.

I shall sleep and when I wake up, he'll be here. I shall lie on his side of the bed and smell the phantom of his head on the pillow. I am so glad that this time, this place has come to pass, that all the universe has aligned such that I should be here now. It seems so clear it could never have been otherwise.

I remember the day my father died, only six weeks ago. There was a horoscope that day. I don't remember what it said, but I know it promised I would fall in love. And here I am. No, I do, I remember a line, what was it? Don't let the past decide the future. There it was wrong – nothing can be otherwise. The past decides everything, I believe that now. Nature, nurture, call it what you like, nothing comes from nothing. I can't say why he loves me. His genes maybe or his upbringing. A moment as a child that set his life on its course. Like the fact the key chain's here, something so small, but in its context, all the universe is never the same again. Or every moment, all the things here, none of which could have been different. He isn't free, none of us is. Free will? There's no such thing, because where does the will come from? Biology or environment or a mixture of both, it doesn't matter, it all has unavoidable causes too. It's all determined.

My father believed in destiny and now at last I see, I acknowledge, he was right, but it's not because of God. It's because there's only one way it can all unfold, that's why none of us is free. I think of my father's smells too, but I cannot recall them, all I remember is his warm dry hand on a cold autumn morning – all the remembrances of things past lost for the moment, along with all their hurt.

Nor can I say why I love him. Only that I do.

And he me. *By the way.*

The ceiling slowly slews above me, the pillow takes my head. I see him as Hamlet and, heavy-lidded, I let the image fill my eyes. The son's duty to his father's ghost. Leo dies again in my mind. We do what we do because of genes, because of mothers, because of fathers, because we're mad, because we're who we are, because that's all we can be, because we have to, because we have to, because we have to. Nothing matters.

Leo.

*

Leo as Hamlet. Chris as Hamlet. None of them free, because of their genome, because of their souls, because of all that has gone before. Gene as Hamlet, free only to fulfil his Holy Father's will. God the Father, God the Son, God the Holy Ghost. God the celebrity. God, the father, the celebrity, the coward. Conscience doth make cowards of us all. Cowardice may cripple freedom, but, even knowing this, it is no easier to be other than what we are.

*

Now. Now. Now, insisting something, and it's the phone and I'm awake and it's half-dark and the phone is by the bed and I'm here. I'm here. Yes, here. Okay. 'Ewo?'

Click-click-click and an American voice asks, 'Leo?'

'Sorry, no. It's not. Who's that?'

'Who's that?' says the voice, but I'm awake enough not to answer and I ask again who's calling, but the American says,

'You his lover, then?'

I don't want to deny it, but I do and then I say, 'This is a private, unlisted number. Who do you want?'

'Just give me Leo.'

'Leo isn't here.'

'Where is he, then?'

'Not here. Can I take a message?' There's a long pause where neither of us wants to give way and I try to work out who I might be talking to and it sounds like he's a friend, but maybe not, work-related perhaps, in which case I'm messing it all up for Leo. Maybe not, maybe the press. Now I'm scared. They know. How do they know?

'Yeah,' says the voice, eventually. 'Tell him Vic called.'

'Any message? Would you like him to call you back?'

'Tell him' – there's more than an American drawl in the voice, a snarl – 'tell him, Helen needs out.'

'Helen wants out,' I confirm.

'No, listen. That's not what I said. Helen *needs* out. It's *my* advice to him, okay? Tell him Vic says Helen needs out, so what's he gonna do about it? Got that?'

'Okay.'

'I'm getting pissed with all this shit.' And the phone goes down at the other end. There's no clock in the room so I get up to check. Only one fifteen. I wash and get undressed and go back to bed.

*

My father's driving and we're going on holiday, but he's going so slowly and I want to get out and walk because I can overtake like all the passers-by in identical T-shirts. Dan is talking to Mummy and Elsi's whispering in my ear, bad things, bad things about Daddy. She's laughing at him and saying he can't drive and he doesn't know anything and 'provincial' she keeps saying and Dan is disagreeing with her and saying 'parochial' but they're laughing together, laughing at Daddy. And all Daddy can hear from the back of the car is the sound of laughter, laughter in the back and he's smiling along and I'm embarrassed because she's my friend and I'm laughing too, laughing along and laughing at him. 'Hateful,

173

too,' I say, 'and dead' and I keep laughing at him despite how I feel and now Elsi and Dan don't think it's funny anymore and I can't see my father's face and I'm not sure if he's annoyed now and I want to say sorry. I want to say sorry. I just want to say sorry for all I've done forever.

Now, we're in a nightclub and my father or Leo is dancing with Mummy and Dan is trying to join in but she won't let him, but I can't dance and so I don't, but then Leo looks over at me and smiles.

Leo is kissing my neck from behind and I'm lying on a soft, soft bed and I open my eyes and I turn to him and press my mouth on his and feel the petals of his inner lips, their buzz as they move on mine, the tickle of his stubbly cheek against my chin. The taste of toothpaste in his mouth and the faint scent of alcohol in his hair, on his neck, as he kisses my face.

I murmur and my own soothed wordless sound comes back to me.

'Don't wake up,' says Leo and his breath trembles on my neck. My eyes stay closed and the quilt moves, weight and warmth shifting and I take shelter against the cool curve of his body behind me, naked, skin against my own, coated in the cosiness of the bed. His arm slides round me and his hot dry palm lays flat against my chest. I nestle further into his shape, our frames settling snugly into each other's. I want to burrow inside him. I feel his hardness tightening against the small of my back and press myself against him as I get harder too. His lips are on my nape and I let myself awake like this.

I turn and face him in the bed and slip my hand around the firmness of his back and I kiss him, kiss him and say, 'By the way, I love you too.'

*

And later we lie together in the lull that follows, my head on his chest, my arm and leg laid across him, my hand at his neck, stroking his hair. His hair runs through my fingers like velvet or milk. My strokes fall in time with his breaths or his breaths fall in time with my hand. As he breathes out in his sleep, he lets out a sound, brief and barely there, a sigh almost or a whimper. A purr, but not so gruff.

I have decided something, or rather, reached a conclusion. I do not need to ask why I love him or he loves me. It is enough. It could not have been otherwise, but I could not have known. It is not sad to know the future is the only path from all that's gone before. It is enough to know the future can never be known. There's nothing free in all the universe, but it feels like choice if you can't predict it. It is enough.

I raise my head to watch his face. It is still, dark shapes of shade cast by his cheekbones. I could not have known this would be and wouldn't have had the imagination to choose it if there'd been the chance. His shuttered eye, the one furthest from my own, is cloaked entirely in the gloom. The long lashes of the other cast shadows almost to his brow, slightly furrowed in sleep. The eyelids do not move. Not at all. I watch them to be sure, maybe seconds, or minutes. His sleep is deep. He is not dreaming. I lay back down.

I want to creep into his sleep. Even when he's inside me, it isn't close enough. I want to be inside him always and for him to be inside me. I want to curl up like a ball and be a part of him always.

I still feel him in my mouth, his size, his motion. And I taste him too, but it is as much a texture as a taste. It is something like almonds or butter-sugar and on my tongue it is like tiny pockets of consistency, reminding me of something. Dunked biscuits. No, those little French cakes they dip in tea that almost melt in the warm liquid and linger on the tongue and throat. What are they called? I can't remember but suddenly images flood back as if the taste reignites a lost sensation, fleetingly and I think of my mother in the old kitchen at Le Noires and giving me the whisk attachment from the electric food mixer to lick. Or I would get the bowl sometimes and Dan would have the whisk.

Quietly, my mind meanders and I know sleep will return soon. I cannot lift my hand to stroke his head now, so I rest it there, on his neck. I kiss his chest. Goodnight. I shall sleep here, like this and when we wake we'll be wrapped in each other, our warmths commingled. Stupor spreads its length across me like a crawling shadow. A calmer stupor.

My closed lids bring me images in the gentle darkness. A thought like a memory comes to me now. In snatches, offcuts of narrative like a half-remembered movie edited by an idiot. I *dreamed* something. And now I know I never dreamt before. It is my own personal film projected inside my head. My father, my mother, my Leo. So much more there than in my memory. And me too. I seemed more certain. I dreamed I was more real, it seems. To sleep. Dream again, dream, dreem, dreeemm, drmmmm, drrrrrrrrrrrrmmmmm

Part Two

Chromosome 13
Are Stochastic Events Free?

'Time present and time past
Are both perhaps present in time future,
And time future contained in time past.
If all time is eternally present
All time is unredeemable.
What might have been is an abstraction
Remaining a perpetual possibility
Only in a world of speculation.
What might have been and what has been
Point to one end, which is always present.'
T.S. Eliot

'There is a history in all men's lives,
Figuring the nature of the times deceas'd,
The which observ'd, a man may prophesy,
With a near aim, of the main chance of things
As yet not come to life, which in their seeds
And weak beginnings lie intreasured.'
Henry IV, Part 2, III, i

At the beginning, Chris Putnam believed he was free. Then he believed he was not, that everything was the necessary effect of all that had gone before. Be it nature, nurture or the complex interplay of them both, it did not matter: free will means to choose and to choose means to have reasons for the choice made, and the reasons, however trivial, are no more than the product of every moment past. If this is ever true, it is true always.

To surrender to the knowledge of such powerlessness might have been intolerable. But Chris Putnam also believed that in the order, there was chaos. Minute interactions, such as the mutation of a single nucleotide or the flapping of a butterfly could dictate all of time to come, but even scintillae such as these are not random. The future might be prescribed by the past, but to know it would be to know the

179

universe and all its hideaways. The future, therefore, is always certain but unpredictable.

Given that Chris's present involved a relationship with Leo Martin, such unpredictability was, for him, promising. If that had not been the case, he might have found himself bereaved and bereft, constricted to a path predetermined from time immemorial, the helpless victim of the whim of circumstance, neither able to know his fate nor to alter it. It was fortuitous for him then, that the previous sentence began with the word 'if' and hence was redundant. For the time being.

There was, however, always that one perpetual certainty in the future. As sure as any moment of his life, and more predictable, would be its end. The end was nigh and it cannot end well.

*

Because there's the illusion of freedom in the air, 'Good morning,' I beam to Peter the old security guard who sits in his hut at the Gower Street gate and who told me once he still likes to fish at weekends and who looks up to see which person is bothering to talk to him. I smile again but I'm already turned right, in through the double doors of the redbrick lab building and up the stairs three at a time. One – two – three – four times three is twelve in all to the landing with the lockers and I can still feel the warm of the sun, even indoors, even in the shade, with the vitamin D and all its little reactions cascading through me, to make me, ultimately, experience the joy of a sunny Bloomsbury good morning.

But that's not all. I feel underslept but overjoyed. Nothing feels so good as this. Being woken gently and making love, once last night and again as the sun rose. His skin scented like toast. Leo phoning for breakfast from the deli, completely casually, as if the apartment were a hotel. Flakes of croissant on the sheets and kissing cappuccino froth from his upper lip. Making love again. Then leaving him cosied in bed, bleary for more sleep, clasping a pillow to his chest as I go to work.

I open my locker and am taking out my lab coat, same stain, and the words 'making love' seem fresh to me now and I realise that's what we do. Leo and I. We forge and fashion love, model and mould it each time we go back to one another's bodies. We have constructed something and we just keep adding storeys and extensions. I don't understand what straights do in bed? I mean, I know what they *do*, but their repertoire seems so limited and surely they can't understand one another in the same way, know how to touch each other? It must be less equal too, always one person doing it to the other. Maybe it's just me. I wouldn't know what to do with a woman because it doesn't concern me. But still, queers have got to be better at it, surely.

I'll set up some reactions on the PCR block now so I won't have to wait for them later and I'm thinking that maybe I've decided I'm going to quit the gay gene project. Why should I do it? I believe I know the answer anyway – part genetic, part environment and you can't divide the two. What's the point in studying it, trying to reduce it to any other conclusion? It's wrong to make me. I don't want to do it on principle. Precisely because I have to. I can't do otherwise – I am caused to be rebellious, however futile it may be.

I'll tell his highness what he can do with it. I'll be standing proud in his office, forefinger stabbing the desk, and I'll be telling him that the passions of the human heart are too complex for study. I'll be saying that love is more than As, Cs, Gs, Ts – it's who I am, who I've been, who I will be. It's all of that and I refuse to be a part of his plans to sequester it, to own it, and, I'm sure if he had his way, to control it. I pick a pair of rubber gloves from the box, reversing them as I pull them down my fingers and snap them to my wrists.

The lab isn't busy yet. I fetch the samples from the freezer. It is not even ten, but I have been up for hours it seems and already today I've had experiences I hope to hold on to forever. I want them to affect the rest of my life and never leave me the same person again. I know I'm not going to tell Sir Hugo I want to quit the project. Not like that at least. I can say it in my head easily enough, write and rewrite my script, but if it came to it, I wouldn't follow it because he wouldn't get his part right. He would have a script of his own. I'd end up leaving too much confused or unexpressed. I am humming a tune to myself which I'm making up as I go along as I'm filling the well-plates, covering them and now putting them in the four blocks of the newest PCR machine. I measure in the primers too. It occurs to me that I always prefer to use this one, even though it is identical, except that the print on the control panel can still be read, but I don't need to read it anyway. I stop humming while I programme it. Now I load the other machines and set them going too.

*

Now I am filling the kettle and will be making coffee for Colin E. – black, two sugars, top it up with cold water – and tea for Nicole – weak and white – and I think I'll have a tea too – strong and white – and I'm prepping each person's mug and now I know what I should do. I will write my objections down. Not in a letter, but a sort of paper on my thoughts about the gay gene. He wanted opinions. Okay then, I'll make it carefully argued – scientific, naturally – and ultimately, even if he doesn't agree with me, which he won't, he'll see the pointlessness of trying to involve me in any of it. Of course, I'll have to come up with something else to suggest as a PhD, but he'll have to let me off the hook on the gay gene. I'm not going to let him control me. I'm not going back on the conclusion I reached last night. All life is predetermined, but it doesn't mean mine has to be determined by Sir Hugo. I may not be free, but I'm not about to surrender the illusion of choice.

The kettle's starting to whisper and mumble quietly to itself and there have been new changes to the sign on the wall. Someone changed it to 'You don't have to be desperate to work here, but it helps', then someone's crossed out 'desperate' and written 'here' – I guess that's a dig at Sir Hugo – and now someone's just crossed out the middle bit and it says, 'You don't have to work here, but it helps', which I don't get. There's a biro on top of the microwave, so I just scratch out 'but it helps' and then scratch out 'work here' as well.

I think of Leo again, as Hamlet last night, when he returned from England and challenged the other guy to a duel. Tuesday, I think it was, or Wednesday, last week anyway, Leo talked to me about the play, about the part, about what he thought about it, and we drank wine, his knee on my thigh ever closer on the sofa. That seems an age ago, when there were still motives couched in the way we said things and sometimes, I suppose, even in what we said. Leo talked about Hamlet like he was our mutual friend. He said he had to come back to face his duty. He couldn't avoid it, but he couldn't have faced it any sooner. Leo cares about Hamlet, as a person, as real to him as us, almost. He imagines him into reality. A creative act, I guess. I pour the teas first and then the coffee and I feel like Hamlet. But I guess everyone does the same. I wonder what's my duty?

Nicole comes in to the kitchen and says, 'That one for me?' taking her mug and Colin's. She stops in the doorway. 'Oh, and Hugo wants to see you when he gets back from Yokohama.'

'Okay. Is it about my PhD?' Maybe finally there's going to be the fallout from what I said and from running out.

'How would I know? I'm *only* the secretary.'

'I'm sorry, I just ... never mind. When's he back?'

'Next week, but his diary's full till the week after. Talk to me later and I'll put you in.'

'Okay, thanks,' I say but she's already gone.

*

I'm sitting at one of the computers and fishing out my teabag now and am going to check my email. I type in 'Sartre' which I should change. I'm bored of it and what I remember about him all seems a bit silly now. Adolescent self-pity. Just plain wrong. I've wised up. There are four messages and I sip my tea while they download. One is from Colin Ng to everyone: who he's assigned to what until the new people start arriving. I'm not on the list yet. Being unimportant has its advantages sometimes. Nicole: a circular about recycling. Elsi: 'mother hen calling chrissy – when are you coming home to roost? need to vet glamorous boyfriend. bring him for interrogation.' And Dan: 'Bro, where you been? Need to talk. Call me on the home number, trashed the mobile. D.'

I don't want these messages. They are intruding on my

time, on time I want to spend with Leo alone. During the day I work, so I only see him each night after the play and on Sundays. Dan sounds like he's being crazy and I don't want to deal with his dramatics. I'll get around to calling him later. Maybe. Also, I still don't want to tell him about Leo. It feels awkward because I don't think he'll understand that it's Leo I like, I love, not, well, not the Leo he thinks of. I'm also worried he'll feel that whatever Leo feels about me is second-hand. He'll make it about himself. But I know it's not. And what right does Elsi have to start talking about 'vetting' him? It pisses me off. Well, a little. I just want it to be him and me without any interference from anyone. I just want everyone to go away and leave us alone. That's all we need.

But I suppose I haven't seen her properly for days and if she's had to resort to emailing me, she must be feeling lonely in the flat on her own. I've neglected her. Maybe Leo and I could have dinner at the flat on Sunday and stay there overnight. We haven't spent the night at mine yet. I guess I don't feel it's my space in the way that his place is ours. I'll check with him before I talk to Elsi about it though.

*

Other people arrive and the main lab fills up. My samples are ready but there's no chloroform buffer to clean them. I ask anyone if they've got any, but it seems no one has, so I'll need to get it from the storeroom. I ask Nicole for the key and she asks me what I need it for and I tell her and she asks if I can wait for one of the lab technicians to get it for me and I say no because we've run out now and they're not around because they're never around and she sighs and she gives me the key.

I switch on the light in the storeroom and the fan starts up, clickety-click-click, and I find the chloroform and I'm holding it in my right hand and checking where I put the key and now there is noise, sudden noise, like glass breaking and there is broken glass on the floor, and liquid suddenly all over the floor and I'm no longer holding the chloroform. Shit, shit, it's everywhere. I grab a wad of tissues and crouch with them to mop it up, moppittup, mottitopitopitup, the wall spins, opmitup pot.

184

*

How do you do did you do what you did did you do? asks the fugu fish, mouthing in deep water focus, in focus and clearer in focus and 'What did you do?' asks a voice to my right and I turn and it's Eve and I'm in the common room and I'm trying to work out what just happened.

'What happened?' I say but it doesn't sound like that. Even to me it sounds like 'wawawen?' There's something huge in my mouth. I chew it gently and realise it's my tongue.

'What did you say?'

'Wawawen?'

'I don't know what you're saying, mate,' she says. 'Are you okay?'

'Unh,' I say.

'Sit him up,' says someone else and I turn my head to the left and it flops disobediently. There's no one there, so I let it flop further back as I feel hands on my back raising me up and I can see another figure, who's behind me, but I don't recognise them because they're upside-down and blurry. 'Give him this.'

Something warm and hard is pressed against my teeth and the smell of strong coffee rushes into my nose and I let my rubbery lips be forced apart by the rim of the mug and feel the liquid run over my bloated gums and down my chin. The mug is taken away and I'm pulled more vertical and the perspective of the room suddenly comes into recognisable shape. Now a rumbling sensation starts between my shoulder blades. It gathers strength like a wave and starts to climb the back of my neck, over my scalp and, breaking, it crashes in a rush of dizziness on the inner wall of my forehead.

'Wa happ'ed?' I manage.

'You dropped the chloroform on the floor,' says Eve. 'You passed out.'

'No, I di-didn't.'

'You did. It was everywhere. They've had to clear everyone out and wait for the specialist cleaners to come in.'

'No. I didn't. I didn't drop it.'

185

'What happened then?'

'He's not with it yet. Let him be for a bit,' says the other voice which is a man but I still don't recognise it. The coffee is pushed in my face again and I take it with my hand to stop them shoving it at me and I drink it for myself. It is black and stewed, thick as treacle and as sweet.

'I didn't drop it though. I know I didn't. I mean, I was holding it. I remember holding it, but I never let go.'

Eve: 'You must have knocked it then.'

'I didn't.'

The man: 'Well, how did it get broken then? It can't have jumped.'

'I don't know, but I was holding it one moment and it was all over the floor the next. The bit in between never happened. The dropping. The falling.'

The man: 'He's not making sense. He's still woozy. He doesn't know what he's talking about. Let's get him outside into the fresh air.'

'I do. I remember. Nothing caused it. It just broke.'

Eve: 'Chris, mate, it's okay. No one's blaming you.'

The man: 'They bloody will be.'

Eve: 'No they won't. Don't worry, Chris.'

But nothing caused it. I want to protest further but it occurs to me I'm wrong. I must be wrong. I just don't remember, which isn't surprising. But it seems clear: it just went from being there to being broken with a kind of absence in the middle, like a drop-out on a tape or finding a page has been torn out of a book, something happening out of nowhere, for no reason, with no cause. Like being beaten up that time. But it can't be. I must have just let go. It's just the effect of the chloroform.

*

Chris believed that if every sub-atomic particle in the universe could be mapped and measured and every law of physics that governed their interaction understood, then the past, the present and the future could be known.

There are those, however, who believe in Randomness, not in the sense of probability, but true uncertainty. There is

186

no cause for this quark's existence here or for that photon's behaviour there; no reason whatsoever why one thing happens and not another or, indeed, nothing at all.

Genetic mutations are sometimes described as 'stochastic' or 'random'. They are like typographical errors that occur without apparent cause. However, it is not the same to say that there is *no* cause for an event as it is to say that the cause is not apparent.

Chromosome 14
Anagrams

'Don't they say that a man who plays with words and makes anagrams and violates the language has ugliness in his soul and hates his father?'
Umberto Eco

'There is something in this more than natural, if philosophy could find it out.'
Hamlet, II, i

It doesn't matter how many times I move Elsi and the ashtray, every time I come back into the sitting room, they're both together again on the sofa.

'Please, Elsi, I'm trying to tidy up.' However much I clean, this flat still looks squalid.

'Relax, Chrissy,' she says. 'You've been tidying all day. The place is spotless. I don't know why you're getting so strung up. It's not as if it's the first date.'

'No, but it's the first time he's been here and it'll be the first time he's met you.'

'Are you more afraid that *I* won't approve of him or that *he* won't approve of me?'

'I—' I don't know which to answer, partly because I think I know, so I bottle out. 'Just, just try to sit there tidily.' She laughs and I return to the kitchen where I've already done everything, but I'm looking around to double-check and I'm checking my list and now opening the wine and now thinking about what else needs to be done so I'm grating some more parmesan and it's not top priority, so I'm wiping down the surfaces again and the doorbell goes. 'I'll get it,' I shout through to Elsi.

'I know,' she shouts back in a sing-song way and I buzz Leo in and I open the flat door as he's bounding up the stairs, one hand behind his back, and looking around and now kissing me passionately on the lips and on the landing. His goatee tickles and he tastes of peppermint and warmth.

'You two going to stand out there all night? Bit public isn't it?' says Elsi and we part from our embrace and see her standing in the doorway. There is only one other flat in the house and that's downstairs so Elsi is being completely unnecessary, on purpose I presume. 'Hi,' she says, 'I'm Elsi, and, of course, *everyone* knows who you are.' Leo is in a linen suit, smart and dashing.

'It's really good to meet you, Elsi. Chris talks about you all the time.'

'Really? I imagined you had more interesting discussions.'

'Okay, well, come through,' I say quickly, 'It's not much, but it's home, as they say. Elsi, Leo has the most amazing apartment in—'

'Holland Park. I know.'

'For you,' says Leo, producing from behind his back a bunch of mixed carnations and a bottle of champagne and presenting them to me. 'For *both* of you,' he says, to Elsi.

'Mmm, lovely,' says she, raising an eyebrow at the flowers and turning towards the sitting room.

We follow and Elsi immediately resumes her residence of the sofa, picking up the joint from the ashtray and the lighter from the table. She relights it. Leo sits on the edge of the armchair, like he's not staying. I've never seen him smoke and I don't really know what his attitude is, but it would be out of character for him to be uptight about anything like that, about anything in fact. 'I'll put these in a vase and get you a drink.'

In the kitchen, I realise we don't own such a thing as a vase and the nearest thing I can find big enough is the spaghetti jar which spills all over the floor when I pick it up. 'Shit,' I say and start to gather them up, crunching some under my knees as I bend down.

'You all right?' calls Leo from the sitting room.

'Fine, fine. Just dropped something. I'll be through in a minute.' And I can hear them talking, Elsi mostly, but I can't make out what they're saying.

I pile the spaghetti strands I've rescued on the side. I'll deal with the rest of them later. I hope I still have enough and I wonder what other pasta we have and whether it's worse to serve macaroni bolognese or to give Leo spaghetti that's been on the floor. I cut the flower stems and have to force them into the jar which is too tall and not really wide enough. Now I realise that although I opened the wine, I didn't get out any glasses, but I can only find two in the cupboard and now I realise I did get them out but I put them on the table in the sitting room. I'll have to take one of those. I pour two glasses of wine but I can't carry the glasses and the bottle and the dish of Kettle Chips at the same time. Okay. That's okay, first I'll take the glasses and the crisps. Then I'll come back with the other glass for the bottle.

When I come in, Leo is drawing heavily on the joint and Elsi's looking at me smugly. 'I've been putting Leo under the spot-lamp.'

'I hope she hasn't been giving you a hard time.' I give them the glasses and put down the crisps. 'She gives everyone the Spanish Inquisition.'

'No, no, it's fine. Makes a change to answer a barrage of questions without worrying about how I'm going to be misrepresented.' Elsi raises an eyebrow at me.

'I've just got to ...' I don't bother to finish the sentence, but I grab one of the glasses and, fishing out the paper napkin I furled into it earlier, I go back into the kitchen. I turn on the gas under the water for the pasta and fill my glass, down it, fill it again and take it, and the bottle, now half-empty, back in.

I balance on the arm of Leo's chair and put my own arm around his shoulders. 'So, has she finished cross-examining you yet?'

Before he has a chance to speak, Elsi says, 'Actually, we were talking about you.'

'I was saying how much trouble you've gone to and that you should come and sit down, join us and relax.' Leo is calm and his calm calms me. 'We don't need to eat for a bit.'

'And I was saying that you're an old fusspot,' says Elsi, 'and you enjoy stressing yourself out.'

'I'm not. I mean, I don't.'

'Whatever,' says Elsi and she refocuses on Leo. 'So, Leo, your age?'

'Twenty-five,' says Leo, laughing good-naturedly.

'Ah, so Chrissy's your toyboy. And how old will you have to be before you can be James Bond?'

'I really don't know. I don't think it's on the cards for quite a while. Besides, I think Pierce is good for a few movies yet.'

'*Pierce*, eh? Good friend, is he?'

'Not really. You've caught me being a luvvie. Apologies.' Leo shakes his head. From behind I can't see his face, but I can tell by the sound of his voice, he's smiling. 'I've met him, but I can't call him a friend.'

Elsi smiles too broadly. I don't know why she's on the attack all the time and I don't know if I should try to stop her. Leo seems not to mind. She changes tack, 'So, *if* you were asked, would you play Bond?'

Leo is taking it all as a joke. I guess the alternative isn't really an option. 'Honestly, Elsi, I really can't say. It might be ...' he pauses and says suggestively, 'dangerous.'

This catches Elsi unawares. 'Why?' she says. I stroke the back of his head.

'I believe there may be a conspiracy afoot.' He stares dramatically at Elsi to ensure he has his audience gripped. 'Brosnan's in on it. Has to be. And the spy forces. The TV companies, I suppose, and the movie studio too.'

'Okay, go on.'

'All right. Well, in what role did Brosnan first make it big?'

'I really wouldn't know,' says Elsi.

'Remington Steele,' I say.

'Exactly,' says Leo. 'And what's the real name of M?'

'Who?'

'M. The real M, head of MI5 or 6 or whatever.'

'I dunno,' says Elsi. 'What is it?'

'Stella Rimington. Stella Rimington, Remington Steele. Makes you think.' He's smiling again.

'Except,' says Elsi, 'that Stella Rimington isn't M anymore.'

'Who is then?' I ask.

'I don't know the name, but it's not Stella Rimington. She retired or resigned or was liquidated or something.' She smiles. 'What you've got there is a problem of cause and effect. Which is supposed to be the cause? After all, Stella Rimington has, presumably, been called Stella Rimington all her life, unless she's married, in which case her husband has probably been Mr Rimington all *his* life. So her name pre-existed Remington Steele's which means that the character

Remington Steele cannot have been the cause of her name. Furthermore, Remington Steele was a character invented, oh, I don't know, in the early eighties? This was,' she starts counting out the points of her argument on her fingers, '*one*, probably before Brosnan was cast for the role, *two*, before anyone knew Brosnan would go on to play Bond and, *three*, before anyone was allowed to know the real name of the real life M. Therefore Stella Rimington cannot have been the cause of the name Remington Steele. Conclusion? What you have there is, in fact, what is commonly called *a coincidence.*' She pauses with self-satisfied gusto. 'But, now you come to mention it,' she begins again, 'you know what is weird?'

We both stare at her blankly.

'Stella Rimington does look one hell of a lot like Judi Dench.'

'You've got me there,' says Leo and I hear the water for the spaghetti hissing as it boils over in the kitchen.

*

I decide to use the macaroni instead and I'm repeating to myself this isn't a disaster, Leo won't judge me on any of this and I'm reminding myself what he sees in me. The thing is, I don't know.

'You don't realise how attractive you are,' said Elsi when I asked her what she thought after that first lunch with him. 'The little-boy-lost thing goes a long way.'

That's become my mantra, my way of convincing myself any of this is really happening.

I'm checking the sell-by on the pasta and it says July 2001 and so I'm pouring it in the saucepan and reminding myself what else she said: 'In all the world, who can Leo turn to? Who's he got? A wife who's having an affair, friends like Dan and endless groupies. Then along comes a great-looking guy, sweet, shy, intelligent and obviously a bit fucked-up – someone who poses no threat. He sees someone he wants to take under his wing, someone he can cherish and be close to. He needs someone he can oversee – all right, *look after*. Anyone who's in it for the showbiz glitz ain't gonna work for him. He needs someone who gets through to him, makes him feel like a big strong hero, him personally, not the mask he shoves up for public consumption. It's all over-compensation for being a closet queer and having fucked up everything for his wife, I reckon.'

So why me? Which is when she said I don't realise how attractive I am and told me to stop fishing.

Then she asked me what I see in him and I said she must be crazy, but I thought about it and I said that, yes, maybe it's because I feel reassured with him, like he can keep bad things at bay.

'It's all Oedipal,' she said. 'You like being mothered.'

'It's not that. It's more male – I guess it's like you said, the big strong hero.'

I pick up the salad bowl and take it through. I don't realise how attractive I am, I remind myself. I don't realise how attractive …

*

'Chris, that was magnificent, a triumph,' says Leo, scrunching his paper napkin, and we give each other a kiss.

'Yes,' adds Elsi snippily, 'very nice fruit salad.'

'I love a tender young fruit,' says Leo, laughing and kissing me again.

'I'd watch those double entendres, if I were you,' says Elsi. 'You'll give the game away.'

'I'm among friends.'

'Oh, yes,' says Elsi, 'I'd forgotten.' And before I have a chance to tell her off, she adds, 'Anyone for a post-prandial?' and she waves her little bag of gear.

'Most kind,' says Leo, who, for my sake I guess, is simply not rising to Elsi's bait. Elsi pulls out a few Rizlas.

Leo looks at ease. Elsi is busy. But I feel the silence is awkward.

'You guys should play Scrabble,' I say.

'And why would that be, Chrissy?' says Elsi, not looking up from her ritual of crumbling.

'Well, you both like it and I'm no good at it, so …' I trail off.

'I'm up for it,' says Leo, 'if you are, Elsi, and if you'll play, Chris.'

'Oh, I'm up for it,' says Elsi, who in these things is always confident of victory and is usually right, especially against me. But Leo does crosswords all the time and the one time we played Scrabble he beat me so soundly he said he didn't want to play anymore because he didn't enjoy beating me. He tried to teach me what I was doing wrong, but I guess it's just not my thing.

I fetch the box from the bookshelf and we relocate, Leo and me to the sofa, Elsi to the armchair, but the seats are too high to play at the coffee table so we squat around it. I lean against Leo, Elsi opposite.

Elsi lights up and we each draw a letter to see who starts. Elsi has A. I have C. Leo has T. Elsi starts. She draws six more letters and a long toke and almost immediately goes all down with JEALOUS with the J on a double-letter and the O on the double-word. I keep score: ninety-four. Leo is not likely to beat her now and I'm kind of relieved.

I have the C I started with and now an F, I, T, another I, O and N. I could do CAT with the A on the board, or ACT. I can put the F in front of it and make FACT. I score nine.

Leo moves his letters around fast on his rack. He is not attempting to keep them hidden from me and I can't help but look. It's not as if it matters whether I know anyway – I'm hardly a contender. A, Y, I, L, E, R and the T from before. I can see a few words that can go down – TRUE, TALES, ROLE, LIES, or LIARS for that matter, but nothing very good. Leo shuffles the letters around some more, plastic on plastic, clickety-click-click, and spells out on his rack REALITY which he puts on the board with Y on the end of JEALOUS. All down as well. He scores eighty-eight. I love him all the more.

*

I have scored ninety-six so far and am left with the Q which I can't use because I haven't got a U and there are no more letters to pick up. Elsi has three hundred and eighteen. Leo is twenty-one behind. It's my go. I put a G before LAD for six. Leo puts UN on the beginning of VEIL and finishes his letters. There's the U I needed, on a triple-letter too. Eleven.

I tot up the scores, taking points off for unused letters and adding them to Leo for clearing out first. Q and E from me – eleven. I and O from Elsi – two. I announce the scores, 'Ninety-one to me. Elsi: three hundred and sixteen. And Leo, at the last minute, just takes it with three hundred and twenty-one.'

'Good game,' he says. 'High scores. And I wouldn't have made it if Chris hadn't got stuck with the Q. Very lucky for me.'

'No such thing as luck,' says Elsi, passing me a joint which I accept for the first time tonight. 'I've got to go to the loo.'

Leo waits till she's out of the room and says, 'I don't think winning was a good idea, do you?'

'I don't know. She's just in a weird mood tonight. Don't worry, I'm sure it's got nothing to do with you.'

'I think it's got everything to do with me.'

'What do you mean?'

'Chris, are you serious?' Leo sees I am. 'She's in love with you herself.'

'Don't be ridiculous.' The idea is beyond contemplation, like incest, but I can't think of any evidence to dispute it. All I can come up with is that she and Gill used to get on great. 'She never had a problem with my, my ex.'

'Okay, when did you first meet her?'

'About three years ago. When I finished as an undergrad. I moved in here as a flatshare.'

'And you were already going out with Gill?'

'Yes, but she didn't know him. Not at first.'

'But there you are then.' Leo strokes my face which must be creased with confusion and concern. 'When you were with him, she could block out her own feelings, just because you simply weren't available. He had the prior privilege. Being gay made you doubly out of the question. Did she get on very well with Gill?'

'Yeah. Really. I think she still sees him sometimes, but I'm not sure. She sided with me when it ended though.'

'I doubt she does see him. Or if she does, it's him who initiates it.'

'Why?'

'Her friendship with him was a way of being close to you. A third party in the couple, almost. When he was no longer in the picture, she had you all to herself and she thought, maybe not consciously, but in there somewhere, that eventually you might come round.'

'But come on, Leo, she knows perfectly well it's not going to happen.'

'Consciously she knows it, but it doesn't matter. Remember what Helen's been through. She's let it destroy her, just because at some level, she can't accept that her love for me cannot be strong enough to make me love her back. Or not in the right way. People never give up hoping that the love of the right woman won't make a poof turn straight.'

I stub out the joint. I don't want any more. If Elsi had not behaved this way tonight – and always towards Leo, not me – and if Leo didn't understand people so much better than me and if I could find anything, any scrap with which to challenge him, then I would not believe it, could not. It is nagging me now and making me feel uncomfortable and there's something else in my discomfort, as if I've forgotten something.

'Don't worry, my love, don't worry. She'll get over it.' He strokes my face again and I take his hand and cup it to my cheek.

It comes back to me. Vic. It was mentioning Helen that reminded me. 'Oh, Leo, I'm sorry,' I say suddenly and he starts.

'What is it?'

'I forgot to tell you, Vic called. Thursday. Thursday night. He woke me up. I'm sorry.' And I tell him what Vic said.

Leo looks pensive and eventually says, 'I'll call him.' Now he is staring at the Scrabble board and says it again. He starts to clear away the letters into their little bag, but stops halfway across the board and selects a few letters and lays them out: V, I, C, H, E, M, I, T, T.

He starts to move them around. 'Look at this,' he says sadly and moves his hands out of the way for me to see: THE VICTIM, it says.

'Did you realise that just now?'

'No, I make up anagrams all the time. I believe they harbour another level of reality,' he says mysteriously, like a clairvoyant. And he tries to smile to show he's just joking, but with the truth in front of us, neither of us is laughing.

'Do another,' I say and he starts to spell out H, E, L, E, N, B, O, S, S, I. Then he rearranges them: SHE IS NOBLE.

'Ain't that the truth,' he says, solemnly comic. The room is silent. I listen to it, like I'm waiting for it to make its move. This isn't funny.

Leo removes some of the letters from Helen's name and rearranges the rest: E, L, S, I, E. 'You see, I told you Helen and Elsi have something in common.' The silence is resilient, oppressive, even when we speak.

'She spells it with no E.'

'What none at all?' he says, trying to make light of it, but these names, what's happening, I can't take it as just a diversion.

'Just that one,' I say, taking the second E away. 'Very particular about it.'

'Well, there you go then,' and he rearranges the letters on the board: LIES, it says.

'I always think of Ethical, Legal and Social Implications.'

'What's that?'

'It's a department of HUGO, the Human Genome Organisation. We get bulletins and stuff from the ELSI Committee and it always makes me think of, well, Elsi.'

'What's her surname?' he asks.

'Tarot. Like the cards.' The lavatory flushes and I realise how long Elsi's been gone. I feel afraid for her, no, it's *pity*. I pity her. Which I have never done before. The balance of our relationship is all new now, now I know what I do. That it's all lies. And the proof is here. The bathroom lock clicks.

Elsi walks in and 'Look,' says Leo, indicating the board. ARISTOTLE, it says. 'It's an anagram of your name.'

Elsi suspiciously rearranges the letters, proving it to herself and then says, 'You're right.'

She picks out L, E, O, M, A, R, T, I and N. Leo starts to spell out my name and I am not sure I want him to. I do, but I don't. It's like staring at an accident or messing with a ouija board. I know, I believe – I mean, I believe that I know it's all rubbish, so much junk, but still, still it has the power to unnerve, to scare, to make goose bumps riddle my skin and my lips become arid. There is the compulsion to do it, to go on, to mess with something I don't understand just to prove to myself there's nothing in it, nothing there. I rub Leo's knee under the table watching. C, H, R, I, S, P, U, T, N, A, M.

Elsi finishes and reveals MINOR TALE with a self-satisfied

'There you go. A bit of a downer for a celebrity like you.' She contemplates it for a second and says, 'Or you could have I'M NOT REAL. That's more suitable for an actor.'

'Spooky,' she adds. She doesn't get it. She doesn't get what's going on here, what's being revealed. The truth. I know he's not real. He's too good to be true. I can touch him, feel him, even be inside him, but still, it all feels like it could vanish.

And I don't want to watch. I can't see what he's doing to my name. I don't want to look but I want to look. Something claws at the cage of my chest. 'How you doing there?' she asks.

Leo opens his palms and moves them slowly from the board, turning it for her to see and on, round, 360 degrees, to me and I don't breathe and I look and I read it, two words: HUMAN SCRIPT.

'It's me.'

'Yes,' says Leo.

'No, I mean, that is who I am. A human script. And it's what I do. The genome.' I see scrolling letters in my vision. The words transfix me. Human Script. Chris Putnam. It's what I do. It's who I am. It's truth. It's just coincidence. No, everything has its cause. But it's too, it's too, too – artificial. It's lies. 'Take it away.'

'You okay?'

'Just take it away.'

*

Leo sleeps beside me. Even when I press against him his presence is too far away. He rests but I am restive. I am staring at the ceiling hearing his breath and I am panicked and lonely. There is so much hidden from me. There is something going on I don't know about. Elsi in love with me? It seems incontrovertibly true in the darkness, like it has always been and I've always been a fool. How much don't I see? My name contrived. Me, contrived. Leo, not real. In this night, it seems everyone's keeping a secret from me. Everyone. They're laughing behind my back. I called 'Daddy' and they're laughing behind my back. It's not possible that no one knows, no consequences. No consequences, no cause. I was beaten by no one. The chloroform. I didn't drop it, I didn't, I believe I didn't, but it fell.

Only Leo. Leo is the one who reveals it to me. Leo will protect me from the secrets. He is reality. He is. Leo. I curl into the curve of his frame and let his heat envelop me. I shall be safe so long as he is with me.

Chromosome 15
Sea of Troubles

'Man that is born of woman is of few days, and full
of trouble.'
The Book of Job XIV, 1

'Each person thinks they are born to be the star of
their own life. No one imagines himself to be a
bit-part actor in another fellow's story, let alone for
his personal sea of troubles to be mere backwash
from that other man's ocean. Think of Stoppard's
Rosencrantz and Guildenstern, or Barth's notion of
a play called 'The Tragedy of Polonius, Lord
Chamberlain of Denmark'. In real life it is our own
personal tragedy to suffer the slings and arrows of
outrageous fortune. But in fiction, you may merely
be caught in the crossfire of a bigger story.'
Simon DeStromp

There is a distinction between a relationship which *has* a
routine (a signifier of depth and durability) and a
relationship which *becomes* routine (which Leo and Chris's,
laden with gentle affection, had not).

In time, relationships must develop their own routine.
Relationships, in this sense, are autopoietic. The degree to
which the routine is planned is irrelevant, since a viable
routine cannot be contrived that would not have evolved
anyway. Should an inviable routine be devised, it will, sooner
or later, be gradually mutated by circumstances into
increasingly workable versions until ultimately it becomes
that routine most fit to survive in the situation. Successful
relationships are driven to adapt quickly. If they do not, they
become extinct as relationships.

In the case of Chris Putnam and Leo Martin, the routine
established itself quickly. It was necessitated by the following
circumstances, among others. (1) Chris worked during the
day. Leo worked in the evening and worked out during the

day. Sometimes he would make such appearances as were necessary to satisfy the need for public relations. (2) Personal relations, however, did not constitute public relations. Therefore being together in public was too much of a risk. (3) Chris and Leo were both acutely but silently aware that their relationship would soon be challenged by a prolonged separation, for it had been ordained that Leo should journey to Hollywood on the fifteenth of August for the filming of *Odysseus*. Were the relationship to survive (as they both hoped), it would not be enough for it to exist, it would be necessary for it also to have acquired the trappings of habit. (4) They loved each other. For what that is worth.

For these reasons, by the twenty-first of June 2000 (one and a half months subsequent to the date both parties had agreed was its inception), the relationship had developed the following routine. Chris would phone Leo several times during the day. Or vice versa. Apart from whispered blandishments, the conversation would consist of arrangements for that night which would invariably be the same. Chris, having usually arrived late at work, would work late and then in the evening go to the flat he shared with Elsi to fetch clean clothes and would enter through the stage door of the Lyceum around eleven o'clock to await Leo, who, depending on the duration of ovations, would arrive around ten minutes later. Within half an hour, they would depart separately, Leo leaving first. However, owing to the nightly throng of autograph-hunters, Chris would usually arrive before Leo at Leo's car (an Aston Martin DB5 in a private car park on Kemble Street). They would drive home (Leo's home, that is), eat together and then go to bed. They were a couple.

Saturdays had their own routine. The morning would be spent in bed. Then Leo would go to the theatre for the matinée performance. In other respects, it was the same as weekdays.

Sundays, however, had no particular routine. This constituted a routine in itself. On three Sundays they took trips to the countryside for wooded walks in such tranquil isolation as they could find, hiding from other walkers like errant schoolboys lest Leo be recognised.

Even Damocles developed a routine.

Wednesday the twenty-first of June 2000 was the twenty-fourth anniversary of the birth of Chris Putnam. Leo performed a matinée on Wednesdays, but had organised caterers to prepare and leave a special birthday dinner for them at his apartment. With, undoubtedly, due recollection of the trials of Helen, Leo experienced the guilt of inadequacy regarding these arrangements given that, circumstances being as they were, he felt unable to achieve a more sufficient observance of Chris's birthday. Nonetheless, with candlelight and romance, he had contrived to stage an intimate celebration.

*

Before any such festivities, however, Chris Putnam had an appointment to keep. It had been two weeks before Sir Hugo Huttenton's secretary, Nicole, was able to find a window in his diary and therefore she scheduled a meeting at one thirty p.m. on Wednesday the twenty-first of June. The delay had afforded Chris the opportunity to produce his document, which at first he entitled 'A Critique on the Genetic Basis for Male Sexual Orientation', then 'A Treatise', and, finally, he called it 'A Commentary'.

It ran to twenty-three sides of A4. The first section provided a précis of some of the most important research, a carefully argued summary of the evidence supporting the genetic basis and a carefully argued summary of the evidence supporting environmental causes. It then contained an explanation (which undeliberately owed much to Elsi's analysis) of how, as Chris saw it, these factors could not be made distinct from one another. Even if a gene or genes could be shown to be significant in the causal chain, it could never be demonstrated conclusively that any one cause was more significant than any other. A factor is only a cause in the context of its relationship with its circumstances. Which then is the true cause: the factor, the relationship or the circumstances?

Next, there was a section about the nature of human sexuality, citing difficulties experienced by researchers from Kinsey onwards in defining homosexuality, and concluding with the claim that human sexual orientation and its causes were too complex to be studied in absolute terms.

Chris then included a section on the eugenic dangers of discoveries in this field: prenatal tests and abortions; gene therapy to treat homosexuality; the unpredictability of expression; *et cetera*. Chris knew that the section on the ethical debate was irrelevant, but having written it and having been satisfied with its sentiments, he decided not to excise it, regardless of whether it would further his case with Sir Hugo.

In conclusion, Chris's 'Commentary' suggested that the cause of sexual orientation could not be identified solely by a clinical study of genetic material, as it cannot be studied in isolation. What, he suggested, would be more rewarding would be to venture into a deeper level of inquiry and study the causes of (apparently random) mutations and whether they arise *ex nihilo*.

Ending his document thus, Chris intended that in his meeting with Sir Hugo he would propose a PhD study on the rôle of the gene RAG1 in influencing stochastic genetic mutations. Chris was pleased with his 'Commentary'. He believed it was well reasoned, reasonable and, most importantly, right. He did not hope to divert Sir Hugo's course, merely to set in train a sufficient eddy that might allow him, without loss of preferment, to be excused from the gay gene project. He had not had time to produce a fully realised proposal on his intended alternative doctoral study, but imagined that there would be time enough for that later.

*

I must at least go through the motions of trying to see Sir Hugo when I'm supposed to even though there's no way he'll be back from lunch before three. I'll call Leo first. At home it just rings. He's the only person I know with no answerphone. That's how successful he is. Of course, he's got a matinée today. I try his mobile. 'Hello,' he says, rising slightly on the second syllable, and even on the phone his voice is emollient and deep.

'Hi, it's me.'

'Hi, you. Happy birthday again. Have you seen your boss yet?'

'You joking? We're only five minutes late so far. He won't be here for hours yet.'

'How you feeling about it?'

'Prepared,' I say. 'What about you? What are you up to?'

'I've just been to the gym.'

'Ogling the hardbody boys?'

'Even if I did, they'd only make me want to be with you.' Somebody coughs officiously behind me and I turn around and it's Nicole pointing at her watch. Her face is all accusation.

'Oh, Le—' and I decide not to say his name out loud because she's still standing there. 'Sweetheart, something's come up. I'll see you tonight. Break a leg.'

'You know what they say, you can't make a Hamlet without breaking legs. And good luck yourself. See you then. Oh, I—' and I realise he was about to say something else but I'm already putting the phone down and don't change my mind in time not to hang up on him and when I lift up again he's gone.

'You're not going to make *another* call, are you?' says Nicole.

'No, I—' and I trail off and say instead, 'I'm ready.'

'Good.'

I follow her into her office the size of a cupboard and knock on the closed door to Sir Hugo's. There is no answer. I look round at Nicole for clues. She's staring intently at her computer screen. 'Is he in there?'

'Yes,' she says, typing, click-clickety-click, click-click.

I try again and there's still no answer, so I open the door slightly and then as it becomes clear there's no one there, I let it swing aside by itself. 'He's not.'

'Yes, he is,' she says.

This is ridiculous. He's not. She knows he's not. Even from where she's sitting she can see he's not there. She knows I know he's not there. Why is she lying to me? It's pointless. I look round at her and I think for a moment that she's not typing but the clickety-click sound is carrying on, now it stops as if I've caught it out and now I realise it may have been the dot matrix printer. 'Look, he's not here. I'll come back in a bit. Or you can come and get me when he gets back.'

'He asked me to tell you to join him in his office.'

'But he's not here,' I say and I'm still saying it as he walks in.

'Ah, Chris. Good. Let's get on with it,' he says and strides past me into his office from where he raises his voice to say, 'Nicole, fish out Mr Putnam's little literary effort, would you? Sit down, Chris, sit down.'

I cross the threshold and sit down and try to understand what he means by my 'literary effort'. Doesn't he like it? Doesn't he see I'm really trying to argue the case here, to look at the issues. I'm not just saying I don't want to do what he wants, I'm giving him reasons, good reasons. Okay, I didn't expect to change his mind, but I thought he'd at least recognise the work I put in. 'Literary effort'? What does that mean? Nicole delivers it to his desk and leaves, closing the door behind her.

He leans forward with his elbows on his desk and picks up my 'Commentary' by the bottom corner. It stands stiffly to attention in his hand and he speaks abruptly. 'Read this last night, Chris. A few questions.' His fingers must have moved slightly because the papers suddenly lose their rigidity and limply droop in his hand. 'First: what the hell is it?'

'I thought I'd submit a few ideas about the gay gene project. You asked for—'

'I didn't ask for *this*.'

'No, not exactly, but I thought—'

'No, you *didn't* think. I said I wanted you on this project. I said I wanted you to come up with a PhD proposal. I said this was an opportunity for you. I did not say I wanted a rambling pile of bunkum which – if I've understood you – suggests that, in *your* opinion, I shouldn't have spent the last nine months traipsing all over the world getting this project off the ground.'

'That's not quite what I—'

'Well, in that case, I don't know what it's about. Chris, Chris, Chris. You're capable of so much more. I'm giving you a break here and I'm doing that because you're equal to the challenge. What is the matter with you? You're all over the place at the moment. I understand you wreaked havoc with some stunt the other week and the whole lab had to be evacuated. And now, you give me *this*.'

'I've appraised the scientific—'

'This, my boy,' he says, waving it in my face, 'is not what science is about. This is.' And he slaps his chest and I'm not sure if he means him, his heart or his wallet. 'Gay genes are interesting. This' – he pushes my commentary back at me – 'is not. Don't ever, ever do something like this again. Now get out. Get out and I don't want to see you in here until you've got a proper PhD proposal, i.e. one that I can write straight into our current budget plans, not this rubbish. You have three weeks.'

'I've got a proposal. I—'

'Well? Where is it?'

'I haven't written—'

'Well, for god's sake, Chris, you piss about on this crap and then say you've not written up what I asked you to. What on earth were you thinking?'

'It's on the RAI and—'

'Don't *tell* me. Write it up and I'll look at it. Three weeks. Now, go.'

'I—'

'Go.'

I go.

*

Nearly six and the platform at Goodge Street is packed with people who cannot possibly all fit on the train which isn't here anyway and it all smells of fury and fumes, end-of-the-day stress. The lighted sign spells out in little red dots that the first train is due in three minutes and it has said the same for at least three minutes and in any case it's an Edgware train and I need Kentish Town which is on the other branch and it doesn't even say how long the second train will be. Two black kids down the platform are pointing at me and saying things to each other behind their hands and now they're laughing hysterically. They're laughing at me and I don't know why. I'm crammed in by crowds all around and they've picked out me to laugh at for no reason. Or maybe it's not me.

Sir Hugo can stuff it. I'm not doing it. I'm not writing any proposals. Forget it. I'll put him off as long as I can and then I'll just tell him, 'So sorry, but I can't do it, just can't, because, you see, I don't want to.' He can sack me if he likes. If it's coming, then it's coming. Now's a good time to be redundant. I've got Leo and, for once, I'm solvent.

The lighted sign click-clickety-clicks like a ticker-tape and says CRAPPY BIRTHDAY, CHRIS but I look again and it doesn't. It's still lying saying three minutes but now I can feel the rumour of breeze that races through the tunnels ahead of the trains and the clickety-clickety-clickety of the tracks. 'Trains', I think, is an anagram of 'strain'. I'm still new at this, but I'm beginning to understand.

*

'Hello?' I say in the flat which is quiet and I'm glad Elsi isn't here. I don't want to confront her. She is lying to me all the time. I think she knows I know, but she's carrying on. She doesn't like Leo or she holds it against him that I do and she makes me feel guilty about it, but it's not my fault, it's not my problem. Besides, Elsi is lies. Elsi is lies and I am a human script. That truth won't go away.

I'm emptying my bag from last night and packing some things for tonight and maybe I ought to do a whites wash and give Dan a call. 'Happy birthday, Chrissy!' cries Elsi in the doorway and she makes me jump.

'Christ, you scared me.'

'Sorry, just a surprise. Happy birthday,' and she gives me a plastic bag and an envelope and goes to kiss me on the mouth as we do, we always do, but I don't want to and she ends up kissing me on the edge of my lip. I say thanks and open the card which has a Gary Larson cartoon that I've seen before, the one with the scientist about to bang a nail in a missile and a colleague behind him about to burst a paper bag. Inside, it just says, 'Dearest Chrissy-wissy, Many happy returns, Love Elsi' and she's underlined 'Love' and I'm not sure if she's making a point or I'm overinterpreting, reading meanings that aren't there, but it seems like they are and the message seems like she doesn't know what to say to me now.

I say thanks again and open the bag. She hasn't wrapped it, but that's not new. It's videos. *The Truman Show*, which I haven't seen, *Liar, Liar*, which seems too ironic and *The Mask*. By way of explanation she says, 'Jim Carrey was on *Oprah* saying he's starring in *Odysseus* with your boyfriend. He's playing the bad guy, the head suitor. I thought you might like to check out the competition.'

'Mm, great. Thank you. Yeah, we'll take a look. I haven't seen this. It's supposed to be good.'

'Indeed it is,' she says and looks awkwardly pleased with herself and I feel bad that I was pleased when I thought she was out and I feel she's more vulnerable than she admits, so I give her a hug and then a quick kiss, on the lips this time.

She disengages first and says, 'I've made a special birthday tea and have plenteous supplies of drink and drugs.'

'Oh Elsi, I'm eating with Leo tonight. He's arranged something.'

'Okay, no worries,' she says turning quickly and heading down the corridor to the sitting room. I follow her apologising and see that she's laid the table and lit candles and laid out three long and perfectly rolled joints.

'Elsi, you shouldn't have bothered. You knew I'd be going out with Leo.'

'You can stay for a bit though.'

'Well, sure, but I don't want to spoil my appetite and I'd better not smoke.'

'Oh come on. It's your birthday.'

'Exactly.'

'I thought,' she says, extending the sound almost to the point of sarcasm, 'that *since* it was your birthday, you might spend an evening with your best friend for once.'

'Elsi. Don't make me feel guilty about it. You knew I'd be going out with Leo.'

'Jesus, there's no point sharing a flat with a flatmate who's AWOL all the time.'

'Don't be silly. I'm here now, aren't I? I'm here every evening. I'm not going anywhere till after ten.'

'Exactly,' she says as if she's proved something and flounces off to her bedroom.

I'd better put the washing in.

Victimised again by the Northern line conspiracy, I'm held hostage in the tunnel between Euston and Warren Street. Names is an anagram of means. Chris Putnam's name = means human script. Dan is an anagram of DNA and and. Name is also an anagram of Amen. The train starts again, but I'm going to be late. There's a man looking at me.

Another man is looking at me too. From the other side. Younger. They've got me trapped between them. They're going to make their move soon. They're waiting for something. A sign. So now I'm waiting for it too, but I don't know what I'm waiting for, what the sign is, what to be afraid of. I don't know what they'll do to me or why. The young one to the right hides his face behind a newspaper. The other pretends to read the ads. The train still waits in the still, dark tunnel. I wait. They wait. I can't watch them both. Not at the same time.

If I move will they follow me? Or will that make it too obvious for them?

I get up and hold my black nylon bag in my hand, gripping it. I could swing it against a face. I feel its weight, its weaponry, its defence. The one who was looking at the ad looks back at me. So I'll take on the other. I put my hand in my pocket and take my keys into my fist, arming my knuckles. I walk past him. He doesn't move.

The train lurches and gasps.

'Leave me alone! Okay? Leave me alone!' and he looks at me in protest but I run, don't wait for a response. I didn't mean to speak. I didn't want to give them reasons to spill into their action, their violence. I am struggling through the door from one carriage to the next and slamming it behind me as the train judders into activity.

As the doors start to close, I get off at Warren Street to shake them and they haven't followed me. I must wait for the next train. I am going to be even later.

Now I wish I hadn't.

Because I'm late getting to the theatre, I have to get through the crowd at the stage door and Norman the doorman insists on ringing through to Leo's dressing room before he'll let me up even though he's seen me every night for weeks now.

'I'll send him up then, Mr Martin. Thank you, sir,' he says and hangs up.

*

The dressing-room door's closed with the star in my face and Leo's name. I'M NOT REAL. There's a voice, not his, and I feel awkward about going right in so I knock and the voice stops and Leo answers 'Come in' but with something absent in the way it sounds, so I open it slowly.

A tall tanned man stands above and behind Leo in the chair and the man looks mid-sentence and he stares at me like it's a challenge.

'Come on in, Chris. Vic, this is Chris. Chris, Vic Hemitt, Helen's boyfriend,' says Leo, getting up and sitting down again.

I close the door behind me, but don't feel I can embrace Leo with Vic, the Victim, in the room. I guess he knows about us, but I don't know what he knows or how much and I feel guilty to be here at all. I feel I've walked in on a situation. Vic acknowledges my presence with a nod and goes on speaking through the stiff rictus of his mouth.

'All I'm saying is that I'm sick of this situation and Helen's done her part. More than that. Now it's up to you to do yours.'

'But Helen doesn't want a divorce.' Leo won't look Vic in the eye or even in the mirror. He looks up at me instead.

'She will if you say that's what *you* want. She only doesn't want one because of your blessed career. All you need is to tell her she doesn't need to go that far. That's all I'm asking you to do. She doesn't need to be a martyr. She's doing it for your career and you're letting her. Come on, Leo, be a man. A divorce isn't going to hurt you. *You* tell him,' he adds looking at me.

'I know that,' Leo interrupts as if to protect me from answering. 'I don't mind. I want a divorce, but it's not that simple.'

'Well, for fuck's sake, why not?' He's shouting now.

'She doesn't want me to.'

'What the hell are you talking about? Jesus, man, this is killing her. Have you seen her lately? I mean, *have you*? Fuck.'

I know why Leo can't explain it to Vic. He can't tell him how much hurt he thinks he's brought on Helen. To Vic, it would seem sanctimonious or callous or arrogant to say it. Nor can he tell him that to cut her off for good would only make the hurt worse. He'd have to tell Vic what everyone but Vic knows, that he's second-best, make-do, and that he's not really what Helen wants. But Vic's right too. Leo has got to do it. Someday soon, he's going to have to tell her that she can't have what she wants. Even though Leo has got it all. And even though she helped him get it.

Leo looks at me and I look at his face, his beautiful face. He's wearing the face of Hamlet in anguish. I keep my gaze on his eyes and nod slowly. 'All right,' he says. 'I'll tell her. I'll tell her I want out, but don't expect me to do any convincing.'

'You'd better. Because if you don't,' Vic is making for the door already, 'I warn you, man, there's shit I can do to make you.'

Leo turns to Vic. 'Come on, Vic, don't get melodramatic. We're all friends.'

'Melodramatic! Good one,' he says leaving the door open and shouting behind him as he heads down the corridor, 'coming from a fucking drama queen. Melodramatic!' His voice fades as soon as the sound of his feet starts to pound down the wooden stairs. People in various states of undress are leaning out of their dressing rooms or standing along the corridor to see what's going on.

There is silence in the room for a moment before I know what to do. I close the door and press my face to Leo's. He sobs. I clench his body to me, its taut, real mass, and I hold him fast, hold him till the sharp intakes of his breath subside and he whispers, 'I'm sorry. Happy birthday.' And I kiss him.

'We'd better go,' he says.

'What did he mean?'

'When?'

'There's shit he can do?'

Leo waves it away with his hand and pulls a tissue from

the box in front of the mirror. 'Nothing. Don't worry about it. I mean, I understand his situation. He wants to be with Helen because he loves her or, I don't know, maybe he just needs to so he can stay in the country with her, but she won't commit. So he blames me. And he's right, because Helen, well, I can't imagine what it was like for her. It's bad enough getting this much attention when the media are on your side, but with everyone in the world thinking you're some slutty bitch when you know, and everyone who knows you knows, that it couldn't be further from the truth.'

'He won't do anything, will he though?'

'What? Like talk to the press? No, no. It'll be fine. I'll talk to Helen tomorrow. Or maybe I'd better have lunch with her. I'll see. Let's get out of here.'

*

It was nearly midnight (the end of Chris's birthday and the beginning of his twin's) when Leo parked in the garage beneath the apartment. On entering the apartment, Leo expected to see a lavish spread resplendently awaiting them. Chris had fewer expectations, but had some inkling of arrangements having been made behind the scenes. However, when Leo opened the door, Chris was not sure in what vein he should react to what they saw. Leo's initial reaction was similarly confused, then besmirched, then belittled, then outraged.

Leo telephoned the police and amid profuse apologies suggested it might be better if Chris weren't there when they arrived. He being Leo Martin, they would not be long and so Chris left on foot, heading towards Notting Hill Gate in the hope of finding a taxi or a night bus. After he had left, Leo had a few moments during which he assessed the losses. A few items were missing, of varying but intrinsically limited value, but which, like Elvis's Q-tips or Napoleon's penis, were potentially valuable by their provenance, being proof of the reality, normality even, of the celebrity in question. There was even the possibility that such items, like a cryptogram or a code, might be carriers of information yielding secrets pertaining to the achievement of fame and fortune. Like the

DNA in a single cell, perhaps such objects contained an entire human script that could be unravelled, read, and so all the secrets of celebrity revealed.

Leo realised that he had not yet given Chris his birthday present, but on searching for it, he discovered that it too was among the items taken by the dissembling caterers.

Chris never discovered what his present would have been and it was several days before Leo had the opportunity to replace it with another first edition, this time of *Peter Pan*, which was, apparently, of particular value on account of the considerable number of misprints in the text, not to mention Barrie's own signature. By the time Chris received it, however, he had other, more pressing concerns.

*

One thirty and I'm too het up for sleep and this click-click-click thing is keeping me awake. It must be tinnitus, but it's click-click-click all the time. I should see a doctor. Maybe I'm just lonely. Maybe I should grow a miniature garden in a window box. Just when I do want to talk to her, Elsi's asleep.

She's barely touched the food she made which is piled on the side in the kitchen. I should be hungry, but I'm too tired for food.

In the sitting room, the table is still laid and the three long joints still lie unsmoked although there is evidence that Elsi has got through several others on her own. I help myself to one, light it and put *The Truman Show* in the video and stare at the story.

I stare and I wonder. Why does he take so long to realise? Why doesn't he see what's really going on? It's all a conspiracy. His life's just a TV show. But even the TV show's just in a movie. It's not real either. They never think of that. The TV director never thinks to himself that maybe he's not real either. He's being directed too. None of it is real. Why do they never think of that?

Sometimes, I feel like that.

Chromosome 16
Poor Dan is in a Droop

'You are yourself. You might change everything about your identity but you cannot change your awareness of yourself as a separate being. The fantasised twin that we carry around in our minds is not only an idealised partner in the experience of being who we are, he is also a means of escape from the life we are living. Twins have often told us that theirs is the most precious relationship imaginable, the closest experience one can have of being with another. Just by being twins, they have been able to reveal many answers to the riddles of existence. But they also show us that no matter how tantalisingly alike we may be, no one crosses the boundary between being alike and being the same. We might, as in this fantasy, be able to exchange lives, but we cannot exchange selves. There is finally no escape from being the people we were born to be.'

Lawrence Wright

'Hypocrite lecteur, – mon semblable, – mon frère.'
(Hypocrite reader, – my likeness, – my brother.)

Charles Baudelaire

Chris awoke in panic at an uncertain hour in front of the television, mumbling to itself, the video having long since finished. At first he was unable to pinpoint the focus of the fear he felt in the dark and suspected a dream. He had by that time begun to remember his dreams vividly nearly every night; however, he still was unsure that what he experienced as dreaming was the same as was commonly reported by others. His dreams had a lucid quality; that is not to say that in them he was aware he was dreaming. On the contrary, increasingly, they were like heretical secrets disclosed to him in whispers in the night. He experienced them as real events, relived rather than invented narratives. Even so, whilst dreaming, he was also aware that there was something suspect about reality, that all this was happening to him, but as someone else, that there were other levels, other truths lurking behind the layers of paint, palimpsestic nightmares just as genuine as what he was experiencing. His dreams, however, were not normally reefs of fear. Even when they were, any lingering dread would shrink into the darkness as he felt the warmth of Leo beside him and sometimes he'd reach out in the blackness to be sure, to be safe. But that night, awaking alone on the sofa, in the flat which was itself made strange by the uncertain light of the television and the strained radiance before daybreak, Chris was disorientated and afraid.

Failing to find just cause for alarm, he felt anxious about Dan, from whom he had not heard the previous day. Despite it being conveniently close to his own, it was not unprecedented for Dan to forget Chris's birthday, although it was unusual. However, after further consideration, Chris could recall no direct communication with Dan for nearly a month and a half. It was not unusual for them often to go weeks without speaking, on the basis that, being brothers and twins, when communications were resumed, it would be *in media res*, as naturally as if there had been no more than a pause in a continuous conversation. Besides, even though there had indeed been no *real* contact, there had been emails (self-obsessed on Dan's part, evasive on Chris's). But, as even he was beginning to acknowledge to himself, Chris had been wanting to avoid Dan for a variety of reasons. In particular, Dan had become, for Chris, the corporeal representation of two of his greatest insecurities: the first being that he still owed some duty to their father and about whose death he was, to say the least, unreconciled; the second being that Leo Martin did not really love *him*. The fact that he now wanted to talk to Dan, indeed was feeling an increasingly desperate need to do so, made Chris believe that, in terms of at least one of these insecurities, he had become ready to confront his fears.

His fears, however, found another foothold. Despite retiring to his bed, Chris was deprived of sleep by the notion that some incubus of his reverie had taken his brother into its grasp. He lay awake watching his ever-slowing clock and wondering how early he could phone Dan to wish him happy birthday and set his mind at rest.

As it happened, he was able neither to set his mind at rest nor to wish Dan anything, for, when Chris telephoned at one minute to eight a.m., neither Dan nor his answerphone responded. Calling his mobile yielded only the vacuity of a click-click-click. Nor did Chris have any more success at ten past eight, nor again at twenty-five past, nor at nine twenty-one when he arrived at the laboratory, nor indeed all day. By the end of the day, Chris had enjoined Leo to try, who had enjoined Helen, who had enjoined various friends and associates including Angel, the Clerkenwell Gallery Manager and Dan's dealers – both artistic and narcotic – all to no avail.

Eventually, Chris, reminding himself most deliberately of Morton's Fork and Occam's Razor and reasoning accordingly, decided that the least unlikely explanation, with as yet no countermanding evidence, requiring the fewest assumptions, was that Dan was either away for a few days and had neglected to inform anyone or that he had fallen prey to no worse a fate than the clasps of some carnal conquest, or, perhaps even conquests. Most probably, whilst Chris had been exciting a small but tumescent body of concern, Dan's own excited and tumescent body was unconcernedly captive in some bawd's bunk. Meanwhile, his answerphone had surely either been filled with messages or had merely been switched off.

Having furnished himself with a reason for Dan's disappearance, Chris was able to accept it for a further week, during which time he experienced the breathless paralysis of a series of panic attacks. These he blamed on Dan's accursed irresponsibility. Leo, meanwhile, afraid to countenance more disturbing possibilities, would provide solace by remarking buoyantly on Dan's frustrating but quixotic charm.

Eventually, Chris decided that not even Dan could remain ensconced with a woman (or even the same few women) for more than ten days and he became quite frantic. Leo therefore arranged that Chris and Helen (who had a key) should meet at Dan's apartment at the Evendam's Warehouse on the evening of Monday the third of July. It was convenient for Leo that he would at that time be otherwise engaged as Hamlet. Coward that he was, for him, every meeting with Helen was a confrontation, with his past, with his guilt and with the breached deal with fortune broken again by each moment he spent with Chris. He was also scared about what might be discovered at Dan's apartment.

Despite his fears, however, Leo had already met Helen as he had promised to Vic. He had realised it had come to the point where he had no choice. He had said he wanted a divorce, for her own good. She had said she did not. She claimed that he should not flatter himself into thinking it was because of any hopes of a reconciliation which she might still cherish, but rather because their marriage was the one reason why she could not remarry. She explained that Vic was determined they should be wed. However, her fondness for him was not deep enough that she was sure that marriage to him was what she wanted. Yet, she was equally sure she did not want to be without him. The self-reliant Helen Bossi had become afraid to be alone. If Leo wanted to help her in any way, she had pleaded piteously, he should tell Vic that it was *he* who did not want the divorce. He should think of some reason. Having failed to think of such a reason that might prove acceptable to Vic, Leo had, as yet, done no more about it.

Doing nothing was as honourable as any available course of action. Think of Hamlet, think of Job, think of Jesus before Pilate. Being a coward has a long and honourable tradition and they all got what was coming to them in the end.

*

It's pissing down and aggressively cold for the middle of summer. I've tried buzzing Dan's flat. No one answers. I'm impatient now. And nervous. Get a move on, Helen. The rain click-click-clicks on the pavement. It's only just past eight o'clock, but already it's getting dark. It's the clouds. They're threatening thunder but don't look like they've got the violence. There's more violence in the faces on the street closing in on mine and passing by. I see faces full of lightning.

I think I keep seeing one face in particular, but I know I

217

must be imagining it. There's a man over there now and he's got the face. Watching me, but never looking my way. Always out of range. He can afford to be closer now, because I can't see the face because of the rain. The hunched shoulders though, the cigarette smoke rising scornfully in the damp. The flak jacket. Who'd be out in the rain unless they were watching me?

I hear the footsteps of high heels now, coming the other way, and I turn and the woman with the black umbrella slapping through the puddles must be Helen, but I don't know because I've only met her once and she looks tighter, frailer, even thinner. But she recognises me and hails me across fifteen foot of splashing pavement and draws the keys from her clutch bag. 'Sorry I'm late.'

'That's okay. You're not really,' I say even though she is and I follow her through the door which she's hardly strong enough to shoulder open on her own so I help her and as I turn I look across the street at the man who's no longer there or who maybe never was or who maybe wasn't there because of me.

We wait in the lobby for the lift to come down. She shakes her umbrella, flapping and wrestling it shut. I don't know what to say to her. I feel guilty in front of her. About Leo. About that night at the gallery. About Dan even. 'Sorry for dragging you out,' I start to say, but she starts to speak at the same time and so I say sorry and let her talk.

'It's very mysterious this, isn't it?' she says.

'Yes, it is.'

'But I'm sure there's nothing to worry about.'

'Yes, I'm sure.'

'Just like Dan, isn't it? To vanish without telling a soul where he's gone.'

'Yes, just like him,' I say and the lift goes ping and even though it takes a while for the doors to open, we don't have to say anything to each other while we wait because that's how it goes with lifts and in the lift we don't have to say anything either or meet each other's gaze. Instead we can each think alone about what we're about to see. It lurches upwards and I look to my left and there is Dan in the lift bedraggled and soaked and I realise it's me and the mirror starts to steam up.

'You okay?' she says.

'Yeah, fine. I'm fine. Don't I look fine?'

'You look fine, just a bit freaked out. Don't be scared. Don't worry. Everything's going to be okay.'

As Helen opens the flat she takes a deep breath and lets it out with a sigh, but the door opens and it's immediately clear there's no one here. The air feels sluggish as it does when it lacks the turbulence of moving bodies or fresh air or heating. The apartment is untidy, but, being big, not very. There's no note on the great glass coffee table. Helen immediately marches through the rooms.

'Nothing. No sign of him. Definitely not here,' she says, 'and it doesn't look like the cleaner's been lately either.'

'He's got a cleaner?'

'Don't you two ever talk?'

'Not often,' I say. 'Not enough.'

'We could call her if I knew her number, but I don't even know her name. I'll see if I can find his Filofax or something. In the meantime you try to think if there's anywhere in particular he might have gone.'

And suddenly I know. I've been so focused on him being here that I didn't think about it, but now I *know* that he's not, it's obvious. 'Le Noires,' I say, 'he'll have gone to Le Noires.'

'Where?'

'Our parents' house, where our parents used to live. It's his now.'

'Well, go on then, call him.' She grabs the cordless phone from its holster on the breakfast bar and hands it to me but I can't get a line and I push a few buttons but it's dead. 'I'll try the one in the bedroom,' but that doesn't work either, so I come back and say, 'It looks like he's been cut off.' A gust of wind blows rain against the wide windows and makes them bang like an animal trying to get in and startling us both.

'Try him on this then,' says Helen handing me her mobile. Her fingers are long and old and cold as I take the phone.

And I can't remember the number – the disconnected memory shocks me – my own childhood phone number, the one Mummy made us practice in case of emergencies since before I can remember. It comes back to me though and I have to practise it in my head first and now I dial and wait for it to connect and it rings. It rings again. Again. Again. I'll leave it for ten rings, I think, and start to count them in my head. One. Two. Three. Four. Five. Six. Seven. Eight. Nine. Ten. Just another five more. One. Two. Thr—

'—king talking to me, you hear?' It's so loud I snatch it from my ear. It's Dan, but he's screaming and must have started talking before putting the receiver to his mouth. 'I said stop fucking with me, okay?'

'Dan, it's me.'

'You fucker. You cunt. I told you, I don't want you 'round me any more. What you want with me?'

'Dan, it's me. Chris.'

There's a pause.

'Hello? Dan?' I say. There is no voice, but a kind of sigh, a rearrangement of sound, at the other end of the line. 'Dan? You okay? What's up?'

'It's all fucked up, bro. It's all fucked up.' His voice breaks up.

'What is? What are you talking about?'

'And this guy won't leave me alone.'

'What guy, Dan?' He doesn't answer. 'What guy, Dan?' The space of silence on the phone stretches out awkwardly with only his heaving breaths to punctuate it. I leave it a moment and now I say, 'Are you on something, Dan? Are you okay?'

'He wants to make me do what he wants. He keeps telling me in my head. I thought he was phoning. He wants to—' and he trails off again but as if he's not stopped talking but just removed the receiver from his mouth. It clicks. He's hung up. But it was absent-minded rather than angry, as if he's forgotten how to use the phone.

'How do I do redial?'

'What's going on?' Helen asks.

'Just tell me how to redial. Quick.'

'Star, star, send.' I do it and wait.

It rings again. This time Dan picks up immediately. '—op fucking with me, Johnny! Stop! Stop! Stop!' and he hangs up again, abruptly and deliberately this time, but again he thinks he's talking to someone else.

'We'd better call an ambulance or the police or something,' I say. 'He's in a bad way. I think he must be on something. Maybe just an ambulance.'

Helen looks at me expectantly. I do nothing. 'Well, go on then,' she says and I press nine, and again. And again. Send.

*

'Well?' says Helen.

'Well, what?'

'What did he say?'

'They're sending someone.'

'No, Dan. What did Dan say?'

'He thinks someone's after him.' I stare out at the Thames, kneading itself in the weight of the rain and I wonder if this glass is reinforced or if I could throw myself against it and tumble down with the raindrops and glass into the water below.

'Who?'

'I don't know. Someone called John, I think, or Johnny. Do you know him?'

'That doesn't help. For God's sake, everyone's called John. Who is he?'

'I don't know, a stalker maybe. Or the boyfriend of one of Dan's girlfriends?'

'Something like that, perhaps.' She pauses and says, 'I don't know how much you know about certain things and it's not my place to tell you.'

'What do you mean? What do you know?'

'Nothing,' she says. 'Really nothing.'

'Or maybe he's just going mad. Do you think he's going mad?'

'He's always seemed relatively stable to me.'

What does she mean *relatively*? She thinks it's me instead. She thinks I'm going mad. 'What do you mean?'

'Well, he's an artist.'

'Oh, I see what you mean.' I pause. 'You two, you've ... I mean, you two are pretty close, right? Someone can seem stable but, underneath, they're losing it, you know?'

'Chris, I know he's not everything he'd have people believe, especially when it comes to women. And he's had his off-the-wall moments, even his inadequacies, but I wouldn't have said he's had more than anyone else.'

'Do you think there is someone though? Someone after him?'

'Who knows, Chris? Let's just get him safe and worry about it then.'

'It's just, it's just I think someone's after me.' Who's been following me and who beat me up that night? Is it him? 'Now he's got Dan. I think he's after me too.' What else can he do? Why does he want to harm me?

Everywhere.

*

It did not take long for the doctors, nurses and psychiatrist of Victoria Hospital in Kirkcaldy to come to the clinical conclusion that the patient's interests might be better served in a specialist institution nearer his London home. Dan Putnam was, therefore, transferred to the Maudsley Hospital on Wednesday the fifth of July, courtesy of his PPP insurance plan, which, fortunately, along with his panoramic rent, had been paid by direct debit. However, as Chris discovered, Dan's red telephone bill (dated the third of June), his council tax and various other items of expenditure had not been met in the month or so since Dan's postbox had last been emptied. Presumably that also explained the absence of the cleaning lady. Further enquiries revealed that no one had seen or heard from Dan since shortly after the beginning of the month.

At work, having just given Nicole another excuse why he would not be able to make the latest appointment she was attempting to arrange with Sir Hugo, Chris scanned the recent emails from Dan for mentions of Johnny. They were all just rants about the show to which he had sent his brief replies. Except one, however, an earlier one, one he had neglected to answer, timed and dated '00:23, Thursday 01/06/00'. He opened it again. It said: 'Bro, where you been? Need to talk. Call me on the home number, trashed the mobile. D.' He feared that particular email represented the critical moment at which by not answering, Chris had placed himself outside Dan's confidence.

Interpolating a parallel with another ignored email, Chris dreaded that his wilful indolence would again cause misery and shame. He nursed a terror that situations were mirroring each other, the same but not quite, reversed perhaps. Things that were habitually together were now coming apart, dividing, bifurcating, recombining. He started to look for pairs of situations, fearing them when he found them, fearing the absent partner even more when he couldn't.

Partly out of guilt for what he felt was his recent neglect of his twin, Chris settled Dan's unpaid bills (expecting to be reimbursed at some future date), overdrawing himself at the bank once again. He decided he could not afford to have the telephone reconnected. When Dan was better, he reasoned, he could do it for himself and in any case, he would not be needing the phone until then.

*

'Hi there, love,' says Leo closing the door and kissing me as he comes into the dressing room, glistening with sweat and make-up and the glow of the curtain call. 'How's Dan?' He sits down in front of the mirror to remove his make-up.

'They're going to let me see him tomorrow.'

'I'll come with you,' he says, pauses, and his reflection looks at me. 'If you want?'

'I really want you to, Leo. Honestly, I'm dreading going in on my own, but they said it would probably be best if visitors were kept to a minimum for the time being.'

'That's good. I mean – you know what I mean,' he pauses again. 'Have they said any more about how he is? About what's wrong?'

'Not really. Just gone schizoid of some sort, I think. They're not very helpful on whys or whens.' I think of my phone call earlier to a psych nurse, clearly immune to anyone who wanted anything more or anything different from what she intended.

'What do you think?' he asks.

'There's this Johnny character. Whoever he is.'

'If he even exists.'

223

'I don't know.' I don't want to tell Leo about the people who follow me. It's not that I don't want to, just that I don't want to talk about it, as if words make it more real. I know I'm imagining it anyway. 'It could be drugs, maybe. Went over the rainbow and couldn't get back.'

'But he doesn't really do anything other than sniff and blow.'

'Yes, but he does a lot.' We both nod but it doesn't seem sufficient so I ask Leo what he thinks.

'His art show, maybe?'

'I know it went badly, but it wasn't that bad, surely? I mean, Dan's got rhino hide, always has done.'

'That's the point,' says Leo. 'He doesn't mind being slagged off, but he hates to be ignored. Dan defines himself by other people's idea of him. Maybe he's just lost himself.'

I can't see it. I can't see how the fact that it didn't get much coverage can harm him. Why can't he just move on to the next one? 'That can't be all it is? Jesus, I'm a nobody and *I* don't care.'

'Despite appearances, my love, you two are *not* the same,' says Leo's reflection emphatically. 'Don't underestimate the importance of Dan's vanity, his constant need to be the centre of attention. If he doesn't get constant approval – or disapproval even, it doesn't matter – if he doesn't get some kind of a reaction, he doesn't even know he exists.'

That's true. As a kid he used to stop still if he was playing and thought no one was watching him. As if he thought there was no point. 'I guess our father comes into it too.'

'Of course.'

'I don't mean just the grief – I don't know how much it affected him that way. Well, not superficially. But the withdrawal of his approval.' That was always there. He's always been the one who got to feel superior, because Dan got through to him, whereas I, I was just able to feel different, my own idea of me. 'You know, suddenly that's gone and his sense of self just disappears.'

'You know, "us" might come into it too,' says Leo tentatively.

'Does he know about us?'

'You haven't told him?'

'No. Have you?'

224

'Well, no,' he says, 'but, I don't know, I just supposed someone must have.'

'What's it got to do with him anyway?' I feel guilty, defensive. I think I make Leo feel guilty too.

'Well, there's always been, I don't know, a frisson between Dan and me. Nothing serious, but he'd flirt with me and, well, I probably flirted back. But now, well, now *we're* together, assuming he knows, maybe he takes it as yet another sign that he's not so attractive because he judges himself by comparing everything about himself to you. As his twin, you're his benchmark. Well, maybe not in everything, but, like you said, his whole sense of self is wrapped up in what other people make of him. He's like a falling tree in the wood – the sound might as well not exist if there's no one to hear.'

Or like a cat in a box. 'All this would explain why he went up to Dunmarrick.'

'How so?'

'For the attention. They love him up there. Local boy made good. And there are the family roots. He could define himself by our parents, our past.' Something's bothering me but I almost don't know how to say it.

'What's wrong?'

'I just thought, we've got the same past, the same parents, the same genes, you know. Maybe it's something back there, in our upbringing or something genetic that's made him ... Maybe I—'

'Oh come on.' Leo turns to face me in the chair and I can see us in the mirror, this selfish fear in my face. He touches my cheek. 'Come on. You're not the same. You're not.' And he turns back to the mirror.

But we are. I have a feeling reality is slipping from me too. Johnny is following me too, trying to get inside my head. It doesn't even matter if he's real. It's just time, a certain inevitable period of time, a clock in our genes, our upbringing. Dan's lost it. And we're the same. I'm losing it too. I'm okay when I'm with Leo, but I'm scared to be alone. I put my hand out just to connect with him, his shoulder. Leo *is* real, touching him is real. But he gets up just as I'm reaching out and he walks over to where his clothes are hanging and starts to take off his costume, baring the softened angles of muscles across his shoulders and down his back. It feels too desperate to go over to him, to press myself against him. I'm on my own in this. Dan has gone over into madness. I've never been without him. There is a genetic imperative here. My time is coming. His madness is coming for me also. We are the same. It is inevitable. It is only a matter of time.

*

I manage to get out of the lab early and catch the 68 which stops just round the back of Queen's College and which goes all the way to the Maudsley but takes forever. I used to do this journey most days as a fresher when I lived in halls on Denmark Hill, but I don't often go south of the river now.

I get a window seat and try to read, *The Dice Man*, but I can't get into it, the type seems to roll and scroll, conspiring to keep its meanings hidden, so I stare out at the real world projected on the windows. The real world gets realer down Kingsway and round the Aldwych as the bus takes on the commuters, but crossing the river, past the IMAX, the reality starts to fade. Most of the people bottle out at Waterloo. By Elephant & Castle we are beyond the normal – the metallic space craft on the roundabout squaring up to the great block of a shopping centre with its tears of pigeon shit staining the walls painted red in a tired attempt to hide the reality of its monstrous hopelessness. 'Behold,' says the sign outside the columns of the Metropolitan Tabernacle, 'my desire is that the Almighty would answer me, and that mine adversary had written a book. Surely I would take it upon my shoulder, and bind it as a crown to me. — Job 31'

The bus edges down Walworth Road like a slow ghost train past faces full of challenge. Now Camberwell – everyone so fucked-up and unreal, living lives that exist only in their heads, railing with their Special Brew at the pubic scrub of Camberwell Green. By the time we get to the Maudsley, no one distinguishes the nervous faces of the diagnosed from the rest of the deranged.

I get off with King's Hospital on my left making the Maudsley look inconspicuous, like a place of normal illness and mortality. Madness is normality here. I belong to this. It wants me too.

Inside the Maudsley, voices call from down the halls like echoes in a swimming baths and the air is tight with disinfectant. Signs hang down everywhere, disorientating me because I do not know where I am supposed to go and I cannot find reception. I am not scared of hospitals. I'm not. I've dissected corpses – well, watched other people do it – and I know what we're made of. Rubbery tubes, plastic bags of blood, inflexible bone compacted under the skin like a well-packed suitcase. But this place, this is an outpost, where people come or are sent when they're at the edge, when there's nothing to be seen, the sickness is packed away, when they can no longer distinguish fear from paranoia, reality from hallucination. The light is heavy. The strip lights are bright and unforgiving and buzz constantly, enough to unnerve anyone, let alone the fucked-up.

I walk down long corridors whose perspective makes me feel bigger and smaller and everyone walking past stares at me, full-eyed. No one offers help or asks for it. I need a plan. I cannot aimlessly wander and so I follow signs saying 'Way Out', guessing the way out must also be the way in and reception must be there, but I turn corners and climb stairs and come to barred wooden doors and I open them and am outside, ejected. I should run. I should get away while I have the chance, while the place does not want me yet. But I fear my path is determined – like Dan, I belong here. I walk around the outside and find another door which is locked and another which now offers me a path to 'General Enquiries'.

Behind glass like a bank cashier, protecting her from the psychosis that drifts in and out, the receptionist is a nurse talking on the telephone and she says my name and is saying something about me, something hateful, and I hear it distinctly I think, but nothing here is distinct and I don't know how she knows my name. I do not want to see my brother here. She notices me and sees I'm trying to listen and she hangs up. 'Can I help you?' she says and I say, 'What were you just saying on the phone?' and she says, 'I'm sorry?' and I repeat the question and she says that she's sorry but it's confidential and I say, 'But it was about me,' and, of course, she says it wasn't and I say that I heard her say my name and she says she didn't, she doesn't even know my name and now I think I can't be sure. 'Now,' she says, how can she help me? I look her in the eye, but she's giving nothing away so I ask her where Dan is and she asks who I am and I tell her and she tells me a ward and room number where Dan is and gives me directions which I cannot follow and she thanks me, which doesn't seem right.

What's she hiding? She's got files on me. On the phone she was getting information about me, instructions. She knows I'm next. Direct him into it, she was told, he'll come quietly.

I head off in the way I think I'm supposed to go and I get lost again until I find a burly nurse all in white whose cap is sticking up like rabbit's ears and I tell her the name of the ward and she says she'll take me and then looks at her watch pinned to her breast and says she's late and hurries away and I have to chase to keep up with her until suddenly she stops and turns around and points and says, 'There you go' and there is a broad smile, like a Cheshire cat, another nurse, a tall black man.

'Excuse me, please, which way do I go from here?'

He grins wider. 'Depends where you're trying to get to.'

'Erm, I'm not sure.'

'Don't matter too much which way you go then,' but he steps aside and there's a door which says in marker pen on card 'D. Putnam'.

'You his brother, then?' says the nurse through his fixed grin and he waits for me to nod. 'Okay. In you go then, but he's doped up at the moment, so you won't get much out of him. But don't worry. That's when it's best, then. That's when you ain't got to worry about what you say, because you just say what's on your mind to them, whatever you want. Don't matter. It's almost like therapy for you as well as them. I'll come get you, then, when he needs to be left alone. Okay?' I nod again. 'Shit, you guys look alike,' he says and shrugs and disappears, smiling to himself.

I open the door.

Dan lies in the bed and stares. Looking like him at the moment is no compliment. He's pale and if I thought there was such a thing as a soul, I'd say it had deserted his body.

He slowly moves his head, repetitively, up and down, as I pad forward. He turns his neck, showing me his face but no recognition and he continues to nod. There are vast bouquets of flowers by the bed on either side and only now does it occur to me I should have brought something, grapes, puzzle books, anything. An offering, a sacrifice, to keep his demons at bay, to make me an outsider here, not a resident of unreality. 'Hi, Dan. It's me. How you doing?' He says nothing, but watches me. 'Who're the flowers from?' and I look to see and I can see the gift tag on the ones over there. They're from Helen. But these, where's the tag? Here. 'Get better soon, Chris and Leo xx.' I didn't send them, it must have been Leo. Unless I did.

I look round for a chair and there's one just behind me, so I try to pull it forward but it's fixed to the floor so I sit on the edge of it and touch his hand which I expect to be cold, but it's warm. Come on, I tell myself, he's not dead. I squeeze it.

'Yo, bro,' he says, slowly, but it still surprises me. I take away my hand. I don't want to touch him with his mind still there, in there somewhere. It's too, too infectious.

'How you doing?' I ask to his face, but he does not react or it takes too long to register, like he's in a different world, the same, just as real, but running at a different pace. Eventually, he nods.

I don't know what to say next and the nurse was wrong, this isn't easy, but maybe it is, maybe it could get worse. Maybe it will. I don't want to be here when it does. I don't want to be here. I feel sucked in already.

I need to say something, so I say, 'I'm okay,' as if he'd asked. 'I should tell you something. I'm going out with Leo. I mean, we're an item, you know. I don't know if you knew. Have been for a while now. It's wonderful. Of course we're always having to sneak around. It's not exactly … free.'

I pause to think of something else. He watches me without expression but even the absence makes it seem that thoughts are going on inside, cold calculations, but the effort to make his face correspond is simply beyond him.

'I've been getting into anagrams. I try to do them in my head.' I pause. 'Maudsley Hospital is "a mad spell hits you". I worked it out on the way over.' I smile trying to make light of it and think that probably I should not have said it even though he does not react. The Dan I know would find it funny or weird at least, even at his own expense, but this replica continues to watch me, his gaze shifting slowly between my mouth and my eyes and back again.

'And my name's "human script" which is kind of funny, don't you think, given what I do? I mean. You know. The human genome. And you're "DNA". Just the Dan bit. Obviously. Daniel is "denial". And our father was called Gene which, well, you know, I don't even need to ...' I stop because he looks like he wants to say something. 'What is it?'

Slowly he mouths words and his eyebrows furrow seriously, furtively, like it's a secret, like we're being monitored. I even look round to check there's no one here. I cannot hear what he says though. I bend my ear closer to his mouth.

'It's not.'

'What's not, Dan? Gene? Yes, it was.'

'No. It's. Not. Eugene.'

'What do you mean?'

'Not. Wendy. Either.'

'What do you mean "not Wendy"? Do you mean Grandma?'

'It's not true.'

'I don't understand.'

'Our family – you asked me. Your email.'

'You mean the pedigree research? You looked into it?'

'You don't know the half of it. None of it's real. Check,' he says and closes his eyes which is enough to show he cannot say more for the moment. I don't get it though. Eugene and Wendy are our family names, our father's family. For generations. The first-born son was always called Eugene. I only escaped the name because we were twins. And Grandma was called Wendy and I think her mother too. Our family was like that. Dan isn't making sense.

Of course he isn't. 'Okay,' I say sympathetically, 'I'll check.' He nods, but not at what I say. He just keeps nodding.

I wait for something to happen. But it doesn't. It won't. There's no clock in here. I can't leave till that nurse gets back because he said he would come and get me and I don't want it to look like I didn't want to stay as long as I could.

230

'You know, I realised something a few weeks ago,' I say, because I can't think of anything else and because, like the nurse said, you just say what's on your mind. 'Our father, he was right. In a way. Everything *is* predetermined. But it's not like what he believed. It's not Fate or Destiny or anything spooky, you know. We're just not free because there's always a reason why we do things, a reason for our choices, even if they're crap reasons, and we can't do anything about the reasons because they're in the past. See? I think it helps, you know, to accept things as they come, to realise there's no freedom, even though it feels like there is because you don't know what's coming.'

He has stopped nodding and just stares at me now as if I'm saying something horrific. Is this a reaction? I don't know if that's a good thing, but I guess it must be. I need to say something else, to keep going, but I cannot look at him to say it. 'Erm, but lately, I feel I haven't been in control. Maybe it's realising I'm not free, but it doesn't feel like I'm even a player. I feel I'm acting out something someone else has set up for me. Everything's lost its edge of credibility, like I'm a bit-part actor in my own life. I don't know, I'm talking junk. Maybe it's what comes of going out with someone who's, well, more than I ever thought I would have.' I pause and think about that and then just carry on, making it up as I go along and listening to what's coming out of my mouth as if it's a stranger talking. 'It's just, I've got this theory. What if I'm right? Everything is predetermined, but it's not all down to cause and effect, instead it's down to' – I search for the word – '*design*? Like a god or a creator *contrived* this whole reality? Made it up? I know it sounds silly and don't get me wrong, it's not what I think, it's just a thought experiment, a hypothesis. But there are things that seem too *neat*, like the anagrams thing and, well, lots of other stuff. For instance, there are times when cause and effect seems to break down. Like this creator got sloppy and skipped a few details. And then things happen for no reason. Like, why are you here? And other things happen, but nothing comes of it. You know, I can handle not being in control of my life, but I don't want someone else—'

Dan starts to laugh loudly and I look up with a start and wonder what to do and he's rocking backwards and forwards in the bed and laughing hysterically to himself and he's trying to speak through the roars and he's saying, 'Johnny. Johnny. Johnny. You too.'

'Who's Johnny?' I'm saying and I'm worried and I don't know what to do and he's laughing so much I think he might be hyperventilating and so I pull the cord for the nurse and pull it again and now I grab his shoulders to stop him rocking but he won't, he won't stop, stop. He rocks into my arms and starts to sob. And I ask him again, 'Who's Johnny?'

The smiling nurse appears behind me. I am still holding on to my brother. He is calmer now. A calmer stupor.

'What's up? Why you pull the cord, then?'

'He freaked out,' I say, without letting go, 'but he's okay now. We're okay now.'

'All right, then. But maybe it's time to leave him alone for a bit,' and I feel his big hands unclasping Dan's arms from around me, disentangling us. I yield to the separation and leave him to lie back on his pillows and begin to nod again. Slowly, up and down. I see myself lying there.

The nurse leads me out without a word. Closing the door, he asks if I'm okay.

'Yeah, fine. I'm fine. Don't you think I'm okay? I'm okay.'

'Yeah, sure, man, you're all right. Don't worry. It's not easy,' he says and I know he's only provoking me, but I am calm. Calm and careful. 'There's someone you need to see.'

'Me? No. I'm fine. Honestly. I'm okay now, just a bit … you know. I don't need to see anyone.'

'No. The consultant. You need to talk to the consultant. About your brother. She'll be able to answer your questions.'

'Okay,' I say, although I did not know I had any questions and he leads me across the corridor, showing me into a room without windows, with chairs, with a long table, each place set out with teacups and saucers as if in permanent readiness.

'She'll be along in a minute, okay?'

And I wait. And time passes. How much is impossible to say.

*

232

Time passes. I drift in and out. As if I cease to be, until I remember to exist again.

*

The door swings open and a short wide woman bustles in, a white coat and a large red novelty heart badge. 'Now,' she's already saying, commanding royally, lowering her red file to the table with the clap of an executioner's axe. 'Daniel Putnam.'

'No, I'm ...'

'*I* know that. You're the brother.'

'Yes.'

'Of course you are. We're keen to have a little chat with you.'

I cannot escape. I cannot escape the feeling that they want to talk to me because they know I too am teetering on the brink. Off his head, she's thinking.

'I'm not ...'

'We wanted to check something with you. About, ahem, "other visitors"?' She says it like there are quotation marks around it.

'Oh.'

'Our understanding is that you're Mr Putnam's "next of kin", but there's someone else we want to contact.'

'Who?'

'A' – she puffs herself up – 'a "special" friend?' She looks at me from beneath raised eyebrows, like I should understand, like I must be mad not to know who she's talking about. 'His – boyfriend, perhaps? Or, he has mentioned someone called Johnny a good deal? Might you know whom he may be? How we might contact him?'

'What?'

'Well, it's clear he's a person of some significance to your brother. We think maybe their relationship has experienced a – hiatus? It is evidently a cause of considerable – distress to him. It is our suspicion that there has, perhaps been an – unsettling relationship breakdown?'

'I was just with him. He was saying—' but she doesn't wait for me to finish.

'You were with him. Good. Can you tell us what he's like?'

'No, I mean with—'

'The relationship, is it abusive, maybe? Would it be helpful to get him in? Or perhaps his presence may be – agitating?'

Time passes.

'I mean, with Dan. I was ...' She opens her mouth as if to speak and then thinks better of it. We are both thinking about what to say next. She cannot mean what she's saying. 'He's not gay.'

'Do you know how we might contact him? This "Johnny"?'

Or maybe it's me. Maybe I'm not saying what I mean. 'It's me. I'm the one who's gay.'

'I see,' she says like she meant nothing by it.

'You've got us all mixed up. He's not gay. He's straight. Christ, he's slept with just about every woman in London. Ask them. Dan is straight.' But then I remember what Helen said. She knew something all along. How could I have missed that?

Off his head.

'Very good. Thanks for coming in, but you may care to leave it a few days before your next visit. I understand there was "an incident". We don't want to – disturb him, do we?' She knows something I don't. She doesn't want me to see Dan any more. She thinks we're not that close because I don't believe ...

'Wait a minute. Tell me. Tell me what you know.'

'Mr Putnam, I'm sure I don't know what you mean.' *Off with his head.* And she's gathering herself up, her papers, her file and bustling from the room and I follow her into the corridor but she's gone, but there's his wide white grin again, the nurse smiling with kind, cat-like eyes.

'Confidentiality,' he confides. 'Your brother's not been sectioned. He's here of his own free will. He's still signing his own consents so I can't tell you nothing, then, nothing he hasn't told you himself.' He looks at me and must see I'm out there myself, out at the edge. Another patient waiting to happen.

'Tell me what's going on, please? He's my brother. I need ...' He is sighing and looking like he might disappear again. 'I only want to know the medical facts.'

He looks happier with this, as if I've stumbled on a password, as if there's a different protocol. 'Okay then. I mean, this is general terms, you understand? Not about him. But it won't hurt if you work some things out for yourself. He sleeps around, yeah? Okay, then. Well you look up satyriasis, then.'

'Where?' I say and he sighs. 'Just tell me.'

'Books, man, textbooks.' He can see he might as well tell me. 'All right, I'm not saying anything in particular here, okay? This ain't no diagnosis. Satyriasis – you know? Don Juan complex – it's promiscuous behaviour usually to compensate for something. Failure. Inadequacy. Homosexuality. It's denial, really. Yeah, *denial*.'

Daniel.

He doesn't wait to be asked any more but says, 'Okay, man. Take care,' and turns on his heel and lopes off again, down the corridor, leaving me lost and alone. Alone because I was a pair and now I'm not. Dan has gone behind a door and I can't get him back. We are more alike than ever I knew.

I look through the porthole in the door at Dan sitting on the bed and nodding again. Nodding to himself, alone in himself. All this denial. It's all gone wrong for Dan somewhere down the line. Dan's gay too, but he must have been hating himself for it. Because of Daddy. He wanted to be the one Daddy loved, because, in the end, he needed it more than I did. For all his outrageousness, it was me, not him, who could admit this to our father knowing he'd hate me for it. And so he found some sadist, this Johnny, someone who'd fuck him over and give him what he deserved for being like me. Someone who's chasing him still, even if it's only in his head. Chasing him because now our father's dead, he's got no excuse to hate himself any more, but he does. All the years I faced our father with this and he was the strong one, but, no, he was weak, weaker even than me. He followed our father's script, allowed himself to be defined by him, have his life written for him until, one day, he wasn't there to write it any more. This is grief, grief denied. Dan nods behind the door.

There's a door waiting for me too.

This was ordained. It has come to pass and it shall for me also. Neither of us will escape. Never. I know that now.

Defiance or denial – every path leads to the same predestination. We are being led. He's after me too. Who? Johnny? Johnny must be the one who beat me up that night? Got us mixed up. Johnny's the one who makes these things happen, everything that has no cause? He's the cause. Dan nods.

Nothing I believed, nothing I thought I knew, turns out to be true. I have to doubt it all, even the evidence before my eyes.

I cannot come here again. I cannot see Dan again, not like this. Maybe never. This is a matter of my sanity. We are the same, on the same course and I must save myself, even if I never see my brother again. We are no longer a pair. Dan nods.

I must try to get away, even if to battle against what will be is futile. Someone has got this planned. Dan thinks Johnny's got this planned.

It's only a matter of time. Johnny's in control now. Maybe Johnny's the god, the creator, the one I'm afraid of. He's making it happen. He's not real, but a fear. Dan nods.

And I turn, turn away from him. I want to get out. I want to get out of here and I am starting to walk down the corridor the way I came, walking quickly and picking up pace. I canter. I run. I hear my footsteps echoing on the hard floor, click-click-clicking behind me. Click-click-click. That noise.

I stop. Still. The footsteps stop. I look behind me. They are my own footsteps. I am not being followed. I walk again. Click. Click. Click. I stop and look again. I am sure the sound is not my own, I am being followed, I am, but when I walk, he keeps perfect time with me. And when I stop, he stops. I look round. There's no one there. A game of Grandmother's Footsteps. But they follow me again when I run away. Click-click-click.

My echo? My imagination? I cannot know. Necessarily I cannot know. I cannot falsify. Click-click-click. I am running, down corridors, lost. Clickety-clickety-click. This is a nightmare. It is a dream. None of it's true. Dan said. Dan warned me. Clickety-clickety-click. Where's the exit? Let me out. Click-click-click. These are not footsteps. I know the sound. Clickety-clickety-click. There are the barred doors I recognise from before. Run and hand on bar and push and clickety-clickety-clickety-click. It is the sound of *typing*.

I shoulder the door and burst out into the open air, warm and bright, and someone catches me and I look up and I see his face and it is Leo, Leo, real Leo, and my arms around his neck, I hold him, hold him till I'm safe.

Chromosome 17
The Book of Job

'Though this be madness, yet there is method in it.'
Hamlet, II, ii

'"But I don't want to go among mad people," Alice remarked.

"Oh, you can't help that," said the Cat: "we're all mad here. I'm mad. You're mad."

"How do you know I'm mad?" said Alice.

"You must be," said the Cat, "or you wouldn't have come here."

Alice didn't think that proved it at all: however, she went on. "And how do you know that you're mad?"'

Lewis Carroll

I'm going mad. I fear I am going mad. At night my dreams reveal their fictions – but they seem just as real – and I am not sure that I am not in a dream now. And worse, I think it isn't even my own. Someone else is writing my dreams. I hear the tapping of typing all the time, as if now that I know He's there, I can understand a higher level of the reality of what's going on. I can decode the script.

My brother is an omen. I cannot put mere distance between us. We're not so different, it seems. We are the same and I am going mad, but knowing the future does not help me to stop it. Perhaps it only draws it on sooner. Perhaps it is part of the plan to draw it on. Nearly a fortnight he's been at the Maudsley now, but Dan gets worse every day. He's on an unstoppable descent. I cannot go to see him again. It is too much like looking in a mirror.

It must have been him, 'Johnny', who beat me up that night, or brought it about. It was not random. It was not without a cause. Even if the reason was a mad reason, vindictiveness, cruelty. It's just I could not have known the reason, perhaps because it wasn't me he was after. Perhaps

Johnny's a real person, like me. In which case I'm not mad. I think there is someone after me though, but maybe it isn't him. In which case I might be. But if no one had beaten me up, I wouldn't be lying here with Leo. Maybe that's why I was beaten up. It was part of the script.

I do not believe I am free. That much I accept. I thought it was because everything, not just me, was predetermined – the past gathered up and unravelling in the present and on inevitably into the future. Now I doubt even that. Now I think maybe I am not free because I am following someone else's script.

If I really think that, I must be going mad. It's easy to believe crazy things when you're half awake in the dark.

I cannot lie here any longer but I can't sleep either. I don't dare. I am too alone. I wish Leo would wake up but I can't bring myself to wake him. It is not yet six. I watch him sleep but I can't do it for long. If I do, the tears well up in my eyes. I don't want him to go away. I'll have a bath and wait for him to wake up.

I run the water and put my hand in the stream to check the temperature. I should be used to this tap's traits and quirks by now, but I never remember until I feel the water. It is a mixer tap, but it doesn't mix, not properly – incomplete entropy – its dynamic physics are its own and the single stream of water is hot on the left and cold on the right and then about halfway down they switch and spiral round each other, a double helix. Only when they hit the enamel do their identities merge.

I have to meet Sir Hugo today. I have managed to put it off for a month now, but this afternoon will come the day of reckoning. Maybe that's why I can't sleep. Should I spend the morning hashing together that RAI proposal just so I've got something to show him? From what he said before he'll turn it down anyway. Perhaps I should tell him I can't do a PhD. My excuse could be determinism, biological or otherwise.

If I lie still in the water, the bathroom is silent. The tap drips at apparently random intervals but nothing in this universe is random, it must be governed by rules I cannot see. Is this planned too? The hanging droplet grows too full of its own weight and can't take it anymore. The drip echoes on the tiled walls and now silence again in which all I can hear is my own breath and the sound of typing constantly in the distance. If it's really there. I think of listening to my own heartbeat when I was a kid trying to get to sleep. With my ear pressed to the pillow I thought it was the sound of some ogre's footsteps pounding up the hill to get me. I would scare myself so much my heart would race and the ogre would break into a run, always getting faster but never getting nearer.

Silent is an anagram of listen.

The door-handle turns and sleepily the door swings open. Leo stands there naked and I think of Greek statues, the way the muscles of his abdomen meet his pelvis, and he squints into the bright bathroom.

'What are you doing up so early?' he says.

'I couldn't sleep.'

'Why didn't you wake me?'

'You didn't get to sleep till after one.'

'Nor did you.'

'But you've got to be wide awake. You've got a matinée today.' This is normal, everything's normal again, now I've got Leo here.

'God, I hate Wednesdays,' he sighs and rubs his face with both hands. 'And, oh shit, what's the date?'

'The nineteenth.'

'I've got that drama workshop this morning too. For the children's charity thing,' he says and steps forward and into the bath. I shift up to make more room for him. He drops down into the water and it rises and slaps the sides. He takes the taps end. He always takes the taps end, unless he lies on my chest – it is one of the things about him which I love. Gently, he is playing footsie in my groin. It is warm and comforting and playful and makes me hard, but it is too early, neither of us have had enough sleep for it to be serious foreplay. 'Why couldn't you sleep?' he asks.

'I don't know. Everything. Dan. And I've got to see Sir Hugo this afternoon.' I don't tell him about the other things that keep me staring in the darkness – that the only conversation I've had with Elsi in the past week was about the growing sculpture of unwashed dishes. I think maybe she hates me. Then there are the fearsome, the mad things – that I am afraid for my sanity or, worse, that I *am* sane but that the cost of sanity is that my life is really at the whim of ... of someone else. These are the things you don't say, even to someone you love.

'The showdown with Hugo the Boss? He of the designer outfits.' He smiles encouragingly. 'It'll be all right. Give him hell.'

'I haven't decided what to do yet. Probably I'll just ask him for more time.'

'Let's go on holiday,' he says.

'We can't. I took all that time off at Easter when my father died. I mean, I don't know if they counted it officially. I didn't like to ask. Even if they didn't, I'm hardly in a position to start asking for holidays right now. Besides, you can't take a break either. You've got two more weeks of *Hamlet* and then, well, then you're leaving me all alone and jetting off to Hollywood next month.'

'Time's wingéd chariot. My point exactly. I've got a fortnight in between. I've got a few things on, but nothing I can't move. Come on, let's.'

I want to. I want to so much. But I'm not free to. It would be my salvation. Abandon all the shit that's mounting in my life, spend time just Leo and me before we spend so long apart. Reclaim my peace from all the chaos. But instead I say, 'I can't afford it.'

'Chris, don't be ridiculous. Do you know how much they're paying me for this movie?'

'I don't want you paying for everything.'

'What's the point of having so much money if I can't spend it on being with you? It'll just sit there or, even worse, I'd have to restrict myself to social contact with people in my income bracket which is the best argument for being broke I've ever heard.' He splashes me to show I'm being silly. 'Anyway, it'll hardly cost anything.'

'Why not?'

'Jocasta – you know, Gertrude? – she's got a villa on a Greek island. She offered to lend it to us. A secluded mansion amid the olive groves of Ithaca. Its own private beach. Scuba instructors with hairy backs ...'

I laugh but say, 'Leo, I can't.'

'Go on.'

'I can't.'

'Think about it, at least.'

*

Leo would go to America and he and Chris would be parted and, ultimately, Chris would die. *Bareich elohim va'mot.* That much could be known. Surely such outcomes were inevitable?

Only the reasons for what would come to pass and the timing of events remained uncertain and, considering the matter rationally, such details do not matter. In the chain of events, it is arbitrary to be sentimental about the passing of any one link. There's always another, no more nor less important than the last.

People do not deserve the bad things that happen to them, but nor do they deserve the good. They come naked from the womb and naked they return to dust. Life is given. Life is taken away. What right has anyone to expect the time between to be worth living? It stems from arrogance, belief that one's own life merits justice when all around the world, justice sits among the ashes. Justice is in the hands of God and if there is no god, justice is just a word.[8]

Such arrogance does not deserve justice. It is arrogance that makes the mad believe they are the only ones who see the truth. And it is arrogance that makes those who are told the truth dismiss it all as madness and lies.

Everyone is arrogant. Everyone is despicable. Everyone deserves the bad things.

*

Chris, in his odious arrogance, denied his God, denied his father. No wonder then that paranoia came to stalk him. No wonder the substitutes for a father's love erupted through his denial. No wonder he began to fear a different creator.

*

---

8 Of course, even if there is a god, God may not be just. As it has been said, 'He is the chief of the ways of God; he that made him can make his sword to approach unto him.' And as it is written, 'For I the Lord thy God am a jealous God.'

Lee Sall puts down his mug and sits at the computer next to me and switches it on. 'All right?' he says, smirking like he's just won a bet.

'Thanks. Yeah. You okay?'

'Stonking, mate.' He sips at his overfull mug through a grin and puts it on the desk. I watch the ring of coffee form round the base.

'Why, what's up?'

'They've put me in charge of stats analysis on the gay gene project.'

'Well done.' I want to be enthusiastic or happy for him, but it's something I'm outside of.

'Too fucking right. Got a raise and, I mean, in a year or two we're going to be publishing papers faster than a whore gets through knickers. I'm on my way, mate, greasy pole and loving it.' His computer has started up, so he turns in his chair to face the screen. He moves the mouse around while the sound of typing carries on in my head. 'You know Sara's in charge of the subject interviews? I thought you'd want a piece of that action. Meet a few men, eh? Suggest conducting a few private experiments, eh?' He laughs dirtily and I join in feebly. 'Weren't interested?'

'Not really.'

'Why not? Found yourself a boyfriend have you?'

It's the first time anyone at work has asked me since I started seeing Leo and I haven't worked out what to say so I bluster a bit and then deny him.

'All right,' he says, 'only asking.' He starts to type. My computer is still processing my sequencing data. I wait. 'What's Colin got you down for then?' He doesn't stop typing.

'What?'

'On the gay gene. What you gonna be doing?'

'I don't know yet. I should be seeing Sir Hugo now but I guess he's running late. '

'Really? Why you bothering with him? Why don't you just tell Colin what you want to do? Be quicker and a fuck of a lot less hassle.'

'Yeah, you're probably right.'

'Too right I'm right,' he says and my computer chimes to say it's finished processing the data and I click to view it.

The nucleotide script scrolls up the screen, laid out in

three-letter codons, fifteen codons to a line, ten lines on the screen at a time. The As, Cs, Gs and Ts flash briefly past, jerkily replacing the line above as they scroll. The randomness of it. I know it isn't random – nothing is random, I just don't know the causes and this is the same. Its meaning is secret and so it seems random, pointless, whimsical. Triplets rush past and I could remember or look up the corresponding amino acids if I tried, but none of it makes sense. Why this and no other? Why GGC, CAG, CAG, TCA? Words that say something jump out at me – TAG, CAT, TAT, GAG – but there is no context, no substance, however hard I look for meaning. Often, the screen repeats and repeats or forms patterns that suggest significance, but then it scrolls onward into nonsense.

It starts to repeat again. ACT. A word, a message. ACT. Like an image brought into focus. 'ACT' it says. 'ACT ACT ACT' it says to me. And again. And again. Meaning materialising before me. The screen fills with the imperative and flashes as the command replaces itself and replaces itself and the click-click-click in my head breaks into a rhythm.

ACT ACT ACT ACT ACT ACT ACT ACT ACT ACT ACT
ACT ACT ACT ACT ACT ACT ACT ACT ACT ACT ACT ACT
ACT ACT ACT ACT ACT ACT ACT ACT ACT ACT ACT ACT
ACT ACT ACT ACT ACT ACT ACT ACT ACT ACT ACT ACT
ACT ACT ACT ACT ACT ACT ACT ACT ACT ACT ACT ACT
ACT ACT ACT ACT ACT ACT ACT ACT ACT ACT ACT ACT
ACT ACT ACT ACT ACT ACT ACT ACT ACT ACT ACT ACT
ACT ACT ACT ACT ACT ACT ACT ACT ACT ACT ACT ACT
ACT ACT ACT ACT ACT ACT ACT ACT ACT ACT ACT ACT
ACT ACT ACT ACT ACT ACT ACT ACT ACT ACT ACT ACT
ACT ACT ACT ACT ACT ACT ACT ACT ACT ACT ACT ACT
ACT ACT ACT ACT ACT ACT ACT ACT ACT ACT ACT ACT
ACT ACT ACT ACT ACT ACT ACT

I know it is for me. I know I must act. I cannot not. An act of will, but not my own, and even though I will decide, the decision will not be mine. Act, it says. I must act. Now.

'Ah, at last, there you are,' says Nicole's voice behind me. 'Sir Hugo's waiting.' And I follow her, to act.

*

'I haven't received any paperwork from you, Chris,' says Sir Hugo, his hands interleaved and resting on his belly.

'No, you haven't.' It is not enough, so I add, 'I haven't done any.' I look at the ceramic pig on his desk. I cannot go through with it if I have to look him in the face. If I focus on the pig, everything else seems absurd, becomes unreal.

'And that would be because ...?'

'Because I didn't want to.'

He repeats my words as if to check: '*Because you didn't want to.*' My legs are shaking, but I must act. I am in a dream, in autopilot, elsewhere, virtual.

'No, I don't want to do a doctorate.'

'Chris,' Sir Hugo is sighing and now leans forward, his elbows on his desk, like a headmaster talking to a child, clipped and patronising, 'I don't think you understand. When I said you *ought* to do a doctorate, I wasn't offering you the choice. I don't want people here who don't want to advance themselves and the lab. I don't want liggers and layabouts.' I choose to stay silent, although this isn't real. It's not my choice. 'You do realise it's not a favour you're doing me by working here? There are queues of graduates willing to do your job, but I pick people who I think will get on. And yet – you "don't want to".' He raises an eyebrow. He's proved his point, he thinks. I will grovel, he thinks, but I must act. I must go on because I can't go back.

'The thing is, I don't want to do what you want me to, Sir Hugo. So I'm not going to.' I've wrong-footed him. He didn't expect me to disbelieve.

'Are you mad?'

'I think I might be, but how would I know?' Maybe he's not in on it. Maybe he plays his part in my script, but doesn't know what he's doing or why. Maybe he doesn't understand why I would say these things. It's possible this isn't a conspiracy. No one knows they're playing a part any more than I did. Everything's exactly as if it's real. There is confusion, yes, real confusion, and it is holding his fury in check. It is there though. I want to get out quickly. 'I think I'll leave now. I don't suppose you want to see me here again. Goodbye.'

I stand up and leave and he says nothing as I go but watches me as if I am disgusting and I find my legs are weaker than I thought and I cannot stride confidently out, but shuffle towards the door and out, past Nicole plotting at the computer, out through the lab to the double doors and I do not dare to stop or look back until they have swung shut behind me and I grab my jacket from my locker and take the stairs one – two – three at a time and out, out into the bright sunshine, like a computer game. I have not said goodbye to anyone but the man whose affronted face I won't forget. I have not collected my things, but what have I got? Some pens, some cough syrup from last winter, a mug with my name on it. In my triumph, it is nothing to leave behind. I have acted. I am free. Even if the freedom is not my own.

I cannot take this seriously. Now I know I should doubt it, it lacks authenticity.

I will go to the theatre and surprise Leo after his matinée and I'll tell him we can go away now. We can be together. I want to take him something, flowers, chocolates. I've got no cash. I'll go to the machine in Malet Street.

*

'Insufficient funds available. Please refer to bank,' it says and I don't feel so clever. I won't refer to bank. Not now. Enough instructions.

What the hell was I thinking? I am mad. I must be. But madness is something you cannot recognise from the inside, so if I know it, either I must be in it deep or I must be sane enough to know I'm mad.

Certainly I feel sort of disconnected. Like my ears are full of cotton wool. But I've heard that's a classic symptom of depression, which is a kind of madness anyway.

How can I test my madness? How can I test whether I'm sane? How can I find out whether I'm real or not? Sir Hugo didn't know, wasn't in on it. No experiment will prove it. None that I can think of now.

I must be real because I know I am. But it's only the same as saying I believe I am. I can't know anything without believing it. And if I sincerely believe something, I might as well say I know it. I must devise an experiment, a test of my reality.

I start to walk to Goodge Street station to go to Leo. Leo seems absolute, the one thing the cotton wool hasn't got to yet. He *is* real, despite stupid anagrams. Actually, that's it. He's the test. If he's not real, why would his anagram tell me so? It's a giveaway. He's the proof. It's fantastic when you think about it. He's the one clear thing.

Chromosome 18
Leviathan with a Hook

'And I will execute great vengeance upon them with furious rebukes; and they shall know that I am the Lord, when I shall lay my vengeance upon them.'
Ezekiel XXV, 17

'This drama is stern. In it truth doubts, sincerity lies. Nothing can be more immense, more subtile. In it man is the world, and the world is zero. Hamlet, even full of life, is not sure of his existence. In this tragedy, which is at the same time a philosophy, everything floats, hesitates, delays, staggers, becomes discomposed, scatters, and is dispersed. Thought is a cloud, will is a vapour, resolution is a crepuscule; the action blows each moment in an opposite direction; man is governed by the winds.'
Victor Hugo

For several days after Chris had brought his employment to a peremptory termination, the answer machine at the flat which he shared (by that time only nominally) with Elsi recorded numerous messages from Nicole, the Queen's College Personnel Office and even one from Sir Hugo himself. Chris did not respond to them, not least because he did not receive most of them since he was now (less nominally) sharing Leo's apartment.

They spent their days together and, in the late afternoon, Leo would depart for the theatre.

Chris would wait for his return, trying to fill the time, which, like the flight of an arrow infinitely halving the distance to its target, would protract exponentially.

Sometimes he watched videos and television, becoming increasingly obsessed with continuity errors.

Sometimes, he would watch films frame by frame to make his own time-frame seem less tortuous, but increasingly he failed to understand the language of film: the quick-cut; the fade; scene structure; motivation; narrative itself.

Eventually, it all ceased to make sense and became just a series of images devoid of meaning.

Then he watched the blank screen.

He counted the items in the flat and wrote down his findings. At a later juncture, he checked them. Often, he would find discrepancies and was confounded in his attempts to devise a test as to whether there was a genuine inconsistency – an intervention or a conspiracy – or whether he had merely miscounted the first time. He suspected that either someone was moving things to upset him or they were forgetting them and therefore they had ceased to exist. They might, of course, have been forgetting them deliberately in order to upset him with their interrupted existence.

And he tried to devise an experiment to test his own sanity and his reality.

At that time, he could not.

He thought of hanging himself, to pass the time.

From time to time he would venture out, but had no money with which to pass the time. His Travelcard would expire on August the sixteenth which was, coincidentally, the day after Leo was to leave for America. For fear Leo might give him money, Chris did not mention his financial embarrassment.

Nor did Chris do anything about his situation himself, such as discuss further credit facilities with his bank. Nor did he seek new employment. Nor did he seek social security payments.

The future had become to him a matter of mere weeks and days, the length of time until separation. Nothing existed beyond that. He did not reflect on life after Ithaca, after parting. He could not contemplate it because he did not wish to do so. To think about it was to bring it into some kind of existence.

Leaving the apartment became similarly trepidatious, requiring the acknowledgement – the creation even – of a world apart.

The world outside was full of confrontation, the contamination of conspiracy. All that was out there were strangers and guilt. He harboured suspicions that he was being followed, tracked, hunted, haunted.

Chris had not returned to visit Dan and had resolved not to see him again so that the trajectories of their lives might diverge as much as possible and Chris might save himself from madness (or so he hoped). Nor had Chris spoken to Elsi for days.

Chris felt watched.

As it happened, he did have good cause for feeling that he was under surveillance. This, at least, was not paranoia; or if it was, it was justified. There was, after all, a small but virtually permanent encampment of *paparazzi* stationed opposite the building, but since it was a large Georgian building with four luxury apartments, extensive security arrangements and subterranean parking from which there was direct access to the reception area above, Chris's comings and goings with Leo were not perceived by the members of the press nor, when he was on his own and came and went through the front door, was it clear to which of the four apartments he pertained.

Chris did not mention to Leo that he thought someone was controlling him, that he was afraid he was going mad. This was not because he felt unable to discuss it with him (nor exactly because he feared rejection – love denied, as his father had done), but because, when they were together, it seemed irrelevant, foolish, lonely.

When he was with Leo, his existence was not an issue. When he was not, there was nothing but absence.

When he was with Leo he was joyous and at ease. When he was not, he wished to be.

Leo, for his own part, relished the need to be depended upon and, in general, the dissolution of solitude whenever he came home and, in particular, the presence of Chris, joyous and at ease.

They both looked forward to Ithaca with as much eagerness as the dread with which they looked forward to what would follow thereafter. They were to fly first-class from Heathrow to Athens on Tuesday the first of August and then by chartered helicopter to the island. Before then, however, on Saturday the twenty-ninth of July, there would be the last night of *Hamlet*.

*

'Take up the bodies: – such a sight as this becomes the field, but here shows much amiss. – Go bid the soldiers shoot,' says the tannoy before a pause and then the applause and the cheering crackling through the speaker like meaningless noise. I time it and it's fifteen – sixteen – seventeen seconds and while I sit and wait and it's three fifty-five – fifty-six – fifty-seven and the thrill infects me too and the greasepaint really does smell and it's nine twenty-nine – thirty – thirty-one and I spin round in Leo's swivel chair and there are roses and champagne on ice all ready and a host of new cards for the last night and fifteen twelve – thirteen – fourteen and I'm thinking how Leo is too good to be true and if this is invented, I don't care, I will happily live happy ever after with Leo and it's twenty-one – twenty-two – twenty-three minutes and twelve seconds before the clapping subsides and subdues into appreciative mumbles as the audience leaves.

Leo is in the room almost before the applause is over and he's carrying more flowers. He's got people with him, congratulating, pandering, so I don't kiss him, but just say, 'Hi' and 'Surprise!' and he manoeuvres them out, thanking them and he closes the dressing room door and kisses me with damp triumph, pushing his whole body against mine. I smell the make-up and the sweat and the joy.

'I didn't think you were coming tonight,' he says, wiping make-up from my face where he pressed his against mine.

'I couldn't very well miss the last night.'

'You know there's the party though?' We don't need to say that neither of us thinks it's a good idea for me to be there. We've been through that before and now we know how to play it.

'Yeah, yeah, don't worry, that's fine. I'll head home and you come and join me whenever you want. I just wanted to surprise you when you came off stage and to find out how it went.'

'Oh, sweetheart. Thank y—' Ringing from the phone cuts him off. 'Hello?' he says, his voice rising because he's happy. He pauses and listens and sighs slightly. 'Tell him, not tonight. No press backstage.' He pauses again. 'Well, tell him if he's got an invite to the party I'll speak to him there, but ... no, I don't want to ... tell him, I don't care what it's about ...' he pauses again, the smile retreating. The phone's internal only, so it must be Norman. Norman the doorman. Because of his name that is what he must be.

'He said what?' Leo looks at me with fear or anger. I gesture to ask if I should go, but he waves me to stay and starts to listen again. 'Okay, put him on.' Now I can hear the faint sound of a new voice on the line.

It's quite a realisation. To know that here, in front of me, is the man who will be old with me. To know that this is the sense it makes. To know, without proof, without needing it, it's the same for him and always will be.

'All right, you'd better come up,' says Leo eventually.

He hangs up and breathes deeply, looks at me and now, suddenly, I think I'm not going to like this. 'What's wrong?'

'It's a journalist, a little weasel called Bill MacRake,' he says. 'He's coming up ...'

'I'd better go then,' I say, turning to pick up my jacket from over the back of a chair.

'Don't bother. He knows you're here. He knows about us.'

'Oh.'

We stand there facing each other. The breath is snagged in my chest. There is nothing to be said now. It's not as if I haven't thought about this. And I'm sure the same is true for Leo. I've almost wanted it. I would like to boast to all the world about my boyfriend. But I didn't think it would happen. Or if I did, I didn't think it would be at any particular moment in time. Not now. Not without warning. I never thought it was beyond our control. But of course it is, everything is. Leo cannot look at me any more and turns to sit at the dressing table and take off his make-up. I watch him in the mirror and watch as he reveals his face, pale underneath the artificial colour. I put my hand to his neck and he raises his hand to place it on mine, but he doesn't, he lifts my hand off instead and, without looking at me, he says, 'Better not. Not while he's here.'

I back off and sit in the other chair.

This is His doing.

There's a knock.

'Come in,' says Leo.

A man in a flak jacket comes in with a pinched face and shit-brown hair which is receding even though he can't be more than early thirties. He flashes a great grin of self-satisfaction. 'Hello, boys,' he says. No one talks to Leo like that.

'Shut the door,' Leo says calmly. MacRake shuts it. 'What do you want?'

'No need to be like that. Really. Don't panic. I know what's going on, but, well, basically, I'd like to help.'

'And how do you intend to do that?'

'Well, let's just say it's lucky it's me who found out about you two first.' He *is* a weasel, Leo is right, but he can't help the wiry way he looks, the estuary wide-boy accent. He wants to help. He doesn't want to ruin everything. Please, I hope that maybe he doesn't want to ruin everything. 'I mean, if *I* found out, who knows who else might have done given enough time. You're hot, Leo. This would be a major scoop for me if I wanted. Some hacks would tear you apart with this.' We say nothing. I watch Leo, his face is stiff, stern patience, nothing revealed. I catch my own in the mirror and my chest heaves suddenly and I think I might start to cry with fear, a child about to be smacked, but instead I scratch my neck quickly and tune in to the background noise of my heavy breath, my thudding heart and the click-click-click of my tormentor. He planned this. He's planned all this. Everything. 'You're looking worried, mate. No need. Honestly. I got integrity. I don't see why I should drag you through it just for the sake of a bit of dirt that'll be old news by next weekend. Besides, there's nothing wrong with gays – some of my best friends, as they say. And it don't affect your acting. I'm one of your biggest fans, you know.'

'So why are you telling us if you're not going to do anything?' Leo is right. I felt relieved for a moment, but what does this guy want?

'Well, put it this way, at first, you know, I was congratulating myself on landing such a big story. I was thinking about all those front-page splashes. I did all the background work. I dug out your exes – I found two, by the way – and got all the dirt on your pretty boyfriend here.' He looks at me properly for the first time, raises an eyebrow and says, 'Christopher Putnam, right? Twenty-four, until recently a bit of a Dr Frankenstein at Queen's College, and twin brother of Dan Putnam, controversial so-called artist. How is he, by the way? Out of the Maudsley yet?'

'All right, MacRake,' says Leo. 'That's enough. What is it you want?'

'As I said, Leo, I was doing all the usual work and then I thought, *I don't want to do this*. I really don't. I don't want to give all this to my editor – who's a complete shit, by the way, no shame – and ruin that poor guy's life. What a time to get a crisis of conscience, I thought. My biggest opportunity and I don't want to use it. Then I started thinking, there's got to be an alternative. There's got to be some way that Leo and I can do each other a favour. I was thinking you might be able to compensate me for not using this.'

'How much?'

MacRake looks shocked, genuinely, as if he hadn't thought of that. 'You've got me all wrong. I don't want your money. I'm a journalist, not a crook. I've got a much better deal. I think you're going to like it.' He's full of boyish excitement and I think it's going to be okay, maybe, he *is* going to help us. Leo will just have to give his kids an autograph or something and he'll forget it. 'It's not going to cost you guys a penny. It might even work out better for you, Leo, mate. You can carry on just as before, bum each other senseless for all I care.' He sits on the corner of the dressing table. It's too high and he doesn't look comfortable, but he doesn't move, he doesn't want to give anything away. He's got control of this. He doesn't want to lose it. 'You need someone to promote you.'

'I've got a PR agent.'

'Oh yes, your *wife*. No that's fine, you can keep her on if you like. In fact, I'm sure it'll make things simpler. I'm not talking about that kind of promotion.'

'Get to the point.'

'Well, Princess Di had her guy at the *Mail* and Charles had Dimbleby, you know, insiders, journalists willing to spin their version. What you need is someone to do all those in-depth interviews, someone who'll pitch the story just as you want it. Maybe we can throw in the occasional juicy titbit just to spice it up. I've got no problem going along with your little white lies. Just enough to keep the public interested in you and reading my copy.'

'That's what you want? To interview me?'

'Well, yeah, basically. I'd like first refusal on your gossip.

Like I said, Leo, you're hot. And you're gonna get hotter too. The way I look at it, how can I lose? How can either of us lose? What do I have to gain by bringing you down when you can take me along for the ride? And then, of course, there are all your celebrity pals. Having you as a contact is worth a lot more to me than having your scalp as a notch on my CV. I'm thinking we can work together. I'll get a good supply of exclusives instead of just one and you get your story told exactly as you want it. Your friends too. I mean I'm not claiming to be no angel. I'm not saying that if we see someone on the way out, that I would be above doing a little exposé. But, hey, fair's fair, and okay, they might be a little pissed off at the time, but, fuck it, when they see how much better publicity is than a therapist, I'm sure they'll forgive and forget. I just don't see any reason to do the dirty on a rising star. What do you say?'

'You really are a low-life.'

'Hang on,' he raises his palms, all offended. 'I don't have to help you here. I'm doing my job. And doing it well. I'm giving you a break because I don't want to see you go down in flames. And, to be honest, what am I asking in return? Nothing. I'm trying to do the right thing here. You're going to have to do these kind of interviews anyway, all I'm saying is that you save the best for me and we can work out how to make the most out of it for both of us.'

'And you're asking me to spy on my friends and colleagues.'

'No, Leo, no. You've got it all wrong. You're just a contact. We're friends, see? You just point me in the right direction. Give me introductions. Leave the espionage to me. But, you know, you save me shoe leather. Come on, it's a fair deal. Fairer than anyone else would give you.' He waits while Leo says nothing. 'Jeez, I thought you'd be grateful.'

'But what if someone else finds out?' I ask. MacRake looks at me, surprised to hear my voice and I realise how irrelevant to him I am.

'Don't you worry about that, Mr Putnam. We'll come up with a pre-emptive strike. We'll run a piece next week about how Leo has employed Dan Putnam's brother as a PA or something. Not much of a story, but it'll be enough to keep people off the scent if they see you together, so long as you don't go snogging in public again.' Leo and I give each other a glance. We didn't. We never. 'No one need know anything unless I will it to be so. And if you don't want that, then nor do I. So, boys, are we partners? Are we friends?'

No one says anything. I can't. I wouldn't know what to say. Anything might be wrong. Leo, you decide. But Leo is staring at his hands and flicking his nail, his face full of agitated thought.

MacRake breaks the silence. 'I wrote the article already,' he says. 'I mean, I don't intend to use it. It was only when I'd done it I came up with this idea. Would you, er, like to see it?' He pulls a bundle of pages from inside his jacket and flattens them proudly on the dressing table. 'All it needs is a quote from each of you. Or "no comment", if you like. I mean, I can prove the whole thing so it doesn't really matter. But, you know, I don't want to run it anyway. So long as you know that.' Suddenly I see how he feels about this. He's nervous. I think even intimidated by Leo, by Leo's fame. He wants this over. That's why he's laid out his story now, a threat.

'I don't want to see it,' says Leo. 'Look, Chris and I need to talk this through, okay? Is that fair?'

'Oh yeah, no problem. I got all the time in the world, but, well, we'd better have a deadline. Journalists love deadlines. How about we say we talk by the end of the day tomorrow? I don't want you running off to your Greek island love-nest before we sort things out, if you don't mind. Of course, if you do, you won't need to catch up on the newspapers when you get back.' He drops down from the dressing table. 'I'll let you keep that copy. Bedtime reading. I'll give you a call tomorrow, Leo, 'round five. Don't worry. It's all gonna be okay. I'll see you, boys.'

Leo shuts the door slowly behind MacRake and doesn't look back at me. His back to me, he watches the closed door where the man just left.

'What are we going to do?' I ask. Leo says nothing. 'How did he find out? I mean we never ...' I realise I'm panting so hard I can't finish the sentence. This is not fair. Leo says nothing. I've done this to him. I've brought all this about and now this man has come and it will be Leo who has to deal with it and not me because he is *someone*. But out of nowhere. We never kissed, never in public, surely.

Except the first time. At La Farfalla. But we were in the basement. At the bottom of the stairs. We couldn't be seen. Surely we couldn't be seen.

The whole thing, our whole relationship. We've been watched all the time.

He must have followed me, followed me everywhere. It was him watching me. And it was Johnny who beat me up – which means I am not mad. I am not paranoid. They really are out to get me. And I feel relief. Because people *have* been after me. People, not ghosts or some author in my head dictating a script for me. And now, now all we have to do is go along with MacRake's plan.

But even so, he could not know all those things. I have doubts again. I have been cheated, my tormentor has cheated me. Perhaps MacRake is an envoy, sent by Him and briefed on everything. There's no cause for this, no reason, no other way he could have known all this. 'Leo, do you think he's bluffing?'

Leo speaks. 'No,' he says, but still does not look round. He hangs his head. 'Vic. It could have been Vic.'

'You think?' Yes, Vic. It makes sense again. I am not mad. If Vic did this I am not mad.

'Maybe, I don't know. Chris, there's only one thing we can do. I have to go along with it. If I don't, they'll rip you apart.'

I can handle it, I think, but it does no good anyway. Whatever they can do to me, they can ruin Leo. 'Jesus, don't worry about me. What about you?'

He ignores the question. 'Chris, I'm not going through this. They did it to Helen. I'm not going to let them do it to you.'

'I'll be fine whatever we decide.'

'You think so?' he says and now he stares straight at me. He is angry, but why angry at me? 'You *really* think so? Look, Chris, there are things I didn't tell you about what they did to Helen and I really don't think you can handle going through that. I love you very much, really, more than you realise, but you're not as strong as she is, Chris. You're vulnerable.' He goes quiet again and sits.

'What? What sort of things?'

'A baby.'

'What? Yours?'

'Vic's,' he says. 'She lost it. And then she got very depressed and she took an overdose, accidentally, she claims … but I don't know and it doesn't matter anyway. I don't want to talk about all that.' He is silent again and I don't know what to say and I think that maybe I whisper 'I'm sorry' or maybe it's just in my head and at last he says, 'So I've got to do it.'

'I know. But, Leo, don't worry about me, I have nothing to lose. Except you. I don't care what's said about me.'

'You don't get it,' he says, his voice rising again. 'Don't you see what I'm saying? I cannot do this to you. *Cannot*.' My face must be telling him I don't understand. He says it again and now he is talking more quickly and he's saying, 'I'm not in control any more. It's all spoilt, Chris. *I've* got to do this. I've got to do it on my own. I had a contract with fate: I didn't bring anyone else into it – that was the deal. The risks I took were for myself. But I've been selfish, Chris, and I've brought you in and now it's all come crashing down. I'm sorry, Chris. I'm so, so sorry. I broke the deal. I've got to mend it.' His eyes are shiny with tears.

'Are you saying we should split up?' This isn't happening. Click-click-click. He's cheating, the author in my head is making this up and cheating. There is no cause. 'But why? I could be your PA, like he said.'

'Don't you understand?' He is shouting at me, but against the violence of his voice, the tears run slowly. Mine do not come. 'That's only for the moment. He *will* run this article—'

'He's not going—'

'He will, Chris, he will. Not this week, maybe, but whenever he chooses, whenever I'm not big news anymore, whenever he gets scared someone else knows, whenever he's got a new sap to suck. *I* have to do this with him. But you don't. And I'm not going to let you, because I loved Helen but nothing like how I love you and I'm not going to be responsible for doing to you what I did to her. And if what I've got to do to stop it is to tell you to get out and we're not going to see each other again, then, then …' and he stops talking. He just looks at me with his mouth open and down-turned and his half-removed make-up running in streaks down his face, his eyes deep set and wet red, a grotesque theatrical mask.

I say nothing. I try to assemble sentences in my head, but everything that comes into my head sounds melodramatic, clichéd lines from movie scripts. I know what is going on. My Author is unravelling me and pulling every part of me apart. This isn't fair. The Author was in my life when I was all alone, but not with Leo. Not when I was with him. It all seemed silly then, but now, he got into this too. He got inside it all and mutated it. I don't know why He doesn't care about me, maybe to him this isn't real. But it is to me. It is to me.

I stand up and Leo stands up. I put my arms around him and hold him and my tears come at last, but now I want to hide them from him. I keep my head down as I turn around and pick up my jacket and cannot face him even as I open the door. 'Thank you,' I think I say as I leave.

*

Chris returned home to the flat he shared (no longer nominally) with Elsi. Leo had no choice but to wash his face, put on a brave new one, and attend the cast's last-night party at Joe Allen's. He did not, however, join the rest of the cast who later repaired to the Green Room Club.

On his way home, waiting on the Underground platform at Covent Garden, Chris stood watching the rails. A passer-by, reeling from their own evening's entertainments, tentatively approached and asked whether he was all right. He replied, untruthfully, that he was. The passer-by then remarked that that was a shame as he'd always wanted to watch someone top themselves and, guffawing loudly, he left Chris alone.

On the train, Chris frantically scrawled the letters of Bill MacRake's name on the back of an envelope. He then rearranged them. BLACKMAILER, it said.

Chromosome 19
Fairy Tales

'Truth is so hard to tell, it sometimes needs fiction to
make it plausible.'
Francis Bacon

'"Beauty is truth, truth beauty," – that is all
Ye know on earth, and all ye need to know.'
John Keats

A young man lies in a bed in a small room in a flat in north
London. He does not stir but his eyes, veined with the
tendrils of spent tears, stare out at the ceiling, at nothing.

This is what self-pity looks like.

There's no need to pity those who do it for themselves.

*

I have realised something. I may have been wrong about Leo
Martin. Maybe he is I'M NOT REAL, after all. Maybe he was
part of the script too, part of my author's plots. Something
that hides reality, not proof of it. I feel certain this is
important.

At least there is something certain beyond these four walls.

I have nothing of Leo. I have no proof I ever knew him.
And now I am beginning to wonder if I did. It seems so
unlikely, too good to have been true, and all my memories
seem like unreliable evidence. I remember flying as a child,
from my bed around the room, but I know I didn't. And I
can't remember my mother's face, but I must have had a
mother and I know I loved her. I loved Leo too, I know I did,
but whether he loved me or whether it was all just fantasy is
something I cannot prove to myself, let alone anyone else.
And why would they believe me anyway?

The room is tepid with the slowness of stale air, but I feel
so cold. Shivery with fever or self-pity, how can I know

which? I only know my eyes and my throat and my chest are so raw with tears that crying now brings no relief, only pain – rough, red, physical pain.

*

Does he leave the room? Who can say? Does it matter?

Let us say he does not.

Let us say this young man has not left this room for many hours, for days perhaps. The fug of unmoving air certainly suggests the whorls of floating dust have not been disturbed by him doing more than shifting occasionally from bed to floor to chair and back to bed.

The bedclothes, the clothes, the tissues and mugs and CD cases and all the other detritus of stasis gather in heaps of disorder.

An alarm clock tick-tocks.

The young man starts to pick up clothes, not to tidy up, but to rummage, to delve in pockets, turning out the shrivelled remnants of worn days. He is searching. Without expectation, without joy, without success.

No, if he found something, that would be too easy.

*

We were so careful not to be together in public, to avoid the camera lenses at the windows, to have none of the ticket stubs, the little notes, the litter from places we went, none of the small souvenirs that lovers treasure to remember the past by. We were so careful to leave no trail.

I have nothing but memory.

Maybe I had no mother. Nor was Leo real either. All my memories are untrustworthy because they're not mine. They're inventions, lies.

We never kissed in public. That's a lie too. That's a damned lie. We were cheated. Cheated. It's all just so unfair. We knew that even so little would be enough to upset everything, less even. The butterfly never flapped. I have been cheated of a cause.

But I'm getting used to that now.

Maybe we kissed. Maybe we did.

I still entertain the possibility that all this is real, that there is no author, that I'm only mad. Maybe I just can't see the cause because I don't want to, because even with a cause it was unjust. I'm getting used to that too. None of it matters any more.

I have almost nothing of Leo. After only ten days, I cannot prove I knew him. All I have is this. This book. And it's not even *his* signature inside. Just a plain white card between the stiff thick pages which says, 'Never grow old. Believe in fairies. I love you.' and then three crosses to signify kisses. Believing in fairies makes me smile again. But smiling draws sharp the contrast between then and now and makes me feel a heaving weight of sadness again and all the pain of tenderness.

I remember Peter Pan from when I was young. I never read it but we – the four of us – all went to a theatre somewhere, but I don't know where or when. I can't prove that either. No, five of us, Grandma was there too. Grandma Wendy. The same name as the girl in Peter Pan. And now again I think of Dan in the hospital – the genetic prophecy of what was bound to happen to me, or maybe it hasn't happened yet – and I remember what he told me. He believed he was being watched, controlled. He told me not to believe in Wendy. Nor in Eugene.

He is my likeness in every way. He draws me on. He has shown me what questions to ask. He's found a way out – madness, medication, treatment. A husk, rocking in a private mental ward. He had the privilege of not seeing it from the outside before he went there. I don't think I can follow him.

*

A young man in a bedroom looks tired but is not looking for sleep. He looks at books, not reading them, but looking for a book, scanning their spines, like friends who have turned their backs on him. Books on biology, biochemistry, bioinformatics, biographies. Some true. Some lies. Stories, fairy tales, fables of pathetic heroes, doomed to suffer and –

if the lies are to be believed – to triumph in the end.

He takes one book, its black and white bird, reduced to the merest representation; its orange and white bands, faded to the colours of London night skies; its Gill Sans, sans eyes, sans teeth; its pages dried, roughened and jaundiced like the skin of a cancerous patient, patiently waiting for death, acquiring the smell of neglect.

This is what we all come to in the end, flaking to dust, unmoving within our walls, ended.

Living only so long as the meaning of the words is remembered.

*

There is a chapter called 'Do You Believe in Fairies?' and because of Leo's card, I open the book there and all of a sudden I want to cry again because he didn't believe, didn't put his faith in us, that we could see it through. Not enough.

'The more quickly this horror is disposed of the better,' it starts and I scan down the page. 'Had she haughtily unhanded him (and we should have loved to write it of her), she would have been hurled through the air like the others, and then Hook would probably not have been present at the tying of the children; and had he not been at the tying he would not have discovered Slightly's secret, and without the secret he could not presently have made his foul attempt on Peter's life.' The writer's just playing with us. All these *if onlys*, as if he hadn't planned it all, as if each thing really caused the next and it wasn't him all along. As if the characters ever really had a choice or a chance.

I read on because there is nothing else worth doing in the world, in my littered, darkened room with the curtains drawn at I don't know or care what time of day. I get to the bit about fairies. Tinker Bell it seems is in love with Peter and so she drinks the poisoned medicine to save his life: '... and now I am going to be dead,' she says and Peter doesn't understand why she drank it. She is dying but she just gives his chin a loving bite and whispers in his ear, 'You silly ass.' And now I feel my face is hot and wet and salty with tears again.

But she is saved. She's saved because the children believe in fairies. 'Do you believe?' asks Peter. 'If you believe, clap your hands.' But I don't clap my hands, because I don't believe in fairies or Father Christmas or three wishes or God or anything that isn't proven. And it isn't for me to prove it.

But I believe in myself. I believe, but I don't *know*. And I have doubts.

There are things I need to prove to myself. In all of this, I must be scientific.

I am losing my reason. My reasons. I am rational, but I am losing it.

Maybe it's just being watched, knowing now that all this time I have been scrutinised, under surveillance, by MacRake, perhaps by Johnny, whoever he is, and who knows who else. That is what has made me paranoid, convinced there is someone else, an author, watching, controlling, inventing. Perhaps I am being watched now. Perhaps he listens in on my thoughts too. Well, do you? Can you hear this now? Can you talk to me?

I guess not.

Perhaps I never knew Leo. It seems improbable.

I don't want to be mad. Not mad, not shrivelled in a corner, shrieking in a silent fit, tears bursting from every inch of my body, tears of mad sweaty fear at what it all could do to me. Don't let me be mad. Please God, don't let me be mad. There is no god – or if there is, he's a spy and a sadist and a puppeteer. I want to cry out for my mummy. I want to hold my father's warm hand or Leo's.

I stand up and walk to the door and nod my head against it. I feel that. I feel that, but it is not hard enough. It is not pain. It is not the pain of proof. I hit my forehead against it. And again. Again. Again. It hurts and dizzies me, real thuds and swirls of colour at the edges of my eyes and it makes the click-click-clicks go away for just a moment but there they are again and I can already feel the bruise proving itself. It's real pain, no more or less real than me.

Perhaps there are levels to reality. Leo is an invention, my father and mother too. Even I am an invention, like a character in a book, say. No more than a human script. We're all the invention of an author. But the thing is, I feel real. They all do. That's because we're on the same level.

But I don't believe in Tinker Bell. Or Peter Pan or Wendy. They're inventions of another level. Inventions within an invention, dreams within a dream, where just to believe in something is the same as to know it and to know it makes it real.

Layer after layer of reality, each just as real to itself, dismissive of the layers beneath, unaware of those above. Perhaps even the author in my head is only an invention? Mine, maybe? Or maybe he has his own author who predetermines his past, his present and his future too.

There must be a highest level, the really real. The question is, am I on it?

I must prove I exist, but anything I do to prove it could be invented too. Leo was my proof. Belief and knowledge felt the same. Certainty. It matters.

Maybe he's just a character that slipped from one level of reality into another for a while. Into mine. I'm slipping too, I think. Seeing the chinks, the causes without effects, the effects with no cause.

I feel certain that if I had proof of him, that would prove he is real, that I don't need to believe any of this. That I can believe in things again. It would prove that anagrams are coincidence, that everything that happens happens only because it does.

If he's real, so am I. There's no need to be afraid. I'm only mad.

But now he's not here. I haven't seen him and I daren't phone him in case he doesn't exist or he hasn't heard of me and now, because of all of this, I don't know anything any more and can believe everything and nothing. I gather the duvet to me, but there's no substitute and yet I have no one, no one in all the world.

Except Elsi, but she is lies. Elsi is LIES. Not to be trusted.

I don't want to go out there. I fear there may be more ways for Him to get at me. In my room, in the dark, in my duvet, things only half exist. I am safer. Not safe. Safer. But alone.

But I must go. It is predetermined.

I have to check about 'Wendy' and 'Eugene'. It may prove something. It may be the difference between knowledge and belief.

I find my alarm clock is under the blanket on the floor. It claims it is three o'clock. Night or day. It isn't ticking anyhow.

*

A man walking down the street. Young, but not young. Unbearded, but not clean-shaven. Alone, but talking. Handsome, but not attractive, not looking like this. Unwashed, smelly (probably, should one get too close), a bruise to the forehead, clotted blood above his eye, and, worst of all, flouting conventions. He doesn't wear enough clothes to keep out the cold. He mutters. His eyes flick side to side, but never meet the gaze of others or when they do, they do so in challenge, immediately brandishing the hostility of the unpredictable, the uncertain, the abnormal. There is danger in the unknowability of what he will feel himself compelled to do next.

He runs sometimes and then stops and dodges, negotiating a path through crowds that are not there and ignoring the wide berth given by those that are. His presence is large for the people around him. They give him space.

'What's wrong with that man?' a child asks her mother, who hushes her and bundles her on to a bus. The child watches the man, staring. The adults look away.

*

The streets are full of strangers, faces come at me fast, staring, expressionless. I have established it is day and it isn't Sunday. It's sometime in the second week of August and the summer's already gone. I don't think I've been out of the flat for nearly a week, but I've missed nothing, nothing but the depression and oppression of faces in the street. May offered promise. Long sunny days, it seemed that could only have got longer and hotter, but it was early yet, but now the sky is dreary and the strangers wear coats and frown and scowl and look me in the eye only to make me scared. They make me scared.

I could scream now. Scream in the street. No one would react. It would be like noise in a vacuum. I'm all alone and the streets are crowded. A sparrow pecks at a dog-end.

*

The public library is full of noise, noises that echo more loudly because the strangers are trying not to make them. I have not been in a public library since I was a child. I cannot recall a single instance though, not one, when I was ever there. I just know I was. In Kirkcaldy. I can recall almost nothing as if my history has been unwritten or never written in the first place. Maybe nothing is remembered, just invented at the time. If I search for recall it comes, instantly, as if it were never not there, like the backgrounds in computer games which fill in when you turn your vision to them but aren't there when you look the other way. I have to keep Him on His toes.

But there are things I can't remember. My mother's face. Leo's smell or his touch. My father. I cannot remember my father, nothing but the box they put him in.

I hear the click-click-click of keyboards. It is there all the time, but when I look round I see that these days they have computers in here. Sometimes I think I'm not imagining the click-click-click.

An old man in ruined clothes coughs and coughs again. He flattens the paper in front of him, blown about by his dry hacking. Now he coughs again and his face goes puce, blood pumped into the stringy veins across his face. He coughs again and at last hawks damply, bringing up whatever sticky mass constricts his throat and, with his left hand, he passes a handkerchief across his drawn-in lips and no doubt deposits the mucus there to dry out crunchily in his pocket.

Reference, I want. I do not want to ask because I cannot remember using my voice since yesterday or the day before or the day before that when Elsi told me she had known all along it wouldn't last with Leo. I wish now I had flown into a rage, proved to myself that it was something more than how she saw it, that it was real. It seems, however, that I could not doubt enough that she was right. Leo did not need me and now I have nothing, nothing to hold on to, nothing to be sure of. There is a whole short aisle dedicated to Catherine Cookson in many versions. Hardback, paperback, large print. Books are strangers, showing me their cold shoulders in their ranks. Hundreds of chapters, thousands of words, millions of letters. Different orders spelling out different stories. What a difference the order of letters makes.

Reference must be somewhere else because it's not here, but now I look I see right beside me the spine of *The Baby Name Book* and I am in Parenting. It is old and cheap with the glossy pink and blue design printed right on to the hardback cover looking like sickly sticky cakes from bakers when I was a kid. The front page says it was published in 1976. So was I. I mean, that's when I was born.

I start flicking from the back, which means, I suppose, I am looking up Wendy first. Wilfred, Wesley, Werner, Wendy: '(f.) invented in 1904 by J. M. Barrie for a character in *Peter Pan*, supposedly inspired by his own childhood nickname 'friendy-wendy'.'

1904. Not according to my family. Forever, they always said. The name went back in our family forever. 1904. That might even have been too late for Grandma Wendy, let alone the generations before.

I flick to go back to Eugene but the page drops open at 'Eugene' as if someone's had it open before me. 'Eugene:' it says, '(m.) from the Greek meaning 'well-born'. Although borne by a few early saints (*C5th*) and Prince Eugene of Savoy (*d.* 1736), the name did not become popular in Britain and the US until the beginning of the twentieth century with the rise and popularity of the science of eugenics. Diminutive: Gene.'

Probably lies too. These are our family names. Dan said they weren't true. How did he know? Another thing with no cause. Is this all he knew? That the names we were always told had been handed down and which we were expected to pass on to our children like some inheritance were just lies? Invented traditions?

It could be true though. Grandma could have been born later than that. She could. And Eugene – *did not become popular*, it says, not that it's a lie. It fits. It's possible. It is not proof.

There are creationists who say that evolution is a pack of

lies, that God put the fossils there to make the world seem older, to test our faith. I did not dare ask our Father if that is what he believed. That would have been too much, evolution is something I believe I know. It is the least unlikely explanation. I know what I know. For chrissakes, it's obvious. But I always have to remain sceptical until I know anything for sure.

My family names, though, my background, my nurture, can that all just be inventions too?

I have no evidence, no fossils. I have no father any more. Nor any mother. I am from nothing, from less than clay. I have no cause. I have no cause. I have no cause.

'Shh,' says someone and 'Go fuck yourself' I tell her loudly in the silence, my voice crackling with the weight of disuse, and I run, hearing the clapping of my feet on the varnish floor. Clapping like children's hands, clapping to show they believe in fairies, and the clapping echoes, clap, clap, clap and out, out, out into the street of strangers again.

*

I have been out some time. All day maybe. The dark is closing in on Kentish Town. No blood-red sun-down, but the mere withdrawal of light, the onset of gloom and the grimy orange of street-lamps smudging the underbelly of the clouds. This is my home, our two-room flat, Elsi and me. But I've left my keys behind and so I ring the bell but no one comes. I must talk it all through with Elsi, even though I don't know if I can believe her. I lean my back against the door. Her hard realities are the way back. I must hang on to those. No sympathy needed, just a clear way through. The practicalities. I ring the bell again. She doesn't come. I have no job, no money. I must sign on. I must get housing benefit or else I won't be able to pay the rent next month. But I haven't done these things. I sit on the doorstep. Realities don't seem real. They are all too much. Or maybe too little. I can't be bothered with them, not when I don't find them convincing. I just want them to go away and leave me in my room. Eventually I'll deal with them or they'll go away or they'll come back when they need to be dealt with. It's too much now to deal with things and people and realities when I think I believe I don't exist. Why the fuck do I need this shit? I don't need food or sleep or warmth or anything. If I'm not real, what's my author going to do with me, eh? Let me die? Let me sit here on the doorstep and die? What the fuck kind of an ending is that?

'Chrissy?'

What? I look up. It's Elsi. I say her name.

'What are you doing on the doorstep?'

'My keys. I forgot my keys.'

'Jesus,' she says and her hand takes me under the elbow and jerks me to my feet and there's a guy with her who's looking at me sarcastically. He's laughing at me. I'm sure he's laughing at me, but he's not showing it. Elsi gets the door open and is pushing me up the stairs and I want to let her and want to lean back and let her take all my weight but I fear she'd let me fall because she's complaining to me and telling me to move it and saying she doesn't need this shit today. 'You realise you can't do this after today,' she's saying. 'You do know that, don't you?'

I'm saying something to show I know, to show I agree, but I'm not sure I do. But I have no will to disagree. At the top of the stairs, there are boxes and bags and Elsi's stereo all along the landing. I sit on a box while Elsi unlocks the flat and I look at the boxes. 'Where are you going?' I say.

She doesn't look at me but gets the door open and shouts over her shoulder on her way in. 'I told you already – I've put my new address on the noticeboard by the phone.'

'I'll get these down to the van, Els,' says the guy who has come up the stairs who ignores me like I'm not here or like I don't exist or like he's been told something about me and he picks up a box and goes back down.

You, hey you, what do you know? Who the fuck are you anyway? I could with superhuman strength tear down the banisters and beat his head to a mash with a baluster, cracking it against his skull again and again, each time bloodier and lower as he slides to his knees there on the stairs leaving behind on the wall a smear of gore and brain and scalp.

His head descends out of view. 'Where are you going, Elsi?'

'Jesus, Chrissy, how many times do I have to say?' She reappears at the door. 'What the fuck is wrong with you?'

'Don't go.'

'For fuck's sake, don't start that again.' She disappears again.

'Don't go.'

I get to my feet and follow her into the flat. Our flat. It is no longer our flat. It is empty. It is not, but it is missing things all over. I follow into her room which has no wall-hangings, no green wicker chair, no candlesticks and ashtrays, no half-empty mugs, no tie-dye bedspread, just a bare mattress. A bare mattress and a duffle-bag, which she slings over her shoulder and she turns around. 'Stop fucking following me!'

'Don't go.'

'Look. I'm gone. I've moved already, okay?' She shrugs her shoulders in the empty room.

'No you haven't.'

'Don't be facetious, Chrissy. I don't want to fall out with you over this but you're pushing it, all right?'

'I didn't know.'

'What?' She is examining my face like it's creased or bent. 'Don't be so fucking ridiculous. I don't fucking believe this.' She pushes past me and continues talking. 'I don't know what kind of shit you're trying, Chris, and I don't know if it's supposed to be funny or spooky or what, but it isn't fair. You simply cannot pretend you didn't know. You fucking promised to help me pack, but you fucked off out of the flat first thing this morning for the first time in a fucking fortnight and left me to it.' She is at the door of the flat, looking around, checking. 'Now, you're trying to act crazy. If it's a plea for sympathy, you can forget it. You cashed in the last of those tokens weeks ago.'

'Why, Elsi?' I want to know the cause. The last fortnight? I remember nothing. As if they haven't been written.

'What's wrong with your face?'

'What's wrong with my face?' I repeat.

'Did you do that on purpose?'

'What?'

'You're not getting my sympathy, Chris. It's pathetic what you're doing.'

'What's wrong with my face?' I say and put my hands to feel it, like a blind man probing a stranger. It twitches and writhes under my fingers and now I feel a muscle in my cheek flick and freak in a nervous spasm. Above my left eye I feel a crust under my fingertips. I look at my hand speckled with rust, like dried blood.

'I walked into a door.'

I did not realise how far I'd got. Because I've been inside me all this time, I didn't realise, not till now, this moment, how bad I am on the outside, how out there I am. And I am out there.

'Chris, I don't know what's wrong with you and I can't help you any more. Every time I try to talk to you, you accuse me of plotting against you. You say I've been lying to you. I know you've had a hard time, I mean, Jesus, you're a walking grief-case. I can see you're unhappy. But you can't take it out on other people as well as yourself. I know you're upset about your dad and Dan and probably about your blessed bloody Leo too, but get over it, Chrissy. Get your act together. Get it in proportion. How many times do I have to say? It was never going to work. Understand? You left your rationality in a box the day you met that guy.'

'Is it because you're in love with me, Elsi?'

'What? No, Chrissy. Would I be moving out if I was in love with you? You're not making sense again. And I don't even love you right now. Not at all. And you want to know why? Because you're being a fucking loony tune, Chris, and I can't handle someone who isn't prepared to listen to reason. I've tried. You know I've tried. But there's only so much I'm prepared to go through. You've gone into overinterpretation overdrive. You can't let anything alone without reading a million meanings into it.'

'But what if the meanings are there?'

'They're only there when you look for them and that means one thing: you're paranoid.' She pauses and examines me, checking something. 'You don't get it, do you? Freakiness is one thing, but violent fits are another. And it's not you. I really don't know you right now. You are way out of my depth and if I don't get out of this flat one of us is going to end up killing the other. And, believe me, I mean that in the nicest possible way. So, Chrissy, get help. Get professional help. I mean that too.' She's lying again. It's because she's jealous. It's a punishment. For Leo.

She's just made it all up. Or He has.

She looks away, out into the landing and I hear the voice of the other guy shouting up the stairs, 'All loaded up, Els. I'll wait in the van.'

Get lost, you fucker, leave us alone.

'I'll drop by sometime soon for any post. Okay?' She fiddles with her keyring intently, working her fingers too fast to do whatever she's doing. 'Okay?' She repeats without looking up. I say nothing. She releases two keys from the rest which she slips in her pocket. 'Here.' She holds out the keys and when I just look at her, at her hand, at the keys, she picks up my hand with hers and turns it over and puts the keys there. 'See you, Chrissy. Take care,' and by the time I look up from my hand the door is closing behind her.

I wanted to tell her. I wanted to tell her I don't believe I'm real. Everything I do is controlled, but so is everything that happens to me. Why did she leave? There was no reason. I don't remember any reason.

She was in on it too. Everyone is in on it. It's all fabrication, invented to torment *me*.

Elsi. Elsi. Why have you forsaken me?

Chromosome 20
Nighttown

Chris need not have thought he was so special. It is not special to be mad.

Anyone can be a story. Everyone is. It is not exceptional and it is mere self-obsession that makes some people think otherwise. Stories run like foul rainwater in the gutters of London at night. The lifelines flow together from many sources, all finding the lowest level on the streets. It is not a decision. It is a destiny, a destination.

Because they are not wanted anywhere, they go nowhere. The arrogant and the self-pitying wander the streets of London unhappily ever after. They are pathetic. Sweep them away.

*

I feel I have been absent for a while. Like I was asleep, but I feel unslept, unslept for days, and as far I know, I am. I do not dare to sleep, to sleep and risk the chance that dreams may come. My dreams are like a death because they obliterate my consciousness, my tenuous continuity of self. I do not remember anything from the past few days and now I am here again, aware.

Also I have not eaten. I think I haven't. I don't remember food or tastes or digestions, defecations. And I have no money so it doesn't seem as though I can have done. I seem to be continuing to exist anyway, but maybe not all the time.

The flat is cold – even though it is warm outside, I can see it is – but that is because it is empty, sparse of furniture, things, people even.

It must be the sixteenth of August. I believe it because the television tells me so, not directly, but by its pictures of Leo. Leo arriving through airport customs. News. They claim it was last night. It is night now and I am alone in this flat, empty of Elsi, empty of her things and, for all I know, empty of me.

Leo looked out at me. He looked out of the screen, straight at me. But he didn't recognise me.

I was mad to think I knew him. That was a story I told myself. Or that I was told.

Or that was told about me.

I am huddled on the sofa, the walls are bare and things are beginning to make sense, I think. There is method in my madness.

I know I am fictional.

I also know I am right or I am mad. But I can't know which.

I only believe I'm not fictional in the same way I believe that God does not exist. But the thing is how to prove such a thing. It doesn't need to be proved, surely? It is too obvious for proof and, besides, you cannot prove a negative. This requires faith. But I have no belief in faith.

I know that I exist, but I am not sure that the one who's inventing me knows it. I know everything must be a lie, but I believe it anyway.

Yes, I now should say I *believe* I am being written. I think I know it, but I can't be sure. I need proof.

Do others feel like this? How do they prove it daily? That things happened even though they don't remember them. I do not feel I have enough memories to fill my life. I have no ever-present backdrop of a past. All this would make sense if He is inventing me. I need a name for Him.

He is my creator, *Author*.

He must be, because He causes my every thought and that is who I think He is.

Johnny, Dan called him.

Is this just me, how it is, being not real, or is this how it is for everyone? No one can ever know what it's like to be someone else. It might well be the same, more or less, but in my case I believe it may be different.

It is what Dan said – it is like I have taken a drug. I'm not free to be doing anything but what I am doing, but even without the choice, it doesn't feel like it's not me doing it.

There is a way of proving I exist, or demonstrating it at least. It's like in the labs. I didn't prove anything there. I filled test-tubes with liquids from syringes. I raced them across tracks of electrophoresis gel. I recorded results. I tried to get it wrong and if I failed, that was proof enough.

It's all falsification. If it cannot be falsified, I might as well believe and check myself into the Maudsley with Dan. Just another regular nutcase. A madman, real enough, but none the worse for that. If I'm mad, I can be treated, but if I'm the Author's creation, well, there's no cure for that.

Besides, I don't think I want to be treated. Manipulated into normality. I want my own solution, my own control, to feel like I'm exercising my will again.

I need to falsify Leo. If I'm right that he's not real, then I'm no more than a human script.

If I can just retrace my steps. Go back. See what I dropped along the path. See what memories are sparked, how real they are. Evidence. 'Chris woz ere' written in graffiti ten miles high. 'Leo 4 Chris'. With him I knew that things were real. Even when I was beginning to find out they weren't. I remember that night in the gallery, being gathered up, my face against his cheek and slowly realising the sound of his breaths as he held me so tight, kept me from my panic, was the sound of his tears.

But, there you go, you see, even that I can't trust, because I couldn't remember that before. Maybe I've just invented it. Or He has.

Now Leo is just a fantasy on the television, a lower reality, like me. Or lower, perhaps, like Wendy or Tinker Bell. That's what I need to find out. If I can go back and find, if not him, at least some unequivocal vestige, then I will be saved. I will have proof enough.

I feel Leo is out there, proof of him, by the theatre or the

276

Thames. The places he used to be. I will search for the spectral traces of him and I will amplify them, clone them, make them visible in my sight. HE IS REAL. I can invent him again and he will save me from this. Either he is out there or He is. One way or another, I feel there are conclusions in the streets. I must go out and look.

I am looking outside and the night looks warm. I am taking my jacket from the floor by the door.

*

Once upon a time, Lance was tall and blond and handsome and pure. However, because he considered himself too good to serve an undeserving employer, having found himself redundant, he remained unemployed for several years.

Eventually, walking in the countryside, Lance met a certain Mr King who owned a gold and silverware supplier based in Cornwall. Mr King recognised Lance's virtues and ability and he made him sales manager for the South East. Lance's pride was satisfied, for Mr King was indeed most deserving of his loyalty and therefore also of his friendship.

Even so, it came to pass that Lance betrayed his noble friend and patron. He betrayed him because he loved a woman, a woman called Jenny, who, as it happened, was married to Mr King.

When Mr King heard the rumours circulating the office, he summoned Lance. Lance, however, was on a not-inconvenient business trip in London, attempting to renew a contract to supply the Hail Glory Cup.

Lance had a reputation as the company's most tenacious deal-maker. Never would he let an honest deal evade him. His tenacity, however, was not so great as his guilt. When he heard word that his treachery was revealed, he vowed never to return to the office nor his home. Indeed, he never even left London. Some might call it honour, but it might also be called cowardice. Among other consequences, the firm lost the Hail Glory contract and did not regain it for many years.

So, because he was not wanted anywhere, Lance went nowhere. The adulterer and cowardly betrayer of his friend wandered the streets of London unhappily ever after.

My keys, I realise, I have left inside, just as I am pulling the door shut. Maybe I realise just before in which case why would I have done it? That thing with effects before their cause again – either way, I am on the street now and cannot get back in. Even if I wanted to. Keyless again – this happened before, everywhere I look, they come in pairs, in twins. I have nowhere to go. I have no money to get there. I walk. Steadily, foot by foot, setting up a rhythm, a solid solitary rhythm which swears blind that I am not a victim.

It is late. I can tell by the traffic on Camden Road and the drunkenness of the crowds spilling around the pubs I pass. Minicabs ferry the drunk and the stoned and the angry. A bus exposes in its strip-light glare sad faces of horror at its windows, people travelling home alone to lonely homes. I'm not going to pity them. I want to poke out their eyes, feeling the warm pop as I plunge my fingers into the sockets. At least they think they're real.

Am I the only one? Do they not exist either? And if not, do they only exist for me or am I not even the centre of this universe created around me? I might, I fear, be just a bit-part character in the book about myself.

The Author, perhaps, is the real hero, the main character at the heart of all of this. Hero? Villain. What's it matter?

*

Once upon a time, Jason's father ran a textile import business. Being a predominantly family affair, after his death, the position of chairman passed to Jason's uncle, who, as it transpired, lacked any of his brother's acumen. He bought inferior supplies and overpriced them. Then, as profits plummeted, he bought yet cheaper materials and hiked prices higher yet.

Jason took it upon himself to save the firm's fortunes. Seeking out new supply channels, he entered negotiations with a Greek source of aurum wool. With favourable terms, he hoped he might attract pump-prime investment and thereby unseat his nugatory uncle.

In the meantime, Jason acquired a wife, the daughter to his principal wool supplier, who proved only too eager to abet his transactions, enriching her husband at her father's expense. Thereafter, however, she enriched only herself; she insinuated herself into the family business and then fleeced it, ruining it dishonestly even more effectively than Jason's uncle had ruined it foolishly. Soon after, having filed for bankruptcy, Jason left her.

So, because he was not wanted anywhere, Jason went nowhere. The avaricious and credulous defaulter wandered the streets of London unhappily ever after.

*

Walking, I am losing myself, not lost, but I feel I am shedding time, what little of it remains. It is not continuous, I believe, in my fictional world. In His world. I can look up one moment and not yet be at Haverhill Road and now again, I look up and no thoughts have passed, just footsteps, but I am past Euston.

I'm losing time. Along with my memory, my mind, my reality, I'm losing any sense of one thing after another. I pass lampposts in the street, evenly spaced presumably, every fifty metres or so, but they flash past me like white lines in the road beneath a speeding car. They strobe above me. Or else, they stretch out, one to the next, a pinprick of light on the horizon, an age ahead, and, now, suddenly, upon me, above me, gone, lost. My father, gone. Just like that. Mummy. Dan. Work. Elsi. And Leo, most of all, Leo. In the past.

The night is not so warm outside, nor is it cold, unless I think of it.

*

Once upon a time, Dr John Foster was a noted academic. Indeed, he was one of the few respected researchers in the dubious field of parapsychology.

Those who can speak with authority on such topics are much pursued by the media. Like all vain men, Foster believed recognition to be superior to achievement and so sought his momentary prominence as greedily as it sought him. After appearing widely as a pundit, he signed a contract to present *You Won't Believe It!*, his own television series on Channel 5, an ill-conceived format following in the wake of *The X Files'* ratings success.

Nevertheless, in the glory of such heady fame, Foster indulged his vanity, believing that his was a charmed life and he could have all that he wanted with never a price to pay. He drank deeply from a cup which academics rarely encounter, the cup of material delights. He slept with beautiful women and developed expensive habits that soon developed into expensive addictions.

Then his show was axed.

So, because he was not wanted anywhere, Foster went nowhere. The vain and greedy sophist wandered the streets of London unhappily ever after.

*

At Holborn a woman reels into me and turns vaguely to look at my face. 'Isn't this bag sad?' she says and her head flops itself to one side towards a man with a green plastic bag.

'What?' I want to commit unspeakable acts of violence against her – pin her to the wall, slice off her ears with a rusty knife, take that bag in my fist and stuff it into her throat till her jaws snap and her cheeks tear. And him. Him, I want to fuck with hate till his anus splits and—

'This bag,' she says, stepping forward and waggling it on the man's shoulder who looks on at her, smiling distractedly. 'Isn't it sad?'

'I wouldn't know.' I want to walk on, but the two of them are managing to move so uncertainly across the whole pavement, I would have to choose to try to pass on one side of them or the other.

'No, guess not.' With a snide grin, she looks me up and down and turns back to the man's face which he buries against hers.

*

280

Once upon a time, Roupesh was a Bhangra musician and kick-boxing champion.

Meanwhile, his girlfriend, an ophiologist, worked in the Reptile House at London Zoo, where one day, whilst simultaneously listening to Roupesh's music and sapping venom from an inland taipan (*oxyuranus microlepidotus*), she dropped the snake and received a bite to the heel. Naturally, the Zoo maintained stocks of antivenin which were administered immediately, but her reaction was unusually severe and she was declared dead at Chelsea & Westminster Hospital before news of the accident had even reached Roupesh.

He did not sleep that night, but cried instead. Next day, however, he received a call from the hospital mortuary where, it transpired, she had awoken that morning from a deep venom-induced coma, weakened but apparently fit. She was asking for him.

The attending Dr Shade, inexperienced in such an unprecedented recovery and afraid for his patient's fragility, did not wish to move her from the mortuary and was examining her there when Roupesh arrived. Afraid to admit him, Dr Shade advised the febrile Roupesh that he feared her heart had been weakened by her ordeal and he should calm himself before seeing her. He, however, was too impassioned and burst through the double doors. As he clutched her up into his embrace, she saw the damage in his face that the long night's woe had wrought and, instantly, she suffered a decisively fatal coronary.

Twice bereaved, Roupesh blamed his own rash passion for his loss and descended into the underworld of a depression from which he was never to recover.

So, because he was not wanted anywhere, Roupesh went nowhere. The reckless and tiresome brooder wandered the streets of London unhappily ever after.

*

The quests of London at night are different from the days. Drink and drugs. Flesh on flesh. A night bus. A taxi.

On Long Acre, flashing lights give clues. Next, one says.

Books, etc. Superdrug. Taxi. Model. Electric, fluorescent, neon, reflected in glass, on the pavement. The sky filthy orange with the afterburn of it all.

Phantom smells reek from the underground kitchens of a late-night Chinese, the stench of soy and chilli and MSG, treacling in my nose and people cackling in the streets as they roll and flail in a drunken haze.

I hate them all, for their ignorance, their dim existence they take for reality.

Drink and drugs, flesh on flesh, all just ways to prove you're still there by escaping from it.

My only quest is to continue to exist and prove it to myself. To hang on to that because it's all I've got left.

*

Once upon a time, the Skipper, as even to his death he was known, captained a trawler operating out of Grimsby.

However, with North Sea fishing stocks depleted and with quotas proscribing the legitimate sale of all but the most paltry catch and with one leg well nigh surrendered to an old seaman's rheumatism, the Skipper grew bitter. He railed against the sea, the fish and the EU, swearing revenge on the great white cod that declined to be caught.

Eventually, he scuppered his own ship for the insurance, but by then was so feeble-minded that his crime was all too evident to the loss adjuster. The police were called in, but the Skipper hopped off to be lost in London.

So, because he was not wanted anywhere, the Skipper went nowhere. The mad and fraudulent deserter wandered the streets of London unhappily ever after.

*

I am in a bubble. People do not notice me as if I am invisible or a ghost. A girl who looks enough like me to be my sister, if I had a sister, jostles me and she just walks by. She hit me so hard I think it may have been on purpose, but she strides purposefully on, with a reason, as if it didn't happen. But still

282

I can feel the heft of her reality against my arm. I have made human contact. I would give her my soul if I had one. I am almost comforted. Even without connection.

*

Once upon a time, Eddie was a soldier, a sergeant major, and it came to pass that he served active duty in the Gulf, in Northern Ireland and in Bosnia.

During his prolonged absences, Penny, his wife, stayed at home with their young son. Fidelity to an absent husband is hard for a young woman to endure and so it happened that a series of men usurped Eddie's rightful place at home.

Eddie, nevertheless, harboured hopes of a joyful reconciliation once he was home again for good. Meanwhile, he suffered further tribulations. He was held hostage by a renegade fighter in a blown-out farm in the Balkans and only escaped by secreting a pencil in his boot with which he blinded his captor. He had been hooked on drugs, along with the rest of the army. And, while stationed outside Sarajevo, he had an affair with a Croatian with high cheekbones and a fondness for seafood.

Eddie, however, was denied his *rapprochement*, for, on leaving the services, he was ill prepared for civilian life. Without employ, he was unable to support even himself, let alone dare to presume he could offer his wife and child more than her latest suitor.

So, because he was not wanted anywhere, Eddie went nowhere. The bellicose and belittled bum wandered the streets of London unhappily ever after.

*

Outside the old actor's church in Covent Garden that looks like a Greek temple there is a busker juggling to himself with an empty hat before him and, now, so late, few passers-by. Three policemen watch him without interest from in front of the Punch & Judy.

The volume of their voices rises as I approach, or is it my

approach that makes it seem louder?

'Stonewall tomorrow.'

'Who?'

He folds his wrist limply and says, 'Nancy boys.'

They are there to offend me, but I am beyond that. It cannot hurt so deeply because I know that is all they are there for. I will let them live, because their existence counts for nothing anyhow.

*

Once upon a time, Henry Flower thought himself an 'entrepreneur'. Forever he had deals afoot, but he never actually conducted any commerce; a hustler without perseverance.

Meeting Molly, then, was fortunate for him. Generally ridiculed by his fellow men, he evoked something more like sympathy in women, not to mention fear. Thus it was that he persuaded her to let him share her two-room flat in the Peabody Estates south of the National Theatre. He also became her pimp, which, in his case, involved nothing more than taking her money from her at the end of the night and clearing out of the flat while she entertained her callers.

So, because he was not wanted anywhere, Henry went nowhere. The selfish and self-deluding parasite wandered the streets of London unhappily ever after.

*

Now suddenly, I am at the theatre, without ever having got here, but he is not here. No graffiti or footprints, no scents. Only the mild night with a few spits of rain as the orange grey sky begins to cry. Just people rushing by towards the Aldwych and the river and the taxis and their homes. I am standing by a stand selling tomorrow's papers. Tomorrow has already come. I know they are there for me to see, for me personally, because beyond what I can see and sense I believe in nothing and because there is the *Mirror* and I am reading its headline: 'OFFICIAL:' it says, 'LEO MARTIN TO DIVORCE!'

'Exclusive,' says the byline, 'by our new Mirror Showbiz Editor Bill MacRake'. I pick it up to read. 'Utopia star Leo Martin will finally divorce PR guru and cheating wife Helen Bossi, we can exclusively reveal.

'Martin has given up any hope of winning back the love of his wife after revelations of her affair with New York city slicker Vic Hemitt.' It's all just a story I read, just characters.

'Thirty-two pee.'

I look up at the voice and see its face, balding and bearded, hand outstretched.

'I don't have ...'

'Piss off, then. Not a fucking library.'

I pull a knife, a small ornamental dirk, from my pocket and plunge it into the fat vein on his neck and watch in gleeful horror at the blood-letting, the treacly tide soaking into his precious fucking papers and on to the street—

Instead I turn away and there are men behind me, night wanderers like me. They have found me at last.

'You're better off trying the bins for something to sleep under,' says the tallest, whose hair was probably once blond, whose features once handsome, whose life once pure.

We walk together and they hand me manna in the wilderness and ask my name.

I am a human script, I say and they say, So are we.

It's true then, I ask and one replies, Insofar as anything is.

Are we real, I ask and another responds, To ourselves.

Is that enough, I ask. No one can ask for more.

Am I a slave, I ask. You are a hero.

A tragic hero, I ask. That depends on you.

On my choice, I ask. On who you are.

Is there no hope, I ask. Not without someone who loves you.

Does anyone love me, I ask. Not if they abandoned you.

Will he come back, I ask. Not if he doesn't love you.

Does he exist, I ask. He was always too good to be true.

When will I die, I ask. When your death has a cause.

Will I live forever, I ask. Only people in stories live forever, they reply.

Now I am alone again. Stranded on The Strand. Gone like ghosts. Sent to taunt and haunt me. No more real than me or Leo. I am walked towards Waterloo Bridge and the black river below.

Now I know. I can prove nothing. I know I will never know. I must put my faith in belief. Leo is not here. I came here to find him, to falsify his absence with a memory of something real. But I find he only exists in the words on the page.

I grieve his loss more than anything. He gave me cause. More of a father than a father was. He was my last hope, but none of it was true, none of it happened, not really. I'm not mad – I'm not anything.

Now I know. The Author is cruel. I know nothing else about Him. I know He is vengeful even though I have done nothing against Him. I couldn't even if I wanted to. He dictates my every move. My thoughts too, I presume. Am I thinking this or is He?

Get out of my head, if you can hear me.

How much does He know? Does He know I know about Him? Did He make me find out?

There are other questions too. So many and I have to ask them. Because He makes me ask? Or because of who I am? And did He invent that too? Or is it just because I am a scientist that I must ask questions? It is my essence, even if science is not now what I do.

Heartless, cruel, tyrant, devil.

If this is a book, what is being read? My Author records it all but what and who for? My thoughts or just some of them? My every move? Do I shit and piss and fuck and wank and fart and everything in His gaze?

Readers. Watchers. Listeners. Spies.

Is there anybody there? Is there? Can you hear me?

I yell it out across the Thames but the river just slaps its banks and flows on. On. To the sea, the great mother of a sea.

I turn back without answer.

All powerful and without pity. He has taken everything from me as if it is a test I cannot win. Tested to destruction, regardless. I know where it will all end.

I must cheat him. I must win, but I cannot, whatever I do. Even defying Him, this will be His will. I must run to the finish line, not let him drag me. Let's be done with it. Come on, then. Come on.

'Come on!' I scream it at the night. 'Coward!'

But nothing strikes me down.

I must do it myself. I no longer need to know. He is going

to make me do that too.

And I will. Just to end it. Then He will not be able to get at me any more, playing with my life. I have nothing left to lose. Nothing to gain either, but long ago I ceased to expect so much. Epitaphs is an anagram of happiest. That tells me what I should do. I should give up the ghost.

Even if I am wrong. Even then, I must do it. Because he makes me. Even if I am mad, then the rational course is still the same. I have nothing left – no job, no money, no friends, no family around me, no Leo. Therefore it is not worth it any more. Never more can I have greater joy than suffering. Even now there is a science, a law, a formula, which even He cannot change. If

$$\frac{inevitable(suffering - happiness)}{+ \ potential(suffering - happiness)} > \text{pain of suicide}$$

then life has no reason.

One thing now is certain for me. Suffering, inevitable and potential. And even the pain of death is as nothing against the pain of life.

I cannot do it here, because He will torture me with redemption, fished from the river by a miracle or missed by the speeding bus. It must be certain. Doubt is no longer any part of me. And this is a private act – it's between me and my maker.

I curse my creator, now let me die. I have decided what I must do. Or at least, it has been decided.

Chromosome 21
The Human Script (II)

'If God does not exist, then everything is permitted.'
Fyodor Dostoevsky

'The characters from my stories go about the world telling everybody that I'm a cruel writer – completely heartless. It would need a very sympathetic critic to make people see how great is the compassion that lies behind that laughter. But where today are there any sympathetic critics?'

Luigi Pirandello

Who is cruel? If freedom is a fallacy, who should be blamed?

Would you want to interfere and attempt to affect some different outcome? What gives you that right? Does Chris deserve to be with Leo? Surely you cannot think that. Chris: mad and pathetic, in love with unreal fantasies and obsessed by lonely, paranoid thoughts in which he believes his fate is determined by an author, a conceit he has conjured because he has defied his father and his god. And Leo: too cowardly to be alone, too cowardly to be together, wanting only the solace of adulation, being made a father figure to someone even more alone than himself.

Would you write this differently? Would you read it differently?

Who is cruel?

*

The human genome is a book in which is written the fate of humankind: to be human. The essence of the species is in its three thousand thousand thousand nucleotide bases. That is where to search for humanity, for civilisation, for original sin.

There are many different versions of the human script, however. Each human's genome tells a different story. No two copies are identical.[9] The differences are there, however minute. They are the alleles – different versions of a gene – which each influence the meaning in their own way. A single base – an A for a G, a C for a T – might be the flapping butterfly that causes skin to be white rather than black, the left hand to be stronger than the right, sexual orientation to be towards the same sex rather than the other.

The gene is the meaning. The alleles are the different ways of saying the same thing, or, perhaps, different things being said. How different do they have to be before they are not the same, before one says: these are not alleles, not different versions, no, this gene is missing and this other is in its place? A book does not remain the same book if you change every sentence for another that supposedly means the same. Perfect translation is impossible.

Genes are signifiers. Words are signifiers. Alleles are the multiplicity of meaning, anagrams, spliced letters, deconstructions and reconstructions: different versions of the same thing. Like lies are a different version of truth, fiction a different version of fact, alleles a different version of a gene.

Context is everything: for genes as well as books. The letters may remain unchanged, but every time the words are read, the context is different. To reread a book is to read a different book. The reader is different. The meaning is different.

Reading is everything: the reader usurps the writer, who may be long dead, just as science usurped god. The reader is more powerful than the writer for he has the power to resurrect life by merely opening a human script.

The human script is nature, but it is nothing until it is read, nurtured in the mind. It has no meaning of its own.

---

9 Except, of course, the genome of monozygotic twins, whose differences must stem from other causes.

Just a series of letters, arranged in triplets[10] and pairs.[11] Three thousand thousand thousand.

On its own, the human script is a tale told by an idiot. He can strut and fret, but it signifies nothing if he is never heard.

*

Suffering is inevitable. It is part of the human condition. It is written in the human script. In pain, man is born, his own pain and his mother's.

Suffering is inevitable. It is part of life. It is part of the pattern that supports it all, red in tooth and claw. To brook no suffering is to want no life. Can there be a story without suffering? Even fey happy endings and tidy romances rest on the anguish begot by other possible outcomes. In pain, the story is born. Only through conflict can change come to pass. And conflict necessitates suffering.

Who then is cruel? Who brings about suffering? Is the baby cruel that brings the pain of its mother's labours? Is the genome cruel that predestines the abnormal, the mutant, the still-birth? Is the writer cruel that makes his characters suffer only to bring them to triumph or tragedy in the end?

Is God cruel?

God created the gourd to shade Jonah's brow and then appointed a worm to smite that same gourd. Was that cruel?

'It is better for me to die than to live,' cried Jonah to his God. And God said unto Jonah, 'Doest thou well to be angry for the gourd?' and by the gourd's suffering and by Jonah's, He granted and justified mercy on Nineveh, that great city. Had He not the right to be cruel to that which he created?

God created the Egyptians, too, whom he drowned to save the Children of Israel in their flight. Had He not the right?

God created Job and placed his fate in Satan's hands, who killed his children and his livestock and deprived him of his

---

10 Trinities such as: codons; God the Father, Son and Holy Ghost; Hamlet the king, the prince and the ghost; Oedipus, Laius and Jocasta; the writer, character and reader; the father, the Author, the God; the need for love, the father's love, the lover's love; and so on.

11 Like twins or mirror images.

riches and smote him with boils. Yet shall he that contendeth with the Almighty instruct Him? He that reproveth God, let him answer it. He the Lord your God was a jealous God and had He not the right to do with His creations what He willed?

The Lord gave. His was the right to take away.

Job was not a God, nor the Egyptians, nor Jonah, nor the gourd. None of them was on His level of existence. He imagined them and He could unimagine them.

And in the end, Job understood that he was nothing more than God's invention and so too was his suffering. His suffering was no more real than he was. When at last he understood this and accepted it, the suffering disappeared and his fortunes were restored.

What then if Job never existed? Nor did his suffering. But to Job (stubborn demander of just reasons), his suffering was as real as he was. Was then the God that let him suffer still cruel?

Is it murder to kill a man if the man never existed? To the man it is. So, to a Christian, the Jews will always be the Christ-killers. Jesus exists, if only in the minds of Christians. They place their Christ's reality on the same level as their own. And so, they believe, his murder was as real as their own. But they are the Christ-killers, for they are the ones who believe he ever lived and therefore it is their invention of his death that killed him.

What happens is as real as the person to whom it happens, even when the cause comes from another level.

But does that mean that God was cruel for killing the gourd?

And what about God? Is man cruel for killing God? His existence is not on man's level and yet man has done away with Him as surely as God smote the gourd.

*

Gott ist tot. God is dead. Or never was. So who does that put in His place?

Mankind.

According, that is, to mankind, which only goes to

demonstrate the importance of who is reading the script.

And does mankind justify its cruelty?

Inhumanity is part of humanity as much as suffering is a part of stories. Cruelty is written in the human script.

Is cruelty still cruel if it is necessary?

Is cruelty still cruel if it is part of a lie? Stories are just lies made to look like truth. And if truth contains suffering, those who perpetrate stories must act cruelly. Again: is cruelty still cruel if it is necessary?

But there are people far crueller than he who perpetrates stories, for he, at least, knows that they are lies: there are those who listen to them, for they must convince themselves that they are true. They write the story again each time they open the book and they place its reality on the same level as their own. They are the ones who see significance in the words. They see the human essence, not the genome. They see the human, not the script. They see the suffering, not the necessity.

They believe it is truth, knowing it's all lies.

There does not need to be an author. *La Morte D'Auteur.* As thoroughly as mankind has killed God, the reader has despatched the author. No one wrote the human genome, the human script. It has no author. It simply evolved. There is no definitive version. Readers sequence the letters and decide on meanings and only when the script has meaning can anyone say it is cruel.

So who is cruel?

You, cruel reader, you are. You. [12]

---

12 I am not sure I like this narrator. I think I shall kill him.

Chromosome 22
Will

'To be or not to be, that is the question'
Hamlet, III, i

'The best of fates is not to be.'
Sophocles

I am huddled on the doorstep outside the flat where I have lived. After a while, some time ago, I cannot say how long, there was no keeping out the cold. All I can do is draw myself in more tightly as if I could fold myself into nothing, a vacuum where sensation and suffering cannot reach.

Slowly the darkness is draining from the orange grey sky and now the streetlights go off, leaving just a muddy grey backdrop to the traffic that gradually multiplies and slows. A line of Latin keeps repeating itself to me: *O lente, lente currite noctis equi.* I don't even know what it means and I know it must be Him messing with my head, but soon He will be gone.

At last a downstairs light comes on and I ring his bell. The man, whose name I have never known and never am likely to know, if he even has one, comes to the door. He's only wearing a towel and the moment seems comical, deliberately inappropriate, as if even now He is trying to undermine me. The man doesn't want to hear my apologies about the key but to get back to his shower or his bath. Nor do I want to tell him.

And so I climb the stairs.

I check the door to the flat. Locked.

I huddle on the landing and wait.

I feel I can switch off time now. I just close my eyes and open them and it will be later.

*

The door slams shut downstairs as the man leaves and brings me back to this reality. Maybe I slept. I no longer make the distinction.

I did not want him to hear me, to intervene.

Creaking and stiff, I stand up and I put my right hand on the banister rail, my left on the wall, and I kick. And I kick again. And the third time, the door panel gives way and as I pull my foot back I feel the sabre-toothed splinters tearing through the leg of my jeans and the skin of my leg. I extricate my foot from the shards of wood and examine my ankle.

It is deep. There is pain. There is blood. I don't want to be stopped. Before the pain can get to me, can remove my will to raise my leg again, I aim another kick at the breach.

My foot goes through and I resist the instinct to recoil and rip my leg further.

I cannot reach up enough through the hole. With my hands I tug at the door's wound, pulling away the plywood, widening it until I can reach the latch and I let myself in. Close the door.

Cum finis est licitus, etiam media sunt licita. Enough with your games, your anagrams, your secrets. You can't do more to me now.

*

I sit in the hallway in front of the broken door and rest my back against the wall. I want someone to come, to ring the doorbell and ask about the noise. I want someone to interfere, to stop me.

There is no one. Just click-click-click.

I have a certain clarity now, I think, but it brings no relief. I am outside my body, my mind, and all I see is the horrible truth of it, the lack of choice – every interpretation another reason for the same end. It makes me breathe uneasily, maybe I am scared or upset, but there's nothing I can do about it now.

I no longer harbour any belief I am real. I'M NOT REAL proved that. I used to believe I was free, but I saw through that one. At first I thought it was because of my genes, my past, that nothing I chose was free, was really mine, but I saw through that one too. Everything I do, even this, is what the Author conducts me to do.

Still there is that delusion though, that irrepressible illusion of ownership of what I decide. Still I feel that to do this deprives him somehow. He may have led me this far, but now he's backed me into a blind alley. He's as robbed of alternatives as I am. And that's because of who I am and who he's made me. I'm the kind of person who would do this now. At least He and I are in this together now.

If I go through with it. My heart is like a rattle in my chest. I'll probably be too scared. Or something will happen. Please, God, Author, whoever you are, make something happen. Stop me.

I can't live like this, if you can even call it living.

Es irrt der Mensch, so lang er strebt.

It begins slowly.

I stand and, in my unslept misery and fear, blood surges to my head, dizzying the walls, dappling my sight. The corridor returns.

The bathroom. Plug the bath. Turn on the taps.

If I can do this, that will be an end to it. He will have to write The End. My end will be The End. No more crying alone without consolation or comfort or the warmth of another person. No more doubting everything, anything. No more fear about what He'll throw at me next. Just no more.

In the living room, I lose my jacket from my shoulders and gather bottles. Less than half-empty, forgotten dregs of Elsi's foreign holidays – rum, schnapps, Metaxa, a miniature Bell's – all the poisons of the world.

He can only make me do this because I want to, because I want to be nothing, more completely nothing. Protected from the pain of barely being by non-existence.

Tov motih m'chayey.

In the kitchen I take up a small sharp knife, the same one I used to cut thin slivers of garlic the first time I cooked for Leo.

But that didn't happen, I remember. If Leo had been real, it might have been worth it to half-exist. If I could believe in Leo, I could believe I too have a self.

He almost caught me again, planting his seeds of memory, of doubt in the unreality of things. Perhaps, even now, He's going to stop me. Through fear or panic or hesitation, He's going to make me back out at the last minute.

All the more reason then to go on, to flush Him out and see what He can pull from the hat.

I must stop thinking like this, thinking that any of this is my doing. It's Him, all Him. Everything else is worthless and void.

I want Him to stop me, to prove me wrong and my raw, painful eyes fill at the prospect that He won't.

If it were done when 'tis done, then 'twere well it were done quickly.

Now the bathroom again. I shed my shirt on the way, letting it lie where it falls in the hall. Place the knife by the bottles. Take off the rest of my clothes.

In the mirrored cupboard, I see nothing, nothing in my face to tell me anything. Just eyes like a wounded bloodhound's. I see ugliness there and I want to obliterate it. I open the cupboard and take out every pill or medicine bottle. Place them by the bottles and the knife on the side of the bath.

I pick up the bleach bottle too from beside the toilet.

O passi graviora, dabit deus his quoque finem.

Turn off the taps. The cold tap drips.

I step into the bath. First I feel the sting of its warmth prickling my feet from which the chill has not yet drained. Now I feel its sharper bite as it washes into the gash on my leg. This pain is comfort. It is the solace of physicality, like a touch. I want to scratch deep into myself to draw out more. Red drifts into the water, dynamically tumbling. I regard my body from above. Once it had form, now it all drifts downwards into the rising vapours. I'll be rid of it soon.

I lower myself into the water's cuddle of heat, letting it envelop me and draw out the cold inside.

This is not so hard, crossing this brink. I had thought it would be more difficult. My hand would tremble on the tap and be unable to turn. Or I would have crouched in the hall for hours, delaying, postponing, losing momentum. It began slowly and now the time draws on. In an hour, maybe more, maybe less, it'll be over. I'll be over. The fear in this is breaking me, but it is not stopping me.

This is my first act of free will. To believe I have free will even though I know I don't. I have but one bare hour to live.

But I've hardly started. I am only taking a bath so far. If I stopped now that's all it would be. Stretch out time. Make an hour into a day, a week into a month, a year. I can kid myself I am defiant, but the truth is that I do not want to die. To be dying or dead. I want just not to be. My face constricts and I'm crying again. Caustic tears creeping from each eye. That is why I can say it's started – because it will end.

I take a bottled medicine, an unfinished prescription, and push down the cap and unscrew. It tastes chalky. I drink it all. Only one mouthful, but it has started. An overdose begins with a little.

The next bottle is eyewash. I don't want to drink it and push it off the edge of the bath. It smashes on the floor and, over the bath's ceramic rim, I watch the keen blue triangles spin across the tiles. My jeans and socks, already spattered with blood from my leg, are splashed with eyewash and splintered glass.

Cough mixture. It smells of a childhood taken from me and tastes of sickly invented strawberries. It is being drunk. I am drinking it.

There's one more. That's not much yet. No harm done. The water ripples around me. My chest is heaving fast and I realise I am panting.

I could be real. Even now, I could be wrong. I must be wrong. I'd be mad to think I'm not real. I must be mad.

But still, does it make any difference? I can chant the mantra to myself – you are mad, you are real – I can know it, but I can't believe it. To be mad is worse than not to be if this is what it is. I don't want the hollow expression, the hollow life. I don't want to be like Dan. I don't want to be.

Or even if they get me sane, what's left? My life is hollow anyway. Everything's gone now. I've fucked it all up. There's reason enough.

I want to die.

The third medicine bottle tastes hot. Maybe it wasn't to be taken internally. I don't care. I want the pills now. Less than an hour. I must be faster now. If I'm doing this, it's better to do it fast. I do not want to get too scared before I've gone too far. I do not want to slip beyond the point where I can see it through, make it certain. Then let Him try and stop me.

I empty a bottle and a plastic pot into my hand and eat the pills like a horse takes a sugar lump. There are too many to swallow, so I crunch them and they taste bitter and dry.

I thirst.

I drink schnapps now and wash it down. And I unpop pills from their plastic blisters and count them down, drinking from the bottle after every one. One – two – three – four – five – six – seven. Out of grappa, Metaxa now. Eight – nine – ten – eleven – twelve – thirteen – unlucky for some – fourteen – fifteen. No more in that pack. Ibuprofen. Sixteen – seventeen – eighteen – nineteen – twenty – twenty-one – twenty-two – twenty-three – twenty-four. Rum. Twenty-five – twenty-six – twenty-seven – twenty-eight – twenty-nine – thirty – thirty-one – thirty-two – thirty-three – thirty-four – thirty-five – thirty-six – thirty-seven. Just when I thought it would last. The miniature of Bell's. Thirty-eight – thirty-nine. Gone.

And now the bleach, the child-proof cap. Can I go that far? *Warning*, it says, *Danger of death*. The bottle smells like urine. I tip it up into my mouth. It's like hot chlorine and makes me gag. I force a mouthful down, but I'm not going to try again. I don't want to make myself throw up.

It burns right down me, like whisky at a wake.

I am breathing like I've run a mile. Already I'm yawning, unable to stretch my jaws enough, yawn again. The water now seems too hot. I push the bottles to the floor and only the schnapps breaks. The others just whizz like pinballs skating on the eyewash and now the Metaxa hits the sink stand and it breaks too. All the glimmering little pieces I see but I cannot prop myself up any more and, I let go, slapping back deep into the bath.

I breathe sharply, but now slowly, controlled. My shoulder-blade hurts from the hard enamel. I am dizzy. I am lying here for a minute, just a minute, before the next thing.

Am I too far yet? Have I done enough?

The moment passes and the next one.

I am not yet ready. I lie here for the next moment too. The moments are long. And they are short. Not long now.

A bluebottle scouts the unlit ceiling lamp, flying in straight lines and crashing against invisible barriers sending it bouncing back around the other side of the lamp only to crash and bounce again.

So now the next thing. The knife is in my hand. This is the worst.

I think of dissections I did, I thought I did, back at college, but nothing comes to me but flashes of distended frogs, flesh pinned back and bowels and organs splayed. I think of blood on white rubber gloves. I don't think I did this before.

I place the cold sharp edge against the soft ridge on my right wrist, pronounced in the heat of the steam. I don't want to. I'll miss this bit out. I've taken enough. I'll be dead soon anyway. Without this.

I knew He'd stop me. In the end. He won't let me do this, because if I don't, I'll survive. I'll still be here for Him to punish, to carry on getting his kicks. I'll bottle out now when I realise I don't have the courage, the nerve to go through with it. I'll get my fingers down my throat and will get through.

I don't want to though. This is misery, pure unretreating pain. None of it goes away if I don't go forward. I am not a coward.

I'll do it then and I'll see, I'll see that the knife can't cut, can't break my skin, can't dig into the vein. It won't work.

The blade presses against the skin and my flesh dips deeply against the force. The skin won't give. It won't.

The skin gives. The blade slips slightly as it slides deeper. I draw it back, down the vein. I watch, from outside, no hurt yet, and the flesh parts like theatre curtains.

Now there is the soft whisper of blood. It pulses and sputters and now seeps out in a rhythmic flow, pumped from within. I have to gasp, a quick breath which returns instantly in a choke of tears in my throat and my eyes. My mouth sets into spasms of sobs. I plunge my hand under the panicked water and the water darkens round me in swirls and fractals of carmine.

I breathe deep. It comes back in a gargle of mucus.

Save me now, you little shit! You cunt! You nothing! Get me out of this if you can. I dare you. Because I don't want to live and without me, you're no more anything than I am.

I am waiting. Time is passing. The dripping tap tells me

how fast, but I lose track between its chimes. The water is red.

Soon He will be here and I am rushing on to meet Him. It's not so easy now, but now I can't turn back. Save me, you cunt. Please.

De profundis clamavi ad te, Domine; Domine, Pater, exaudi vocem meam.

My arm rises out of the wine-dark bath, still bleeding, still refilling the wound as fast as it flows into the water. I take the knife in my right hand and I regret not doing the left wrist first – now I have to cut with my weaker, and now wounded, arm.

I try to line up the knife and it is not in focus and I think maybe I am trembling. It's unsteady and I can't do it. I steady it against a wall tile and press the knife, but I can't press hard enough against the wall because I haven't the strength there and so I draw the arm into my stomach. I double up to press harder, harder against the skin and I almost hear the skin's mute pop now as its resistance breaks. I draw the knife down.

A little blood. I have missed the vein.

I'm running out of time now. He's trying to stop me.

I raise the knife and flick it against my arm, slashing, shallow cuts that open deeper as I slash again, again, again and criss-cross red lines of tearing.

Now the blood flows. It flows.

A curl of skin flaps in the flow like paper.

It hurts, but feels like nothing in the scheme of things, distant unreal pain.

The knife is dropped somewhere. The water, maybe, and I lay back and there is the warm pulse of my arms under the water and my breaths come softly. I had not thought it would be so hard.

Eli, eli, lama, sabbachthani?

Nothing can save me now. I am saved.

He can't make anything happen now. No more unrealities. Too late.

I have done the right thing. He can't hurt me now. No more. Even if it is He who did this, it was me too. Either He controls me, my every act, in which case, I could have done no other. Or I had the choice and now this will end it all. This has been an experiment too. Hypothesis: I am the Author's invention. By showing that I can kill myself, I falsify. I will not be able to observe my results, but I am content to let the proof stand. Even if I prove nothing, I deny Him whatever pleasure He derives from all of this.

He can't do any more to me.

I'll close my eyes.

I'll destroy his book.

It hurts.

Either way, it is over now.

I'll sleep.

It is at an end. His end. Mine.

My eyes are closed.

Mehr Licht!

*

In the distance, there is noise.

Far away, down a corridor, in an echoing other place. I am sleeping now maybe.

There are still the drips. I am aware of them again, but there's something else. *Ring ring.* The sound I think is in my head. The sound of dying, perhaps. *Ring ring.*

My eyes are heavy, but I would like them open. That may be more than I can do. *Ring ring.* The light floods in, the white-tiled walls, all misty in steam, no, the water seems too cold now for steam, too cold. *Ring ring.*

I am remembering. Remembering. The phone. *Ring ring. Click-click-click.*

I am back. I can hear. I can hear the answer machine. Picking up.

Elsi's voice, but, no, not her. 'Elsi and Chris aren't around right now, but you know the routine.' I hear the beep.

'Hello? Chris? Are you there?'

The voice is full and gentle and far away. A silence follows.

'If you're there, please, pick up. Please. It's me.'

Yes, Leo, I know. You're not real.

'Chris? No?' He sighs. 'Well, I was just phoning to say hello, see how you are. You know. Things are fine here, I guess, and I just wanted to say hi, well, to talk to you.'

It's him. It's all all right. Everything's going to be all right. He is real. He's here. Hang on a minute, Leo. I'll be right there, just give me a moment.

'I mean, things are fine, but I wanted to say, I wanted to say that some things haven't been going too well and I just really wanted to hear you.' There is silence, but he doesn't hang up.

'There are just some things I was going to say. I've been thinking, you see, that perhaps I should exercise more control over what goes on in my life. I mean, one of the things I love about being with you is that I feel I've got a handle on things, but I think that got me scared too. I think I've been a bit cowardly about taking what I want. I don't want to be here. I'd rather be there. I've decided that now.' Silence again. 'I still love you. I'm sorry. I got it wrong. I don't want it all to end.'

All this time you have been real. You weren't contrived to add to my torture.

Wait a moment, Leo, I'm coming. I raise my arms from the water, thin, pellucid, tattered. The cuts have opened and spilt out the grey insides.

'Listen, I'm coming home tonight. My flight gets in at some ungodly hour and I'll come over to you if I may. I mean, if you don't mind.'

The sides of the bath are slimy walls. I am climbing them but all that happens is splashes of cold dark water and back I slide, my face plunged under, the ferrous taste of blood in my nose, and I arise again, choking. 'I'm not going to tell them about you. And you needn't worry about MacRake or Helen or Vic or anybody. I've been doing some sorting out. Everyone's happy. You needn't worry about anything. Give me a call on my mobile to let me know if it's okay to come over. I'll pick up the messages.'

Wait, Leo, please wait. I'll make it there. Now I know, now I know you're real and there's some point of certainty in all of this. I have been wrong. There is no author. I've decided I want to live.

'Let me know what you decide. I love you, Chris. I love you.' Click-click-click and now the sound of the dialling tone and now a final click and just the sound of the dripping tap again.

I am in the bath, glass on the floor.

Jesus wept.

My will is sending messages of movement but my body is far away, far far away. The water's no longer cold. The room's no longer bright. I am closing my eyes. To sleep, to sleep.

Teleteserai. Teleteserai.

The X or Y Chromosome
This Mortal Coil

'Cogito, ergo sum.'
Rene Descartes

'Allah takes the souls at the time of their death, and of those that do not die during their sleep. Then He keeps those for which He has decreed death and releases the others for a specified term. There are messages in this for those who apply reason.'
The Qu'ran, 39:42

I'm dead. I must be dead. Surely, I must be dead.

This is what death is like. Or rather, this is death. I did not think I would exist at all.

But what is *I*? 'I' does not exist, I think. I do not feel. No pain, no sense, nothing. There is not even the dark I have when I've closed my eyes. I have no eyes. I think I have no eyes. I have lost everything: no possession, no body, no life, no self. No matter, never mind. All I know is what I know directly, not what I see through the prism of my eyes – what eyes? – or, worse, through the veil of His invention. I can doubt everything else, everything but what I know directly. Like the good rationalist scientist I think I am. I was.

'I' is consciousness, for, I think, that is all I am.

My consciousness survives in emptiness. My self survives in death? Then what is death? Not an end. This is not what I thought, not what I thought at all. Not what I thought I knew. Not what I believed. But I *must* be dead.

Unless it's Him.

It must be Him. He keeps me here, His final vengeance against my self-destruction. He has not let me die and become nothing, like any other death, but keeps me here in this lingering non-existence. There is no afterlife so long as life is real in the first place, but for me, I will spend eternity in this wilderness, in this hell. I was right all along – little good it does me now. He torments me even with the truth. Forever!

Take it away. Take it all away. I do not want to be alone.

What else could He do? Save me or let me go to live or die happily ever after? No, this way He wins in the end. I have nothing. I cannot stop myself from being.

Please. I do not want to be.

Dear God, just let me end.

Be calm again. Be calm. There's time to fret. There's time forever.

Am I even someone? Wouldn't a no one do as well as a someone about whom nothing can be said? For I know nothing. I doubt everything. I am detached, detached from the sanity of a cause. Now we're getting somewhere. Just my thoughts, endlessly sustained, full of the knowledge that Leo was coming back. I remember now, he was coming back. Leo was coming back. Too late. But Leo was my proof. I'M NOT REAL was not real. I have been wrong. I have been mad. I am real after all.

I am real. It has all been delusion. There was never proof, just my mistaken belief. Nothing happened without a cause. Eugene was real. Wendy was real. It was merely people, real people watched me, followed me and beat and bruised me in alleys. Anagrams are just anagrams. Sounds in my head weren't really there or they were, but were not what I feared. It was all coincidence, just coincidence, searching for patterns of meaning where there are none. Over-interpretations, searching for sense where there was no sense to be found.

I am not dead then. Dying. Perhaps I am dying. My brain shutting down. My cerebellum gone. No senses streaming through the hypothalamus. No communication between what finally is me and my body in a bath in a flat, beyond saving.

Not for me the distant white light dimly glimpsed at the end of the long passageway. Coming out into brightness where my past lost loves are here to greet me. My mother. My father. I can want them, but they are not coming. Where is my Daddy now?

Or perhaps I am in an ambulance or a hospital. A doctor with charged paddles orders 'Clear!' and all the time I'm drifting off further into blackness until the line is flat and then these thoughts, even these very thoughts, will be gone too. Or maybe they have given up the ghost already. My body lies frosted and naked in the steel drawer, tag on my toe. Now we're getting somewhere.

Perhaps Leo found me. And I was not yet dead. He pulled me cold and drained from the rusty water and pressed his lips to mine again, breathing his life into me and I'll wake up soon and be with him again. Soon. How soon? How long have I been gone already? Moments, hours, weeks, years? I am in a coma, plugged into a hospital bed with no visitors and no open eyes to see the view from the window. And maybe they don't know I am alive in here and any moment they'll just shut me off and – mid-thought – I'll stop.

When will I stop? Why don't I stop? Why haven't I stopped?

I am asleep, in bed, at Le Noires. I am just a boy who dreamt he wasn't real. I never used to dream, perhaps that is why – the dream within a dream is too precarious. Dreams are safe, the mind floats free, but I do not feel safe or free or even anything but fear. The horror. The horror!

I will wake up soon and it will all have been a dream.

Okay, now we're getting somewhere. Maybe what I believed was true. Or maybe it wasn't. Either I am dead or I never lived. Without God, the Author takes his place. Without the Author, there is God. One is invented or both or neither. And perhaps me too. And who's inventing whom? Am I creating them or are they creating me?

I did away with God and He came back to haunt me. I did away with myself and my self remains. I am not substance, my body gone, but He continues to use my mind to keep my story, His story, going. Who is my creator? Who tortures me this way? Who fathered me, blessed me with the burden and the crime of life?

His grey beard. His tender, learned eyes. His careworn brow, frowned in concern. After all this time, now I know I loved him, love him most of all. Our father who art ... I pushed him away. All this, it has all been grief. I thought I could do without him, but when he was gone, it was only a matter of time. I needed him to exist to make me be. I created him again. All this time I have been wanting his absence, it is only because I think it'll make me exist all the more, but the truth is that *he* is my creator. I am made in his image, of his genes and of his nurture. He is my father.

Mitochondria
Revelations

'What distinguishes works of literature is that they have no "signified", nothing to which they ultimately refer. They are in a particular sense, not about anything.'

Roland Barthes

'The rest is silence.'

Hamlet, V, ii

The End

Index of Epigraphs

Part One
Rabbi John D. Rayner, from *Gate of Repentance*. Reproduced by kind permission of the Union of Liberal and Progressive Synagogues.

Chromosome 1: Genesis, Genetics and Gemini
Genesis I, 31
Jean-Paul Sartre, *Existentialism and Humanism*. Reproduced by kind permission of Éditions Gallimard. Originally published as *L'existentialisme est un humanisme* in 1946.

Chromosome 2: The Calvinist Tulip
William Shakespeare, *Hamlet*, IV, v
Romans XIII, 30

Chromosome 3: The Human Script (I)
Robert Cook-Deegan, *The Gene Wars (Science, Politics and The Human Genome)*. Reproduced by kind permission of the author.
Douglas Adams, *The Hitchhikers Guide to the Galaxy*. Copyright © 1979. Reprinted by kind permission of the Estate of Douglas Adams.

Chromosome 4: Inheritance
Exodus XX, 5
Henrik Ibsen, *Ghosts*

Chromosome 5: Ante hoc ergo post hoc
National Lottery slogan
James Joyce, *Ulysses*

Chromosome 6: Ars Magna
Oscar Wilde (attributed)
Hans Christian Andersen, *The Emperor's New Clothes*

Chromosome 7: Improbability
Kurt Vonnegut, *Slaughterhouse 5*. Reproduced by kind permission of Curtis Brown Group, London on behalf of the Estate of Kurt Vonnegut. Copyright © Kurt Vonnegut, 1969.
Arthur Schopenhauer, *On the Freedom of the Will*

Chromosome 8: A Question of Identity
Francis Galton, 'The history of twins as a criterion of the relative powers of nature and nurture' (*Fraser's Magazine*, 1875)
John XVIII, 37–38

Chromosome 9: Relief, Grief, Belief
Jean-Paul Sartre (attributed)
William Shakespeare, *Hamlet*, III, i

Chromosome 10: Chaos and Strange Attraction
Traditional
Pierre-Simon de Laplace, *Analytic Theory of Probabilities*

Chromosome 11: Superreality
The ontological argument of St Anselm from *The Proslogion*
Fanny Burney, *Tristessa: or The Sign of Invention*

Chromosome 12: Calmer Stupor
Charles Darwin
Marcel Proust, *À la recherche du temps perdu*

Part Two
Charles Dickens, *David Copperfield*

Chromosome 13: Are Stochastic Events Free?
T. S. Eliot, 'Burnt Norton', I, *Four Quartets,* taken from *Collected Poems.* © Estate of T. S. Eliot and reprinted by kind permission of Faber & Faber Ltd.
William Shakespeare, *Henry IV, Part 2*, III, i

Chromosome 14: Anagrams
Umberto Eco, *Foucault's Pendulum.* © Umberto Eco, *Il pendolo di Foucault*, RCS Libri S.p.A. – Milano, Bompiani 1988–2013.
William Shakespeare, *Hamlet*, II, i

Chromosome 15: Sea of Troubles
The Book of Job XIV, 1
Simon DeStromp, *Hamlet and the Postmodern Fallacy*

Chromosome 16: Poor Dan is in a Droop
Lawrence Wright, *Twins (Genes, Environment and the Mystery of Identity).* Copyright © 1997 by Lawrence Wright. Reproduced by kind permission of John Wiley & Sons, Inc.

Charles Baudelaire, *Les Fleurs du mal*, Preface

Chromosome 17: The Book of Job
William Shakespeare, *Hamlet*, II, ii
Lewis Carroll, *Alice's Adventures in Wonderland*

Chromosome 18: Leviathan with a Hook
Ezekiel XXV, 17
Victor Hugo

Chromosome 19: Fairy Tales
Francis Bacon, *On the Advancement of Learning*
John Keats, 'Ode on a Grecian Urn'

Chromosome 20: Nighttown
Karl Popper, *Conjectures and Refutations*, iv. Copyright ©
1963 by Karl Popper. Reproduced by kind permission of the
Estate of Karl Popper.
Ivan Turgenev, 'Hamlet and Don Quixote'

Chromosome 21: The Human Script (II)
Fyodor Dostoevsky, *The Underground Man*
Luigi Pirandello, 'The Tragedy of a Character'

Chromosome 22: Will
William Shakespeare, *Hamlet*, III, i
Sophocles, *Oedipus Coloneus*

The X or Y Chromosome: This Mortal Coil
Rene Descartes, *Le Discours de la méthode*
The Qur'an, 39:42

Mitochondria: Revelations
Roland Barthes, *Elements of Semiology*. Reproduced by kind
permission of Editions Denoël.
William Shakespeare, *Hamlet*, V, ii

Acknowledgements

As these pages try to show, the factors that cause something to come into being are many and varied, too many and too varied to hope to capture them all adequately. For that I apologise to those who are not directly thanked below. You know who you are and the inestimable roles you have played in my life and in the creation of this novel. Thank you.

As for the others, I am very grateful to the following, too many of whom are sadly no longer with us:

Matt Parker, my close friend, who drew me into writing and kept me drawn in – my constant reader and literary foil. Someone hit life's dimmer switch when we lost you.

Andrew Motion, Malcolm Bradbury, Lorna Sage, Jon Cook, Max Sebald, Paul Magrs and the faculty of the School of English & American Studies and all my fellow students on UEA's alchemical MA course in Creative Writing, particularly Tim Guest.

Mike Shaw and Jonathan Pegg, latterly of Curtis Brown, for their support, albeit to no avail.

All those who helped me in my research: the staff of the Sanger Centre at the Wellcome Trust Human Genome Campus in Hinxton, in particular Dr Tom Freeman (of the Gene Expression Group); Jenny Doak (then Jenny Sackin of the Natural History Museum); Prof Steven Rose (not least for his superlative book *Lifelines*); Prof Steve Jones (and his many wonderful books, but particularly *In the Blood*); Dr Rex Scaramuzzi (for a spot-check of my science; any remaining errors, however, are mine not his); Chandler Burr (and his book *A Separate Creation*); Peter Tatchell; and Prof Carl Djerassi. Other excellent books that deserve a mention, although I had no contact with their authors, are: *Twins* by Lawrence Wright; and *Not in our Genes* by R. C. Lewontin, Steven Rose (again) and Leon J. Kamin; and *Chaos* by James Gleick.

Although I find his views on many subjects abhorrent, I should also thank Rev Dr Alan C. Clifford of the Norwich Reformed Church for welcoming me into his home to explain the tenets of Calvinism.

Dr Jan Piggott for being an inspiration to many

generations of pupils.

My many other supportive friends and family, including – among the more vocally supportive – Tom McCarthy, Henry Phillips, the Bradbury family, Shane Brighton, and my wicked uncle David Benedictus (whose wickedness in making a livelihood – if not a living – out of being an author made the act of writing both more and less acceptable at the same time, and whose feedback was greatly treasured).

The writers, lyricists and copyright owners who have so kindly allowed me to quote from their works.

Karen Ings and Caroline Goldsmith of Red Button Publishing for taking a punt when few others would.

Also to Nicole Linhardt-Rich, ever patient with me, supportive and motivating (who could not be further from the character called Nicole in the book, who is called that for wholly other reasons). And to Thalia and Naia for being a constant delight.

Finally I would like to dedicate this book to the two people who had more to do with making me able to write it than any others ...

To my progenitors, my primal cause,
my extraordinary parents, Michael and Janice.
Any credit is theirs. Any blame is mine.

About the Author

After taking his first degree at the University of Durham, Johnny Rich returned to education as a mature student in 1999, completing an MA in Creative Writing at the University of East Anglia, where he wrote the first draft of *The Human Script*. Apart from his work as a writer, Johnny is well known in the world of higher education as an expert on student life and careers and appears regularly on TV and radio discussing education issues. Johnny lives in London with his wife and two daughters.

About Red Button Publishing

Founded in 2012 by two industry insiders, Red Button aims to give a voice to talented writers who are often overlooked by the mainstream.

Our mission is to find books that are simply crying out to be published.

For more fantastic fiction visit

www.redbuttonpublishing.net

12949556R00180

Printed in Poland
by Amazon Fulfillment
Poland Sp. z o.o., Wrocław